Nothing to Lose

Joanna Brady Mysteries

Desert Heat

Tombstone Courage

Shoot/Don't Shoot

Dead to Rights

Skeleton Canyon

Rattlesnake Crossing

Outlaw Mountain

Devil's Claw

Paradise Lost

Partner in Crime

Exit Wounds

Dead Wrong

Damage Control

Fire and Ice

Judgment Call

The Old Blue Line: A
Joanna Brady Novella

Remains of Innocence

Random Acts: A
Joanna Brady and
Ali Reynolds Novella

Downfall

Field of Bones

Missing and Endangered

Walker Family Novels

Hour of the Hunter

Kiss of the Bees

Day of the Dead

Queen of the Night

Dance of the Bones: A
J. P. Beaumont and
Brandon Walker Novel

Nothing to Lose

A J. P. Beaumont Novel

J. A. Jance

HARPER LARGE PRINT

An Imprint of HarperCollins*Publishers*

HarperCollins books may be purchased for educational, business, or sales promotional use. For information, please e-mail the Special Markets Department at SPsales@harpercollins.com.

FIRST HARPER LARGE PRINT EDITION

ISBN: 978-0-06-321125-4

Library of Congress Cataloging-in-Publication Data is available upon request.

22 23 24 25 26 LSC 10 9 8 7 6 5 4 3 2 1

To Niesje, the judge who almost lives next door

Nothing to Lose

Prologue

H ey, babe," Mel called to me from the bathroom doorway, "the shower isn't draining, and neither is the toilet."

At six thirty on a cold, dark winter morning, those were ominous words indeed, and for more than one reason. In some relationships being addressed as "babe" might be regarded as a term of endearment. Coming from Mel Soames, however, the word landed with the same impact as when, without ever raising her voice, my mother used to address me as Jonas Piedmont

Beaumont. In those instances, and in this one as well, it was time for me to wake up and smell the coffee.

I didn't make the strategic mistake of getting out of bed to go see for myself or of asking, "Are you sure?" If Mel said that was the situation, that *was* the situation. Nor did I caution her to avoid flushing again. My wife happens to be a very smart woman, and my offering her unneeded advice is never a good idea.

Her words were worrisome for another reason, and that's this: I am not now nor have I ever been a handyman. Yes, I've seen all those *America's Funniest Home Videos* clips where the kids yell, "Hey, Dad, there's water coming out of the bathroom!" The panicked father races to the scene only to discover that his rug rats have set out a long line of plastic water bottles marching in single file from an open bathroom door and out into a hallway. The disgruntled father is left muttering a series of bleeped-out words while the happy pranksters double over with laughter. That joke might be funny on TV but not in my own bedroom and certainly not at that ungodly hour of the morning.

With Mel still occupying the bathroom, I crawled out of bed and headed for the kitchen. When Mel and I purchased and remodeled our sixty-five-year-old Mid-Century Modern home, I had no idea that the house came with radiant heat throughout. As I padded from the bedroom to the kitchen, I was grateful for the comforting warmth of the heated flooring on my bare feet. A check of the kitchen sink showed no sign of a backup there, and so, with a thankful heart, I turned on the coffee machine.

While our DeLonghi Magnifica put itself through its morning warm-up exercises, I turned around expecting to find Sarah, our recently adopted Irish wolfhound, at my side and ready to go do her morning necessaries. She was nowhere in sight. When I went looking, I found her still in the bedroom, curled up in a ball and snoozing away in her toasty nest next to my side of the bed.

Before I go any further, a word about dogs. I'm not a lifetime dog lover. The dog that had dragged me into this new and relatively unfamiliar territory was another Irish wolfhound named Lucy. Mel serves as the chief of police in Bellingham, Washington, north of Seattle. She's still gainfully employed while I am a not-so-happily-retired househusband. Lucy came into our lives in the aftermath of a domestic-violence incident in Mel's jurisdiction. When the battered wife took her children and fled to a shelter situation, they were unable to take Lucy with them, so Mel ended up bringing her home.

After years of chasing bad guys first for Seattle PD

and later for the attorney general's Special Homicide Investigation Team, aka SHIT, I have now become the person tasked with keeping hearth and home in order. As a consequence Lucy became my responsibility, a job I grudgingly accepted but only with a good deal of griping and a singular lack of grace. All that changed, of course, when the abusive husband from the domestic-violence incident got out of jail on bail and came gunning for Mel—knifing for her, actually, rather than gunning. When the chips were down, Lucy had come racing to Mel's defense at considerable harm to herself. If that isn't enough to turn a guy into a dog lover, I don't know what is.

I would have been happy to keep Lucy permanently, but that wasn't in the cards. Mel and I might have fallen for her, but once Lucy met our new granddaughter, Athena, Lucy voted with her paws and made her preferences clear. We might have loved Lucy, but Lucy loved Athena, and that's where she is now, living with Athena and her other grandfather in Jasper, Texas. But by the time we gave up Lucy, Mel and I both knew there was bound to be another dog in our lives sooner or later. When "sooner" arrived, we took pains to locate another wolfie.

Sarah is a former mommy-dog rescued from a now-shuttered puppy mill outside Palm Springs. Lucy was coal black. Sarah is a whitish gray—white when she's dry, gray when she's wet. The first time I saw her, I thought I was seeing Lucy's ghost.

We had adopted Sarah in early October, but since she'd spent most of her life living in a metal shed giving birth to one litter of puppies after another, she had no social skills and almost no muscle control in her hind-quarters, leaving her rear end so weak that she could barely stand. After arriving in Washington, Sarah had spent six weeks at the Academy for Canine Behavior in Woodinville, regaining her physical strength and learning how to be a family dog with some basic command training thrown in on the side. She finally came home to live with us only a couple of weeks earlier on the Friday after Thanksgiving.

As with Lucy, since I'm Sarah's primary caregiver, she's now clearly *my* dog as opposed to *our* dog—and her side of the bed happens to be my side of the bed, so that's exactly where she was when I went looking for her. Lucy always bounded up and out the moment my feet hit the floor. Sarah is your basic slugabed and has to be coaxed into rising and shining, especially on cold winter mornings.

"Out," I ordered, pointing at the door. Sarah delivered a series of sleepy-eyed blinks before slowly unfurling her very long legs. Once upright, she gave me a floppy-eared shake of her head as if to voice a personal objection on being rudely awakened before sauntering reluctantly out of the bedroom. Due to her Southern California roots, Sarah does not like the cold, so I followed along to make sure she didn't take an unexpected detour somewhere along the way. After all, at that very minute it was cold indeed in our corner of western Washington, even for people who are relatively acclimated to winter weather.

Two days earlier what meteorologists refer to as a polar vortex had plunged a long knife of frigid weather down through British Columbia and into the United States, with Bellingham right on its westernmost edge. At the same time, what our weather gal calls a "Pineapple Express" was rolling in off the Pacific, bringing with it drenching rains all up and down the West Coast. The two opposing weather patterns had merged somewhere north of Seattle, resulting in blizzard conditions that had brought our small city to a complete standstill.

Mel's and my house on Bayside Road in the city's Fairhaven neighborhood sits on a bluff overlooking Bellingham Bay. Because we're so close to the water, we're usually in a banana-belt situation as far as snow is concerned—usually, but not this time around. If it hadn't been for the all-wheel drive on Mel's Interceptor, she wouldn't have been able to make it up and down our driveway. My S-Class Mercedes is an older model 4Matic, but when it comes to driving on snow and ice, I'm not especially proficient, and as much as possible I try to avoid driving and walking in that kind of weather.

The previous morning, before the snowstorm hit, it had already been icy cold outside. When I sent Sarah out into our frigid backyard to do her thing, I assumed she'd completed the job. That was an error on my part. Sarah evidently likes walking on icy-cold ground as much as I do. A lot later in the day, I learned she had avoided freezing her huge but dainty paws by leaving an Irish-wolfhound-size gift for me under the roofline of the front porch. Rather than walk around the house to the proper receptacle, I had resorted to the lazy man's shortcut of flushing the by-then-frozen pile of doodoo down the guest-room toilet. Standing in the kitchen the next morning and waiting for the coffee to brew, I should have been smart enough to put two and two together and figure out what had happened with the plumbing, but as I mentioned earlier, I'm no handyman.

After filling Mel's and my thermal mugs with coffee, I made a pit stop of my own in the powder room without attempting to flush. Then I picked up my iPad and found the number for Roto-Rooter in the home-vendors section of my contacts list. That's another side issue of owning a home that dates from the middle of a previous century. It's a good idea to have a talented plumbing guy and an electrician or two on speed dial.

By the time I'd managed to get an ETA on the plumber, Mel was dressed and having her typical on-the-go breakfast, which generally consists of a piece of buttered toast accompanied by a couple slices of pepper-jack cheese.

"What's on your agenda for the day?" I asked, joining her on an adjacent stool at the kitchen island.

"A working lunch with the mayor at noon," she replied, "and a city-council meeting this evening, unless they call it off due to weather. The trucks are out plowing and spreading sand, but the streets are impassable again almost as soon as the plows are gone. You probably didn't hear them," she added, "but they already did our street and driveway."

"Rank hath its privileges," I observed.

She gave me a beaming smile. "It certainly does," she agreed.

"When's the cold streak supposed to end?" I asked.

"Tomorrow," she answered, "but don't hold your breath. It's going to warm up tomorrow or the next day, but before that happens, they're predicting another record snowstorm."

"Great," I grumbled. "Alternating layers of snow and ice. Looks like I'll be settling in for a long winter's nap."

Mel gathered her coat, purse, and coffee and then on her way out stopped by where I was sitting.

"As long as you're stuck at home," she suggested, giving me a wifely good-bye peck on my cheek, "why don't you think about putting up the Christmas decorations?"

She said it with a smile and a kiss. It was more of a hint than an order, but once again, just as with the water problem in the bathroom, I knew I needed to pay attention.

Chapter 1

Lars Jenssen, who started out as my AA sponsor and ended up becoming my stepgrandfather after marrying my widowed grandmother, used to tell me, "We get too soon old and too late smart." I like to think I wised up before it was too late. That's why, once I finished my morning coffee and my daily roster of crossword puzzles, I got my rear in gear and set about dealing with the Christmas decorations, starting by hauling a dozen or so boxes in from the garage.

Supposedly we have a three-car garage. That's what the real-estate agent told us. The reality is somewhat different. Once we came to Bellingham and Mel had the use of a company car, she had unloaded the Porsche I'd given her years earlier. So now one of the three bays holds my S-Class Mercedes and one holds Mel's Police

Interceptor, while the third bay is devoted solely to Christmas—Mel's doing rather than mine.

The Christmas-only space in our garage is a direct result of Mel's lifelong conflict with her father. She grew up as an army brat and always had a problematic relationship with her dad, who retired as a full-bird colonel. He's gone now, and I'm more than happy to take her word for it that he wasn't a pleasant person. For him Christmas was nothing but an annoying afterthought. Naturally Mel begs to differ.

When she divorced her first husband and moved to Seattle to go to work for SHIT, she drove cross-country towing a U-Haul trailer loaded with—you guessed it— her vast collection of Christmas decorations, which for years were stowed in a rented storage unit. After we married, whenever it came time to decorate our condo for Christmas, Mel would go to the storage facility and come traipsing home with a collection of boxes that turned our high-rise condo into a winter wonderland that the grandkids absolutely adored. The whole family loved it, yours truly included, but I couldn't help but wonder how she did it, because each year the end result seemed to be totally different from the year before. The reality of the situation didn't come into focus for me until after our move to Bellingham. That's when she shut down the storage unit and transferred her amazing collection to our garage.

Mel is nothing if not organized. The boxes are loaded onto four heavy-duty rolling shelving units. The three boxes containing the pre-lit tree are pretty much self-explanatory: top, middle, and bottom, with the tree skirt neatly folded in the one labeled "Bottom." The rest of the otherwise identical moving boxes are labeled on every visible side: "Red Balls," "Silver Balls," "White Balls," "Blue Balls," "Poinsettias, one Red and one White," "Holly Sprigs," "Ribbons," "Bows," "Angels," "Santas," "Nutcrackers," "Christmas Linens," and "Wreaths." As I surveyed the assortment of boxes, I realized this was like one of those gigantic Lego sets my grandson, Kyle, loves so much. Everything I needed was there—some assembly required.

Since I didn't remember seeing blue ornaments on any previous tree display, and since blue is my favorite color, I chose the box labeled "Blue Balls." It seemed to me that white poinsettias would be a good bet with blue balls, so I took down a box of those as well as ones labeled "Angels," "Santas," and "Nutcrackers." I also set aside boxes marked "Christmas Linens" and "Ribbons." After hauling all those inside, I went to work.

Before Karen and I divorced, I remember Christmas decorating mostly as an ordeal of organized chaos. I wasn't exactly encouraged to participate, and for good reason. Because I'm over six feet and Karen was only five-five, it was usually my job to install the angel at the top of the tree, a task that was always accomplished *after* the tree was fully decorated. One year, having had a bit too much holiday spirit (I believe I already mentioned I've been in AA for years now), I came to grief with the ladder, and so did the tree, right along with a large number of decorations. Karen started speaking to me again sometime after New Year's, and from then on my help with the angel was no longer required.

This year, doing the job on my own and determined not to repeat that disaster, I decided to put the angel on the top of the tree *before* I put the tree together. I unloaded the angels from their box, lined them up on the kitchen island, and picked out one with a blue skirt. Then, using a pair of zip-ties, I fastened that angel to the top in a fashion that I doubt even an earthquake could dislodge. Only *then* did I finish putting the tree together. Fortunately, all those little multicolored LED lights lit right up without the slightest hesitation.

I was somewhat disappointed when I opened up the box labeled "Blue Balls." What I'd had in mind was something truly blue—royal blue, I suppose you'd call it. These were more turquoise than deep blue—some shiny and some frosted. I didn't use all the balls in the box, but I think I hung most of them. Then I filled in the blanks on the tree with dozens of white poinsettia blossoms and punctuated those with a flock of silver bows and ribbons.

I was standing there asking Sarah what she thought of my decorating job. (Yes, I do talk to my dog when no one else is around.) That's when the doorbell rang. Sarah beat me to the door, but due to our security system's monitor in the entryway hall, I knew without cracking the door that the person pressing the bell was Ken, our regular Roto-Rooter guy, come to present his bill.

After putting Sarah on a sit-and-stay command, I opened the door. "All done?" I asked.

"Yup," Ken said.

"What was it," I asked, "a tree root of some kind?"

Ken glanced at me and then sent a reproachful glare in Sarah's direction. "I wish," he said. "By the time I was able to scope it, it looked to me as though someone had tried to flush a gigantic dog turd down a toilet. The damned thing got hung up on an ice dam in the main sewer pipe and stopped everything cold—at this point very cold," he added with a chuckle. "Fortunately, I finally managed to break it up. That'll be three-fifty—card, cash, or check?"

I used my Amex and paid the $350 with a happy heart, grateful as all hell that Mel hadn't been home to hear the cause and effect, both of which, as it turns out, were entirely my fault. Then I went back to decorating. I lined up the angels, Santas, and nutcrackers on the kitchen island in preparation to actually distributing them. Then I opened the linens box. The top layer of that was a selection of holiday-themed guest towels. I knew from past experience that those needed to be rolled up and put in the basket on the counter in the powder room. Then I sorted through the holiday tablecloths, runners, and doilies. Once I had those on various flat surfaces throughout the house, I deployed the angels, nutcrackers, and Santas, placing them in sad little groupings of three, like so many trios of mismatched carolers.

It wasn't exactly the elegant effect Mel usually produces. My results were more ham-fisted than beautiful, but I figured Mel could do some embellishing once she got home. In the meantime, giving myself a pat on the back, I settled with a newly made cup of coffee into my favorite chair by the gas-log fireplace to survey my handiwork.

The whole process had become more or less a meditation on Christmases past, first the memory of that Christmas-tree screwup with Karen and the kids and then going all the way back to Christmases when I was a kid. My mother was a World War II–era unwed mother. She was engaged to my father and pregnant with me when he died in a motorcycle accident. Rather than give me up for adoption, she had—against her father's wishes—chosen to keep me and raise me on her own. We lived in a small two-bedroom apartment over a bakery in Seattle's Ballard neighborhood. She supported us by working as a seamstress, making clothing on a treadle Singer sewing machine next to a worktable that took up a good third of her bedroom.

Naturally she was always busiest in November and December as clients wanted new duds for holiday events. On many of those cold winter nights, she was still up working long after I went to bed, but at some point she'd be done, and the next morning something magical would have happened. I'd come out of my bedroom and find that the living room and dining room had been transformed overnight into a Christmas wonderland. We always went to church on Christmas Eve and then hung our stockings on the mantel of our nonworking fireplace. Christmas morning both of our stockings would be filled, but it wasn't until after I was

old enough to get a job as an usher at the Bagdad The-
atre that she finally opened her stocking on Christmas
morning to find something she herself hadn't put there.

I was sitting there, half drifting and half dozing,
thinking about what an unsung hero my mother had
been, when the doorbell rang again. Since I wasn't expecting any visitors, I thought maybe Ken had come
back to give me a revised bill of some kind, but the
security screen in the hallway revealed the presence of
a stranger wearing a long woolen coat—unusual in the
Pacific Northwest—and carrying what appeared to be
an old-fashioned satchel. He was a handsome-looking
guy in his late twenties or early thirties. The distinctive
white collar around his neck told me he was also most
likely a priest. That made me wonder. Was the local
Catholic parish dispatching priests out to pass collection plates door-to-door these days?

I sent Sarah back to the living room, ordering her
to wait on the rug before I opened the door. Thanks to
her academy training, she did exactly as she was told.

"May I help you?" I asked the stranger out front.

"Detective Beaumont?" he said.

People who know me now don't call me that, so obviously this was a voice out of my past.

"Yes," I replied uncertainly.

"You probably don't remember me. I'm Jared," he

said, "Jared Danielson—Father Danielson now. I hope you'll forgive me for stopping by without calling first."

The name "Jared Danielson" took my breath away and opened a window on one of the darkest days of my life. I needed a moment to gather myself after that. It had been close to twenty years since I'd last seen him.

"Why, of course, Jared, you're more than welcome," I said hastily, offering him my hand and ushering him into the house. "So good to see you. How are you, and what are you doing these days?"

He stepped inside and stood there on the entryway rug, stomping off the ice and snow that had clung to his boots. "I'm here because I need your help, Detective Beaumont," he said.

The last time I'd seen Jared Danielson was years earlier when he'd been a lanky kid of thirteen who had just lost his mother. Now he was a well-built grown man, but a shadow of that long-ago tragedy still lingered in his eyes.

"Call me Beau," I told him. "I stopped being Detective Beaumont a long time ago. Come have a seat and a cup of coffee while you tell me what you've been up to since I saw you last. Black or cream and sugar?"

"Black is fine," he said.

As I walked Jared Danielson into the house, it seemed as though all my recently installed holiday cheer had instantly vanished. Suddenly I was traveling through time and space into a very dark place in my life, headed somewhere I definitely didn't want to go—a hell I had visited in nightmares countless times through the intervening years.

First there is an explosion of gunfire from somewhere out of sight. When nothing more happens, I realize the bad guy is dead and turn back to check on my partner. Shot in the gut, a bloodied Sue Danielson sits leaning against a living-room wall. She is holding my backup Glock in one hand, with the weapon resting on her upper thigh. As I watch in horror, her fingers slowly go limp and the gun slips soundlessly to the floor.

In real life that's when I knew for sure that Sue was gone. Her ex, Richard Danielson, had shot her dead.

Chapter 2

While I fussed with the coffee machine to give myself some emotional distance, Jared Danielson seemed to make himself at home. He wandered over to the westward-facing windows and stared out at our water view. When he dropped down to one knee and gave Sarah a pat on the head, she acknowledged the gesture by thumping her tail.

"I've always liked Irish wolfhounds," he said. "What's her name?"

"Sarah," I replied. "She's a rescue."

Straightening up, he caught sight of a framed photo on the mantel. It's a photo of my granddaughter, Athena, and Lucy. Both of them are sound asleep, with Athena's head resting on the dog's massive shoulder.

"A grandchild and Sarah's sister?" Jared asked as I carried a loaded serving tray into the living room and set it down on the coffee table. My hands were shaking badly enough that I'm surprised I didn't slop coffee in every direction.

"You've got the grandchild part right," I told him. "Her name's Athena. The dog is a previous wolfie—Lucy. We adopted her, but she ended up adopting Athena. They live in Texas now."

By the time Jared and I were both seated on the sofa, I had a better handle on myself. "So," I said, "I believe the last time I saw you was at your mother's fallen-officer memorial."

I remembered that event distinctly. After Sue's death her parents had flown in for the memorial service from somewhere in the Midwest—Ohio, I seemed to remember. The grandparents, whose names I had somehow forgotten, had taken Sue's boys—Jared and his younger brother—back home with them. Right that minute I couldn't recall the brother's name either, but they had all flown back into town months later to participate in the ceremony when Sue's name was added to Seattle PD's memorial wall in downtown Seattle.

"I believe you said at the time that you might want to be a policeman when you grew up," I added.

Cops learn to read faces. It's something that's drilled into your head starting on your first day in the academy, and there are times over the course of a career when being able to capture and decode a fleeting expression on a suspect's face can mean the difference between life and death. I saw the muscles in Jared's jawline twitch. He chewed on his lower lip for a moment before he spoke.

"I tried that," he said at last. "I got a degree in criminal justice and went to work for Monroe PD in Monroe, Ohio. It's outside Cincinnati. They're the ones who sent me through the academy."

I wasn't sure how his going through police-academy training jibed with his showing up in priestly attire. I was about to ask, but something in his expression kept me from opening my mouth.

He sighed and then, after taking a deep breath, continued. "I made it through training fine. But then, my first week of being in a patrol car on my own, I got a call to do a welfare check."

A wave of gooseflesh passed over my body, because I knew what was coming.

"A domestic?" I asked.

He nodded. "A woman and two little kids—a boy and a girl—all of them dead, stabbed to death in their beds. The perpetrator was down in the basement. He'd taken himself out with an overdose."

I said nothing because there was nothing to say.

"I called it in," he continued. "I stayed there until the homicide detectives showed up so I could give them my statement. The lieutenant wanted me to be part of the house-to-house canvass. I told him I couldn't do it. Instead I drove my patrol car back to the department, where I turned in the keys, my badge, and my weapon. Then I went home, got good and drunk, and stayed that way for a month."

He paused and sat there staring into his coffee cup as though the liquid there might be able to deliver some enlightenment. I knew it wouldn't.

"I think most people given those circumstances might have stayed drunk for a lot longer than that," I offered. "What happened?"

"My grandmother sent her parish priest to talk to me, Father Joel." Jared gave me a sidelong glance. "Did you know we were Catholic?"

"Not until your mother's memorial service," I answered. "Somehow our respective religious affiliations never came up in casual conversation."

Jared nodded. "That's one of the reasons my mother's divorcing my father was such a big deal. They were both good Catholics, supposedly, and they had married in the Church. It's why she put off getting a divorce for as long as she did."

Again I managed to resist the temptation to speak. That's another thing they try to teach you in the academy. When a suspect or witness is busy telling his or her story, don't interrupt—just shut up and listen. I've had years of experience in that regard, so I kept quiet.

"Father Joel was a good guy," Jared continued. "The last time I'd seen him was two years earlier when he officiated at my grandfather's funeral. By the time he showed up at my apartment, I'd been shit-faced drunk for days. I wasn't eating or sleeping, had lost close to twenty pounds, and hadn't bothered to shower in I don't know how long. The place was filthy, and yet there he was. The first thing he did was make me shower and put on clean clothes. Then he threw out the booze, made me drink coffee, and ordered a pizza. While I was drinking coffee, he started cleaning the apartment—throwing out garbage, washing the dishes. He told me Grandma had sent him to check on me because I wasn't answering the phone."

I nodded. "Sounds like she was right to be worried."

"I was busy feeling sorry for myself—not for the people who'd been murdered whose bodies I'd found, but sorry for me. Father Joel asked me if I wasn't going to be a cop, what was I going to do with my life? I told him I had no idea. I knew I couldn't be in law enforcement anymore, even though I had a degree in criminal justice. It seemed to me as though the four years I'd spent going to college had been a total waste of time and money."

"'We should pray about it,' he said. I thought he was nuts. 'Pray?' I asked. 'Right here? Right now?' 'Why not?' he said. And that's what we did. We both got down on our knees next to the couch where I'd been lying and wallowing in my misery, and we prayed. When we finished, we got up off our knees, and he said, 'My grandmother always used to tell me that those who can, do and those who can't, teach.' I was astonished. 'You think I should teach criminal justice even if I can't do it?' I asked him. Father Joel nodded, and that's what happened.

"He pulled some strings and helped me get into the graduate program in criminal justice at Notre Dame, and one thing led to another. By the time I earned my master's, I had entered the seminary. I received my doctorate in May and was ordained this past July. Starting next fall I'll be an associate professor of criminal justice at the University of New Mexico at Albuquerque."

Thank you, Father Joel, I said to myself. Just then

the name that had been eluding me turned up in my little gray cells. "So what about Christopher?" I asked. "What's become of your little brother?"

Jared's telltale jaws tightened again. "That's why I'm here," he said finally. "Chris has fallen off the face of the earth. I need your help in finding him."

Chapter 3

Without warning, Jared abruptly lurched to his feet, mumbling something about needing to use the restroom.

"That way," I said, pointing him toward the powder room. Fortunately, after Mr. Roto-Rooter left, I had gone through the house and made sure everything was draining properly. Jared probably did need to use the restroom, because I heard him flush a minute or so before the door opened and he emerged, but I'm pretty sure the real reason he fled the living room was to avoid letting me see his sudden onset of tears. Too bad for him, because I already had.

While he was gone, I refilled our coffee cups and released Sarah from her wait on the rug. By the time he returned, Sarah had stretched out full length on the sofa with her head resting in my lap. (Yes, we're the kind of household where dogs *are* allowed on the furniture.) As a result Jared took a seat facing me, and that was exactly what I'd intended. When we'd been sitting side by side, I'd only been able to observe him in profile. When it came time for him to tell me the rest of the story, I wanted to be able to look him in the eye.

Jared picked up his coffee mug and stared into the dark depths of it the same way I used to stare into glasses full of MacNaughton's. I knew from experience that the answers he was seeking still weren't to be found there, but I had the good sense to wait him out by changing the subject.

"How'd you find me?" I asked. Mel's chief of police, so we don't exactly post the location of our residences in public forums.

"Molly," Jared replied. "Molly Lindstrom."

Molly is the widow of Big Al Lindstrom who was once my partner, too. After he was injured on the job, I ended up being partnered with Sue Danielson, but he had known her as a fellow member of the homicide squad, and both he and Molly had attended Sue's memorial service. The last time I saw Molly had been at Big Al's funeral. I felt a pang of guilt that I hadn't done a better job of staying in touch with her. While she, on the other hand, had clearly made the effort to stay in touch with Sue's mother and the two boys. And I had no doubt she had done so the old-fashioned way, with handwritten cards and letters rather than emoji-filled texts and e-mails. In other words two black marks on my name as opposed to just one.

Awash with an added layer of self-recrimination, I gave Jared a nudge. "What's really going on, Jared?" I asked. "Why are you here?"

"Chris blames me," he answered at last.

I was baffled. "Blames you for what?" I asked.

"For our mom's death," Jared said, almost choking on the words. "He thinks if I had called the cops sooner instead of running away from the house the way we did, maybe Dad wouldn't have killed her."

I felt an instant flash of outrage. Jared had been a true hero that night. With his folks arguing in the living room and with Christopher still asleep in his bed, Jared had called to alert me about what was going on. I'd been south of Seattle outside Auburn when his call came in, but I knew that having squads of patrol cars show up with sirens blaring and lights flashing would likely make things worse. So I had told Jared to throw whatever cushioning he could find outside the window to soften their landings and then take his little brother and run, and that's exactly what Jared had done—he followed my instructions to the letter.

Were those instructions wrong? I've certainly questioned them myself often enough over the years. Maybe having armed officers show up on the scene might have resulted in a different outcome, and Sue wouldn't have died. But in no way was Jared to blame for any of it. I believe to this day that if the two boys had remained in the house, they would have perished right along with their mother.

"You know that's not true," I offered quietly.

"Do I?" he asked bleakly.

"Jared, you were only a kid," I told him. "What you did that night to save your little brother was brave beyond belief."

"It's beyond belief, all right," Jared retorted, "at least as far as Chris is concerned."

"What makes you think he blames you for what happened?"

"He told me so," Jared replied, "time and again."

Passing blame around made it sound to me as though maybe Christopher Danielson was a chip off his father's old block. "So tell me about Chris," I said. "What's his deal?"

Jared sighed again before he answered. Whoever wrote that line "He ain't heavy, he's my brother" never met Jared Danielson's little bro.

"With both our parents gone, our mom's folks—our

grandparents, Annie and Frank Hinkle—took us back home to Monroe, Ohio, to live with them. It was a good place to grow up, or at least it was for me if not for Chris. I graduated from high school and won a scholarship to Ohio State. By the time Chris was in eighth grade, he was already smoking, drinking, ditching school, and sneaking out of the house at night. Gramps was an Eagle Scout kind of guy. Whenever he tried to get Chris to straighten up and fly right, Chris backtalked like crazy. He barely made it through eighth grade, but right after graduation he snuck into their bedroom one night, stole money out of both Grandma's purse and Grandpa's wallet, and then took off.

"Naturally they were worried sick about it and reported him missing. The cops looked for him but couldn't find him anywhere. Three months later our dad's mother, Linda Danielson, wrote to Grandma Hinkle saying that Chris had turned up on their doorstep in Homer, Alaska, asking to stay. She said he claimed he'd run away because Grandpa Hinkle had beaten him with his belt, something I can tell you for sure never happened. Gramps wasn't that way. She said that since Chris wanted to live with her and Grandpa Danielson, she needed his school transcripts and shot records so she could get him enrolled in high school there."

"Your other grandparents went along with that?"

Jared shrugged. "What else could they do? They had done their best by both of us, and they decided there wasn't much sense in trying to force him to come back. They figured he'd just take off again, so why bother?"

"What happened then?"

"I'm not sure. He stayed on with the Danielsons for a while—I don't know for how long. He ended up dropping out of high school without graduating and took off again."

"Did you try contacting your grandmother over the years?"

Jared shook his head. "I didn't really know that side of the family. We weren't ever close, not even before Mom died to say nothing of after. Maybe you remember that none of them bothered to come to Mom's memorial service, and if they had one for our father, Chris and I never heard about it."

"You weren't even invited?"

Jared shook his head again. "So other than that one letter requesting Chris's school information, we—meaning my grandparents and I—never heard another word from my father's side of the family. It was like they had disappeared off the face of the earth."

I'd seen situations like this countless times before. When domestic violence results in a homicide, the lingering aftereffects can continue to tear a family apart for generations.

"Obviously all this happened years ago," I observed, "so why are you on a mission to find Chris now, and why come to me?"

"Gram Hinkle isn't well," Jared told me. "She's in assisted living and wants to make things right with Chris before she passes on. I think she wants to see him one last time, and I took a leave of absence to try to help her get that sorted."

"This sounds as if your grandmother took the parable about the prodigal son to heart," I suggested. "The kid who goes AWOL gets the brass-band treatment when he comes home. As for the son who never ran off in the first place? He's more or less taken for granted and brushed aside."

Jared favored me with another nod accompanied by a rueful grin. "Right, he's the guy who gets sent out searching for the one who isn't there—if he still exists, that is."

"You think Chris might be dead?"

"Maybe or maybe not," Jared replied. "I have no idea. No one on our side of the family has heard from him directly since he left Ohio at age thirteen."

"Have you filed a missing-persons report?"

"Chris may be missing from our lives, but that

doesn't mean he's missing as far as other people are concerned, so no. We haven't filed a missing-persons report."

"Have you tried contacting your other grandmother?"

He nodded. "She died two years ago."

"Have you checked with the cop shop in Homer?"

"I gave them a call, and they mostly gave me the runaround."

"Have you looked into NamUs?" I asked.

"What's that?" Jared returned.

For someone who was about to be teaching criminal justice at the college level, it seemed to me that NamUs shouldn't have been a mystery to him. "The National Missing and Unidentified Persons System," I said. "It's an open-sourced program that allows law enforcement and even family members to upload personal information on missing loved ones so it can be compared to unidentified remains."

Jared shook his head. "Never heard of it," he said.

"That would be my first step. I'd start by entering every detail I could about Christopher Danielson into their database. Providing a sample of your own DNA would also be helpful."

"I see," Jared said.

"Is your DNA in CODIS?" I asked.

CODIS is the Combined DNA Index System. Fortunately, that piece of law-enforcement jargon was something Jared did recognize. He probably also understood the thinking behind my question. If Chris had grown up to be a clone of his biological father, there was a good chance he had ended up in enough trouble with the law to be marking time in a prison cell someplace where his DNA would have been collected at the time he was incarcerated. The same possibility might have occurred to Jared, but he didn't mention it in his reply.

"I'm pretty sure Monroe PD took a sample of my DNA for elimination purposes when I first joined up," he said. "That might have been uploaded into CODIS, but I'm not sure."

Not necessarily, I thought. What I said was, "We should check and find out."

"Does that mean you'll help me?" he asked.

"Not so fast," I admonished. "You still haven't explained why you came to me for help."

"I watch a lot of true crime on TV," he replied. "Last fall I saw that *48 Hours* episode about Justice for All getting an exoneration for that guy from down in Seattle who spent sixteen years in prison for a murder he didn't commit. You weren't interviewed for that show, but as soon as the name Beaumont was mentioned as part of the case, I knew it had to be you."

He was right on that score. I had indeed been involved in the Mateo Vega wrongful-conviction situation. At the time I had made it clear to the folks at Justice for All that I didn't want my participation in the case to become public knowledge. Good luck with that. Having my name mentioned on national TV was exactly what I *hadn't* had in mind.

I nodded. "You're right. I didn't want my involvement made public, but as they say, no good deed goes unpunished."

"But that's why I thought of you when Gram asked if I'd try to find Chris for her. At least you're someone I used to know."

"I am that," I agreed.

"So will you help me, then?" Jared asked.

"I guess so," I agreed.

Jared's face brightened. Reaching across the coffee table, he took my hand and pumped it. "Thank you so much, Mr. Beaumont."

"You're welcome, Father Danielson, but wouldn't it be easier if, for now, we stuck to Beau and Jared?"

"Yes," he said quietly. "I'd like that."

I pried Sarah's head off my lap, got up, and went in search of my iPad. "Okay," I said once I returned to the sofa. "Now it's time to go to work. Tell me everything you can about your brother."

"Before we do that, don't I need to put you on retainer or something?" Jared asked.

"No," I answered. "Whatever the bill turns out to be, it's marked paid in full. Your mother already took care of it."

Chapter 4

If you're dealing with a missing-persons case, what's needed is information. "All right," I said, "let's start with the basics. Do you happen to have a recent photo of Chris?"

When Jared had entered the house, he'd placed his satchel on the floor near the end of the couch. Now he opened it and pulled out a volume of some kind. When he passed it over to me, it turned out to be a copy of the 2006 high-school yearbook for Homer High School, *The Log.* If the school mascot was the Mariners, then calling their yearbook a log made perfect sense. Since Ballard, Washington, used to be the shake-shingle capital of America, the Ballard High yearbook is called *The Shingle.*

Inscriptions inside the book were addressed to someone named Edwina. "Who's she?" I asked.

Jared shrugged. "No idea," he answered. "I bought this from a yearbook dealer on eBay."

"What was Chris in 2006," I asked, leafing through the book, "a senior?"

Jared nodded. I thumbed through the pages until I found the entry for Christopher Danielson. Like his brother, Chris was a good-looking kid, but one whose features clearly resembled those of his deceased father. Jared, on the other hand, bore more of a resemblance to their mother. Even in the head shot, Christopher Danielson exuded "attitude." The smirk on his face said he saw himself as something of a wiseass. He probably drove his teachers nuts.

Beneath the photo there was nothing listed other than his name—no clubs, no honors, no sports affiliations. Chris had been a senior that year, but in name only—apparently putting in his time without actively participating in any school-related activities. If memory served, class pictures were generally taken at the beginning of a school year rather than at the end.

"Did he graduate?" I asked.

Jared shook his head. "Not as far as I can tell."

I studied the photo again. It was a dozen years old at this point, so without going through the relatively expensive process of computer-generated age enhancement, it probably wouldn't be helpful. Appearance has a lot to do with lifestyle, and drug use, booze, and other bad choices tend to speed up the aging process—and not in a good way.

"When was he born?"

"September eighteenth, 1988," Jared answered.

"Where?"

"Group Health in Seattle."

"What's the connection to Homer?" I asked.

"That's where my father's parents were born. His father was a halibut fisherman. They lived in Seattle while he was working in the fishing fleet out of Ballard. They moved back home to Alaska after he retired."

The Ballard fishing community is small and tight. There was a good chance that Jared's grandfather and my stepgrandfather, Lars, had known each other.

"Our dad was still in high school here at the time," Jared continued. "He went back to Alaska with them for a while, but once he graduated from high school, he came home to Seattle and enrolled at the U-Dub. That's where he and Mom met—at the University of Washington. She was there on a nursing scholarship."

You'd think that in the course of working with Sue Danielson for a couple of years, I would have been familiar with some of this family history, but I wasn't.

As far as partners go, she was anything but a Chatty Cathy. Considering the complexities of her home life, that wasn't too surprising.

"Nursing?" I repeated.

Jared nodded. "Turns out she didn't like it. She dropped out of nursing after her sophomore year. Without the scholarship she couldn't afford the out-of-state tuition, so she quit college completely. My dad had graduated by then, so they got married. I'm pretty sure she was already expecting me at the time, and that's why they tied the knot that summer, but they didn't exactly live happily ever after."

That last bit wasn't news to anyone.

"Your dad was in banking?" I asked after a moment.

"Insurance, actually," Jared replied. "Something bad must have happened—I never knew what, but he ended up losing his license for one reason or another, and then his job. That's about the time things started going downhill. With him out of work and drinking more and more, Mom went to work at the 911 Call Center. Sometime later she hired on with Seattle PD, and then she got pregnant with Chris. I'm not sure, but I suspect getting pregnant with him was some kind of last-ditch effort in trying to save the marriage. If so, it didn't work, because Dad kept right on spiraling. She ended up throwing him out shortly after Chris was born. That's when Dad moved back up to Homer to live with his folks. Mom didn't get around to finalizing the divorce until . . ." Jared's voice faded momentarily. "Not long before everything happened," he finished. "You know all about that."

Unfortunately, I did know about that, all of it, far more than I was willing to discuss with Jared right then. While the couple was separated and later, after the divorce proceedings, Richard Danielson had been required to pay child support. Because he wasn't working, as far as anyone knew, the court-ordered amount had been little more than a token, but he hadn't bothered to pay a penny of it. The week before Sue's death, Richie had played the oldest card in the divorced-deadbeat-dad playbook—the one where the noncustodial parent appears out of nowhere offering to treat the kids to some kind of expensive gift that Sue, as a single mom struggling to keep food on the table and a roof over her kids' heads, could never afford.

In this case the jackpot on offer was an all-expenses-paid trip to Disneyland. Without consulting Sue, Richie had booked the flights and the hotel room for the week *before* Jared and Chris's spring break rather than *during* their spring break. Sue had absolutely put her foot down, telling Richie that she would not allow him to pull the boys out of school in a way that would leave them with five days of unexcused absences. Eventually Richie had caved and changed the reservations, but I'm pretty sure he was pissed about it.

Then, when he finally showed up in Seattle, he did so with brand-new luggage—fancy Rollaboard bags— one for each of the boys to use and something else Sue would never have been able to spring for. I don't know exactly what happened that night, but something about those pieces of luggage—maybe their weight when they were supposedly empty—must have aroused Sue's suspicions. She had sliced open the interior lining on one of them, an action that had revealed that both the top and bottom were chock-full of cocaine. It turns out Richie Danielson was a drug runner, and the trip to Disneyland had been a ploy that would have enabled him to use his sons as unsuspecting mules.

And there's a good chance he might have gotten away with it. This was back in the nineties—before 9/11 necessitated all kinds of new security measures at airports all over the world. At that point luggage wasn't screened the same way it is now, and I have no doubt Jared and Chris would have pulled their drug-laden bags through the airport and had them loaded onto the plane without incident.

But somehow Sue must have suspected what was up. Her fingerprints and no one else's were found on the box knife in the bottom of the shredded piece of luggage. Richie most likely arrived on the scene shortly after she'd sliced it open. Jared had awakened to the sound of quarreling. As the argument escalated, he'd called me, and that's when I advised him to take Chris and get the hell out. That's why the boys were safely away from the house by the time gunfire broke out.

I, on the other hand, arrived moments too late. Neighbors were calling to report hearing gunshots at almost the same time I stopped my vehicle outside the residence, and that's the part that haunts me to this day. Had I arrived a mere thirty seconds earlier and pounded on the door, might it have been enough of a distraction to prevent Sue's untimely death? Of course it's impossible to know one way or the other, and the bottom line is the fact that Sue Danielson is still dead.

Needing to rescue both Jared and me from this topic of discussion, I tried changing the subject to something less emotionally charged.

"What can you tell me about your brother?" I asked.

Jared thought about that before he answered. "I guess I really didn't care for him much," he admitted. "For one thing he always acted like a know-it-all—a snotty spoiled brat who always got his way. He was smart—he knew his times tables up to ten before he got out of first grade, but he never did his homework, and even when he did, he didn't bother turning it in most of the time. But he could draw like crazy. Whenever I tried to draw, I never managed anything more than stick figures. No matter what Chris drew, it looked real. Years after Mom died, he drew this for Grandma Hinkle for Mother's Day."

Opening the satchel again, Jared pulled out an eight-by-ten gold frame and handed it to me. Inside was a pencil drawing of Sue Danielson's face, so true to life that it took my breath away. The hand-drawn image could just as well have been a photograph.

"He drew it from memory," Jared said, answering my next question before it was asked.

I studied the picture for a time in silence. Chris had captured all of Sue's features, including the direct gaze in her eyes and the determined set of her jaw. At the time I knew her, Sue was a struggling single mom with a complex job, two kids, and far too much on her plate. I don't remember ever seeing her smile, but in her son's re-creation of her, there was a hint of a smile playing around the corners of her lips.

"No, Jared," I said, handing the portrait back to him, "I think you're wrong. I don't believe Chris drew this from memory. This drawing of your mother came straight from his heart."

Jared stayed on for the next couple of hours, telling me everything he'd learned and everything he could remember. Somewhere along the way, it dawned on me that we'd both missed lunch, so I went out to the kitchen and whipped up a couple of grilled-cheese sandwiches.

Listening to Jared's recitation of his investigation so far, I realized that although he might have been a priest, he was also a young priest. Including his tracking down that physical copy of *The Log*, all his research had been done online, where he'd found no trace of Chris since his sudden disappearance during the second semester of his senior year in high school. Back then Facebook was in its infancy. There was no such thing as Instagram or YouTube. In fact, Jared couldn't say for sure if Chris even had a cell phone. If he'd owned one, knowing when and where it was last used might have provided a clue as to his whereabouts, but without access to the number that avenue was closed to us.

"Have you found any indication that law enforcement was contacted about his disappearance?"

Jared shook his head. "As I said, when I called Homer PD, they had no record about that, but I don't think the person I spoke to looked very hard."

Even if a missing-persons report had been filed, cases concerning runaway teenagers—especially repeat runaways—don't garner a whole lot of attention from law enforcement. Still, that was a line of inquiry worth pursuing. It occurred to me that I just happened to know someone who might have a better chance of tracking down that kind of information than Jared Danielson, but there was no point in mentioning it at the time. He was feeling useless enough as it was about his inability to further the investigation, and I saw no reason to pile on more misery.

At last Jared glanced at his watch. I checked mine, too, and was surprised to discover it was getting on toward four.

"I need to take off," he said. "I'm supposed to be back in time for dinner."

"Where are you staying?" I asked.

"At a monastery on the far side of Bothell," he replied. "It's not a good idea for newly minted priests to be out running the streets," he added with a grin. "They let me use their vehicle."

"Are newly minted priests allowed to have cell phones?" I asked. "If I'm going to work on this, I'll need to be able to be in touch."

"Of course," he said. Jared gave me his number, and I typed it into my phone.

If Jared's hunch was correct and Chris was already deceased, then DNA would be essential, and I didn't want to have to rely on a DNA profile that might or might not have been loaded into CODIS years earlier. Any resulting profile also needed to be somewhere we'd be able to access it without having to go through official channels.

"Can you receive mail at said monastery?" I asked.

"Yes."

"Then why don't you send off for one of those Ancestry.com DNA kits," I suggested. "Having your DNA profile on record and readily available could come in handy, and be sure you sign permission for your profile to be accessible to others."

"Others as in homicide investigators?" he asked.

I was relieved to hear that he understood that finding a DNA match would most likely not be good news. "As in," I agreed.

"Okay," Jared said with a nod. "I'll get on that right away."

He left a few minutes later. I let Sarah outside where it was positively bone-chillingly frigid. With snow still on the ground, our canine refugee from California once again avoided freezing her huge but tender paws by doing her job on the porch. I flushed that time, too, but on this occasion I did so before the pile had a chance to freeze solid.

I had learned my lesson, and I sure as hell wasn't going to make *that* mistake again!

Chapter 5

Not surprisingly, the city-council meeting was indeed canceled due to weather. Since it was Mel's turn to cook, she showed up with an armload of takeout from a new Thai restaurant in Fairhaven. Over generous helpings of pad thai and coconut prawns, we told each other about our day. Her meeting with the mayor had gone fairly well. The former mayor had been a piece of work. As far as Mel was concerned, this one was a much better fit.

She expressed delight with my ham-fisted stab at Christmas decorating, although I noticed that before dinner she had quietly made a few discreet adjustments. She was also relieved that I'd managed to solve the plumbing issue. I explained that the blockage had

to do with an ice dam that had formed in the main
sewer line. Had I been a better man, I would have admitted straight out that I was the primary cause of said
ice dam, but I'm not and I didn't. We devoted most of
our dinnertime conversation to discussing Father Jared
Danielson's unexpected visit.

Mel and I have been together long enough that she
knows all about Sue Danielson's death. For years after
that dreadful night, I simply refused to partner with
anyone. Mel and I met when we were both working for
Special Homicide, and I balked at first when someone
suggested we become partners. The falling-in-love and
getting-married parts came about much later.

So Mel listened to my recitation about Jared's visit
mostly without comment. "You pretty much have an
obligation to take this on," she concluded when I finished.

"Yes, I do," I agreed. "I'm just not sure how to go
about it."

"Tomorrow will be plenty of time to figure it out,"
Mel announced, getting up to clear away the leavings
of dinner. "But tonight, with the council meeting canceled and more snow on the way, I believe we should
declare this to be our date night with Charles Dickens."

Each December we create a time when the two of us

can sit by a fireplace and listen to Jim Dale's CD version of *A Christmas Carol.* I love that moment when Scrooge wakes up to discover that everything that had gone on had happened to him overnight. That it was still Christmas morning and there was still time for him to make some changes in his life. It's a lot like emerging from spending years in a drunken stupor and then suddenly discovering you're still alive. At least that's how it's always seemed to me, and the life I live now is a lot like Mr. Scrooge's Christmas morning.

When Mel and I finally went to bed, my heart was full of holiday cheer, but it didn't last, because that night Ebenezer Scrooge wasn't the only one plagued by disturbing dreams. So was I. Mine was the same nightmare I've had countless time before, only this version was worse than usual.

The dream always starts in the same awful way. I drive up to Sue Danielson's residence and see lights burning inside. I switch off the engine and exit my vehicle as quietly as possible. I hold my breath as I step up onto the wooden planks of Sue's creaky front porch. The front door is unlocked, and the knob turns in my hand. I enter a scene of utter carnage and find Sue, bloodied, wounded, and weaponless, sitting propped against the living-room wall. Only this time another awful element has been added. The two boys, Jared and Chris, both wearing pajamas, lie sprawled in pools of blood just outside their bedroom door.

Knowing that Richie is armed and dangerous, I hand my backup weapon, my Glock, to Sue and start toward the hallway. Right then a gunshot splits the night. I turn back to Sue just in time to see the Glock slip slowly from her now-lifeless fingers.

I woke up then—sweating, shaking, and fighting the covers.

"Are you all right?" Mel asked, touching my shoulder.

"I'm fine," I told her, "just a bad dream."

Not wanting to disturb her any further, I staggered out of the bed, grabbed my robe, and headed for the living room. I walked over to the window and stood staring outside, where the muted illumination provided by a neighbor's yard light revealed thick, feathery snowflakes blowing sideways in the wind.

A few minutes later, after I left the window and settled on the couch, Mel padded out of the bedroom and sidled up beside me. By the time she leaned against me and lifted my arm over her shoulder, my cold sweats had finally subsided.

"Better?" she asked.

I nodded. "Some," I replied.

"You can't change history," Mel murmured.

It was hardly surprising that she knew exactly what had happened. She'd witnessed the shattering aftermath of this particular nightmare countless times before.

"I know," I agreed.

"We both know, however, that there's a good chance you can change the future," she added. "Jared Danielson and his grandmother are looking for answers, and I'm pretty sure you're the only one who's going to provide them."

That's the strange thing about being married to Mel—she often seems able to read my mind, because while I'd been staring out at the swirling snow, I had arrived at the same conclusion.

"You're probably right," I acknowledged.

"So come back to bed now and try to get some sleep," she told me. "We'll sort all this out in the morning."

Chapter 6

I awakened on Wednesday morning to the noisy racket of heavy machinery lumbering around outside our house. Mel, seated on her side of the bed, was pulling on a pair of boots.

"What's all the noise?" I wondered aloud.

"The snowplows are here again," she told me, "but it's better than our having to clear the driveway ourselves."

"Has Sarah been out?"

"Not yet."

"How deep is the snow?"

"According to the TV, another nine inches," Mel answered.

That was several more inches than I liked. In the

kitchen I found that the coffee machine was already up and running. As I waited for my cup to brew, I noticed a large rectangular package lying on the kitchen island, one that bore clear indications of its Nordstrom origins.

"What's that?" I asked, pointing at the box as Mel entered the room, settling her last earring into place.

"It's your Christmas present," Mel said. "You need to open it."

"It's not Christmas yet," I objected, "not nearly."

"Close enough," she told me, "and you should open it now."

So I did. Inside, under a layer of white tissue, I found a carefully folded, bright blue parka. It was lightweight but puffy and constructed of some slick material that, I was sure, made it waterproof.

"Try it on," Mel urged, unzipping it and holding it out for me to put on over my pajamas. Feeling more than slightly silly, I complied. Naturally it fit perfectly.

Mel stood back and observed me for a moment before nodding her approval. I wasn't exactly convinced.

"I feel like the little brother in *A Christmas Story*," I objected, "not the kid with the BB gun but the one who gets trapped in his snowsuit."

"It may not be your typical look," Mel agreed with a slight frown. "I got it for when you're out walking Sarah in bad weather, but if you're heading off to

NOTHING TO LOSE · 57

Alaska in the next day or two, you're going to need this a whole lot sooner than Christmas Day."

"But wait," I objected, "if I'm heading for Alaska, who's going to look after Sarah during the day?"

"I will," she said, "and I'm guessing she'll be coming to work with me."

"Can you do that?" I asked.

Mel looked at me and grinned. "I'm the chief," she said. "If I can get my driveway plowed, I can sure as hell take my dog to work."

After she left, Sarah and I went through our usual morning rituals with me making sure things were handled in a way that wouldn't clog the plumbing. Once I downed sufficient amounts of coffee, I picked up my phone and dialed Todd Hatcher. He's another holdover from Special Homicide.

Todd hails from southern Arizona originally. He dresses like a cowboy and looks for all the world like your basic good ol' boy, but he's a forensic accountant and one of the smartest people I've ever met. People sometimes go by appearances and dismiss him as a country hick without realizing that his home-spun appearance—western shirt, jeans, and boots—disguises the brilliant, nerdlike mind lurking under his customary Stetson.

Once SHIT folded, Todd began doing his consulting

gigs from a ranch outside Olympia, where he lives with wife, Julie, and daughter, Sabrina. As a private investigator, I've used his services before on occasion, and I felt as though Todd was my best bet for picking up any kind of financial or public-record trail for Christopher Danielson.

"Hey, Beau," Todd said when he answered the phone. "How's it going? Are you and Mel ready for the holidays?"

I glanced around the room. Mel had made a few more subtle adjustments to my Christmas decor. The place was looking suitably festive.

"Pretty much," I said. "How about you?"

"We're getting Sabrina a pony for Christmas," Todd told me, "a mare. We'll be picking her up later today."

I had enough trouble looking after a dog. I didn't want to consider the complications of having a pony, especially in the doo-doo department. "Good for you," I said.

"So what can I help you with?" Todd asked. "You don't usually haul off and call me out of the goodness of your heart."

"You're right," I said, "because I do need some assistance. I'm working a missing-persons case. A kid named Christopher Danielson went missing in 2006. His older brother, Jared, is looking for him. Annie

Hinkle, the grandmother in Ohio who raised the two boys after their mother was murdered, is on her death-bed. She and Chris had a falling-out when he was a kid, and he took off for Homer, Alaska, to live with his paternal grandparents. Annie is hoping for some kind of reconciliation with Chris before she kicks off, but when Jared went looking for him, he found out that Chris had disappeared from Homer in 2006."

"You mentioned that their mother was murdered," Todd put in. "Was this one of your cases?"

I believe I already mentioned that Todd's a smart guy, but it took a moment for me to formulate a response. "Their mother was my partner at Seattle PD," I said at last. "She was murdered by her ex, who put a bullet in his own head a couple minutes later."

The silence that followed seemed to last forever. Todd spoke first, simply picking up the specifics of this case without delving into any of the painful issues from the past.

"How old was Christopher when he disappeared?" Todd asked.

"Seventeen," I answered, calling up the information from what Jared had given me the previous day. "He disappeared sometime during his senior year at Homer High School. After leaving Ohio he spent several years living with his paternal grandparents, Gary and Linda

Danielson. By the time Chris went missing, the grand-father had passed away."

"Do we have an exact date for that disappearance?"

"No," I replied. "We don't."

"Date of birth?" Todd asked.

"September eighteenth, 1988."

"Social Security number?"

"No idea," I replied, "but I'm sure you'll find one. Given the nature of the boys' parents' deaths, the two sets of grandparents weren't exactly on the best of terms, and that kind of information wasn't passed along to the folks in Ohio."

"Was a missing-persons report filed at the time?"

"Maybe, maybe not. We're not sure."

"We?" Todd asked.

"Jared and I," I answered. "Jared, Chris's older brother, is a newly ordained priest now—Father Dan-ielson. He's looked as far as he's been able to but hasn't found anything. Unfortunately, he isn't blessed with your kind of Internet search skills. Neither am I, for that matter."

As Todd and I talked, I was thumbing through the copy of *The Log* that Jared had left behind. That par-ticular yearbook's original owner, a girl whose name was Edwina Moran, had been a sophomore the year Chris was a senior. As I glanced at all the very young faces pictured there, I wondered which of the guys in Chris's class might have been pals with him. Were any of those people still living in Homer? Did any of them remember him? Had they wondered and worried about Chris's sudden disappearance from their midst? And if so, why hadn't there been more of a reaction to his absence? Although, since Chris's grandmother hadn't seen fit to file a missing-persons report, I could see why none of his friends might have done so on their own. After all, since they were just a bunch of kids, who was going to pay any attention to them?

"All right," Todd said finally. "This gives me a starting place. I'll see what I can do, and I'll send you whatever turns up."

"Thanks," I said. "You know where to send the bill."

"Didn't you say that the boy's mother was your partner?" Todd asked.

"Yes," I said quietly. "Yes, she was."

"In that case there won't be a bill."

That blue line may be thin, but it's very strong, and there was a lump in my throat when I answered. "Appreciate it, Todd," I said, "more than you know."

After the call ended, I studied the senior section of *The Log* once more, thumbing through it a page at a time, studying the earnest faces pictured there as well as the captions underneath each photo. Some-where along the way, I remembered something about my mother and me. During eighth grade I fell in with some of the tough kids at school—a gang of five boys, all of them seemingly determined to go in the wrong direction. Somehow my mother got wind of it, prob-ably through the principal. That summer she kept me on very short boundaries. When I asked her why, she told me, "Birds of a feather flock together, and I don't want you hanging out with those guys."

When it came time for my freshman year at Bal-lard High School, she told me, "Okay, there's football, basketball, or track—pick one." I was tall and scrawny, so naturally I chose basketball. Eventually I became reasonably proficient at it and moved on to the varsity squad during my sophomore year. As a result I ended up in a completely different social milieu from that gang of young toughs.

As for my eighth-grade pals? Two of them never graduated from high school and went to work on family fishing boats in Seattle. One of the boats sank, and my former friend's name along with those of his father, two brothers, and a cousin are all engraved on the memo-rial at Seattle's Fishermen's Terminal. As for the other one? He took his fishing money and opened a small used-car dealership that eventually morphed into two large new-car dealerships.

Of the three of us who did graduate, one got drafted right out of high school. His name is engraved in black granite at the Vietnam Memorial in Washington, D.C. The second one went to prison in his early twenties on a vehicular-manslaughter charge after killing two people, an elderly couple, while he was driving drunk. I have no idea what became of him after that. As for number three? That would be yours truly, who ended up in law enforcement as a homicide cop. I may not be a police officer anymore, not officially, but that's how I still think of myself—as a cop.

Suddenly all those innocent-looking young faces in the yearbook took on a whole new meaning. I flipped back through the pages again, studying the captions more carefully this time, looking for the kids who might have been shoved aside, bullied, or dissed. I ignored the people who were student-body or class officers. I ignored the valedictorian and salutatorian. Ditto for the guys who played varsity sports or were in the National Honor Society. Instead I went searching for guys like Chris who had nothing at all in their captions—no honors, sports, or club affiliations whatsoever. If Chris Danielson had been a nobody—an outsider—chances are his best friends would have been cut from the same cloth.

I ended up with a list of seven names and immediately sent that off to Todd. Take a look at these guys, I told him in a text. Any current contact information would be greatly appreciated.

Then I made a call to the non-emergency number at Homer PD. After speaking to a clerk in the records department, I learned that the information Jared had come up with earlier was absolutely true. Christopher Danielson might have disappeared off the face of the earth sometime in the spring of 2006, but no official missing-persons report was ever filed. The poor kid had vanished into thin air, and no one had given a tinker's damn.

I might have been years late to the party, but I cared now, and so did Jared. Together we would find out what had happened to that younger brother of his, or as my mother would have said, we'd both know the reason why.

Chapter 7

While I waited to see what, if anything, Todd Hatcher might turn up, I showered, dressed, and then puttered around the house for a bit—putting out the trash, emptying the dishwasher, starting a load of clothes. In my old age, I seem to have become quite accomplished in the househusband department. Then, as a reward for doing the chores, I sat down in front of the fireplace to work my crosswords. I was coming to the end of those when Todd called back.

"Guess what?" he said. "Your missing person has a son."

I was floored. "He does?"

"Yup, Christopher James Danielson," Todd replied. "According to the state of Alaska's Department of Public Health, he was born December twelfth, 2006, to one Danitza Annette Adams and Christopher Anthony Danielson."

That was a showstopper.

"Does that mean that Chris and Danitza are living happily ever after somewhere in Alaska?"

"I doubt the happily-ever-after part," Todd said. "I'm unable to locate any marriage or divorce records for Danitza Adams and Christopher Danielson. My guess is the child was born out of wedlock after Chris did his disappearing act. I did find marriage records for Danitza Adams and a guy named Gregory Howard Miller. They were married by a judge in Anchorage on June seventeenth, 2011. Gregory died in March of 2013. His cause of death is listed as accidental drowning."

I was making notes as we went along, but it seemed pretty clear that in order to gather any information on Christopher my best source would be the mother of his child.

"Any idea about where I can get in touch with this Danitza? Miller's her last name now?"

"That's correct—Danitza Miller. She lives on Wiley Loop Road in Anchorage and works as an ER nurse for Anchorage General Hospital."

"Address and phone number?"

Todd read them off to me. Once I wrote them down, he continued.

"Danitza Miller was born in Homer, Alaska, on March fourteenth, 1989, to Roger and Eileen Adams."

"Did you say 1989? That would make her a year younger than Chris. They probably attended high school together."

To confirm my suspicions, I reached around and picked up my copy of *The Log*. This time I turned my attention to the pages devoted to the junior class, and there she was in the very first photo at that top of the page. Danitza Adams's head shot revealed a cute blonde with a pixie haircut and a winning smile, but a 1989 birth date meant that most likely she had been only sixteen at the time she gave birth to her son. So what we were dealing with was a sixteen-year-old unwed mother with a boyfriend who most likely hadn't bothered to hang around long enough to do the right thing once he knocked her up. If that were the case, it's no wonder that when Chris headed out for parts unknown, he hadn't bothered to leave a forwarding address. Had I been in his shoes, I probably wouldn't have either. I would have been too ashamed to show my face.

That was my first thought. It took a moment for me to remind myself that considering the existence of my own out-of-wedlock daughter, Naomi Dale, I was being a judgmental hypocrite.

"Did Danitza graduate from high school?"

"Nope," Todd replied. "According to her college transcripts, she first earned a GED. Then, in 2008, she enrolled in the School of Nursing at the University of Alaska in Anchorage, where she graduated with honors four years later."

That was a surprising outcome. For a single mother raising a little kid on her own to graduate from anything in four years was commendable. To do so with honors? That was downright remarkable.

"She must be pretty smart," I said.

"Agreed," Todd replied.

"What about the kids on the other list I sent you, the unaffiliated ones from the yearbook?"

"One of those, a guy named Augie Pardee, is deceased—accidental drug overdose. Two, John Borman and Bill Farmdale, live in Anchorage. Three more— Alex Walker, Phil Bonham, and Ron Wolf—still live in Homer. The last one, Kevin Markham, is an Army Ranger currently deployed to South Korea. I've got addresses and phone numbers on everyone in Alaska other than the dead guy, but I managed to locate a home phone number for his parents. They're still in Homer, too. As for tracking down the Ranger? Good luck with that."

"I'm guessing he's somebody who got tired of being pushed around and decided to push back."

"I wouldn't be surprised," Todd said. "I also found

Chris's driver's license. I'm sending along a copy of it because of the photo on it, but that original license has never been renewed."

That wasn't good news. In the world as it is now, no one goes anywhere without some kind of currently valid government-issued ID.

"Okay," Todd concluded. "I just pressed send on a file containing everything I've located so far, and I'll pass along whatever else I find as it becomes available."

"And thanks for all this," I told him. "It certainly gives me somewhere to start."

Once Todd's e-mail came in, I opened the file folder and then sat for a time scrolling through the material. The driver's license showed up first. The photo had probably been taken within months of the one in the yearbook, so that wasn't much help.

As I shopped through the various names, each was a bread crumb that might or might not lead me in the right direction for investigating Christopher Danielson's disappearance. As Todd had pointed out, other than the guy doing a tour of duty in South Korea, everyone else was still in Alaska. That probably meant that I needed to be in Alaska, too.

I suppose I could have picked up my phone and started shopping through the collection of phone numbers Todd had helpfully supplied, but I didn't. In my experience if you want truthful answers to difficult questions, you need to be looking at the person you're interviewing—meeting that individual face-to-face and eyeball-to-eyeball. Talking over the phone is not the same thing. But going to Alaska in the dead of winter? Even with a brand-new parka in hand, that hardly sounded inviting.

I glanced out the window. By now the clouds had parted. Bright sunshine glittered off the thick layer of snow covering our backyard, and my iPad indicated the temperature in Bellingham right then had risen to a balmy eighteen degrees. Just for the hell of it, I checked the temperature in Anchorage. According to Accu-Weather, the temperature there coming up on noon was an almost toasty thirty-nine in comparison, and the predicted low that night was thirty-three—both of which were far higher than I had expected.

Then I checked for flights. The ones from Bellingham to Anchorage all went by way of Seattle, but at the moment every flight from Bellingham to anywhere that day was either canceled or delayed due to issues with the airport's deicing equipment. The flights going to and from Seattle and Anchorage were fine. In other words, the only way to catch a flight to Anchorage that day was to get my butt to SeaTac Airport.

Meteorologists will tell you that somewhere between

Bellingham and Seattle there's what's called a convergence zone, a spot where competing weather systems meet up and duke it out. That's exactly where the previous day's Pineapple Express had collided with the polar vortex, just south of Mount Vernon. Above Mount Vernon it had been all snow all the time. By now our weather had moved east, leaving behind roads covered with ice and snow. Below Mount Vernon the drenching rains continued, triggering a spate of flash floods and mudslides.

There was a 5:45 P.M. flight from SeaTac that would have me in Anchorage by eight thirty. I called Mel first, to see if she could come pick up Sarah and her goods at lunchtime to take the dog back to police HQ. Then I booked a seat, packed up, and headed south.

Out of deference to Chief Soames, the snowplow folks had not only cleared our driveway but had made a path from our place straight down to the main drag. From there it was only a hop, a skip, and a jump to southbound I-5, and that had been sanded to within an inch of its life. I started toward Seattle under clear blue skies, but those disappeared the more I traveled south. At first the landscape was covered with snow, but as I neared Mount Vernon, the fields along the freeway were bleak, wall-to-wall mud. By the time I reached Everett, it was raining pitchforks and hammer handles, but I managed to make my way to SeaTac without any problem.

Once at the airport, I took note of the level and row where the car was parked, then went inside. I was plenty early, so I checked into the lounge and spent the wait booking a hotel room and renting a car.

"Yes," I told the car-rental agent, "I definitely want four-wheel drive, heated seats, and a heated steering wheel."

"And Blizzak tires?" she asked.

If those were some kind of winter-weather tire, I had never encountered them before. "Are those recommended?" I asked.

"Definitely," she said.

"Okay, then," I said. "Blizzak it is."

I had purchased a first-class seat on the plane, so I had dinner—a grilled hot sandwich, a salad, and a bag of chips. It wasn't exactly sumptuous, but it did the trick. I spent the rest of the time continuing to sort through the material Todd had sent me.

He'd helpfully let me know that Danitza Miller was currently working day-shift hours—7:00 A.M. to 3:00 P.M.—in the ER at Anchorage General. As a single woman with a relatively young child, she probably wouldn't be thrilled to have a complete stranger show up on her doorstep at home unannounced and late at night. It seemed to me that it might be better for me to track her down at her workplace the next day. That way I could at least introduce myself in public. These days guys can't be too careful in those kinds of situations. Even with the best of intentions, it's far too easy for private male/female interactions to end up being deemed inappropriate.

So once I got to Anchorage, I collected my car—a Ford SUV model that Mel and I used to refer to as "Exploders." As ordered, it came with four-wheel drive, heated seats, and the highly recommended Blizzak tires, so I was good to go. I dialed the Captain Cook Hotel's information into the vehicle's internal GPS and let the car direct me to where I was going. I know I've had my issues with technology over the years, but when you're in a strange city, a GPS system with audio included has it hands down over a physical map.

Once in my room at the hotel, I spoke to Mel. Sarah had behaved herself admirably in the office and was now welcome to visit Bellingham PD whenever she wished. After touching base for a few minutes, we said our good-nights. I tried watching TV for a while after that, but I kept dozing off. It was ten o'clock Anchorage time, eleven in Seattle, when I turned off the TV and bedside lamp.

Dreaming about Sue Danielson had cost me most

of the previous night's sleep. Tonight, maybe because she knew I was looking for her son, Sue left me alone. The next time I looked at the clock, it was 7:00 A.M. The sky outside was nowhere near daylight, but I awakened with a sense of purpose. I had a job to do, and it was time to drag myself out of bed and get with the program.

Chapter 8

Over the years I've learned that the best way to gain access to a hospital emergency room is to bypass the reception desk altogether. I was approaching the ER entrance when an ambulance pulled up and began unloading a patient. As they rolled the gurney inside, I positioned myself a step and a half behind the medic and made my way inside as though I had every right to be there.

As my patient decoy was wheeled into a curtained cubicle, I looked around. At nine on a weekday morning, the ER wasn't exactly filled to the brim. Thanks to the yearbook photo and the fact that Danitza Miller still wore her ash-blond hair in a pixie cut, I was able to pick her out on my own without having to ask for help.

I spotted her, dressed in a pair of brightly colored floral scrubs, standing next to the nurses' station, chatting with someone on the far side of the counter.

"Ms. Miller?" I asked, approaching her from behind. "May I have a word?"

She spun around and faced me. She was a little bit of a thing, only five-four or so, but she wasn't short on spunk. "Is this about a patient?" she wanted to know.

"No," I replied, holding out one of my cards. "This is actually something of a personal nature. If I could have a moment or two of your time."

She glanced at the card briefly, pocketed it, and then peered up at me. "As you can see, I'm working right now and—"

"I'm a private investigator looking into the disappearance of Christopher Danielson."

The change in both her attitude and expression was instantaneous. "You're looking for Chris?" she asked.

I nodded.

She turned back to the woman on the other side of the counter. "I'm going to take my break now," she announced. To me she added, "We can talk in the coffee shop."

Leading the way, she walked briskly through the ER, out another entrance, and then across a granite lobby area into a coffee shop. She proceeded through the room to a table at the far back.

"Sit there," she ordered, pointing. "I'll get the coffee. Black or with cream and sugar?"

"Black, please," I murmured.

I had no doubt that Danitza Miller ordered her ER patients around in exactly that way, and I'm equally sure they did the same thing I did and complied without a word of protest.

She reappeared a few minutes later carrying a tray bearing two paper cups loaded with steaming-hot coffee. She put the cups on the table and then shoved the tray aside before staring me in the eye.

"Who's looking for Chris?" she demanded.

I had expected to be the one doing the interviewing, but that wasn't the case.

"His brother," I answered.

"Jared?"

I nodded.

"Why?"

"Their grandmother is dying," I said, "their other grandmother, Annie Hinkle, back home in Ohio. She's evidently hoping to make things right with Chris before she passes on."

"You're saying Chris isn't in Ohio?" Danitza asked.

That surprised me. "Not as far as I know," I replied. "From what I've been able to determine, he hasn't set foot in Ohio since he ran away from home right after he graduated from the eighth grade."

Danitza's cheeks paled, as though some long-held forgone conclusion had at last been verified. Then she took a deep breath. "He's dead, then, isn't he?" she murmured.

Before I could reply, she stood up abruptly. "I can't talk about this here. Do you know where I live?"

I nodded.

"I get off at three. I'll be home by three thirty. Come by then. My son, James—we all call him by his middle name—has his Dungeons & Dragons club meeting right after school and won't be home until around four thirty. I don't want to discuss any of this in front of him."

Abandoning her unfinished coffee, she walked away, leaving me sitting there wondering exactly what had happened, but one thing was pretty sure. There was no point in wasting my time looking for any of those unaffiliated boys from Chris's high-school yearbook, at least not right that minute. Danitza Adams Miller was willing to talk to me, and I had a feeling she would be able to tell me most of what I needed to know. The finality of the way she'd said the words "He's dead, then" made me think there was a lot more to the story than I'd managed to glean so far.

To while away the time, I spent the remainder of the morning and part of the afternoon doing some strategic Christmas shopping. Faced with either buying more luggage to get home or using UPS, I had most of the items wrapped and shipped, some to Bellingham for the kids who would be coming there for Christmas and some to Kelly down in Ashland, since she and her family were going to spend the holidays with Jeremy's folks this time around. I sent another enormous package of wrapped presents to Texas, including an almost life-size plush husky for Athena and a rugged rubber walrus chew toy for Lucy. Naturally all the items had some kind of Alaskan connection.

I also bought a few things I didn't ship home, including a pair of sturdy snow boots, not quite mukluks but good enough. Mel had gotten me a parka, but she'd neglected to buy a pair of gloves. I could hardly blame her for that. After all, at the time she was out doing her Christmas shopping, she'd had no idea that Alaska was about to become part of my agenda.

I already knew that at some point I'd have to make the four-hour-plus drive to Homer. In case something went haywire with the rental on the trip between Anchorage and there, I wanted to be prepared. To begin with, I told the clerk I was looking for a pair of fur-lined gloves. Much to my surprise and on her recommendation, I came away with what she said were highly insulated mittens instead

Back in my hotel room, I turned once more to *The Log*. This time, rather than focus on the junior-class head-shot photos, I scrolled through the various groupings of kids involved in extracurricular activities, scanning through the captions on the bottom, and found Danitza Adams's name listed again and again. She was a member of the varsity cheerleading squad. She was in both the National Honor Society and the Quill and Scroll, an organization that recognizes high-school kids involved in journalism of one sort or another. Sure enough, Danitza was pictured as part of the yearbook crew. She had also played Juliet in that year's school presentation of *Romeo and Juliet*.

That set me to thinking. Her family and Chris's weren't exactly the Montagues and the Capulets, but still, how could a bright young girl who had all the potential of being voted Most Likely to Succeed have ended up with an apparent loser of a kid like Chris, someone who seemed hell-bent on turning himself into a deadbeat? How had the two of them become a couple? I suspected that neither family would have been any too thrilled by the prospect.

As a consequence I wasn't just Johnny-on-the-spot at Danitza's place for our scheduled three-thirty appointment—I actually arrived fifteen minutes early, bringing with me, I confess, a preconceived notion about what I'd find there.

Danitza Miller was a single mom. Having been raised in a two-bedroom apartment by an unwed mother, I knew something about that reality. Growing up, I'd always envied kids who were able to live in actual houses. We never did, and my mom was a renter until the day she died. Since Danitza and her son were also a one-income family, I expected to find them living in somewhat humble surroundings. Instead when I pulled up outside the address on Wiley Loop Road, I found myself parked in front of a respectable-looking two-story house in what appeared to be a prosperous suburban neighborhood. The tall wooden fence surrounding the yard was strung with an array of multicolored lights, and a fully decorated Christmas tree glowed in the front window. Given that this was Alaska in the winter, I suspected Christmas lights stayed on around the clock. In fact, although it was barely midafternoon on my watch, the pinkish glow of the sky overhead said it was close to sunset.

When Danitza drove up in a late-model Honda, I noticed that she pulled in to a two-car garage with an

SUV of some kind parked in the other bay. Hers might have been a one-income, one-driver family, but she had a two-car garage with two cars parked inside. My first thought was that maybe her folks had been helping her out financially, but of course I turned out to be dead wrong on that score. I was about to discover that the Adams family, not unlike my mother's, never lifted a finger to help either their single-mother daughter or their fatherless grandson.

A shoveled walk led to the front porch, but Danitza motioned me over to the driveway and into the garage. Being ushered into her house like that, through the back door and into a small but tidy kitchen, made me feel as though I were being treated as a longtime acquaintance or friend rather than a complete stranger. In the mudroom she encouraged me to strip off the parka (warmer than I actually needed) and my boots before she led me on into the living room, turning on more lights as she went.

I paused at the fireplace and looked at a framed photo of a young man sitting in a place of honor among the Christmas decorations on the mantel. At first glance I thought it was Christopher, but closer examination revealed that wasn't the case. The haircut and clothing didn't work. This had to be a recent school portrait of Christopher James Danielson rather than one of his absent father.

"Your son's a good-looking kid," I commented, sensing that Danitza had walked up behind me and was gazing past my shoulder toward the photo.

"He is that," she allowed. "Jimmy looks a lot like his dad. He's also a straight-A student, plays in the jazz band, and helps out around the house. He's the one who put up all the Christmas decorations."

Having just accomplished that complex task on my own for the first time ever, I was suitably impressed.

"Won't you take a seat?" she invited. "Can I get you something?"

"No, I'm fine, thank you," I said sinking down onto a nearby sofa.

Danitza took a place in an easy chair across from me, laid my card on the intervening glass-topped coffee table, and then looked me in the face. "You're a private detective, Mr. Beaumont?" she asked.

I nodded. "Most people call me Beau."

"And most people call me Nitz," she told me. "You said Jared Danielson hired you to look for Chris?" I nodded. "All right, then," she continued resignedly. "What do you want to know?"

I decided this was no time for playing games or pulling punches. "Your initial response this morning surprised me," I said.

"How so?"

"Once I said Chris has never returned to Ohio, you immediately concluded he had to be dead. Why?"

"When he left Homer without saying a word to me, that's what I assumed—that he'd gone back home to Ohio. A couple of months earlier, he had gotten into a big fight with his grandmother in Homer, left her house, and dropped out of school. He was renting a room at a friend's house and waiting tables at a local hamburger joint, Zig's Place, trying to save up enough money to pay for a trip back to Ohio later that spring. He said he owed his brother an apology, and he wanted to deliver it in person. When he came back to Alaska, he told me he planned on getting a job on one of the fishing boats. You don't have to have a high-school diploma to do that."

"Wait," I said. "What's this about an apology?"

"As soon as I saw your card this morning, I recognized your name." Nitz paused and gave me a piercing look. "You're the detective who urged Jared to grab Chris and leave the house the night their parents died, right?"

I nodded. "Guilty as charged."

"Chris and I talked a lot about that night," Danitza

said. "He was still a little kid when it happened, and that terrible event haunted him. He was angry that his parents were dead, and why wouldn't he be? When he was shipped off to Ohio to live with his maternal grandparents, things got worse. He was rebellious and acting out. By the time I met him, he was starting to feel guilty about how much trouble he'd given his grandmother before he finally ran away and came to live with his other grandparents in Homer.

"While he was living in Ohio, his mother's parents only told him their daughter's side of the story. Once he got to Homer, his father's family did the opposite. They filled him full of his father's point of view. The Danielsons claimed that Richie was the real victim—that he'd been driven to do what he did because Sue was such a poor excuse for a wife and mother."

"So one set of grandparents said one thing and the other ones said something else?" I asked.

Danitza nodded. "Which meant Chris ended up not knowing who or what to believe. Not only that. To begin with I believe Chris was under the impression that if he and Jared hadn't left the house that night—if they had still been there—they could somehow have prevented what happened."

With the horrendous scene from my recent nightmare still fresh in my mind, I shook my head.

"That's not true," I declared. "When Richard Danielson turned up at Sue's house that night, he came armed to the teeth. I'm pretty sure that before he ever set foot inside, he had already made up his mind about what was going to happen. I believe that if the boys had been there, Richie would have murdered them right along with their mother." I paused for a moment before continuing. "Did you know that Sue was my partner in the homicide unit at Seattle PD?" I asked.

Nitz nodded. "Once Chris and I started talking about it, I made it my business to look up everything I could find about that night. The fact that the two of you were partners was mentioned in one of the articles I read online."

"Take it from me, Sue Danielson was a terrific partner and an amazing mother," I said. "No matter what Richard's parents might have told Chris about his father, the man was a violent and abusive drunk. He was also up to his eyeteeth in the drug trade."

Nitz nodded. "I found out about that, too," she told me. "Back then the Web wasn't what it is now, but I was able to track down several news accounts written at the time, and those made his involvement in drug dealing pretty clear. Chris was stunned when I told him about it. Somehow Grandpa and Grandma Danielson had neglected to mention anything about that. As far as I'm concerned, what they did to Chris was nothing short of brainwashing."

I have to say I was impressed. When all this had happened, Chris and Danitza had both been teenagers, seventeen and sixteen years of age respectively, yet it sounded as though they had discussed some pretty serious stuff.

"You cared for him a lot, didn't you?" I suggested quietly.

She nodded.

"How did the two of you meet—at school?"

Nitz smiled and shook her head. "Not at school. As far as school was concerned, we were never in the same class and ran in totally different circles."

With that, Danitza rose from her chair, walked over to a bookshelf, and retrieved what I assumed to be another framed photograph. When she handed it to me, however, I realized that it wasn't a photo at all. Instead it was a pencil drawing of Danitza, not as she was now but as she must have been back then—pert, cute, and sweet, with glowing eyes and a bright smile illuminating her face. I was instantly reminded of the pencil portrait Chris had done of his mother.

"He drew this for you?" I asked.

She nodded. "He was working in a restaurant at the time."

That's when I noticed that the image had been drawn on something that looked like a used paper place mat, complete with a circular brownish stain from what was probably the bottom of a coffee cup. Under the drawing was a hand-scrawled message: "Would you like to hang out sometime?"

I gave the drawing back to Danitza. "Sounds like a killer of an opening line to me," I said with a smile, "the kind of invitation no right-thinking girl could possibly refuse."

All through our conversation, Danitza Miller's facial expressions had been entirely serious. Now, for the first time, she gave me something that resembled a smile. "Yup," she said thoughtfully. "I said yes and gave him my phone number on the spot. After that he reeled me in, hook, line, and sinker."

Talk about the same old story—the local "it" girl becomes involved with the poor loser kid from the wrong side of the tracks. Not exactly *Romeo and Juliet,* but close enough.

"I take it your parents didn't approve?" I ventured.

"Are you kidding? Not at all," she agreed. "Homer's not a very big a place. Unfortunately, there was a good deal of history between my father and Chris's dad, Richard Danielson. While they were in high school, they were head-to-head rivals when it came to their varsity sports teams. To make things worse, they ended up chasing after the same girl—my mother, as it turns out."

"And once your dad was declared the winner, the two of them became mortal enemies?" I asked.

"Something like that," Nitz admitted. "I didn't know anything about it until one night when Chris came to the house to pick me up for a date. My dad wasn't home at the time, so I introduced him to my mother. When my mom told Dad about it later, he hit the roof. He was waiting up for me that night when I came home, and he was absolutely livid. He ordered me, 'Stay away from that no-good Danielson kid. He's a piece of crap, just like his father.'"

"Which you chose not to do?" I suggested.

Danitza smiled again. "Why would I?" she returned. "What's better than the taste of forbidden fruit? From that moment on, Chris and I took our dating underground. My friends were all in on it and helped make it happen. I think they thought there was something romantic about our sneaking around behind my parents' backs. When I wanted to go and be with Chris, my friends always claimed I was with them."

"When's the last time you saw Chris?"

"The morning of the final Sunday in March 2006," she answered at once.

It was telling that she remembered the exact day and time.

"My folks were out of town that weekend. After Chris got off work on Saturday night, I spent the night at his place. The next morning I woke up sick as a dog. Chris borrowed a roommate's car and took me home. I never saw him again after that. I didn't even talk to him on the phone."

Given her son's birth date, it wasn't difficult to put two and two together.

"Morning sickness?" I asked.

Nitz nodded. "I thought it was some kind of flu bug. I'd been having symptoms for a week or more. I was naïve and had no idea what was happening, but when I was sick again that Monday, my mother figured it out. She went to the drugstore and bought one of those home pregnancy tests. It came back positive, of course.

"When my father found out, he went berserk. I was a minor. He demanded the name of the father so he could call the cops and put the SOB behind bars for statutory rape. I wasn't going to let that happen, so I told Dad he'd have to take his pick, because the father could have been any one of three boys, and I wasn't going to tell him any of their names."

I had to give the girl credit for gumption. Hearing her claim she'd had more than one lover must have been a stunner for her father. It's a wonder he hadn't suffered a coronary on the spot.

"That must have sent your father around the bend," I suggested.

Nitz nodded. "Absolutely," she said. "Dad had always been a bully. I'd spent years watching him boss my mother around. I hated it that she always gave in to him no matter what. I decided my best bet was to fight fire with fire."

"What happened next?" I asked. "I suppose he demanded paternity tests all around?"

Nitz shook her head. "Nope, I didn't give him a chance. I had seen him angry before, but never that angry. I decided to get the hell out of there, so I went to my room, loaded some clothes into a backpack, and let myself out through my bedroom window. I'd gotten pretty adept at that by then," she added with a grin.

"Did Chris know about any of this—the pregnancy test, I mean?"

Again Nitz shook her head. "He was at work that night. I knew he couldn't talk on the phone, so I left a message saying I needed to talk to him. He never called me back."

"He had no idea you were pregnant?"

"I don't think so."

"What happened then?"

"I went to his place, expecting Chris to turn up there as soon as he got off shift, but he didn't. I waited around as long as I could, but it was freezing cold. Finally I left another message. Then, since I couldn't very well go back home, I walked out to the highway and caught a ride to Anchorage."

"You hitchhiked from Homer to Anchorage?" I demanded in disbelief. "In the middle of the night?"

"And in the snow," she added.

"How far is it from here to there?"

"Four and a half hours, give or take. It turns out that the guy who gave me a ride was someone I knew from school, so it wasn't like I rode with a complete stranger. He gave me a ride to Aunt Penny and Uncle Wally's place and dropped me off there."

"And they are?"

"Penny and Wally Olmstead," Danitza explained. "Penny is my mother's younger sister. My mom always claimed that Penny was her mother's 'change of life baby,' and the two of them were fifteen years apart. Penny's only eight years older than I am, so as I was growing up, she was more like an older sister to me than she was an aunt. When I showed up on her doorstep early the next morning and told them what had happened, she and her new husband took me in. I stayed with them for the next five years.

"They'd never had any kids of their own, but once James was born, they looked after him while I went back to school. Uncle Wally was a counselor at West Anchorage High. He helped me get my GED and managed to find a scholarship that allowed me to enroll in the nursing program at the UAA—the University of Alaska Anchorage. I worked while I was going to school, of course, but I never would have been able to manage on my own without their help."

"Did you keep reaching out to Chris?"

Danitza nodded. "I kept calling his number and texting him, too, but I never heard back from him. Eventually I got a recorded message that the number was no longer in service."

"So you're saying Chris did have a cell phone?"

Danitza nodded. "He couldn't afford either an iPhone or a calling plan, so I gave him what they call a burner for his birthday and paid for it out of my allowance."

As a kid I never had the luxury of being given an allowance. My mother couldn't afford it. If Danitza's allowance had been generous enough that she could afford to provide her boyfriend with a cell phone, she had grown up in far more luxurious circumstances than I, and I respected her that much more for walking away from all that in order to keep her child. And the fact that

Chris had been in possession of a phone made me feel as though we were making progress. Maybe even years after the fact, there might be a way to track his phone's location.

"You wouldn't happen to remember the number, would you?" I asked.

Danitza picked up her phone, tapped a few buttons, and then handed it over to me. She had her contacts list open to a page that said "Chris." No last name was given, but there was a phone number. I jotted it down and then returned the device to her.

"I'm surprised you kept his number," I said.

She nodded. "Whenever I've gotten a new phone, I've kept his number and all his messages and texts, too. I kept them for Jimmy so that someday, when he's a little older, he'll be able to hear the sound of his father's voice."

That touched me, and I had to swallow the lump that suddenly caught in my throat. When I spoke again, I changed the subject. "So you thought Chris had gone off to Ohio and that eventually he'd come back?"

Danitza nodded. "I believed it as long as I could. In fact, until this morning when I met you, I still hoped it was true—that somehow he was still alive and well out there somewhere, living his life without me. In fact, that's why I named our son Christopher, so that if Chris ever came looking and found that name, he'd know it was us."

"But he never did."

"No," she agreed quietly. "He never did, and although my son's first name is Christopher, he goes by James or Jimmy. Calling him Christopher hurt too much."

Unsure of how to respond, I took a moment to glance around the house. It wasn't ultra-posh by any means, but it certainly would have been out of reach of most single moms left to raise kids on their own.

"So how did you end up here," I asked, "on Wiley Loop Road?"

"Eventually I met a guy," she said, "a very nice guy named Greg Miller. He was a part-time nursing student at the UAA. He was two years older than I was but a year behind me in school since he went to school part of the year and supported himself as a crabber the rest of the time. He made good money fishing, but working on a crab boat wasn't what he wanted to do for the rest of his life.

"Greg and I became friends first. He was great with James. Took him fishing. Taught him how to ski—did all those boy things with him. We ended up falling in love. Greg was ready to get married a lot sooner than I was, but in time he won me over. He had bought this place on his own before we got married. It was way more expensive than I could ever afford, but he told me not to worry. He said that when he bought the house, he signed up for mortgage insurance. He had to pay a higher premium because of his job, but he told me that if anything ever happened to him, the house would be paid in full, and it was—five years later he went down with the *Snow-Queen*."

Ballard, the area where I grew up, is still ground zero for Seattle's fishing fleet, and the world of commercial fishermen is a tight-knit community. If a boat goes down somewhere, people from Ballard pay attention, because there's a good chance someone they know might have been on board. So I remembered the *Snow-Queen* incident. The vessel had lost power, iced up, and capsized during a raging storm in the Bering Sea. Crew members abandoned ship, but they had all succumbed to the cold long before the coast guard was able to reach them. No one survived.

"I'm so sorry," I said.

Nitz nodded. "Thank you. I still miss them both," she added, "Chris because he was my first love and Greg because he was such an incredibly good man. As far as love is concerned, I consider myself a two-time loser—except for James, of course."

As if on cue, the front door slammed open. "Hey,

Mom," a young voice called. "I'm home. What's for dinner?"

Christopher James Danielson had announced his arrival before he ever closed the door. As soon as he did so, he saw his mother and me sitting in the living room. "Oh, sorry," he said quickly. "I didn't know we had company."

"This is Mr. Beaumont," Danitza said. "He was a friend of your birth father's back when he and his brother were living in Seattle."

James was a long-legged and good-looking preteen whose striking resemblance to his uncle, Father Jared Danielson, was downright spooky.

I held out my hand. Slipping off his backpack, James walked over and returned the gesture with a surprisingly firm grip and a ready grin. "Glad to meet you, sir," he murmured respectfully. "Did you really know my father?"

I nodded. "Your dad was several years younger than you are now, but yes, I knew him and his older brother, Jared, too."

"What was he like?"

In all of James's twelve years, I suspect I was possibly the only person alive, other than his mother, who had actually known Chris Danielson in the flesh.

"He was a good boy," I answered truthfully. "He and

his brother both were, and neither of them deserved to lose their parents the way they did." I wanted to add the words "and neither did you" to that statement, but I didn't. And it turns out I didn't have to. Looking me in the eye, James favored me with a tiny nod that told me he got it. As someone who had already lost two parents—both his birth father and his stepfather—he understood all too well.

"How are you fixed for homework?" Danitza asked, interrupting our conversation and precluding any further discussion.

"I've got some math and a lot of social studies," he answered.

"Go upstairs and work on that while I finish with Mr. Beaumont here," she said. "Once you're done with schoolwork, we'll order a pizza."

James's face brightened. "Sounds good," he said. With that he gathered his backpack and disappeared up the stairs.

For a moment I couldn't speak past another catch in my throat. Christopher James Danielson was clearly a terrific, well-brought-up young man. It broke my heart to think that his grandmother never got to meet him. Sue Danielson would have been so very proud.

Chapter 9

It had been overcast and getting dark when I parked in front of Danitza Miller's home an hour or so earlier. When I left a little after five, I came outside to discover it was pitch dark and had started to snow. So far it didn't amount to much—mostly light flurries. In Seattle it would've been enough to have people crowding grocery stores' aisles to do "panic" shopping. Once some of the white stuff stuck, drivers on Seattle's roadways would have gone nuts and started slamming into one another. In Anchorage it was business as usual.

Back at the hotel, I sat in my room for a while and perused the notes I'd made during my long conversation with Danitza Miller. With each detail I began putting together a timeline on Chris's disappearance. The last Sunday in March of that year would have been the twenty-sixth. Nitz had spent the previous night at Chris's place, and then he'd taken her home the next morning because she wasn't feeling well. The big fight with her parents that had resulted in her leaving home had happened the following day, on Monday evening.

That night Nitz had gone to Chris's place and waited for him to get off work, but he hadn't shown. Whatever had happened to him had most likely occurred on either Sunday or Monday. Had he actually gone to work that night? The only way to find out about that for sure was to get boots on the ground in Homer itself, which gave me another reason for making that side trip.

So who all was involved in Chris's disappearance? I instantly removed Nitz herself from my list of possible suspects. Yes, either the boyfriend or the girlfriend is usually involved in love-gone-wrong homicides, but in this case I couldn't see it. Had there maybe been another boy involved? Maybe someone else had been competing with Chris for Danitza's attention. If that were the case, she hadn't mentioned it.

That brought me around to her parents, most specifically Danitza's volatile father. It was interesting to know that Richie Danielson and Roger Adams had been in each other's crosshairs as far back as high school. It must have driven Roger nuts to find out that years later his longtime rival's son had knocked up his

sixteen-year-old daughter. Remembering the murderous thoughts in my heart when I first discovered that
my daughter, Kelly, and her boyfriend, Jeremy, were
in the family way, I could see how Nitz's father might
have gone off the rails. With that in mind, I picked up
the phone and dialed Todd Hatcher.

"Have you been getting what I've been sending
you?" he asked once he came on the line.

A glance at my mailbox revealed I had fifteen separate messages, all of them from him and all of them un-
opened. "They're here," I said. "I've been tied up with
an interview, so I'll get to them in a while. Do any of
them have to do with Roger Adams, Danitza's father?"

"Not so far," Todd replied. "Why?"

"I think he might bear some looking into," I suggested. "Around the time Chris went missing, Danitza's
parents had just discovered that their sixteen-year-old
daughter was pregnant and that one of the boys in
question was none other than the son of Roger's longtime rival from back in the day, Richie Danielson."

"That probably didn't go over very well," Todd observed.

"You could say that. There was a huge father-
daughter spat that resulted in Danitza packing a bag
and leaving home that very night."

"Which night would that be?" Todd asked.

"That would be Monday, March twenty-seventh, 2006," I told him. "After leaving her folks' place, she went to Chris's apartment and waited for him, expecting him to come home once he got off work. When he didn't show, Danitza hitchhiked from Homer to Anchorage, where she moved in with her aunt and uncle—her mother's younger sister and her husband. She never saw Chris again."

"So when was the last time she *did* see him?" Todd asked.

"That would be the day before, when he dropped her off at her house."

"Unfortunately, there's no way to track his movements."

"There might be," I suggested. "It turns out Chris did have a cell phone—one Danitza gave him. I know it's possible to track locations on those now, but I'm not so sure it was possible back then."

"Nice try but no time," Todd said.

I've been around Todd long enough to know that's rodeo speak for some poor guy who's just been pitched off a bucking bronco sooner than the buzzer, only now the guy biting the dust was yours truly.

"So no way to track the phone?"

"In terms of telecommunications, 2006 is the dark

ages," Todd replied. "Smartphones weren't all that smart back then, and GPS didn't show up on cell phones until several years later. As for finding out the last time the phone was used? Wireless companies don't maintain call records that long."

To say I was disappointed would be an understatement. I had hoped tech magic would somehow come to my rescue, but that wasn't going to happen. Chris Danielson's disappearance, long gone cold, would have to be solved the old-fashioned way—by interviewing witnesses and acquaintances and asking questions rather than counting on the basics of current forensic science—DNA profiles and cell-phone pings.

"Did you have any further luck finding a missing-persons report on Christopher Danielson?" I asked.

"Nope," Todd replied. "I'm coming up empty on that score. None of the agencies I've checked with have any record of one."

Hearing those words made my heart hurt. Twelve years earlier a seventeen-year-old boy had vanished off the face of the earth, and not one person had cared enough to mention his disappearance to the authorities.

"Do we have any idea about Chris's last known location?" Todd asked.

"Danitza believed he was at work at a restaurant

called Zig's Place in Homer that Monday night. She expected him to come home once he got off shift, but he didn't."

"FYI," Todd continued, "Homer has no record of any homicides at all—solved or unsolved—in 2006. They had a couple of suicides and an accidental death or two, but no homicides. In a place as small as Homer, with a population of five thousand, give or take, even a disappearance would have been big news."

"It wasn't because no one knew it happened," I told him. "Suppose Chris was attacked on his way home from work. Any killer with half a brain wouldn't be dumb enough to leave a dead body lying around near the crime scene or inside a relatively well-populated area where someone was likely to find it. Alaska is a vast, wild, and mostly empty space, and a killer would have used that to his advantage."

"So you're saying the killer would have transported the body out into the wilderness in hopes it might never again surface?"

"And even if it did," I added, "had the body been stripped bare, with nothing to assist in confirming an identification and no matching missing-persons report, how would anyone make the connection?"

I asked the question, and for a long moment neither Todd nor I had a ready answer. But then I thought of something. There was still no official report, but I now knew for sure that Chris Danielson was missing.

"Can you tell me who's in charge of unidentified skeletal human remains found in the state of Alaska?" I asked.

After a few moments of swift keyboarding, Todd had an answer. "Unidentified bodies go to the state crime lab in Anchorage. Skeletal remains go to Harriet Raines, a professor of forensic anthropology at the UAA. She teaches there, but she's also the director of a state-funded laboratory on campus where they try to identify skeletal human remains and determine causes of death wherever possible. At that point she turns her findings over to the Alaska State Police, or AST as they're usually referred to—the Alaska State Troopers."

"Can you give me an address and a phone number for that anthropology lab?"

"Sure thing." Todd's voice was interrupted by a beep on the line. "Oops, Beau," he said. "I need to take this call. Once that's done, I'll send along Professor Raines's contact information and start gathering whatever I can on Roger Adams."

"No rush," I told him. "And thanks."

Once off the phone, I started scrolling through some of the information Todd had already sent, including addresses, phone numbers, and employment information on the two unaffiliated guys from The Log who lived in Anchorage—John Borman and Bill Farmdale. Since those two individuals were here in town and so was I, looking them up seemed like as good a starting point as any. There was nothing to say they were close to Chris Danielson or even knew him from a hole in the ground, but with nothing else to go on, even remotely possible leads needed to be tracked down. Better to start out in Anchorage and head for Homer once I'd exhausted the leads here. Not knowing how long any of this would take, I figured it was just as well that I'd left my return flight open.

By then it was coming up on dinnertime. I went over to the desk and examined the in-room dining menu. I used the hotel phone to place a room-service order, and then I used my cell to call Mel.

"Where are you?" I asked.

"Sarah and I are on our way home," she answered. "I don't think she's accustomed to the kind of adoring attention she received yesterday and today. She's done, and so am I. What are you up to?"

"I just ordered dinner from room service."

"All right," she said. "Once I get home, I'll feed her and then give you a call. We'll have a long-distance dinner together with you eating whatever you got from room service—"

"A hamburger and fries," I supplied.

"And I'll have my PB&J," she said. "That way neither one of us will be dining alone."

"Sounds good," I told her.

And that's what we did. We both put our phones on FaceTime and chatted away, with Mel eating her peanut-butter-and-jelly sandwich at our kitchen island while I suffered my way through the meal seated on the only available chair in the room, an ergonomic nightmare—a rolling torture machine made of metal and plastic with scrawny armrests and supposedly lumbar-supporting lumps in all the wrong places.

"How's your room?" Mel asked.

"The room's fine," I said, "but this chair? Not so much. And since this is supposedly a double room, shouldn't they have at least two decent chairs?"

"Quit your bitching," Mel advised, "and tell me about your day."

So I did. She was especially interested in my long conversation with Danitza Miller. "To launch off on her own while pregnant at age sixteen and be able to put herself through school, she must be one tough cookie," Mel observed. "Most of the girls I knew growing up would have swallowed their pride and gone crying to their parents for help, and I'd like to think that most of those parents would have been more than willing to do so."

"Only if said parents were somewhat more open-minded than Roger Adams," I observed. "Once Danitza left his household, her father effectively banished her. At some point after Danitza moved out of the home, her mother was diagnosed with cervical cancer. A year and a half later, when Eileen was dying, Nitz tried to visit her, but her father had left orders with the hospital staff saying she wasn't welcome. And later, when it came time for Eileen's funeral, Roger banned Nitz from that as well. He was in the state legislature at the time and claimed that his daughter was disturbed and dangerous. When she turned up at the church, an off-duty Alaska State Trooper was stationed at the door to prevent her from entering."

"That takes the cake," Mel declared. "Have father and daughter ever reconciled?"

"Not so far, and not just over the funeral situation either," I told her. "There's an issue with Roger's second wife, Shelley. Penny Olmstead is the maternal aunt in Anchorage who took Danitza in after she left home. Penny is only eight years older than Nitz, so the two of them were more like sisters than auntie and niece.

"It turns out that before Shelley hooked up with Roger Adams, she was married to one of Roger's best friends, a guy named Jack Loveday. Shelley and Penny went through school together. Penny was newly married and living in Anchorage when she went to a friend's baby shower at some fancy Anchorage hotel. While there, she spotted Roger and Shelley being all lovey-dovey in the hotel restaurant, even though they were both still married to other people at the time. Penny spotted the lovebirds, but they didn't see her. Shelley's husband, Jack Loveday, was already a goner by the time Eileen Adams passed away. Shelley and Roger tied the knot three and a half months after Danitza's mother's death."

"Did Danitza know about the affair?" Mel asked.

"Not until after their hurry-up wedding," I answered. "That's when Aunt Penny finally broke down and ratted them out to Nitz."

"So Roger was pissed off about his daughter getting knocked up, even though at the same time he himself was carrying on a long-term affair?"

"Yup," I said. "That's the way it was."

"What a hypocrite!" Mel exclaimed.

"Indeed," I agreed, "although after all these years he might have decided to bury the hatchet."

"What makes you say that?"

"Nitz mentioned that her father has handed off his law practice to a partner and is currently dealing with some kind of serious health issue. A couple of weeks ago, his longtime secretary reached out to Danitza, letting her know that he's in pretty rough shape and hinting that maybe she should go see him."

"I wouldn't if I were her," Mel declared, "not on a bet."

"I doubt Danitza will either. At least it didn't sound like it."

"So what's your next step?" Mel asked.

"Tomorrow I'll be checking out some of Chris's classmates from high school, the ones living in Anchorage. After that I plan to head for Homer."

"Have you bothered looking at a weather report?" Mel asked.

"No, why?"

Glancing out the window, I could see a thick cloud of swirling snowflakes dancing in the glow of now-invisible streetlights several stories below. The flurries I'd seen earlier had become much more serious while I wasn't looking.

"Because I just did," Mel answered. "It looks like Anchorage is in for a hell of a snowstorm tonight—probably more than we had here. How far is Homer from where you are?"

"Four and a half hours," I answered, "but my rental has four-wheel drive. I should be good."

"Should be," Mel repeated, "but the questions is, will

you? I hate to be the bearer of bad tidings, but you're a seventy-four-year-old man with two fake knees. I don't like the idea of you driving around by yourself on unfamiliar roads and in questionable weather conditions. If you happen to run off the road into a ditch, you're not in any condition to dig yourself out, and I don't want you standing around in the cold waiting for a tow truck to show up either. Hire a driver."

In case you're wondering about that distant rumble you just heard, it wasn't thunder. It was the sound of Melissa Soames lowering the boom. In my mind's eye, nothing has changed, and I'm still perfectly capable of doing all the things I used to do. Usually a glance in the mirror is enough to correct that misapprehension, but right that second there were no mirrors handy, and even though her remark might have come as a blow to my ego, I knew she was right. I wasn't in any better shape to deal with a foot or so of snow than our Sun Belt–raised Irish wolfhound was. Male pride, or maybe just plain cussedness, meant that I couldn't concede the point without at least voicing an objection.

"I'll look into it," I grumbled, "but I'm not making any promises."

Our conversation was winding down. "Sarah and I miss you," Mel said. It was her understated way of apologizing for hurting my feelings, and I accepted it as such.

"I miss you, too," I said, "but I feel like I need to be here. If Jared hadn't taken my advice, grabbed Chris, run for their lives that night, there's a good chance that Chris's son, Christopher James, would never have been born. So I feel like I owe him and Danitza, too. It's as though I've been personally designated to give Chris Danielson's family a final answer as to what happened to him."

"What a surprise!" Mel said with a laugh. "After all, isn't that exactly what you've been doing for most of your adult life—providing those kinds of answers to grieving families?"

And as soon as she said it, I knew it was true. I was spending that night in snowy Anchorage doing exactly what I was supposed to do—finding out once and for all what had happened to Chris Danielson, not only for his still-grieving lover and fatherless child but also for someone who was no longer with us—for my former partner, Sue Danielson. She deserved answers every bit as much as they did.

So now, instead of having one pro bono client, I had three—Jared, Danitza, and Sue Danielson. I'll give you one guess which one was most important.

Chapter 10

I awakened the next morning to a dark sky and the sounds of dead silence. You don't realize that you're hearing a constant din of traffic in the background until all of a sudden it isn't there. The room was so dark I thought it had to be the middle of the night, but the bedside clock said 8:05. I got out of bed, hurried over to the window, and looked outside. It had stopped snowing, all right, but by the light from the still-glowing streetlights I could see that cars parked on the street below were literally buried in snow, and if the pavement had been plowed at all overnight, evidence of that was no longer visible. A quick glance at the local news told me that due to the storm schools were closed and all but essential workers were advised to stay home.

Great, I thought. *Just what I need. I'll be stuck here*

at the hotel all day and won't be able to accomplish a
damned thing.

With that unhappy thought in mind, I threw on some clothes and went down to breakfast. If the kitchen was going to run out of supplies, I wanted to be sure I had something to eat well before that happened. While I was eating, I heard a few sounds of machinery moving outside on the street level, so someone had finally gotten out the snowplows after all. Better late than never.

I went back to my room determined to let my fingers do the walking, since due to the snow being out and about didn't appear to be an option. I had those three guys to look up in Anchorage, but until I had a better idea about driving conditions, there was no point in attempting to make appointments with any of them. Instead, realizing that police officers are considered to be essential workers, I picked up my phone, checked my contacts list, and dialed a number at Anchorage PD. Then I waited for Detective Hank Frazier to pick up the phone.

As a homicide cop or as an investigator for Special Homicide, I was pretty much assured of a cordial response when calling in to unfamiliar police departments. As a private investigator? Not so much. Since Homer PD was a totally unknown entity as far as I was concerned and because I wanted a positive result, I felt the need to have an intermediary, and Hank Frazier was it.

A couple of years earlier, while still employed at SHIT, I had teamed up with him on a case where a guy named Winston Hale had murdered both his mother and stepfather before fleeing to Alaska. Because the parents were retired and lived in a cabin out in the boonies, the homicide wasn't discovered for several days. The son's name came up early on, because friends and neighbors knew that he despised his mother and hated his stepfather even more, but by the time he was on law enforcement's radar, the killer had already fled Washington State and flown to Anchorage. Frazier was the guy who had picked up the Alaska end of the investigation. Between us, and without ever meeting in person, we'd managed to bring Hale to justice. A year after being given two life-without-parole sentences and being remanded to the Monroe Correctional Complex, Hale committed suicide—thus sparing taxpayers a lifetime's worth of trouble and expense.

But the connection between Hank Frazier and me had been forged, and as soon as he knew who was on the line, he sounded pleased to hear from me. "Hey, Beau," he said. "How the hell are you? Still working for SHIT?"

When you worked for the unfortunately named

Special Homicide Investigation Team, that line was always good for a laugh. It still is.

"Nope," I said. "The new attorney general shut us down as soon as he came on board."

"Too bad," Hank said. "That was a good outfit. What are you up to now?"

I told him, giving him a quick overview of the whole Chris Danielson missing-person saga. "How can I help?" Hank asked when I finished.

"I was hoping maybe you could run interference for me with Homer PD," I answered. "I was planning on taking a drive out there today—"

"In this weather?" Hank interrupted with a hint of disbelief in his voice. Perhaps it was more concern than disbelief.

"Well, there is that," I conceded, "but the thing is, whenever I get there, whether it's today or tomorrow, most cop shops don't exactly welcome visiting PIs with open arms, so I was wondering if you could put in a good word for me at Homer PD."

"Turns out you came to the right place," Hank said with a laugh. "It so happens I went through the academy with a guy named Marvin Price who's now in charge of investigations in Homer. I'll be happy to give Marve a call on your behalf and let him know you're a straight-up guy. I'll also text you his contact information, including his cell and direct number. Anything else I can do for you while you're in town?"

There was another unknown entity on my list—the forensic anthropologist at the University of Alaska Anchorage.

"Ever heard of someone named Harriet Raines?" I asked.

Hank let out a hoot of laughter. "Of course I know Harry," he said. "That's what everybody calls her. She's a character with a capital *C*. Smokes like a steam engine and prefers cigars to cigarettes. Do you ever watch that show *NCIS: Los Angeles*?"

Most cops I know wouldn't watch a scripted crime TV show on a bet, and if they do, it's usually a closely guarded secret. Personally I'm partial to *America's Funniest Home Videos*. I love watching people do stupid stuff without ending up dead as a result. But the interesting thing about getting married is that you sometimes don't find out all your spouse's dirty little secrets until *after* you say "I do."

Along with her propensity to collect Christmas decorations, that was another of Mel's closely held secrets— she does watch those shows. Because she was raised as a military brat, she adores anything that has NCIS in the title. She watches all three of those shows—*NCIS, NCIS: LA,* and *NCIS: New Orleans*—avidly. Since spending time with Mel is my favorite thing to do, I end up watching them right along with her.

"I've seen it a time or two," I allowed. "Why?"

"You know that funny little woman on *NCIS: LA*, the one who sits at the front desk drinking either tea or scotch. She never seems to do much of anything herself, but she sees all and knows all."

"You mean Hetty?"

"Yeah, that's the one," Hank replied. "Well, Harriet Raines is a whole lot like Hetty. She's a little bit of a thing, but smart as all get-out, and if you give her any guff or try to pull a fast one on her, she'll fix you with a cold, hard stare that'll shrivel your balls. But when it comes to piecing human skeletons back together, no one can top her. If someone turns up in her lab with a banker's box full of bones, she's all over it. Those remains are real people to her. They can be a month old, decades old, or a hundred years old—it doesn't matter. She takes the bit in her teeth and runs with it."

"So scary but good," I said, "sort of like my old high-school English teacher. But in weather like this, what are the chances she'll be in her office today?"

"One hundred percent," Hank told me. "She's pretty much a one-woman show, and I have it on good authority that on snow days she sleeps on a cot in her office just in case she's needed. So you're thinking your missing kid ended up dead somewhere?"

"Seems like a real possibility," I answered.

"Well, give Harry a call, then," Hank said. "I'll text you her direct number, too. You're welcome to tell her that I suggested you be in touch."

When Hank's texts came in, I added those names and numbers to my contacts list, but I was a little leery about making phone calls. If I'm meeting someone for the first time, I like to take measure of them face-to-face. That's especially true if I'm going to be asking for a favor. So I got up, went over to the window, and looked out again.

The snowplows had now worked their magic. Traffic was moving slowly on the street below. The traffic lanes were relatively clear, and the pavement had probably been treated with some kind of deicing material. I checked the map on my iPad. The route from the hotel to the university was fairly straightforward and seemed to feature mostly main thoroughfares. If the street outside the hotel had been cleared, most likely the ones leading to the university had been as well. Since my rental came with all-wheel drive and those top-rated winter tires, I figured I was good to go. Donning my new coat and stuffing my even newer mittens into the pockets, I grabbed my iPad and phone and headed out.

Once in the Explorer, however, I didn't make it far. At the garage exit, I was stopped cold—and I mean that in every sense of the word. The snowplow might have cleared the traffic lanes out on the street, but it had left a six-foot-tall mound of plowed ice and snow blocking the garage exit. Stymied, I went back up to the lobby to ask when they expected to have the exit cleared.

"There's a crew coming," the young woman at the desk explained, glancing at her watch, "but they're a little backed up right now and probably won't get here for another hour or so."

That's when I remembered Mel's sage advice about my hiring a driver. "Any taxis or Ubers working today?" I asked. "In fact, since I need to make several stops, I'd probably be better off if I could hire someone to drive me around for most of the day."

There were two people at the desk—the woman I was speaking to and a somewhat younger guy at the far end of the counter who was handling checkouts. "TW maybe?" the guy suggested helpfully.

The clerk working with me sent her partner a disparaging look along with a small grimace of disapproval.

"Who's TW?" I asked.

"That's TW Transportation," the man supplied. "It's a one-woman operation. Believe me, it's nothing

fancy, but she'll get you wherever you need to go, regardless of weather or road conditions. Would you like
her number?"

"Since I can't get my car out of the garage, I guess
I'd better have it," I said.

Frowning, the female clerk typed something into her
keyboard and then wrote a number on a slip of paper,
which she handed to me. I took a seat in the lobby and
dialed away. The call was answered on the second ring.

"TW," a female voice said.

"My name's J. P. Beaumont," I told her. "I'm a guest
at the Captain Cook. I need to see several people here
in Anchorage today, but a snowplow just buried the
garage entrance, and I can't get my car out. I was wondering if you have a vehicle available."

"Where all do you need to go?"

"The University of Alaska here in Anchorage for
starters," I told her.

Over breakfast I had looked up the addresses on what
I still called the "unaffiliated boys" from Homer High
School now living in Anchorage. Both appeared to live
out in the hinterlands, one on Mount McKinley View
Drive and the other in what looked like a subdivision
off Potter Creek Road. The squiggles and curves I'd
seen on the map had made me rethink the idea of doing
face-to-face interviews, but hopefully TW Transporta-

tion had the capability to get through any snowbound streets that might stand in my way.

I read off the addresses.

"Sure," the woman on the phone said. "No problem. I can get you there and back. How long do you think you'll be?"

"That's the thing," I said, "I'm not really sure. Could I just hire you on an hourly basis so you could hang around and wait until I'm finished?"

"Five hundred bucks with a four-hour minimum, nine-fifty for eight hours, paid in advance, cash or credit card."

If I had been billing a client, I might have had second thoughts, but seeing as how the only person I might have to answer to was Mel and since getting a driver had been her bright idea in the first place, that sounded like a fair deal.

"How soon can you be here?" I asked.

"Fifteen minutes work for you?"

"Sure," I said.

"Wait inside," she said. "I'll pull up out front."

"How will I know it's you?"

"Oh, you'll know me all right," she said with a short laugh followed by a surprisingly serious cough. "By the way," she added once the cough subsided, "if you've got sunglasses, you'd better bring them along."

"Sunglasses?" I echoed, thinking she was pulling my leg. When I'd been packing to leave dreary Bellingham for wintertime Anchorage, the idea of bringing along sunglasses hadn't occurred to me. And since it was still mostly dark outside, the idea of wearing sunglasses seemed laughable.

"Sun'll be out later," the woman warned. "Believe me, if you don't have sunglasses on you, you'll wish you did. And be sure to dress warmly. The heater core's toast. I've got the part on order, but it's coming from someplace in Pennsylvania and taking forever."

That sounded ominous. The desk clerk had said TW's services were "nothing fancy," but it seemed to me that having a functioning heater inside a vehicle for hire in wintertime Anchorage should be mandatory rather than optional. I took her advice to heart, however. Because I'd been on my way out, I was already wearing my boots and had my coat and mittens with me. During my fifteen-minute wait, I went into the gift shop and invested in a knit cap and a scarf along with the suggested pair of sunglasses.

The garage exit might still be an issue, but someone had shoveled the front driveway. I was standing next to the sliding doors at the entrance a few minutes later when a brown-and-yellow seventies-something vintage International Harvester Travelall pulled up outside. A snowplow attachment of some kind, also painted bright yellow, occupied the spot where the front bumper should have been. A blue tarp lashed to a luggage rack on top covered what appeared to be an extensive collection of various-size boxes. Snowplow aside, it was the kind of vehicle I might have expected to encounter either when setting off on a desert safari or else lined up on display at an antique car show.

The woman who hopped down from the driver's side and came around to greet me was a tall, ruddy-cheeked, salt-and-pepper brunette, probably somewhere in her early sixties. Her burly build would have made her a respectable lineman on any college football team, and I suspected that any overly enthusiastic male who attempted to get out of line with her would end up on the floor and wishing he hadn't in short order.

She was dressed like a lumberjack, complete with a plaid flannel shirt and a voluminous Carhartt jacket that appeared to be several decades older than my puffy blue parka. My pull-on boots had been brand-new and fresh-out-of-the box that morning. Hers were well-worn metal-toed lace-up work boots, and the only perfume in the air surrounding her was the thick scent of cigarette smoke that permeated her hair and clothing.

"Mr. Beaumont?" she asked, holding out a rough, chapped hand and offering a disturbingly firm hand-shake.

"Yes, ma'am," I said, "and you are?"

"Twinkle Winkleman," she replied.

The name struck my funny bone, but I had the good sense to keep my expression as stone-faced as hers.

"Most folks call me Twink," she continued. "My old man was like that jerk who named his poor son Sue, and he's the one who stuck me with that handle when I was born—said he thought it was cute. I've cussed him about that every day of my life since I first set foot in kindergarten, but since he was also the guy who gave me Maude back there," she added, gesturing with her head in the direction of the idling Travelall, "I guess it pretty much evens out in the long run. Shall we? You want to ride in the front or in the back?"

I could have told her I didn't like my given names any better than she did hers. Rather than go into any of that, I simply answered her question.

"Front," I said, and Twink held the passenger door open for me, allowing me to clamber up onto the front bench seat. It wasn't a short step by any means, and as I settled in and fastened my seat belt, I muttered a mental thanks to Dr. Ault, the orthopedic surgeon who had installed my two fake knees. Fortunately, they worked flawlessly. I could only hope that the same held true for Twinkle Winkleman's aging Travelall.

With what looked like eighteen inches of snow on the ground, I didn't want to be stuck outside walking around, no matter how good my new knees were. On that score my Irish wolfhound, Sarah, and I were on exactly the same page.

Chapter 11

Twink Winkleman heaved herself onto her side of the tattered bench seat, fastened her seat belt, and then held out her hand. "Cash or credit card?" she asked.

I dug out my credit card. Twink might have been driving an antique vehicle, but her iPhone was up to date, and it came equipped with one of those little Square credit-card readers. "Whole day or half?" she wanted to know.

What the hell? I thought. Since I had at least three people I needed to track down in an unfamiliar city where road conditions were less than optimal, having a driver who knew her way around seemed like a good idea, so I went for it. "Make it the whole day," I said.

"Suit yourself," she replied. "If you've got the money, honey . . ."

I was old enough to know the missing lyrics, and if Twink did too, maybe she was a bit older than I had first thought.

"Mind if I smoke?" she asked after stowing both the phone and the chip reader in one of her jacket's many pockets.

The interior of the Travelall already reeked of so much secondhand smoke that adding in a little more to the mix hardly mattered. "Okay by me," I said.

Although the heater in the antique vehicle was clearly history, much to my surprise the cigarette lighter worked perfectly. Twink lit up and then, with a satisfied sigh, blew a column of smoke into the air. My side window and hers were both cracked open. When I reached to close mine, she stopped me.

"You'll need to leave it open," she said. "With the heater core busted, if I don't leave the windows cracked open, the place steams up so much that I can't see a thing."

Driving around in Anchorage in the snow with the windows open? Calling TW Transportation "nothing fancy" was one thing, but this was ridiculous. Maybe I shouldn't have signed up for the full day after all.

"Where to?" Twink asked.

I read off the address on the UAA campus, including the name of the building.

"You a detective?" my driver asked as she put the Travelall in gear and eased out into the plowed but almost deserted traffic lanes.

Her question startled me. I wasn't exactly walking around wearing a name tag and a badge.

"Private investigator," I answered. "How'd you know that?"

"You're going to see the bone lady, aren't you?" Twink asked. "Harriet Raines is famous around here. Everybody in Anchorage knows about her. I saw her interviewed on one of those true-crime shows once. She said that it's her mission in life to see that the bones of the people she deals with end up going back to wher-ever they belong. That's especially true when it comes to the bones of indigenous folks. No matter how long those dead bodies have been lying out in the weather, she likes to see to it that they end up where they're sup-posed to be, back with the right people. Makes sense, of course. I understand she's half Tlingit and half white. I believe those Tlingit folks are of the opinion that once someone is dead, they're best left alone."

I felt a shiver up my spine. I knew something about those kinds of indigenous beliefs. Years earlier, back when goths were the big thing in Seattle, some of them had collected a set of bones from over on the Kitsap Peninsula west of the city. The grave robbers laid the bones out in a forested area of Seward Park, using them as props to scare the hell out of stupid people who were willing to pay good money to be terrified.

Unfortunately, said bones were those of a beloved medicine man, and they carried with them the long-held belief that anyone who handled or disrespected them was subject to a curse. In the course of the next several days, more than one of those Halloween pranksters met untimely deaths, as did Sue Danielson, who happened to be one of the detectives assigned to collect the bones from Seward Park. I was out of town at the time and hadn't been part of that crime-scene investigation. Yes, Sue might have died as a direct result of a gunshot wound in an act of domestic violence perpetrated by her former husband, but a part of me still believed that the curse from being in close contact with those sacred bones also had something to do with it.

"That's what homicide investigators do, too," I said after a long pause. "They try to make sure that the remains of loved ones go back to where they're supposed to be and, if they happen to be victims of foul play, that whoever did it gets what's coming to them."

"I thought you said you were a private eye instead of a homicide cop," Twink offered.

"I *was* a homicide cop," I corrected, "for most of my career. One way or another, I guess I still am. Right now, though, I'm working a missing-persons case."

We rode in silence after that while Twink finished one cigarette, ground the stub out in an overflowing ashtray, and promptly lit another.

"Here we are," she said at last, pulling up in front of a low-rise three-story building that would have looked perfectly at home in any self-respecting business park in the country. "The campus cops don't much like visiting vehicles hanging around on campus, but maybe on a snow day they'll give me a pass. If I end up having to move and park off campus, though, you can call me when you're finished."

"I have no idea how long I'll be," I said. "I don't know for sure if Professor Raines is in today, but what number should I use?"

"You called me earlier, right?" Twink replied.

I nodded.

"Use that number," she advised. "I only have one. That's all I need."

Someone on the UAA campus had been busy. The walkway from the street to what turned out to be the anthropology building had been shoveled clean and deiced. I pushed the entry door open and stepped into a tiled and polished interior that mirrored buildings of higher learning all over the planet—mixed-use arrangements with classrooms and offices scattered throughout. After tracking down a building directory and learning that the Alaska State Department of Forensic Anthropology was located on the basement level, I went in search of an elevator.

When the door slid open on the B. Level, I found myself in a surprisingly chill corridor with industrial-chic overhead fluorescent fixtures lighting the long, narrow hallway. From the looks of it, I guessed this had originally been wasted space that had eventually been repurposed.

Directly across from the elevator was a wooden door topped by a milk-glass window. Stenciled on the glass in black all-cap letters were the words DEPARTMENT HEAD. Since Forensic Anthropology was the only office listed for the B. Level, I assumed this had to be where Professor Raines hung out. There was a combo buzzer/speaker device on the wall next to the doorframe, so I gave the button a solid push.

After a considerable pause, a disembodied voice came through the speaker. "School's closed today. Come back tomorrow."

"I can't," I said. "I'm only in town for today."

"Are you a student?"

"No, my name's J. P. Beaumont," I answered. "I'm a private investigator from Seattle."

Professor Raines probably knew good and well where Bellingham was, but Seattle has a slightly better ring to it.

"You're here on a case?"

"Yes, ma'am."

There was an audible click as the lock released. As soon as I opened the door to step inside, the scent of a burning cigar assailed my nostrils—cigar smoke mixed with something I suspected to be microwaved Top Ramen. Between cigars and cigarettes, as a former smoker I suppose I prefer cigarettes, and after years of living the single life, I'm all too familiar with the Top Ramen style of home cooking. I was in a dimly lit laboratory with only a few security lights providing illumination through a collection of stainless-steel tables. At the far end of the room was what appeared to be a window-walled private office with plenty of lighting inside that. When no one came to greet me, that's where I headed.

I walked into a cluttered office where almost every flat surface, chairs included, was covered with an assortment of books and/or a scatter of papers. Seated behind a wooden desk, Professor Harriet Raines, an elfin woman if ever there was one, was barely visible behind yet another dangerously crooked mound of papers and books. In the small cleared spot directly in front of her sat a bowl of some kind with a spoon in it, a mostly-empty rocks glass, and an ashtray with a still-smoldering cigar. Nearby sat an almost-full bottle of Crown Royal.

The woman's iron-gray hair was plaited into thick braids that wound around the top of her head, creating what looked like a crown. Her bulldog face, lined and wrinkled, was reminiscent of Winston Churchill's, including a pair of horn-rimmed glasses. Professor Raines stared up at me silently for a long assessing moment, then reached down, opened a drawer, and pulled out what was presumably a clean rocks glass. She slammed it onto the desk and then looked up at me again.

"Care to join me?" she asked.

"No thanks," I said. "I gave it up for Lent."

"It's not Easter—it's Christmas," she declared, pouring herself a generous two-shot portion into the other glass. "What can I do for you, Mr. Beaumont?"

"I'm retired Seattle homicide," I explained. "I'm here working what may turn out to be a cold case."

She leaned back in her chair, took a slow sip of her drink, and then shook her head. "This is Alaska," she told me. "In the winter it turns out all our cases are cold cases."

She said the words with a totally straight face and then leveled an icy stare in my direction as if waiting to see how I would react. I felt as though I were undergoing some kind of evaluation. Depending on whether I arrived at the correct response, Professor Raines would either help me or tell me to piss off.

"This one may be colder than others," I said. "It's from 2006."

A glint of interest appeared in her otherwise expressionless eyes. She set down the glass. "An Alaska case dating from '06?" she asked.

I nodded. "Yes, ma'am," I said. "I believe so."

"Have a seat, then," she invited, waving at a chair. "Just put that junk on the floor. And none of this 'ma'am' crap, please. Most people call me Harry."

As far as I'm concerned, the name Harry now and forever belongs to Harry Ignatius Ball, aka Harry I. Ball, my old boss at Special Homicide. "If you don't mind, I'll call you Harriet."

"Fine with me," she said with a shrug, "and you are?"

"J.P.," I said, "either that or Beau. Take your pick."

"I'll opt for J.P.," she said.

Since I evidently had just passed some critical point in Harriet Raines's acceptance process, I did as I'd been told by clearing the nearest chair and taking a seat.

"Tell me about your case," she said, and so I did.

"In 2006 a kid from Homer disappeared off the face of the earth."

Harriet nodded. "Your missing-persons case," she said. "What's the name?"

"Chris—Christopher Danielson. He was seventeen at the time he went missing. The problem is, this isn't officially a missing-persons case because he's never been reported missing."

"What exactly happened?"

"Chris's family life was complicated. When he was younger, his father murdered his mother. That happened down in Seattle. His folks were divorced at the time of the homicide, and his mother, Sue Danielson, was my partner at Seattle PD."

I'm not sure why I added that last bit, but somehow I felt a sudden need to provide full disclosure.

"So this is personal for you, then," Harriet Raines observed, nodding sagely.

"Yes," I agreed. "I suppose it is."

"Go on," she urged.

"After the deaths of their parents, Chris and his older brother, Jared, went to live with their maternal grandparents in Ohio. That lasted until Chris was about thirteen. At that point he ran away from home and came to Alaska to live with his father's parents in Homer. At the time he went missing from Homer, he was estranged from all his surviving grandparents. He'd dropped out of school, but he evidently had a serious girlfriend, a sixteen-year-old girl named Danitza Adams. The night Chris went missing, Danitza had just discovered she was pregnant. Unfortunately, so had her parents."

"Sounds like there was a good deal of family drama going on at the time," Harriet surmised.

I nodded. "You could say that. Danitza and her parents had a huge row. It was serious enough that when it was over, she packed up and left home that very night. She went to the place where Chris had been living and waited, expecting him to show up after work. When he didn't, she hitchhiked from Homer to Anchorage, where she moved in with an aunt and uncle. They looked out for her, and Danitza stayed with them up to and after the time her baby was born. Chris had been telling her that he was hoping to save enough money to go back to Ohio and fix the rift with his maternal grandmother. When Chris disappeared without a word, Danitza assumed that's what had happened—that he'd gone back to Ohio. As a result she never reported him as missing. The problem is, neither did anyone else.

"This week Chris's older brother, Jared, contacted me asking for help in locating him. The grandmother

in Ohio is evidently close to death and hoping for a reconciliation."

"So everybody in Ohio thought Chris was in Alaska,"
Harriet put in, "while everyone in Alaska thought he
was in Ohio."

"That's about the size of it," I acknowledged.

"If you're a hammer, everything looks like a nail,"
she said, giving me a piercing look accompanied by
a wry smile. "Since you're a homicide cop—an ex-
homicide cop—I suppose everything looks like a
murder. Does this seem like a homicide to you?"

"You've got me there," I admitted. "That's what I
suspect—that Chris was murdered."

"And I'll bet you've even got an idea who did it," she
added.

"According to Danitza, her father had a temper. He
was also beyond furious when he found out she was
pregnant."

"Can't say as I blame him," Harriet Raines allowed.
"Under the circumstances I'm pretty sure I'd be furious, too, but there's angry and then there's homicidal.
Do you think it's possible this Mr. Adams might be
responsible for whatever happened to Christopher?"

Harriet might not have been taking notes, but if
she had plucked that name detail out of what I'd just

told her in casual conversation, she had definitely been paying attention.

"I don't know that for sure," I said, "but I'd certainly like to have the opportunity to ask him about it face-to-face."

A long, thoughtful silence ensued. At first I wondered if she was about to send me packing. Instead, while I watched and waited for Harriet Raines to say something more, an odd thing happened. A subtle change came over her, as though she'd just made up her mind about something.

At that point the very atmosphere in the room suddenly shifted. It was as if some kind of emotionally charged barometer had just dropped. Even though I hadn't said a word, Harriet nodded as if I had. Then she picked up the bottle of Crown Royal and the clean glass she'd offered me earlier and shoved both of them into the bottom drawer of her desk. Next, after stubbing out her smoldering cigar, she turned back to me with yet another appraising look.

"What do you know about bears?" she asked.

That question, coming out of the blue, caught me totally off guard and left me thinking I had somehow missed a turn and wound up in a whole other conversation.

"Not very much," I admitted. "Why?"

"We have a lot of 'em up here," she replied, "all kinds—black, brown, grizzly, and polar. When it comes to bears, Alaska is all for diversity."

It took a second for me to realize that "Cold Case" Harriet Raines had just cracked another joke. By my count that was number two. She was on a roll.

"And we've got a bunch of people around here," she continued, "naturalists, biologists, and the like, who make it their business to know everything there is to know about those different kinds of bears. Some of those folks go out in the wild each spring to track down hibernating bears in their dens and put battery-powered collars on the big ones and tag the little ones."

"Not my kind of job," I said.

At that point Harriet actually smiled at me. "Not mine either," she agreed.

With that, Professor Harriet stood up abruptly. "Wait here," she said. "I'll be right back." She collected her empty soup bowl and spoon as well as her empty glass and placed all those items on a serving tray that was sitting on the credenza behind her desk. Then, after donning a lab coat from a nearby coat tree, she picked up the tray and headed for the door.

"Oh," she added as an afterthought while pausing in the doorway, "would you care for some coffee?"

"Please," I said.

"It's instant."

"That's fine," I told her. "I'm not fussy."

"How do you take it?"

"Black." I answered.

"Okay," she said. "I'll be right back."

Through the glass walls of her office, I watched Harriet's progress through the lab, turning on lights as she went. Eventually she paused in an area that appeared to be a tiny kitchenette where she put her dirty dishes in a sink and switched on an electric kettle. At the far end of the lab, she stopped in front of another door where she had to punch a code into an electronic keypad to unlock it. She disappeared inside, letting the door close behind her,

Several long minutes passed before she emerged once more. She did so carrying a banker's box. The contents couldn't have been very heavy, because small as she was, she appeared to carry the weight with little or no effort. She deposited the box on the lab table closest to her office door and then beckoned for me to come join her, which I did. As I approached, I caught a glimpse of the label on the end of the box, which read "Geoffrey. 4/25/2008."

"Bones?" I asked.

Harriet nodded. "Not just bones," she replied with

a smile, "my personal specialty—unidentified bones. A lot of the time when skeletal human remains are located in wilderness areas, they turn out to be Alaska Natives, indigenous people who succumbed to natural causes decades earlier. Often we locate remains of people like hunters, hikers, or skiers who wander out into the woods and end up dying due to misadventure such as accidental falls or drownings. Occasionally we find the remains of homicide victims, and that's apparently the case with this one," she added, giving the lid of the box what appeared to be an almost affectionate pat.

"In the spring of 2008, just before the breakup—"

"Breakup?" I interrupted, thinking the topic of conversation had somehow veered into some kind of marital discord. "Whose breakup?"

Harriet sighed. "That's what people in Alaska call that time of year when the ice breaks up—usually in the late spring. One of the bear-tagging teams working near Eklutna Lake some distance north of here went into the den of a hibernating black bear and noticed something that appeared to be a partial human skull. In the old days, some nitwit most likely would have straightaway gassed both the mama bear and her cubs to death without ever allowing them out of the den. And chances are the bear in this particular den had nothing at all to do with the bones in question, since they looked to have been there for some length of time.

"In any event, since we're now living in more enlightened times, the tagging team simply notified us about the existence of the remains and sent along the coordinates of the den so we'd be able to locate it later. You'll be happy to know that we waited until the den was abandoned before sending out a team of graduate students to do the actual work."

"Graduate students instead of CSIs?" I asked.

"We're a bit on the underfunded side here," she said. "We can't afford CSIs."

With that, Harriet carefully lifted the lid off the box. I could see there was only one item inside—a partial human skull with jagged holes showing here and there. It resembled a nightmare jigsaw puzzle with several missing pieces. From the multitude of cracks spread across what remained, I could tell that the skull had once been smashed to pieces and then painstakingly glued back together. A few of the teeth were there, but most were missing. There was a deep indentation in the back of the skull.

"Would a blow like that have been fatal?" I asked.

"This is all speculation, of course, but I believe so. If the skin was broken, the wound would have bled profusely, but the real damage would have been from a subdural hematoma."

"A brain bleed, then?"

Professor Raines nodded. "The angle of the blow suggests that the victim was most likely in either a kneeling or a sitting position when he was struck from behind. At the time of death, I believe the skull was still intact. I suspect a hungry bear cracked it open later in order to devour whatever remained inside."

"So the victim was dead long before the bear came along."

"Correct."

"And the weapon?" I asked.

"Most likely a round metal object approximately three or so inches in circumference," Harriet replied. "Had the instrument of death been a tree branch, for example, we would have found tiny wooden splinters still embedded in the bone. However, there weren't any of those."

"How do you know the guy's name was Geoffrey?" I asked.

"I don't," Harriet answered. "That's the name I assigned to him when he first came into the lab. At first, with nothing more than the shattered skull to examine, I didn't know if the victim was male or female, but I allocate names to victims the same way meteorologists dub hurricanes—alphabetically, according to the year, alternating male names with female ones. Since 2008 was quite busy, by late April I was already up to the G's, and by then it was time for a male name."

"So you give each set of bones an individual name?"

"It humanizes them for me in a way that calling them Jane or John Doe doesn't. It helps me keep in mind that these were once real people who walked, talked, breathed, and lived before being reduced to this."

"What else can you tell me about Geoffrey?" I asked.

"My grads managed to locate several teeth. From those we eventually learned that our victim had received reasonably good dental care. We were also able to obtain a DNA profile that told us Geoffrey was both male and *dleit ḵáa*."

"I beg your pardon?"

She repeated whatever she'd said before, but I couldn't come close to pronouncing it to say nothing of spelling it. "And that would be what?" I asked.

"It's what my mother's people, the Tlingit, call whites," Harriet explained. "Based on bone development, I estimate Geoffrey was in his mid- to late teens at the time he died. Naturally I brought the AST— the Alaska State Troopers—into the picture. As far as they're concerned, he's what they like to call a UU—an unidentified and unsolved homicide victim, but do you know what I think?"

"What?" I asked.

"I believe, between the two of us, that we might have just identified this one as your missing Christopher Danielson."

I couldn't help but be amazed. When I started out in homicide, the best forensics could do was type any blood found at crime scenes. Blood typing eliminated some suspects but did nothing to identify the actual perpetrators. And although fingerprint evidence was often collected, the only prints it could be compared to were those on file cards stored in local police agencies. There was no such thing as a CODIS, the Combined DNA Identification System. And the Automated Fingerprint Identification System, AFIS, was still in its infancy. Under those circumstances the remains of unidentified homicide victims, those Harriet designated as UUs, were destined to remain just that—unidentified and unsolved.

Nodding in agreement, I stared down at the empty skull and thought about the little boy I'd last seen years earlier at his mother's fallen-officer memorial. The Hinkles had brought both boys to the event wearing matching black suits with clip-on bow ties. The realization that I was most likely looking down on the only earthly remains of Sue Danielson's younger son hit me like a punch in the gut. I was relieved when Harriet silently returned the lid to the box, shutting the skull from view. Then she reached over and laid a comforting hand on my arm.

"The water in the kettle should be hot by now," she suggested. "Let's go have that cup of coffee."

A small kitchen table and two chairs sat in what evidently served as a break area. I stumbled over to one of those, dropped down onto it, and rested my elbows on the table. I'm not sure how long I sat there with my head buried in my hands while once again, as I had done countless times before, I second-guessed all my actions from that awful night years earlier. If I'd made different choices and decisions back then, would Christopher Danielson have led a completely different life? In fact, maybe if I'd simply stayed out of it and let things play out, Chris would still be among the living and so would his mother.

That merry-go-round of useless thoughts was still spinning in my head when a steaming cup of coffee appeared in my line of vision as Harriet set it down on the table directly in front of me. The coffee inside was black, all right, and strong as it could be. Once I raised it to my lips, it turned out to be by far the vilest cup of coffee I've ever tasted but also the kindest. A moment later a second cup was placed on the table across from me with Harriet Raines's lined and weathered face forming a backdrop.

"Why don't you tell me about what happened to your partner?" she urged quietly.

That's when I remembered what Hank Frazier had said about her—that Harriet Raines was someone who knew all and saw all, and maybe it was true. So I told her the story then—the whole story from beginning to bitter end. I related each action I'd taken that night and explained how those actions had affected what came later. I regaled Harriet with every detail of the incident that had shown up in the official police reports, but along with those, I related the rest of the story, too. I had told Mel about it, but this was the first time I told anyone else.

The official determination was that that Sue Danielson had perished as a result of homicidal violence at the hands of her estranged former husband, Richie Danielson, but for me there had always been that other thing lurking just in the background, so I told Harriet about that as well—about how, in the process of recovering the stolen bones of an indigenous medicine man, Sue had somehow become targeted by an age-old curse. I might have been a homicide cop, but strange as it may seem, I'd never been able to shake the lingering idea that, in some way I didn't understand, the medicine man's curse was ultimately the root cause of Sue's death.

Over the years that idea had seemed so off the wall and woo-woo that I'd never discussed it. As for why I spit it out now, after all these years? I don't really know, but it seemed to me as though Harriet Raines might be someone who understood that part of the story, and I wasn't wrong.

"Mishandling the bones of a powerful medicine man can indeed be dangerous," she commented softly once I finished. "But let me assure you, Beau, nothing you did or didn't do that night would have made the slightest difference in the outcome. Sue Danielson's death wasn't your fault, and neither is her son's."

In that moment I felt something I had never expected to feel about what happened that awful night—a sense of forgiveness—of self-forgiveness.

"Thank you," I murmured, and I meant it with every atom of my being.

Harriet leaned back in her chair then and regarded me over the tops of our respective coffee cups. "As I said earlier," she began, instantly and effortlessly making the switch from shaman to scientist and from comforter to investigator, "we were able to obtain a

DNA profile, but even though we've continued running it through CODIS from time to time, so far there are no matches."

"Did you find anything else in the den?" I asked. "Things like items of clothing might help us identify the victim?"

Harriet shook her head. "We found nothing," she said, "not in the den and not anywhere around it either. We searched the whole area, checking bear scat for something that shouldn't have been there—buttons, rivets, or zipper fragments—that would have indicated the presence of clothing. Nada. The den was close enough to the lake that I suspect anything else might have gotten washed away during the breakup, something most people in Anchorage would find disturbing, since Eklutna Lake is the main source of the city's water supply."

"Do you think the victim was killed there or somewhere else?" I asked.

"In my opinion it's likely the homicide occurred somewhere else before the body was transported to the lake and dumped. The lack of clothing suggests some effort to make identification of the remains as difficult as possible, but things have certainly changed on that score, haven't they, Mr. Beaumont?" Harriet added with a small smile. "Do you happen to know if there's a way for me to access Jared Danielson's DNA?"

At the time Jared was leaving our house in Bellingham three days earlier, I'd suggested that he submit a DNA sample to something like Ancestry.com, but even had he done so immediately, getting his profile would probably take several weeks. What was needed now was a much faster turnaround. In the old days, I'd had friends in the crime lab who would have helped out in a heartbeat. Now, however, there was a good chance that train had gone off the rails.

"I might be able to get one," I said dubiously. "Why?"

"I'll need to notify AST about this development," she said, "but before I call them in, I'd like to be able to provide a positive ID."

I knew exactly what Harriet was doing—allowing me a short window in which I was free to proceed with my own investigation before she was obliged to call in the home team.

"Do you happen to have Geoffrey's case number handy?" I asked.

She nodded. "It's on the box," she told me. "Hang on. I'll go get it."

Chapter 12

While Harriet went to retrieve the banker's box, I hauled out my phone. A few months prior, I'd been embroiled in an investigation into what eventually turned out to be a case of wrongful imprisonment. Close to twenty years earlier, a young man named Mateo Vega had been a recent college graduate living and working in Seattle when his girlfriend, a young woman named Emily Anne Tarrant, was murdered shortly after she and Mateo attended a summertime beach party. Unfortunately for Mateo, other guests at the party had witnessed and been willing to testify to the fact that the two of them—Mateo and Emily Anne—had engaged in a heated argument as they were leaving the party shortly before her homicide.

The flawed police investigation that followed had

focused totally on the boyfriend, to the exclusion of any and all other potential suspects. Two separate male DNA profiles had been found on the body, and one of those belonged to Mateo. That was no surprise, since Mateo told investigators that he and Emily had engaged in consensual sex prior to attending the party. Nonetheless, at the urging of his public defender, Mateo had eventually accepted a plea deal to a lesser charge of second-degree homicide in order to avoid going to trial on first-degree homicide and risking a possible life sentence.

Released on parole after serving sixteen years in prison, Mateo had gone to work for the same people who'd employed him prior to his being sent to prison, and it was his employers who brought me into the case by way of my involvement with TLC, The Last Chance, a volunteer cold-case outfit for which I've done some work in retirement.

In the course of my investigation, I discovered that neither of the two profiles taken from the homicide victim's body at the crime scene had ever been uploaded into CODIS. One of those profiles had, of course, belonged to the boyfriend, who was also the presumed killer. The second profile wouldn't have rung any investigative bells at the time, because at that point the person involved was still a juvenile with no police record. It wasn't until much later when I came along that the second crime-scene profile was finally uploaded into the system. Once that happened, alarm bells started going off all over the place, because by then that innocent-looking kid from way back then had turned into a convicted serial killer, and Emily Anne Tarrant had been his first victim.

Over the years I had done a lot of work with the folks at the Washington State Patrol Crime Lab, and I knew many of them personally. When I had asked Gretchen Walther, one of the crime lab's DNA techs, to look into the Emily Anne Tarrant homicide, she did so as a personal favor to me. Although she hadn't been responsible for the clerical error that resulted in the profiles not being uploaded in a timely fashion, she happened to be the one who discovered the oversight.

After that all kinds of hell had broken loose, and I don't doubt that a crime-lab head or two had rolled as a result. Not long ago I'd heard that Mateo's wrongful-imprisonment lawsuit had been settled for "an undisclosed amount." That generally translates into big bucks, in which case a few more people might have found themselves out of jobs.

As for me? My involvement in the Mateo Vega debacle probably meant that I was definitely persona non grata at the crime lab these days. Still, fools rush in where angels fear to tread. I found Gretchen's name in my contacts list. Since she usually works swing shift, I tried calling her cell phone. She answered after two rings.

"Are you kidding me?" Gretchen demanded once she figured out who was calling. "You actually have nerve enough to call me after all the trouble you caused?"

"That's me, all right," I answered as cheerfully as I could, "more nerve than a bad tooth."

To my relief, Gretchen laughed aloud at that. "You ended up taking a couple of obnoxious muckety-mucks down a few pegs, which wasn't such a bad thing, so the grunts who have to work around here don't mind you all that much, me included. What's up?"

By then Harriet had returned with the banker's box in hand.

"I'm working a case," I said.

"Big surprise there."

"A seventeen-year-old kid named Christopher Danielson went missing from Homer, Alaska, in 2006. Unfortunately, he was never reported as missing, not at the time he disappeared and not anytime since either. I've been talking to Professor Harriet Raines up here in Anchorage. She has a set of unidentified human remains that were found in the spring of 2008. It's possible they might be a match."

"Oh, I know Dr. Raines," Gretchen said quickly. "We've worked together a couple of times. Tell her hi for me, would you?"

I held the phone away from my mouth. "Gretchen Walther from the Washington State Patrol Crime Lab says hello." I wasn't doing a FaceTime call, so there was no video, but I put the phone on speaker.

"Hi right back at you," Harriet said.

"What do you need, Beau?" Gretchen asked.

"I got involved because the presumed victim's older brother, Jared, sent me searching for him," I continued. "My client's name is Father Jared Danielson, and he's a priest currently staying at a monastery in Woodinville. Professor Raines asked if I had a DNA profile for him, which I currently don't have. I was wondering if it would be possible for me to send him by so you could collect a sample and create a profile."

"I can't do it for you," Gretchen said at once, "but we have a mutual-aid agreement with the state of Alaska, and I could certainly do it for Dr. Raines. Does she have a case number on that?"

"We're on speaker, so why don't you ask her directly?" I suggested.

For the next several minutes, the two women talked back and forth, still on speaker, with Harriet Raines providing all the necessary details Gretchen needed to create a case file on her end. Finally Gretchen asked me for a phone number for Jared.

I started to give it to her but then thought better of it. I needed to talk to him about what Harriet Raines and I had discovered and what we suspected before anyone else did. I was the guy Jared had sent searching for Christopher, and I was the one who needed to tell him that his brother was most likely deceased.

"I'll need to do the next-of-kin notification first," I said, speaking from across the table. "How about if I give Jared Danielson your number and have him call you?"

"Good thinking," Gretchen agreed. "Have him call me whenever he's ready. I'm working swing shift tonight, so if he wants to drop by this evening, we could probably have a profile for you in short order."

I ended the call feeling as though things had gone far better than I could have hoped. Still, phoning Jared to deliver the news wasn't going to be easy.

"Do you want me to leave you to it?" the all-knowing Harriet Raines asked.

"No," I told her. "I'd rather have you here in case he has questions I can't answer."

I glanced at the time before locating Jared's number. I had spent far longer in Harriet's basement lab space than I had expected, and unless she'd found refuge in a coffee shop, Twink Winkleman could well be frozen to her unheated car seat by now. Since it was already close to noon here in Anchorage, that would make it a little later in the afternoon in the Seattle area. I found myself hoping that priests had something urgent to do at this time of day so Jared wouldn't answer the phone, but of course he did.

"Hey, Mr. Beaumont," he said at once. "Have you found him?"

His voice sounded chipper and happy. Now was no time to remind him to call me Beau.

"I'm afraid I have some potentially bad news for you," I replied. "I'm sitting here in Anchorage in a forensic-anthropology lab with the director, Professor Harriet Raines. She has some unidentified human remains dating from 2008 that may or may not be a match for Christopher."

What followed was a moment of stark silence. "You're saying Chris is dead?" Jared asked finally.

"He may be dead," I cautioned. "We're going to need a sample of your DNA in order to know for sure."

Additional silence followed. I've done more than my share of next-of-kin notifications through the years. Initial reactions from loved ones can be all over the place, ranging from absolutely nothing to screaming hysteria. I prefer the latter, because in those moments my heart is usually screaming, too.

"I sent my DNA sample to Ancestry.com yesterday," Jared said when he finally spoke. "I don't have any idea how long it takes to get a profile back."

I had to give the guy credit. He'd gathered himself far more quickly than I could have, switching within a matter of seconds from hearing the shocking news to looking at all the practicalities.

"We'd like to move a little faster than that," I told him. "I've been in touch with one of my friends at the Washington State Patrol Crime Lab, a DNA tech named Gretchen Walther. Professor Raines here has forwarded the applicable case number to her. If you could drop by her office this evening sometime, she can take a swab and create a profile. That would be the fastest way to get this settled."

"How do I find her?" Jared asked.

"I'll text you her number and address as soon as we finish this call. She's expecting to hear from you. That way she can tell you where to be and what time."

"Should I call Grandma Hinkle and tell her?" Jared asked.

"No, not yet," I told him, "not until we know for sure. I'm sorry about this, Jared, so very sorry."

"But you said the remains are from 2008? If Chris has been missing all this time, how come we never knew a thing about it?"

"Because he fell through the cracks," I replied. "According to Chris's girlfriend at the time, he'd been saving up money for a trip back to Ohio, primarily because he wanted to talk to you. According to her, he was finally starting to realize that the versions of events told by your two sets of grandparents couldn't both be correct and that the truth lay somewhere in the middle. I also think he was coming to understand that he'd been wrong in believing that had you boys been in the house at the time of the incident, you might have been able to prevent your mother's murder. Danitza said Chris specifically wanted to apologize to you about blaming you for what happened."

I heard a slight sputter on the phone that sounded suspiciously like a partially suppressed sob. That was followed by another long pause. "Chris had a girlfriend?" Jared asked in a hoarse voice that was little more than a whisper.

"He did," I answered. "Her name is Danitza Adams Miller. She goes by Nitz. Earlier, on the day Chris disappeared, Nitz and her parents had both learned that she was pregnant." For the next few minutes I filled Jared in on everything I had learned about the case since my arrival in Anchorage.

"Did Danitza ever have the baby?" Jared asked when I finished.

"It turns out that baby is now a twelve-year-old boy," I answered. "His name is Christopher James. Nitz calls him Jimmy, and he looks a lot like you."

There was another choked sob. "Sorry, Beau," Jared said quickly. "I need to go. Send me the number for the lady at the crime lab."

"Will do," I said into the phone, but Jared had already hung up by then, and I couldn't help but be grateful for that. I hate hearing grown men cry.

Chapter 13

When I finally emerged from Harriet Raines's basement lab, I was in for a surprise. It had still been a strange kind of pinkish twilight when I first walked into the anthropology building, but when I stepped outside almost three hours later, I was astonished by the blinding sunlight glinting off my snow-covered surroundings.

Belatedly I understood why Twink had advised me to bring along sunglasses. It took a moment to fumble them out of my pocket and onto my face. I was about to use my phone to call her when I spotted the Travelall sitting with its hood up in a lot that, under normal circumstances, was probably reserved as faculty parking off to the side of the building. As I walked in that direction, Twink Winkleman appeared from under the hood. She had shed her jacket in favor of a pair of grease-stained gray coveralls.

As I walked toward her, Twink gave a monkey wrench a quick polish on her pant leg before dropping it into a battered toolbox. After that she carefully closed the Travelall's hood, giving that a bit of a polish, too, in the process. By the time I reached her, Twink was wiping her hands on a thick blue paper towel.

"Car trouble?" I asked.

"Nope," she said, "I just finished installing that new heater core. My daughter-in-law, Cindy—my ex-daughter-in-law, actually—" she corrected, "knew when I left the house this morning that I'd been waiting for it. When the UPS driver dropped it off, she called to see if I'd like her to bring it to me. God knows she's a hell of a lot more dependable about things like that than my son ever was. She stayed on with me after my son walked out on her, and I'm happy to have her. She looks after the house and does most of the cooking. What could be better than that?"

When I didn't comment, Twink continued. "Once Cindy brought me the heater core, I figured what the hell. I could either continue sitting there freezing my ass off or I could get off my heinie, go to work, and install the damned thing. With a cheechako riding around with me for the rest of the day, I figured the sooner I got the heater fixed, the better."

Remembering the Tlingit words Harriet had used to refer to white men, I wasn't at all sure what I'd just been called, but I suspected it wasn't exactly complimentary.

"With a what?" I asked.

"A cheechako," she repeated. "That's a newcomer to Alaska—someone from Outside who just arrived and doesn't know up from down about life around here."

Presumably in Alaska the word "Outside" stands for anyplace else, but the part about my being a new arrival was absolutely true. I had visited Alaska only once before, and that had been on a cruise ship. Being in Anchorage in the depths of winter wasn't at all the same thing.

"Sounds about right," I admitted.

Twink hefted the toolbox up off the ground. Lifting loaded toolboxes is no mean feat, but she did so effortlessly, shoving it over the Travelall's rooftop luggage rack and into what was clearly its designated space. Before she could tug the blue tarp back into place, I caught a glimpse of some of the other items stowed up there—a spare tire and a pair of ten-gallon gas cans along with several sturdy wooden crates.

"What's in all the boxes?" I asked.

"Spare parts mostly," Twink replied, manhandling the tarp back into position. "With the exception of replacement heater cores, I keep an inventory of anything and everything I might need with me at all times—alternators, generators, spark plugs, sun visors. You name it, I've got it. And thanks to my old man, if I break down out on a lonely road somewhere between hither and yon, all I have to do is haul out my handy-dandy toolbox and fix whatever's broken.

"Last week I had some smart-ass kid throw a rock through the rearview mirror on the passenger side. After I cleaned the kid's clock, I grabbed the spare mirror out of the crate and fixed the problem on the spot. You wreck one of them newfangled SUVs with all those fancy-schmancy cameras built into 'em and you've got yourself a five-thousand-dollar repair bill and a minimum three-week wait for parts."

Once Twink finished tying down the tarp, she turned to me and said, "Where to next?"

I had been wondering that very thing. "Let me check," I said.

I climbed into the passenger seat, fastened my belt, and consulted Todd's incoming e-mails. The two unaffiliated boys from Homer High School who lived in Anchorage were John Borman and Bill Farmdale. John was a bartender at a place called the Anchor Bar and

Grill, so depending on his shift he could be either working or at home sleeping. According to Todd, Farmdale was a social-studies teacher at East Anchorage High. Since this was a snow day, there was a good chance he might be at home.

When Twink got into the driver's seat, she had stripped off and stowed the coveralls. Having shed her jacket as well, she was down to nothing more than her faded flannel shirt. Whatever the outside temperature might have been right then, it was clearly not an issue for her, while I was still zipped back into my parka. I guessed I was seeing an example of one of the differences between people who actually live in Alaska and a chucka-something—whatever it was she'd called me earlier.

Twink settled into the seat, punched the lighter, and lit her next cigarette. "Well?" she prodded, still waiting for me to decide where we were going.

"How far is South Salem Loop?" I asked.

"Not far," she said, reaching for the key. "Not far at all."

I gave her Bill Farmdale's address. She didn't need to enter the address into a GPS before putting the Travelall in gear.

As she drove, I thought about Danitza's place on Wiley Loop Road and wondered aloud, "Why are there so many loops around here? Seattle has streets, avenues, courts, roads, and lanes, but I don't know of a single loop."

"Beats me," Twink said with a shrug. "Nobody bothered consulting me when it came to naming streets, but did you find out what you needed to know from the bone lady?"

"Pretty much," I replied.

"Good news or bad news?"

During my years as a cop, I was taught not to discuss ongoing investigations with outsiders. Just now, however, not engaging in polite conversation with the woman who was driving me around seemed downright rude.

"Probably bad," I said.

"So the guy you're looking for is dead instead of missing?"

She had correctly assumed that my missing person was male, and I let it go at that. "Most likely," I replied, "although that has yet to be confirmed."

"By DNA?" she asked.

I nodded.

"I like those true-crime shows on TV," she added. "Seems to me that DNA must make you guys' jobs easier."

"Seems like," I agreed.

What I really wanted just then was for Twink Winkleman to be quiet so I could think, but that didn't seem to be in the cards.

"Where's he from?"

I was trying to decide how I would approach Bill Farmdale. Eventually I figured out Twink was asking about Chris. It turned out, however, that the answer in both Farmdale's case and Chris's was the same.

"Homer," I replied.

"My dad grew up there," Twink said. "Only way out for him was to join the military, so he came to Anchorage via a long stint in Korea. Never wanted to move back to Homer. I've been there on occasion for work. Homer's not really my cup of tea."

Must not have been Bill Farmdale's either, I thought.

Thinking about our next stop, I changed the subject. "What kind of place is the Anchor Bar and Grill?" I asked.

"It's mostly a dive," she answered. "Not exactly high on our list of tourist attractions and probably doesn't have any of them Michelin stars."

"I'm not a tourist," I grumbled aloud. "I'm working."

The new heater core might have been humming along like a champ, but the atmosphere inside the Travelall turned suddenly frosty. "Well, pardon me all to hell," Twink responded huffily. Obviously I had offended her, although I wasn't quite sure how.

A few minutes later, we pulled up in front of a raised ranch on a well-plowed street. I was glad to see that the walkway and front steps leading up to the house had been cleared of snow.

"How long are you gonna be this time?" Twink wanted to know. "According to the terms of my contract, I believe I'm due for a lunch break pretty soon."

"We'll have lunch after this interview," I assured her, hoping to get back on her good side. "You choose the spot. I'll buy."

After leaving the Travelall, I made my way to the front porch and rang the doorbell. The hefty guy who answered the door was in his late twenties and was wearing a pair of East Anchorage High School sweats. Behind him I heard the voices of some young kids squabbling.

"Mr. Farmdale?" I said, offering my hand.

He peered over my shoulder and took in the Travelall before giving me a wary look. "Who's asking?" he wanted to know.

"My name's J. P. Beaumont," I explained, pulling a business card out of my pocket and offering that in place of the handshake. "I'm a private investigator from Seattle, and I'm looking into the 2006 disappearance of a young man named Christopher Danielson. I was wondering if there was a chance he might be a friend of yours."

Bill Farmdale's eyes widened. "You're looking for Chris?"

I nodded.

The wariness he had exhibited before vanished. "It's about damned time someone did!" he exclaimed. "Come on in."

The kids I had heard were two boys, maybe ten or eleven, duking it out in some bang-bang-shoot-'em-up video game on a big-screen TV hung over a gas-log fireplace. Bill Farmdale invited me to take a seat on a somewhat saggy sectional with more than a few crumbs and bits of popcorn showing here and there. Meanwhile he spent the next five minutes booting the kids out of the living room. They weren't happy about having their video warfare uprooted, and it took a promised bribe of snacks in the kitchen to finally dislodge them. I hoped Mr. Farmdale, the teacher, had better disciplinary skills with his students at school than Bill Farmdale, the father, did with his kids at home.

The house had been built long enough ago that "open concept" had yet to be an architectural requirement. When Farmdale returned to the living room and shut the kitchen door behind him, the two kids were

in an entirely separate space and completely out of ear-
shot.

"So you knew Chris Danielson?" I confirmed as he
flopped down onto the sofa beside me.

"I did," he said.

"And you were friends?"

Bill nodded.

"Close friends?" I asked.

"I guess," Bill admitted, "as close as anyone ever
got. Chris was kind of a loner who didn't have many
friends. He had a pretty rough life, you know."

"You mean because of losing his parents?"

"He didn't just lose them," Bill said. "Chris's
father murdered his mother and then committed suicide. After his folks died, Chris and his older brother
were farmed out to live with their grandparents.
One set of grandparents blamed Chris's father for
what happened. The other grandparents blamed his
mother. Made Chris feel like he was in the middle of
a tug-of-war."

Of course I knew all the details of that far too well,
but I was gratified to have found not just one of Chris's
friends but a good one at that, and I was eager to learn
more.

"I understand Chris was living with his paternal
grandmother in Homer and moved out after some kind

of disagreement with her. Do you know anything about that?" I asked.

"Chris didn't just *move* out," Bill corrected. "His grandmother *booted* him out. He came home from school one day in the dead of winter and found all his stuff left in a heap on the front porch. She had also changed the locks on the doors. He didn't have a car or anyplace to stay. I came over in my folks' car and loaded all his crap into that. Some guys I knew were sharing a house. They'd just lost a roommate and had an extra room to rent, so he moved in with them."

"I was under the impression he'd stolen money from his grandmother and that's why he moved out."

"That's what she claimed, but it wasn't true," Bill said with a firm shake of his head. "That woman was a witch and mean as a snake. Once Chris's granddad died, his grandmother couldn't wait to get rid of him. She made his life miserable in hopes of getting Chris to leave on his own. When he didn't, she was the one who made it happen."

"Is that when he dropped out of school?"

Bill nodded. "His grades weren't all that good even before then, and he was already in danger of not being able to graduate, so he just quit. He hoped to hire on with one of the fishing boats eventually. In the meantime he wanted to earn enough money to go back to

Ohio to visit the rest of his family—his brother and his other grandmother. That's when I helped him get a job washing dishes in my uncle's restaurant."

"Zig's Place?" I asked.

Bill seemed taken aback that I knew the restaurant's name, but he nodded. "My Uncle Sig—Siegfried—is my mother's older brother. Everybody calls him Ziggy, and when he decided to open a restaurant, that's what he named it—Zig's Place. Chris and I worked there together. I was out front waiting tables while he was mostly in the back doing the dishes, but sometimes he worked out front, too."

"And that's where he met Danitza?" I asked.

Bill literally winced at the sound of her name. "Yes," he said, shaking his head. "It was love at first sight for both of them. It was like he'd been living in a dark cave and she was his bright ray of sunshine. She was a nice girl—smart, too. At first I thought she was just being kind to him because that's the sort of person she was, but I believe now that she liked him as much as he liked her."

"When's the last time you saw Chris?"

"It was the end of March, the year we were seniors."

"So 2006, then," I supplied.

Bill nodded. "We were both at work. It was on a Monday night, I think. He came in from dumping the trash and said he was going to take off early because there was a lady outside who needed help with a flat tire."

"What lady?" I asked.

"I have no idea," Bill said. "Just some lady with car trouble. I never saw her. He left the restaurant to go help her, and I never saw him again."

I thought about the deep indentation on the back of that skull in the banker's box from a blow that had most likely rained down on the victim from behind. Could the weapon involved have been a tool of some kind—a tire iron maybe? No, that would be far too narrow. The business end of a monkey wrench maybe?

"What happened then?" I asked.

"Like I said, the last time I saw him was at work on Monday. I had the next day off. When I came back to work on Wednesday, Uncle Sig was all bent out of shape because Chris hadn't shown up for his shift on Tuesday, and he wasn't answering his phone either. When I went by his place, his roomies hadn't seen him and had no idea where he'd gone. After that I went by his grandmother's place to see if she knew anything. She said he'd most likely run off to go back to Ohio."

Hearing that shook me. In the aftermath of Sue Danielson's fallen-officer memorial, when the Hinkles had taken Jared and Chris from Seattle to Ohio, I'd had every reason to believe that the boys would be in good hands and living in a secure, loving environment. Obviously, as far as Chris was concerned, that had been wishful thinking on my part. For some reason he'd fled Ohio in search of greener pastures with his paternal grandparents in Homer. Only that had gone sideways, too.

I gave myself a moment before continuing. "So you didn't try to report him missing?"

Bill shook his head. "I didn't believe it was my place. I mean, after all, Mrs. Danielson was his grandmother. I was just a kid, and she was the grown-up. If she wasn't worried enough to do it, why should I? And then all the rumors started."

"What rumors?"

"It turned out that Danitza Adams disappeared that same weekend. When school started on Monday morning, she was absent. Pretty soon kids at school started saying that she'd gotten pregnant and that they'd had to run away to get married. That wasn't a big surprise."

"What do you mean?"

"Everybody in town knew that Nitz's parents disapproved of Chris. I mean, her dad was a big deal around Homer, and Chris was just . . ."

"A kid from the wrong side of the tracks?" I suggested.

Bill nodded. "Eventually one of Chris's roommates

called me. He said they had gathered up all of Chris's stuff and asked if I wanted it. It wasn't much, only a couple of boxes. I still have them, I think, probably out in the garage somewhere. And that's how things stood for a long time. I was busy going to school, and Chris and Danitza were like out of sight out of mind. I didn't really think about them. I just assumed they were together someplace else. When Nitz's mother died, I went to the funeral expecting she'd turn up there, but she didn't.

"Then, years later, shortly after I landed a teaching job here in Anchorage, the *Snow-Queen* went down. It was big news, of course, more so for me because one of my students lost his father on that crabber. I was watching the evening news, and there was Danitza being interviewed by one of the reporters as the widow of one of the guys lost on board, except her last name wasn't Danielson by then. It was something else."

"Miller," I supplied.

Bill nodded. "Obviously she and Chris weren't together anymore, and that made me wonder what had happened to him. But I couldn't very well show up at her husband's funeral and say, 'Hey, whatever happened to that other guy, your old boyfriend?' So I just let it go. Know what I mean?"

He gave me a hopeless shoulder shrug. The regret I heard in his voice was all too familiar. I'd pulled a similar stunt on occasion. Then Bill Farmdale looked me straight in the eye. "You think he's dead, don't you?" he said.

I nodded. "I believe there's a good chance that he was murdered soon after he left the restaurant the night you saw him last, and—"

"Wait," Bill interrupted. "You think Chris was murdered?"

I nodded. "Human remains that may be his were located a number of years ago, but since no missing-persons report had been filed, they've remained unidentified. At the moment they still are, but once we have access to Chris's older brother's DNA profile, that may change."

Bill's eyes clouded with tears. "Crap," he said. "As soon as he was gone, I should have reported him missing. This is all my fault."

"You don't need to blame yourself," I said. "If his grandmother wasn't worried, why should you have been? But this is where we are now—trying to solve a homicide that more than likely happened in 2006. And that's why I'm here."

"How can I help?" Bill asked.

"Is there anything you can tell me about the woman who needed her tire changed—"

"Wait, you mean it might have happened that very night, right after work?"

I nodded.

Bill took a deep breath before replying, "There's really nothing to tell," he said. "Like I said, I didn't see her, and as far as I know, no one else in the restaurant did either. But you think maybe she did it?"

"It's possible." I pulled out one of my cards and handed it to him. "If you remember anything else, please give me a call."

"All right," he said. "I will."

I stood up to leave. "I'll be going," I said. "I've taken up far too much of your time and kept your kids from their video game long enough. But you should probably know that all the rumors you heard back then were right. Danitza was pregnant when she left home. She still lives here in Anchorage and is an ER nurse at Anchorage General. She has a twelve-year-old son named Christopher James Danielson. His mother calls him Jimmy. He seems liked a pretty squared-away kid, and I'll bet he'd be thrilled to meet someone who was friends with his dad."

Bill used the back of his hands to mop tears from his eyes. Then, leaving him sitting there staring off into space, I showed myself out. I had meant to ask if Bill thought there was anything to be gained by my talking to John Borman, but I didn't bother. I had already brought the poor man enough bad news for the day. There was no point in piling on more.

Chapter 14

When I made it back to the Travelall, Twink was inside, still in her shirtsleeves, sitting in a cloud of smoke and reading a tattered Louis L'Amour paperback. When I climbed inside, the interior was warm enough that I suspected she'd idled the engine a time or two in my absence in order to maintain the temperature.

"Lunch?" she asked, tossing the book on the seat between us and turning the key in the ignition.

Figuring I was still in the doghouse with her for some reason, I simply nodded. As I fastened my seat belt, I saw that the title of the book was *The Iron Marshal*, with a gun-toting lawman on the cover.

"I see you like Louis L'Amour," I said. "Me, too."

"When Chad and I were little, our dad used to read

us to sleep with Louis L'Amour stories. When Dad died, he had a whole bookcase full of 'em, and I inherited those right along with Maude here," she added, patting the steering wheel. "I usually keep a couple of 'em in the glovebox, and if it turns out I've read them before, it doesn't bother me a bit."

Twink pulled out, and we headed back in what seemed to be the general direction of downtown. "We're going to Simon & Seafort's," she informed me. "It's a bit too swanky for my blood, but a lot of my customers rave about the food, and I figure you're good for it."

If treating Twinkle Winkleman to a high-end lunch would put her in a better mood, it would be money well spent. I'd been to a near relative of that restaurant, Stanley & Seafort's in Tacoma. The food there was reasonably good, and I was pretty sure the same would be true at this one.

We were no sooner moving when Mel called. "How's it going?" she asked. Mel was taking a late lunch and expected a full briefing on my morning's worth of activities. I wanted to talk to her, too, but I didn't want to discuss my adventures with TW Transportation or my meetings with Harriet Raines or Bill Farmdale with Twink listening in on every word. I latched on to what I hoped sounded like a reasonable excuse.

"We're on our way to lunch right now, and I need to catch up on what Todd Hatcher just sent me," I said. "Can I call you back a little later?"

"I suppose," Mel said, and hung up.

That was not a good sign. Mel obviously didn't approve of having to take a backseat to incoming messages from Todd Hatcher, so now, through no fault of my own, I had managed to land in trouble with two separate women fifteen hundred miles apart.

Back downtown, after turning onto L Street and barely a block away from my hotel, we encountered what has to be an only-in-Alaska traffic jam. Three vehicles ahead of us, a humongous moose was ambling slowly down the middle of the snowplowed traffic lanes, looking for all the world as if he owned the place, and maybe he did. Taking his antlers into consideration, he was taller than the topmost layer of the Travelall's rooftop luggage. Since he didn't appear to have a working turn signal, no one wanted to risk trying to pass him, on either side. Suddenly our previously speedy trip turned into a slo-mo, moose-led parade.

"I guess moose . . . whether one or in a herd . . . always have the right of way. It's not mooses, correct?"

"You've got that right, city boy," Twink said.

"What do you expect?" I asked her. "After all,

aren't I one of those chickadoodles—or whatever it is you called me earlier."

"*Cheechako,*" she corrected with the hint of a grin twitching at the corners of her mouth. "And you've got that right, too. You're a cheechako in spades."

"And moose always have the right of way around here?"

"Indeed they do," Twink told me.

It turns out that the restaurant was within a stone's throw of my hotel, the Captain Cook. When we turned into the restaurant parking entrance several minutes later, the moose parade was still moseying on down the street.

Inside the restaurant the lunch crowd was beginning to clear out. Given a choice between being seated immediately or waiting for a window, Twink opted for a window. Clearly now that she had arrived, she was going to take full advantage and enjoy the experience to the fullest. Once we were shown to our table, I have to admit that even for someone who lives with a seaside view, the panorama visible from the restaurant's windows was well worth the short wait.

When it comes to eating out, I'm not big on fish— I'm more of a meat-and-potatoes sort of guy. Since this was Alaska, I was afraid the menu would be all salmon all the time. When Twink ordered the waitress-recommended meat-loaf sandwich, so did I. You know how that old saying goes—when in Rome, et cetera, and I wasn't sorry. For beverages Twink and I both chose coffee. Thankfully, coffee at Simon & Seafort's was far less lethal than the bitter brew served up by Harriet Raines.

"Where to next?" Twink asked.

I scrolled through e-mails from Todd until I found one with a subject line containing John Borman's name. Yesterday Todd had supplied me with both Danitza's place of employment as well as her shift, and this time he came through again.

"It says here that John Borman is working at the Anchor Bar and Grill today. What can you tell me about it?"

"Like I said earlier, the Anchor's not exactly a favorite hangout as far as I'm concerned," she said. "It's a bit on the sleazy side. Why?"

"That's our next stop. How far away?"

"Eight blocks or so," Twink replied, "but I wouldn't recommend walking. I also wouldn't recommend going to the Anchor after dark. It's one of those places where hard-core drinkers go to get drunk or laid, not necessarily in that order. Who's John Borman?"

"Someone from Homer who went to school with the

guy we're looking for and who may or may not be a friend of his."

Twink accepted my answer. Thankfully, she didn't ask for any further details.

The artichoke-dip appetizer arrived and disappeared in short order. As soon as it was gone, Twink grabbed her purse and went outside for a smoke. Left on my own for a few minutes, I sent Mel a brief text explaining my reasons for dodging her call.

Then, for the first time since leaving Bill Farmdale's home, I had a chance to think. What he had told me about Chris's going out late that Sunday night to change someone's tire resonated with me. A blow from a tool of some kind could easily have left the deep indentation in the back of the skull in Harriet's banker's box. It also squared with the idea of the victim's having been in a kneeling position when the fatal blow was struck. Once she had Jared's DNA and, presumably, a positive ID on the human remains, investigators from the AST would be summoned en masse, and my presence in the mix would become problematic.

Jared Danielson was my client. If the homicide victim's remains resting in Harriet's banker's box really did belong to Chris, I wanted to be the one providing that confirmation to his survivors, even if the painful truth that his brother was dead was the last thing Jared ever wanted to hear. More than that, though, I wanted to be the one who answered the questions Jared and his grandmother would ask next: Who did this and why? That's what homicide investigators do. Retired or not, that's still who I am and what I do.

I had no doubt that once Harriet confirmed the victim's identity, AST would launch an investigation, but the urgency of a twelve-year-old cold case would depend entirely on how much else the agency had going on right then. My personal urgency and theirs were two entirely different things.

Twink returned, bringing with her the indelible scent of cigarette-smoke-drenched clothing that was obvious from several feet away. She had barely regained her seat when our entrées arrived, and we both tucked into our marvelous meat-loaf sandwiches. During lunch, in an attempt to carry on polite conversation, I mentioned Twink's proficiency as a mechanic.

"I'm not sure I would have known what a heater core was, much less been able to install one on the fly like that," I told her.

"That's all because of my dad," she said. "Our mother was a lot younger than he was. She took off and was totally out of the picture early on. Daddy had us out in the garage crawling under cars and handing him tools before we could walk and talk."

"Who's us?" I asked.

"Me and my older brother, Chad."

"Is he a wizard mechanic, too?"

"Not with cars," Twink said. "His specialty is airplanes. Chad and Daddy had a falling-out when Chad was a teenager. Chad joined the air force. He went to Vietnam for a couple tours of duty and came home a trained airplane mechanic. Alaska is a big place, and lots of people use planes to get around here—especially them little Pipers that can land three ways—wheels, skis, or floats.

"Chad managed to turn himself into the go-to guy doing maintenance for bush pilots and family planes alike. Occasionally a pilot will keel over dead, leaving behind a plane in need of offloading. That's especially true when some expensive FAA-required maintenance overhaul is in the offing. Chad keeps his ear to the ground. When he hears about some orphaned aircraft, he buys it up at bargain-basement rates, does the necessary maintenance work, and then resells it."

"Sounds like an interesting guy."

"More ornery than interesting, if you ask me," Twink supplied. "He makes good money. Never married, lives out in the boonies all by himself. He has a condo in Hawaii and one in Palm Springs. It's winter, so he's probably at one or the other at the moment. I couldn't tell you for sure—we're not exactly close."

This was way more Winkleman family history than I had anticipated hearing or knowing. I suspected that when it came to being "ornery," Twink would have given her brother a run for his money, and there could be little doubt that both had come by that trait by way of their father's side of the family tree.

The food was wonderful and more than either Twink or I could eat. We both passed on ordering dessert. At the end of the meal, when our waitress brought the check, Twink asked for a box and then loaded my remaining fries into the container right along with her own.

"No sense in letting good food go to waste," she said. "Next stop the Anchor Bar and Grill."

In better weather it would have been an easy walk from the restaurant to the bar, but we drove instead. As we approached the place, a pickup of some kind pulled out of a parking place in front of the army-surplus store next door. That told me pretty much all I needed to know about the neighborhood and what I could expect to find inside. Twink declined my invitation to come along.

"I'll wait here," she said, picking up her book. "Take your time."

The Anchor Bar and Grill lived up to its advance notices. It might have been a piece of Alaska's colorful history, but it was all too familiar to me. I had spent decades of my life hanging out in joints just like it— ones that came complete with acres of scarred but polished wooden bars, damaged pool tables, and worn-out dartboards. The single bright spot in the otherwise gloom-filled room was a well-lit oil painting hanging on the far wall. It featured a generously endowed young woman, reclining seminude to better display her impressive wares. Her presence hinted that at sometime in the distant past, booze hadn't been the only temptation for sale on the premises.

It was now verging on 3:00 P.M., and the place was crowded with a motley assortment of barflies I recognized all too well—the Friday-afternoon regulars, otherwise known as serious drinkers, who show up early and stay for the duration. I found an empty stool and bellied up to the bar.

Todd had sent me a photocopy of John Borman's driver's license, so even though the bartender was at the far end of the bar, I knew he was the guy I wanted to see. Bartenders need to be reasonably gregarious, but they're generally not wild about talking to detectives of any kind—sworn officers and private investigators alike. It's usually considered bad for business. They do, however, engage in conversations with paying customers, so when the barkeep came my way, I ordered a ginger ale.

"Not a drinker?" he asked as he delivered my alcohol-free beverage.

"Turns out it was bad for my health," I replied. "You're John Borman, right?"

"Depends on who's asking," he said. "Who are you?"

I slid one of my cards across the bar. He picked it up and studied it for a moment.

"A private detective?" he asked with a frown. "What's this all about?"

"I'm looking into the disappearance of Christopher Danielson."

The frown deepened into a scowl. "From Homer, you mean? That's yesterday's news," he said. "Chris disappeared years ago, while we were all still in high school. You thinking maybe I had something to do with it?"

"I'm just trying to talk to people who possibly knew him back in the day and might have an idea about what became of him."

That was a giveaway. Had Chris and Borman been close, he would have been aware that Chris had already dropped out of school before he disappeared.

"I'm not going to be of much use to you," Borman said, confirming my initial assumption. "I mean, I knew who he was, but I didn't really *know* him. We weren't friends or anything. We were maybe in a couple of classes together, but that's it. He was sort of a sad sack. I think something bad happened in his family when he was little, but I don't know much about it."

I nodded. "Domestic violence. His dad killed his mother and then committed suicide." Sometimes you have to give a little information in order to get some.

"I never knew that part," Borman conceded.

"What *did* you know?"

"Just that Chris was mostly an odd duck, a perpetual outsider, so it surprised the hell out of me when I heard he was hanging around with one of the most popular girls at Homer High. How does that happen? Then, a while after that, he was just gone. Word was that his girlfriend was pregnant and they ran off to get married. That's the last thing I remember hearing."

A customer down the bar caught Borman's eye and summoned him with a wave of his finger. As he walked away, I could tell that although my "unaffiliated boy" theory had come up winners with Bill Farmdale, it was a dud here. Chris had regarded Bill as a friend—someone Chris had turned to in his time of need. John Borman had been Chris's sometime classmate, but that was it.

When the bartender returned, I dropped a ten-dollar bill on the counter. "Thanks for the help," I told him. "Keep the change."

Setting foot outside the bar, I noticed that the sky was once again that weird shade of pink that made it look like late afternoon. Inside the smoke-filled Travelall, Twink assured me that that pinkish glow was what passed for afternoon daylight in wintertime Anchorage.

"Where to now?" Twink wanted to know as she punched the button on the cigarette lighter.

The truth is, I had no idea. Danitza Miller, Bill Farmdale, and John Borman had been the only three names on my Anchorage to-do list. Two of the three had produced worthwhile information. I had already told Jared Danielson that his brother was most likely dead, but I'd had to do that in order to rush the DNA comparison. The next time I spoke to Nitz, I wanted to have a clear answer one way or the other—either the human remains in Harriet Raines's lab belonged to Chris Danielson or they did not. Until I knew for sure, there was no reason to see her again.

Bill Farmdale had told me about the mysterious woman whose tire had needed changing the night Chris disappeared. She was certainly a likely suspect in my opinion, but would a random stranger show up at his work, lure him away, and then murder him just for the hell of it? No, I was sure someone with motive must have been behind it. The most promising suspect there was an irate father who'd just discovered that his unwed daughter was pregnant. I needed someone who wasn't Danitza herself to shed some light on her dear old dad. Suddenly it occurred to me there might be another person in Anchorage who could do just that.

I had evidently been sitting there thinking for far too long. "Well?" Twink demanded impatiently.

"Hang on," I told her. "Let me give someone a call."

I pulled out my cell phone and punched in Todd Hatcher's number. "What do you need now?" he asked. I got the distinct feeling he was growing weary of my constantly badgering him for information.

"I'd like the address for a Penny and Wally Olmstead. Maybe it's Walter instead of Wally. I understand they live here in Anchorage, but I have no idea where."

In a matter of seconds of rapid-fire keyboarding, I heard an incoming text arrive on my phone. "Sent," Todd said.

"And received," I told him. "Thanks."

I read the address aloud to Twink Winkleman. "Peck Avenue is due east of here," she said, turning the key in the ignition. "Maude and I will have us there in a jiffy."

Exactly one and a half cigarettes later, we pulled up in front of a small frame residence in the 8000 block of Peck Avenue. It was a modest one-story tract house that looked as though it had been built in the sixties. There were lights on inside, which led me to believe someone was home. Twink pulled in to the cleared driveway and parked.

"Don't worry," she told me. "I'll wait."

Chapter 15

Once outside the vehicle, I followed a narrow cleared path from the driveway to the front door. Clearly people in Alaska are serious about shoveling their walks.

After ringing the bell, I waited the better part of a minute before a woman finally came to the door. When she opened it, an enticing aroma of cooking food wafted through the air. All day long my beleaguered nostrils had been assailed by secondhand smoke, both from Twink's chain-smoked cigarettes and Harriet Raines's cigar. Whatever garlicky delight Penny Olmstead was cooking up in her kitchen—beef stew maybe?—served as a welcome antidote.

The woman standing in the doorway was tiny, with short blond hair. I guessed her to be somewhere in her late thirties or early forties. If I had encountered Penny and Danitza Miller walking down a street together, I probably would have assumed the two of them to be sisters rather than auntie and niece.

"Yes?" she inquired, staring up at me.

"Penny Olmstead?" I asked.

She nodded. "Who are you?"

I handed her one of my cards, and she studied it for a moment before saying, "You must be that private detective from Seattle. Nitza was telling me about you."

"Who is it, Pen?" asked a male voice from somewhere deep in the house. I assumed the person asking the question had to be Nitz's Uncle Wally.

"It's Mr. Beaumont, that detective Nitza spoke to yesterday," Penny said, calling over her shoulder, "the guy who's looking for Chris."

I made a mental note of that. Danitza Miller might be Nitz everywhere else, but in this household and as far as her Aunt Penny and Uncle Wally were concerned, she was Nitza.

"Well, have him come inside so you can shut the damned door," the man ordered irritably. "It's freezing, and we don't need to pay to heat the great outdoors."

"Won't you come in?" Penny Olmstead invited. Once inside, she pointed toward a collection of shoes sitting just beyond the door. "If you don't mind," she said.

I was standing on a welcome mat–style rug in a small entryway, but the flooring in the next room was a highly polished hardwood. Clearly Aunt Penny didn't want anyone tracking snow or melted salt water inside. There was a small bench there, and so I complied with her wishes by sitting down and slipping off my boots. I was grateful for the bench. My fake knees are a miracle for most things, but standing upright while removing boots isn't one of them.

"You and your niece look a lot alike," I observed.

Penny Olmstead gave me a tentative smile. "Yes, we do," she agreed. "We always have."

When the boots were off, I looked down at my stockinged feet, grateful that I wasn't wearing socks with holes in them.

From the small entryway, Penny led me into the wood-paneled interior of the house, where it felt as though the temperature had to be somewhere in the eighties. Obviously the baseboard heaters were working overtime. We walked past a compact dining area complete with an old-fashioned table and six matching chairs. The polished tabletop was decorated with a gorgeous Christmas centerpiece made of freshly cut evergreen branches studded with white and red candles.

Beyond the dining room was a cozy seating area. Much of the far wall was taken up by a large brick fireplace with a wood fire crackling inside. The large flat-screen TV, perched on the mantel, was tuned to the Golf Channel. On-screen some guy whose name I didn't recognize was teeing off at a green, palm-tree-lined golf course far away from wintertime Alaska. In the corner next to the fireplace sat a petite but fully decorated Christmas tree. It was pretty enough, but unlike the wreath on the table it wasn't real.

The walls on either side of the fireplace contained a gallery of framed photos, almost all of them featuring Christopher James Danielson. Taken together they showed a chronology of the boy's young life. There were photos of birthday celebrations, complete with cakes and candles. One school head shot after another showed his gradual facial changes from year to year. Several showcased him in a Cub Scout uniform while others had him dressed in a Little League outfit, glove and all. Those kinds of over-the-top photo displays are usually limited to the walls of doting grandparents. In this case the doting was being done by a loving great-aunt and -uncle.

Seating arrangements in the space consisted of two leather recliners directly in front of the TV set with a narrow end table standing between them. Off to one side sat an upholstered love seat. A rolling walker was stationed within easy reach of a graying fifty-something man seated in one of the recliners.

"I'm Walter Olmstead," he said, holding out his hand in greeting. "Have a seat. I hope you'll forgive me for not standing. Football injury," he added in explanation, patting one hip, "a new one rather than an old one. I'm the coach, you see. The first game of the season was a doozy. In the middle of a crucial play, I saw two players charging straight for me. Unfortunately, I dodged to the right when I should have dodged to the left. Broke my hip and had to be stretchered off the field. The doctors tried screwing it back together, but they finally gave up and did a hip replacement. With any kind of luck, I'll be back at school after Christmas break."

"Ouch," I said, settling onto the love seat while Penny sat down on the other recliner.

"Them's the breaks," Walter said with an offhand shrug accompanied by an engaging grin. "But the Wolverines went on to win state without me, so you can see how much my coaching is worth. What can we do for you, Mr. Beaumont?"

"As your wife said, I met with Danitza yesterday— with her and James both. He looks like a great kid," I added, gesturing toward the collection of photos.

"He *is* a great kid," Walter declared proudly, "no

question about it. His mom has done a terrific job of raising him."

"But not without a good deal of assistance from the two of you."

"We do our best," Penny agreed with a modest smile.

"But what can we do for you today?" Walter insisted. "Why this sudden interest in finding Chris now? Why not twelve years ago?"

"Because twelve years ago it wasn't clear he was missing," I answered. "Since Chris was estranged from both sets of grandparents at the time he disappeared, no one ever got around to reporting him as missing. Now, though, his only remaining grandmother, Annie Hinkle, is likely on her deathbed back in Ohio. She asked Chris's brother, Jared, to try to find him in hopes of having a last-minute reconciliation. Jared's the one who brought me into the picture."

"I don't see how we can be of much help," Penny said. "Wally and I never actually met Chris. All we know about him is what Nitza has told us over the years."

"From what I've heard, you two were part of a very limited group of people who knew much of anything about what was really going on at the time Chris went missing."

"You mean about her being pregnant?" Penny asked.

"Yes," I answered. "I guess Nitza's parents weren't too thrilled with the news. What can you tell me?"

"Saying they weren't thrilled doesn't come close!" Penny objected. "Roger Adams was downright furious, and when Roger is angry, he's a force to be reckoned with. As for my sister, when it came to choosing between her husband or her daughter, Eileen always went along with whatever Roger said. That's one of the reasons I tried to stay close to Nitza over the years, even when she was little. I wanted her to feel like she had someone on her side."

"You must have succeeded," I remarked, "because that night when the chips were down, she trusted you enough to come straight here."

"And we're both glad she did," Walter declared, sending a smile in his wife's direction. "I was always troubled by the way Roger and Eileen treated their daughter, but when Roger refused to let Nitza attend her own mother's funeral? That was the last straw in my book."

"Did you go?" I asked Penny.

"To the funeral, you mean?" she wanted to know.

I nodded.

"I tried," Penny said. "Nitza and I wouldn't even have known it was happening if one of Shelley's friends hadn't called and told me about it."

"One of Shelley's friends?" I asked. "You mean Roger himself didn't let you or Nitza know that Eileen had passed away?"

Penny shook her head. "He never said a word! One of Shelley's good friends, Betsy Norman, was working in the hospital in Homer when Eileen was undergoing chemo. Back when we were kids, Bets and I knew each other from youth group at church. When she got to high school and started running with Shelley and the rest of the cheerleader crowd, the two of us drifted apart. Still, if she hadn't called to express her condolences about my losing Eileen, Nitza and I wouldn't have known her mother was gone."

That struck me as odd. Using my iPad, I made a quick note of Betsy Norman's name. "No one else called to notify you?"

"Bets was the only one." There was more than a hint of bitterness in Aunt Penny's reply, and I didn't blame her. It was as though once Aunt Penny had taken Danitza's side in the quarrel between her and her parents, the whole town of Homer had closed ranks against the two of them, with the sole exception being this

Betsy person, who happened to be pals with Roger's longtime mistress and soon-to-be bride.

"Anyway," Penny continued, "Nitza and I found out when the funeral was scheduled to happen, and we drove over to Homer together, taking Jimmy with us. Except when we got to the church, there was an Alaska State Trooper stationed outside on the front steps. He wouldn't let Nitza and Jimmy inside, so I didn't go in either, but Shelley was there in all her glory. She came waltzing up the steps, big as you please, just as we were turning to leave. She was dolled up in head-to-toe black, looking like your basic mourner-in-chief. Knowing what I knew, just seeing her there acting like a full-fledged member of the family made me sick to my stomach. I wanted to grab that woman and strangle her on the spot. How dare she!"

"When you mentioned knowing what you knew, I'm assuming you mean that you were aware your brother-in-law and Shelley were having an affair long before your sister died."

Penny nodded.

"How long had you known?"

"A year or so before Nitza came to live with us, I was at a restaurant here in downtown Anchorage for a friend's baby shower when I spotted the two of them together. I recognized Shelley right off. I saw them, but they didn't see me. They were too busy acting like a pair of love-starved teenagers who couldn't keep their hands off each other."

"Did you tell your sister?" I asked.

Penny shook her head. "I suppose I should have, but I didn't. For one thing, Eileen was totally besotted with Roger, and knowing he was cheating on her would have broken her heart. Besides, I kept thinking the fling would run its course and go away, but with Shelley Hollander Loveday in the picture, I should have known better."

"Wait, are you saying Roger's other woman was someone you already knew?"

"Oh, I knew Shelley, all right," Penny sniffed. "I was in school with her, too. I was a junior when she was a freshman. She was the kind of girl who always went for older guys. Even as a freshman, she only dated upperclassmen. She likes her men to be older and well-to-do."

"Maybe when it comes to liking older men," Walter observed with a grin, "people who live in glass houses shouldn't throw stones."

Penny returned his grin with a fond smile, as though this older-man/younger-woman issue was a longstanding joke between them. "I dated lots of guys my age before I ended up with you," she teased.

"So Roger Adams isn't Shelley's first husband?" I interjected, trying to steer the interview back on course.

"By no means. Shelley was always a bit of a wild thing. When everybody else was talking about going off to college, she was dead set on becoming a bush pilot, and that's exactly what she did. As soon as she graduated, she signed up for flight school. Jack Loveday not only owned the school, he was also Shelley's flight instructor. He might have been twenty years older than Shelley and married at the time, but that didn't keep her from putting the moves on him. She got what she wanted. Jack and his first wife, Lois, divorced. Lois went away, and Shelley became the second Mrs. Jack Loveday. Jack gave Shelley her very own Piper Cherokee as a wedding present."

"Generous," I commented. "Where's Jack now?"

"Dead," Penny replied. "He was badly injured in a plane wreck and ended up committing suicide, but I don't know any of the details on that," she said. "What I do know is the whole time Shelley was pretending she and my sister were the best of friends, she was screwing Roger behind Eileen's back. I wanted to tell Nitza about what was going on between them on our way home from the funeral, but she was too upset. I kept my mouth shut then, but when Roger and Shelley got married barely two months later, that was it. That's when I finally broke down and told Nitza."

In that moment my heart went out to the late Eileen Adams. While in high school, she'd been pursued by not one but two of the local hunks—Richard Danielson and Roger Adams. When she opted for Roger, I'm sure she thought she was making a good choice. I knew now, with the benefit of hindsight, that neither of them had been decent husband material. Eileen would have been far better off going after someone who wasn't close to being a high-school stud.

"So let's go back to when Chris went missing," I said, changing the focus of the conversation. "I've been working on a timeline. The weekend before Chris disappeared, he and Nitza spent Saturday night together. The next day when Nitza woke up, she was ill so he took her home. When she was still sick on Monday, that's when her mother must have stumbled onto what might really be going on and had—"

"Nitza take that home pregnancy test," Penny supplied.

I nodded. "When the results came in, all hell broke loose. Nitza went to Chris's place, thinking he'd come home after work. When he didn't, she came here to you."

"And never saw Chris again," Penny said.

"Exactly," I agreed.

Wally had been quiet during most of this conversation, but now he spoke up. "I've always thought Roger
had something to do with that boy's disappearance," he
asserted.

His comment caught my attention and Penny's, too.
She was clearly surprised.

"You did?" she asked. "How come you never mentioned it?"

"I don't always say everything I'm thinking," he
replied. "Besides, things between you and Eileen and
between Nitza and her folks were already complicated
enough. I didn't see any reason to heap more fuel on
the fire."

I had made no mention of Harriet Raines or the
human remains, and it sounded as though Walter was
still sold on the idea that Chris had simply taken off.

"Mr. Olmstead," I asked, "what makes you think
Roger Adams might be involved in Chris's disappearance?"

"Please call me Wally," he said. "As for Chris? I've
always suspected Roger paid the kid off, telling him to
get lost and stay that way."

"You think Roger bribed Chris to leave town?"

Wally nodded. "I do indeed. From what Nitza has
told us, at the time Chris was barely scraping by and

trying to save up enough money to go back to Ohio for a visit. For someone like that, it wouldn't take much money to make him feel like he'd stumbled into a gold mine. As little as a thousand bucks or so would have done the trick, and Roger always made it a point to let me know that he kept a pile of cash handy, either in his wallet or in the safe in his den."

"I never knew anything about that either," Penny said. "How come you did?" She sounded more than slightly put out.

"Because he told me so," Wally replied. "Why bother you? We both know that Roger Adams is nothing but a blowhard and a braggart. Back when we used to hang out with them from time to time, Roger always rubbed my nose in the fact that he was the big-deal attorney, raking in the dough, while I was nothing more than a dirt-poor schoolteacher. I always regarded those kinds of comments as coming from a bad case of brother-in-law one-upmanship. Once Nitza came to live with us and we ended up cutting off all communication with him, it was no great loss."

"You're saying that you haven't maintained any contact with him and his new wife?" I asked.

Wally shook his head emphatically. "Not at all! I was appalled that Roger wouldn't let Nitza come visit her mother while she was in the hospital let alone not allow her to attend the funeral. I wouldn't cross the street to spit on that man's shoes."

"Back to the money question," I put in. "You're saying you believe Roger Adams kept enough loose cash around, either on his person or at the house, that he could have tossed a thousand bucks or two in Chris Danielson's lap at the drop of a hat?"

"No question," Wally declared. "Roger's grandfather was well-to-do in the twenties and then lost it all when banks went bust during the Great Depression. As a result Roger's dad grew up dirt poor and so did Roger. That's why he swore he'd never let himself end up in the same kind of fix, and that's why he always kept a bundle of cash on hand. It's also why he was always investing in real estate. He said that way if things went bust, he wouldn't be left high and dry."

"I still think you should have told me something about all this," Penny interjected.

Wally might have believed that keeping his thoughts and suspicions about his ex-brother-in-law to himself all these years had been a wise move, but I had a feeling that once I left the house, Penny was going to give him hell about it.

"You told me earlier that you don't really have any contact with Roger and Shelley, but you're aware he's ill now."

Wally and Penny both nodded in unison.

"Nitza told us Helen had been in touch," Penny explained.

"Helen?" I asked.

"Helen Sinclair," Penny answered. "She's been Roger's secretary for as long as I can remember. She dropped by Nitza's place a week or so ago to deliver the news. She was hoping Nitza would agree to come visit, but that's not going to happen. Nitza told me she has no intention of doing so, and I don't blame her. Yes, Wally and I helped her once the baby came along, but Roger had far more wherewithal than we did, and he never lifted a finger. As far as I'm concerned, regardless of what's going on with Roger right now, Nitza doesn't owe that man a damned thing!"

From all I'd heard about Roger Adams to this point, I wholeheartedly agreed. In terms of my investigation into Chris's disappearance, I was now willing to move Roger's name up the ladder of my suspect chart from person of interest to prime suspect. As far as I could tell, he was the only person with a strong motive for having Chris Danielson out of the picture.

If it hadn't been so late in the day, I would have been tempted to head for Homer the moment I left the Olmsteads' cozy home. I wanted to be in the same room with Roger Adams, speaking with him face-to-face while trying to determine what the man was all about. Up to this point, the general consensus seemed to be that Roger was a self-important bully who liked to throw his weight and money around and wasn't above cheating on a dying wife. Those were interesting asides, but I'm a homicide investigator. For me there was only one question: Was the man also a cold-blooded killer?

Once I had a firm yes or no on that score, I'd be able to figure out what to do next.

Chapter 16

When I exited the Olmsteads' house, it wasn't quite five, but it was already dark—not just twilight dark but very. As I approached the Travelall, illumination from a streetlight allowed me to see that Twink was sacked out in the driver's seat. Her only concession to the weather was the well-used jacket tucked under her chin and covering her front.

When I opened the passenger door, she started awake. "Sleeping on the job?" I asked.

"Just resting my eyes," Twink told me. She turned the key in the ignition but didn't put the vehicle in gear until after she'd lit her next cigarette. "Did you get what you needed?"

"Pretty much," I answered.

"Are we done for the day?"

"I think so."

"Back to the hotel, then?" Twink wanted to know.

"That's fine," I said.

We rode along in silence for a minute or two before she mentioned, "That's what I always wanted to be when I grew up, you know—a cop."

"Why didn't you?" I asked.

"Oh, I did," she replied, "but it didn't last. I got hired by Anchorage PD and made it through the academy without a lick of trouble. But then, my first week on the job, I was out on patrol with my field training officer. It was after midnight. We got called to a public disturbance in the parking lot of a place called Boomer's. It was located on Fourth, just up the street from the Anchor Bar and Grill. When we arrived on the scene, guys from two separate motorcycle gangs were whaling away on one another, and we waded into the melee, trying to break it up. When someone took a swing at me, I turned around and decked him. Unfortunately, I knocked him colder'n a wedge. Took out his two front teeth, and he ended up in the hospital with a concussion."

"I guess his mother never taught him that he shouldn't pick on girls," I suggested.

Twink laughed aloud at that. "I guess not," she agreed.

"So what happened?" I asked.

"Anchorage PD claimed I'd used excessive force and dropped me like a hot potato. I waited tables for the next twenty years or so. In the meantime my dad had started this shuttle service, moving people back and forth from the airport to homes or hotels. He used nice cars when he could, but when it came to taking folks out into the boonies where all the other drivers refused to go, he used this—trusty old Maude here. Before Daddy passed, I drove for him sometimes when he was overbooked. Once he was gone, I ran the shuttle service full-time. Ended up selling out the operation for a damned fortune a few years ago, but people still know that if they're going out into the back of the beyond or if they need to get around in rough weather, I'm the one to call. I enjoy it, too. Chauffeuring people around keeps me off the streets, and I meet some interesting folks from time to time, you included."

I couldn't help but be struck by the comparison between her story and Jared Danielson's. Both had started out to become cops. Once those dreams came to nothing, they had both settled on completely different paths.

"Sounds like you haven't done too badly for yourself," I said.

"Nope," she agreed. "I get to come and go as I please, and I don't have to answer to anybody, which is just the way I like it."

That's probably the way your one-time FTO likes it, too, I thought.

By then we were pulling up in front of the hotel. As we turned in toward the lobby, I could see that the snow had been cleared from the parking lot's entrance. I'd seen a weather report saying that no additional precipitation was expected for the next two days. In other words, exiting the hotel garage the next morning wouldn't be a problem.

At the entrance I got out of the vehicle, told Twinkle Winkleman thank you for all the help, and headed inside thinking I'd never again see the Travelall or its driver. Naturally it turns out I was wrong on both counts.

Inside the lobby I found that a weekend conference of some kind was getting under way. I dodged through the crowd and made it to the bank of elevators. After that heavy-duty late lunch, I wouldn't be needing much of a dinner that evening.

Up in my room, I was happy to shed the boots I'm not accustomed to wearing. I was also glad to ditch my smoke-drenched clothing and take a shower. Had my room had windows that worked, I might have opened one and hung my clothes on a curtain rod to air out.

I used the pod machine in the room to make myself a passable cup of coffee and raided the honor bar for a bag of peanuts. Then I turned on my iPad and read through the extensive biographical material Todd Hatcher had managed to amass on Roger Adams. He was clearly a big deal in Homer. As far as I could tell, until recently he'd been the top-rated attorney in town. Before being sent to the state legislature, he'd served on the city council and done at least one term as mayor. He was also past president of the Homer Rotary Club, to say nothing of being on the local school board.

Todd had already told me that the population of Homer was right around five thousand people. In that small pond, Eileen and Roger Adams would have been very big fish, and in a place where everyone knew everyone else's business, having your sixteen-year-old daughter turn up pregnant by a ne'er-do-well kid would have been a terrible a blow to an overly developed ego. The professionally photographed portrait on the Roger Adams, Attorney at Law Web site showed a robust middle-aged man smiling confidently into the camera lens. Dressed in a well-cut tailored suit and sporting a headful of dark brown hair, Adams appeared to be downright urbane, far more so than I would have expected to find in small-town Alaska.

It wasn't difficult to conclude that Roger was someone for whom appearances were everything,

And how would someone like that regard the kid who had knocked up his teenage daughter? With utter contempt. He would have seen Chris as little more than a bug on his windshield, an annoyance to be brushed off at the first opportunity. With Chris gone, Roger's expectation most likely would have been that his daughter would shape up and come home. Instead she'd chosen to ship out.

From what Wally Olmstead had told me, I knew that Roger had looked down on his less well-to-do in-laws, so it must have driven the man nuts to know that Penny and Wally were the very people from whom Danitza had sought shelter and aid in her time of need, thus allowing her to deviate from the path her father had laid out for her and enabling her to chart her own course. As for what might have happened had Danitza knuckled under and come home? Most likely Roger would have pressured her into having an abortion or giving the baby up for adoption. In either case Christopher James Danielson would not exist.

In my years as a cop, I've met plenty of abusive

spouses. Male or female, they show the world one face, charming the hell out of everybody lucky enough to live outside the four walls of the family home. In the Web site's photo, Roger Adams seemed harmless enough, benevolent almost, but who was he behind closed doors? Had he simply used his money and power to manipulate Chris into leaving town, or had he resorted to something worse?

At this point most of the world still regarded Chris Danielson as a missing person. Harriet Raines and I both believed he was dead. I suspected that Roger Adams was the only person alive who knew the truth, and I wanted to be the one who confronted him with questions about it.

Would I be interfering in an AST homicide investigation by doing so? Yes, but only if there *were* an ongoing investigation, and at this point there wasn't one. Until Professor Harriet Raines told me otherwise, I fully intended to keep on keeping on—including conducting a one-on-one interview with Roger Adams.

That's how things stood when Mel called once she and Sarah got home. Over the phone I gave her a play-by-play rundown of my day's worth of activities. It was only when I told her about my plan to drive to Homer the next morning to interview Roger that things came to a full and complete stop.

"Are you kidding me?" she demanded.

I was a bit befuddled. "Kidding about what?" I asked.

"You're planning on going to Homer in the morning, all by your little lonesome, to have a heart-to-heart chat with the guy you think murdered Chris Danielson?"

"Well, yes," I allowed.

"So what part of Lone Rangering don't you understand?" Mel wanted to know. "I refuse to have you come home from Alaska in a frigging body bag. If you do, it'll ruin Christmas for everybody."

In the world of law enforcement, Lone Rangering, aka Tombstone Courage, means failure to call for backup. The middle-aged guy I'd seen in that official Web-site portrait didn't appear to be especially dangerous, but what if he were? If Roger really had killed Chris Danielson and had spent all this time thinking he'd gotten away with it, what would happen if I turned up asking a few uncomfortable and very pointed questions?

"Well?" an impatient Mel prodded.

Obviously she was waiting for my answer, and believe me, I was struggling to find one, because in my heart of hearts I knew she was right. Finally I hit on a response that might possibly pass muster.

"What if I contacted the lady who drove me around today and had her drive me tomorrow as well?" I asked.

"Twinkle whatever?" Mel asked.

"Yes, Twinkle Winkleman," I replied. "Years ago she served briefly with the Anchorage PD." I didn't say exactly how briefly. "She washed out when a suspect took a swing at her and she punched his lights out. She was suspended for excessive use of force."

"Sounds like my kind of girl," Mel murmured. "If you got into trouble, do you think she'd be able to help?"

I thought about the effortless way Twink had hefted that loaded toolbox up and into the rooftop luggage rack earlier in the day. With her around, if I ended up encountering some kind of trouble, Twink would probably be able to do more than just call for help.

"In my opinion," I told Mel, "anyone who underestimated Twink's physical capabilities would be making a serious error in judgment."

"Good," Mel said. "Do you think she'll agree to go?"

"It depends on whether she's already booked for tomorrow."

"Call and find out," Mel said, "and then let me know. I don't want you bearding Roger Adams in his den without someone there as backup. Got it?"

"Yes, ma'am," I said. "I hear you loud and clear."

Mel hung up then. I checked my phone for recent calls and figured out which number had to be Twink's. She answered instantly. "TW Transportation," she said. "Who's calling?"

Standing on ceremony wasn't exactly a Twinkle Winkleman thing.

"J. P. Beaumont," I said. "What are you doing tomorrow?"

"Depends," she said. "What have you got in mind?"

"I'd like to hire you to drive me to and from Homer."

"For all day?"

"All day," I replied.

"Same as today, but to go that distance I'll have to charge for mileage and meals."

"Fair enough."

"What if things go long and we end up having to stay over?" she wanted to know. "I don't want you thinking this is some kind of driver-with-benefits arrangement."

Twinkle Winkleman was a long way from being my type, but I didn't mention that. "Absolutely," I said. "If we end up staying over, I'm good for separate rooms. Believe me, if I weren't, my wife would kill me."

"Sounds like my kind of woman," Twink said.

I almost laughed aloud at that. At least she and Mel were on the same page.

"What time?" Twink asked.

"How about eight?" I suggested.

"It's four and a half hours from here," she said. "If you want any time on that end, we'd better make it earlier. What say seven instead of eight?"

"Seven it is," I replied. "See you then."

Chapter 17

The next morning at six, with it still pitch dark outside, I went down for breakfast and stopped by the front desk on my way to the restaurant. Since I didn't know exactly how long the Homer visit would take, I wanted to know if I checked out that morning, would I be able to check back in that evening in case Twink and I finished up earlier than anticipated. The clerk—the guy who had actually recommended Twink in the first place—told me that due to overbooking for a conference, once I checked out, getting back in probably wasn't an option.

I immediately walked to the far side of the lobby and called Twink. "Do you have a two-day rate in case we have to stay over in Homer?" I asked.

"I figured as much," she said. "Fortunately, I'm not

booked for either one. The multiple-day rate is seven-fifty, plus mileage, meals, and hotel."

"Done," I said.

"Have you made a room reservation in Homer?" she wanted to know.

"Not yet," I replied. "Why, do you have any suggestions?"

"I can recommend the Driftwood Inn," she told me. "The one in town rather than the one out on the Spit. They usually give me a good deal."

"I'll look into it."

That's what I said, but I didn't do it right away. I figured there was plenty of time. Back in my room after a quick breakfast, I packed, realizing as I did so that once I got back home, I'd need to air the lingering cigarette smoke out of my luggage as well as my clothing. Then I called the car-rental folks and made arrangements for them to come pick up their vehicle from the hotel garage.

By seven o'clock I had checked out, left the Explorer's keys at the front desk, and was waiting by the door when Twink showed up. Once my luggage and I were safely stowed, I offered my credit card.

She waved it away with a shake of her head. "Not to worry," she said. "I figure you're good for it. 'Sides, if you try to skip out on me, without a car where ya gonna go?"

"Good thinking," I said.

"Where to first?"

I gave her the address Todd had given me for Roger and Shelley Adams on a street called Diamond Ridge Road in Homer.

"Got it," Twink said. "That'll be in the high-rent district out where all the hoity-toities live."

With that she put the Travelall in gear, and off we went. There was no electronic GPS visible in the vehicle, but obviously the one in Twink's head was functioning just fine. She pulled in to traffic with the confident air of someone who knew exactly where she was going.

Thanks to Todd, I already had addresses for the three of Chris Danielson's classmates who still lived in Homer—Alex Walker, Phil Bonham, and Ron Wolf. My plan was to start with Roger Adams and move on to the others later. I had also asked Todd to locate an address for Helen Sinclair, Roger's longtime secretary and the woman who had reached out to Danitza about her father's current health issues. Taken together, it was quite a list, and if contacting some of these folks took as long as some of yesterday's appointments had, it was probably a good thing Twink and I were already planning on an overnight stay.

Once it was actually daylight, the sunglasses came out. Twink seemed content to drive along humming some tuneless melody under her breath and feeling no need to engage in idle conversation. That gave me time to go through the dossiers Todd had provided and to map out a possible game plan.

Sometime well into the trip, Twink was forced to slow the Travelall to a crawl to avoid hitting a solitary moose meandering along in the middle of the highway.

"I guess these guys have the right of way no matter what," I said. "In town or out of town, they own the roads."

"That's right," Twink said after we finally drove around the beast and got back up to speed. "I hit one once, you know," she added, "a big sucker. Ran out of the woods right in front of me. There was no way to avoid him. What saved my bacon was the damned snowplow. The angle of it worked like a cow-catcher on a train. It pushed him away from me and off onto the shoulder instead of throwing him up over the hood and into the windshield. I could see the poor thing wasn't dead, so of course I put him out of his misery and then took the carcass home to butcher and eat. It was more than my freezer would hold, so I shared him with a couple of neighbors."

"Of course you put him out of his misery," I agreed. "How'd you do it, with one of the wrenches from your toolbox?"

I was making a joke, or at least trying to. Twink wasn't buying it.

"With the 350 Magnum I keep under my seat," she snapped, "and there's a Colt .45 in the glovebox, in case you're interested. You don't think I'm out here on the road all by my lonesome at all hours of the day and night and in all kinds of weather without being armed to the teeth, do you? I'm not exactly stupid, you know!"

I was beginning to learn that it took very little to push Twinkle Winkleman's buttons. A long period of silence followed that minor skirmish. The Travelall motored along at a sedate sixty miles per hour, which was probably pretty close to its top speed. I took the time to write a long e-mail to Jared Danielson. I didn't have a lot to say, but I gave him a detailed report of my efforts so far and let him know what the game plan was for today. I wrote that e-mail and one to Mel as well, but due to spotty coverage I wasn't able to send either one of them.

We arrived in Homer on schedule, right around eleven thirty. Much to my surprise, Twink pulled in to a restaurant parking lot rather than the residential address I'd given her at the start of the trip. A glowing neon sign announced we had arrived at Zig's Place.

"Wow," I said, staring at the sign. "I had no idea this place was still open."

Twink seemed taken aback. "You know about Zig's Place?" she demanded in disbelief. "They serve the best burgers in southeast Alaska, but how the hell would a cheechako like you know about that?"

"I don't know about the burgers," I allowed, "but Chris Danielson, the person I'm looking for, was working here at the time he went missing."

"Okay," Twink said, "so let's go get some grub, then. In case you haven't figured it out on your own, I'm a three-meal-a-day girl, no exceptions. If I don't eat on a regular basis, I can be downright cranky."

I didn't want Twink any crankier than she already was. "By all means," I agreed. "Let's go try one of those burgers."

Inside, Zig's Place was your typical fifties-style diner, complete with red-upholstered booths and actual working jukeboxes on each table. A sign at the entrance invited us to seat ourselves. Once we did so, a smiling young woman wearing a uniform that included a frilly white apron stopped by to deliver our menus. Twink and I ordered coffee.

"Is Zig in?" Twink asked.

"He's in the back. If you wanna talk to him, you'd better do it now. There's a basketball game going on across the street. It's about to get over, so you should probably order now, too. Who should I say is here?"

"Tell him Twinkle Winkleman wants to say hi."

I had already noticed that the scoreboard for the Homer High athletic field was directly across the street from the restaurant. That meant that the gym probably was somewhere nearby as well. Bill Farmdale had mentioned that the restaurant was close to the high school, but I hadn't realized how close.

"We'll take two Ziggy's Specials with everything on them," Twink said, ordering for both of us. She did so without bothering to consult me, and I had the good sense to make no objection.

A moment or two later, a man emerged from the kitchen wiping his hands on a surprisingly spotless apron. He was a tall, balding beanpole, somewhere in his late sixties who bore absolutely no resemblance to his nephew, Bill Farmdale. He was beaming as he approached our table and holding out his arms outstretched in welcome as though he and Twink were long-lost friends.

"Hey, Twink," he said, as she rose to her feet and allowed herself to be wrapped in his enveloping hug.

"How the hell are you? What brings you to these parts?"

"I'm here with him," Twink said, nodding in my direction. "His name's J. P. Beaumont."

"Glad to meet you, Mr. Beaumont," Siegfried said, holding out his hand. "People call me Ziggy. What brings you to town?"

"He's a private detective looking for a missing person," Twink supplied.

"Someone from here in Homer?"

"It's a kid who used to work for you—" I began, but Zig stopped me cold.

"Chris Danielson?" he asked.

I was shocked that he knew the name of the missing person in question with only that tiny smidgeon of information.

"You remember him?" I asked.

Some unidentifiable surge of emotion crossed Zig Norquist's face. Without another word he turned on his heel, strode away from our table, and disappeared behind the swinging door that led into the kitchen. I wasn't sure what had just happened. Had I somehow offended the man?

A moment later he came back, carrying something that turned out of be a framed picture. As soon as he handed me the pencil drawing, I recognized Chris

Danielson's work. This sketch featured a light-haired, pleasant-featured woman who was most likely somewhere in her forties. The shape of her face and the set of her eyes, however, were a perfect match for those of her nephew, Bill Farmdale.

"It's my late wife, Sonja," Zig explained softly. "She was working the front of the house when Chris was here. She was terribly shy when it came to cameras, so whenever anyone took a photo of her, she always looked like death warmed over, but Chris caught her off guard. He drew this one night when we weren't very busy, and she had no idea what he was doing. It's the best picture I have of her. She passed away two years ago, and I keep this in the kitchen so I can have her with me while I'm working."

Remembering Chris's lifelike drawings of both his mother and Danitza, it was no wonder Ziggy hadn't forgotten Chris Danielson.

"Clearly Chris was a talented kid," I said, "and I really am trying to find him. Can you tell me anything about him?"

"Nothing much," Zig said. "I always felt sorry for him. It turns out I knew the whole Danielson clan, including Richie, Chris's asshole of a dad. His grandfather, Gary, was a helluva nice guy, but his grandmother?" Zig shook his head regretfully. "Linda Danielson was a piece of work, beginning to end. Too bad her son took after her instead of his old man. As long as Gary was around, everything was hunky-dory with Chris being here. Once the old guy was gone, Linda moved heaven and earth to boot Chris out of the house. She had all kinds of excuses, claiming he'd taken money from her and was giving her no end of grief.

"Chris and Billy, my nephew, were friends. Billy was the one who let me know what was going on, and that's why I offered Chris a job. I worried that he'd be a problem, but turns out he wasn't. He was dependable as all get-out, did his work, never gave anybody any lip or trouble. And then one day he didn't turn up for his shift and didn't call in either. As far as I know, that's the last anyone ever saw him."

"But no one bothered to report him as missing?" I asked.

"After Chris disappeared, Billy went to see Linda Danielson. She claimed Chris had gone back home to Ohio of his own accord. Since she hadn't bothered reporting him missing, why should anyone else?"

An outside door slammed open, and a group of ravenous-looking teenagers surged into the room. "Oops," Ziggy said. "The basketball game must be over. Duty calls. See you later."

As soon as he walked away, I turned toward Twink. "How did you manage that?" I asked.

"Manage what?"

"Find me someone who knew the kid I'm looking for?"

Twink shrugged. "Wasn't hard," she said. "Places like this are so small that pretty much everybody knows everyone else."

The room quickly filled to standing room only. As more kids entered, the din level rose until I could barely hear myself think. Carrying on a conversation was out of the question. Once our burgers came, they were every bit as good as advertised, but while Twink and I ate our meals, I couldn't help thinking about Chris Danielson.

I had now seen three of his drawings, and if those were any indication, he'd had the potential to become a real artist. Instead both his life and his growing talent had been cut short. Something he had dashed off in a matter of minutes during a slow spot in a shift was now a treasure for Siegfried Norquist. Chris must have captured Sonja Norquist in the same subtle way he'd rendered both Danitza and his mother, embodying their personalities with a depth of feeling no intrusive camera lens could ever have delivered. And having seen those three examples of Chris's extraordinary artwork made me that much more determined to learn exactly what had happened to him.

Twink had requested separate checks, but when our waitress dropped them off, I grabbed both before she had a chance to reach for hers. When I paid the bill, I added in a hefty tip. Having lunch at Zig's Place would have been worth every penny at twice the price.

Chapter 18

S ounds like Chris Danielson had a pretty rough go of it," Twink commented once we were back in the Travelall and headed for Diamond Ridge Road.

There was no point in denying it. Twink had heard about the case fair and square as a result of her accidentally choosing Zig's Place for lunch. Now that I had another side of Chris's story, I owed Twink a piece of it.

I nodded. "He was just a kid when his father murdered his mother and then committed suicide. Chris and his older brother, Jared, went to live with their mom's folks in Ohio. When that didn't work out, he came to Homer to live with his other grandparents."

"Which didn't turn out to be a bed of roses?" Twink asked.

"Exactly."

"How old was Chris when he went missing?"

"Seventeen."

"Sounds like he had a tough life. You think he's dead?"

I wasn't ready to give Twink a straight answer on that one. "That's what I'm trying to find out," I told her.

The houses along Diamond Ridge Road were all set back from the street, but the address Todd had sent me took us to a large two-story timbered place that looked like a chalet that had escaped from somewhere in Switzerland. Twink rounded the circular driveway and pulled to a stop next to the front steps.

"Here we are, and take your time," Twink announced. "See you when you're done." She lit a cigarette, drew out her paperback, and settled in for the duration.

There was no way to know what to expect from this visit, but as I approached the door, I gathered myself for a possible confrontation. I'd already heard that Roger Adams had a temper, and when he learned the reason for my visit, I was relatively sure he wouldn't be thrilled to see me. I rang the bell and waited and then waited some more. Finally a key turned in the dead bolt, and the door swung open.

The barefoot man I saw standing before me wasn't at all what I expected. Scrawny to the point of being gaunt, he was dressed in a pair of flannel pajamas that appeared to be several sizes too large for him. He resembled the guy I'd seen in the photograph on the Roger Adams Web site, but if this was the same man, he seemed to have aged several decades. His hair stood straight up, as though he'd just crawled out of bed.

"Mr. Adams?" I asked uncertainly.

Swaying slightly, he used the doorjamb to steady himself while studying me with a bleary-eyed stare. At last he nodded. "Who are you?" When he spoke, his voice was raspy, as if weakened from lack of use.

"My name's J. P. Beaumont," I explained, offering him a business card. "I wanted to talk to you about—"

Before I could say anything more, he brushed the card aside. "A detective?" he asked. "Are you here to help me?"

Help him? Believe me, that was not at all the greeting I had expected. While I struggled to find an appropriate response, a woman dressed in a terry-cloth robe materialized in the entryway behind him. Just visible over Roger's pajama-clad shoulder, she had a towel wrapped tightly around her head and appeared to have just stepped out of the shower.

She dodged around the man in the doorway as though he weren't there and then stopped directly in front of me. "Who the hell are you?" she demanded furiously with her eyes drilling into mine. "And what do you want?"

Nice to meet you, too, I thought.

"As I was just telling Mr. Adams here, my name is J. P. Beaumont," I said aloud. "I'm a private investigator from Seattle. I'd like to speak to Mr. Adams about the disappearance of Christopher Danielson."

"Who?" the man asked vaguely, putting one hand on the woman's shoulder as if using her to help himself remain upright. "Has someone disappeared? Do we know him?"

The robe-clad woman, clearly the second Mrs. Roger Adams, covered his trembling hand with a solicitous one of her own. "It's all right, Roger," she said. "This is nothing for you to worry about. Just let me handle it."

"But who's gone missing?" Roger insisted.

Shelley turned to face him with a smile that was all sweetness and light. "Come on, now, honey-bun," she said. "It's too cold for you to be standing here in your bare feet. Not only that, it's time for your afternoon nap. Let's get you back in bed."

"But what about this man here?" Roger objected, waving his free hand in the air and sounding more agitated. "If someone is missing, we should help."

"No, we shouldn't," she said firmly. "Whatever this is, it isn't our problem. Come on, now, let's go."

As Shelley drew Roger away from the open door, I noticed that she paused long enough to deftly remove the key from the dead bolt and slip it into the pocket of her robe. She then led Roger off with him protesting like a two-year-old who's not the least bit inclined to take a nap. As they went, however, I noticed something else. When he'd waved his hand in the air, his oversize pajama sleeve slipped back down to his elbow, revealing a distinctive pattern of bruising around a painfully thin wrist.

In my experience marks like that usually result when someone has been held in restraints for a considerable length of time. If that was the case, maybe the question he'd asked me earlier had some basis, and he really did need my help.

Shelley hadn't slammed the door shut in my face or told me to get lost, so I stayed where I was, awaiting her return, except I couldn't help but wonder what the hell was going on inside this house. What if things with Roger weren't okay? If he were being held against his wishes, what was my responsibility here? And if I tried to tell someone here in Homer that odd things were happening on Diamond Ridge Road, shouldn't I have some kind of proof to back up that claim? With that in mind, while Shelley was still out of sight, I slipped my iPhone out of my pocket and set it to record before putting it away again.

When the woman of the house returned a minute or so later, she was still dressed in her robe but had shed the damp towel. As she approached the doorway, she appeared to have had a sudden change of heart as far as I was concerned.

"I'm Shelley Adams, by the way, and you are?"

"J. P. Beaumont," I replied. "I'm a private investigator."

"Come in so I can shut the door," she invited. "Sorry about snapping at you. I have to keep an eye on my husband every minute, and sometimes the pressure gets the best of me. The last I saw, he was sitting there in his room, quiet as can be and watching TV, so I thought it was safe for me to jump in the shower. I had no idea he had somehow located the spot where I kept the key to the dead bolt. He goes wandering, you see, and that's why I have to keep the doors locked. The last time Roger went walking around barefoot in the snow, it's a miracle he didn't come away with frostbite."

That went a long way to explaining the necessity of using restraints. "I had no idea your husband was ill," I said. "What's going on with him, Alzheimer's?"

Shelley shook her head. "Not exactly," she answered. "The doctors say it's some form of early-onset dementia. No cure, of course. We just have to wait it out. As for your missing person? When I realized you were asking about Chris, that little creep from all those years ago, it rubbed me the wrong way. Roger can barely remember his own name these days. How could he possibly remember Chris?"

Dealing with a mentally challenged patient in need of constant supervision was a legitimate explanation for the bruising I'd seen on Roger Adams's wrist. Suddenly I felt ashamed of the fact that my pocketed cell phone was still busy recording our conversation, but since there was no way to turn it off at that moment, I let it be.

Shelley had ushered me into a wood-paneled living room with a roaring fire burning in an enormous river-rock fireplace. The room was filled with comfortable pieces of well-used, overstuffed leather furniture.

Shelley settled into an easy chair situated in front of the fireplace and motioned me into the matching one next door. As she crossed her legs, the robe fell open slightly, revealing a pair of shapely legs that clearly matched the rest of her. Shelley Adams was a good-looking woman. Even with wet hair and no makeup, she was a natural beauty, with clear skin, good bones, and fine features. I knew from Penny Olmstead that Shelley was considerably younger than her husband, but at this point the difference in ages could have been thirty years rather than half that. Shelley was still youthful and vibrant. Roger was a frail, used-up shell of an old man.

"So what's all this about Christopher Danielson?" Shelley asked.

"Did you know him?" I wondered.

"We never met in person," she said, "but I certainly heard about him, and none of it was good. Jack, my first husband, and I were close friends with Roger and Eileen, Rog's first wife. The four of us had lots of great times together, but our relationships were such that we shared some of the bad stuff, too. As far as Roger and Eileen were concerned, Chris Danielson was bad news."

"Because he was a high-school dropout or because he and their daughter were expecting a child out of wedlock?" I asked.

"All of the above," Shelley said with a nod. "Of course, a dozen years later when gender-reveal parties routinely precede both engagements and weddings, that whole premise seems almost quaint, but that was what her parents believed at the time—that their bright, promising daughter was squandering her future on some low-life loser. They wanted her to graduate from high school, go off to college, and do something useful with her life."

Which is just what she's done, I thought, *and without an ounce of help from either of her parents.*

Before I could ask another question, I heard a key turn in the front door and a man and woman let themselves into the house. The pair appeared to be in their thirties or forties and looked a bit sketchy and unkempt. Between them, however, they carried several grocery bags, and Shelley wasn't the least bit alarmed that they had entered on their own.

"That's my cousin Nadine and her husband, Duncan," Shelley explained as the new arrivals disappeared down a hallway without any words of greeting. "They stop by from time to time to help out. This is a big place to manage on my own. Nadine does a lot of the cooking and most of the housework. Dunk handles the firewood supply and makes sure the vehicles are all in good working order. And as long as they're around, whenever I need a break, I have someone on hand to look after Roger."

I knew from Todd's dossiers that the house on Diamond Ridge Road had belonged to Roger and Eileen Adams long before Shelley had officially entered the picture, but clearly it belonged to Shelley now—lock, stock, and barrel. She was in charge, and I suspected

Roger had very little say in how things were managed, one way or the other.

"Now, where were we?" Shelley asked.

"We were talking about Danitza and Chris," I prompted.

"Oh, yes," Shelley said. "Roger believed that if Chris was out of the picture, Nitz would see the error of her ways and come home."

"But that's not what happened."

"No, it's not," Shelley agreed. "No matter how much Eileen and Roger disapproved, she was hell-bent on keeping that baby, and that's what she did."

"So what do you think happened to Chris Danielson?" I asked.

"I don't have to think about what happened to him because I know what happened," Shelley asserted. "Roger offered him an armload of money in order to convince him to get lost, and that's what he did. That no-good worm of a kid took the money and ran, just like the scumbag everyone always said he was. But even with him out of the picture, Danitza never came back home. Apparently she's every bit as stubborn as her father. I don't believe she and her father have exchanged a word since."

For good reason, I thought. *Being barred from my mother's funeral would have done it for me.*

"What about Eileen?" I asked. "Did she ever reach out to her daughter in hopes of a reconciliation?"

"Not as far as I know," Shelley replied. "Part of her problem was disappointment with her sister, Penny. Eileen felt that Penny and her husband, Wally, enabled Danitza's bad behavior by giving the girl a refuge when she ran away from home."

And by allowing Nitz to keep her baby, I thought.

It was an odd conversation. As Shelley spoke, I seemed to be taking mental exception to every word out of her mouth, and that left me somewhat conflicted. Here was a relatively young woman stuck caring for an older husband with what appeared to be some very serious health issues. Rather than feel empathy, however, I couldn't get beyond the way she'd come to have that older husband in the first place—by screwing around with him while his original wife, and a woman purported to be a friend, lay on her deathbed. Call me judgmental if you like, yet in a way I couldn't help but feel that Shelley Hollander Adams was getting just what she deserved.

Needing to steer the interview back on track, I moved away from Danitza's longtime estrangement with her parents.

"You said Roger paid Chris an armload of money to leave town," I suggested. "Do you happen to know how much?"

"I know exactly how much," Shelley said at once. "He told me it was ten grand."

Ten thousand dollars? I wondered. "What did he do, write Chris a check?"

"Good heavens no," Shelley replied. "Rog paid the kid off in cold, hard cash."

Piece by piece I'd been putting together a timeline surrounding Chris's disappearance. I knew from Bill Farmdale and his uncle, Zig Norquist, that Chris had been at the restaurant on Monday night and that he'd left work early. From Nitz I knew that she'd run away from home that same night shortly after the pregnancy-test quarrel with her parents. She had gone to Chris's place and waited for him. Despite having left work early that night, he never came home. As far as I could tell, all this had taken place in the evening hours—at a time when most banks are locked up tight.

"You're saying Roger Adams just happened to have that kind of cash lying around loose here at the house?"

Shelley laughed aloud at that. "Not loose," she said. "He always kept money in the safe in his den. Rog has never been particularly trusting as far as banks are concerned. It has a lot to do with things that happened to his father's family during the Depression. Back when Jack and I started hanging around with Rog and Eileen, he told us that he always kept at least a hundred thousand dollars in cash here at the house just in case. That's what he called it, in fact, his 'just in case' money."

I wondered if he still did that and if Shelley happened to have access to the safe's combination, but I didn't ask. Instead I changed the subject. "When did you first learn about Danitza's pregnancy?" I asked.

"About the time Rog and Eileen found out, or maybe a little before," Shelley replied. "Eileen had told me Danitza had been dealing with the flu for several days in a row. Since I wasn't her mother, it was easier for me to suspect what was really going on well before Eileen did. As a matter of fact, I believe I was the one who actually suggested Eileen pick up an at-home pregnancy test to find out for sure, and we all know how that turned out."

"Yes, we certainly do," I agreed. *His name is Christopher James Danielson. He's twelve years old and a hell of a nice kid!*

"So Roger handed the money over to Chris in person?" I asked.

"As far as I know," Shelley replied with a shrug.

"Did Chris give Roger any hints about what his intentions were—about what he planned to do with the money or where he was going?"

"If he did, Roger never mentioned it, at least not to

me. As far as I know, once Chris had the money, he was supposed to leave town, and he did. My understanding was that he intended to go visit some of his relatives in Ohio."

That sounded plausible enough, except I was pretty sure Chris had never left the state of Alaska. With ten thousand bucks in his pocket, he could have purchased a vehicle, but in a post-9/11 world and without a valid passport, he wouldn't have been able to drive through Canada to reach the Lower Forty-eight. As for leaving by air? With a driver's license, he could possibly have boarded a plane for U.S. destinations, but had he?

I noted in my mental to-do list to ask Todd if a passport had ever been issued in the name of Christopher Danielson. But my bottom line remained unchanged. I was relatively sure Chris had never set foot outside Alaska, because he'd been murdered and left lying dead along the shoreline of Eklutna Lake. My problem now centered on the fact that Roger Adams, one of the last people to have seen Chris alive, no longer knew up from down. And even if he was arrested and charged with murder, Roger was in no condition to aid in his own defense. There was no way he could be tried, convicted, or held accountable for any crime at all, to say nothing of murder.

In other words, I had just run smack-dab into a dead end.

"I should probably let you get back to your day," I told Shelley, rising to my feet. "You've been most helpful. I trust you'll forgive me for just barging in the way I did."

"You're forgiven," she said with a smile. "In fact, I'm grateful you stopped by. If you hadn't, I might never have known that Rog had discovered where I was keeping the key. From now on I'll have to find another hiding spot."

I couldn't help hoping that at some time in the not-so-distant future I wouldn't end up in the same situation as Roger Adams—in such bad mental shape that Mel would find herself compelled to hold me prisoner in my own home.

Shelley rose to walk me as far as the door. I was out on the porch when almost as an afterthought she asked, "Why all this interest in finding Chris Danielson now? Is Danitza the person who hired you?"

I found it interesting that Shelley wanted to know who had sent me snooping around and asking questions, but the identity of the person who hired me was none of her business.

"I'm working on behalf of Chris's other grandmother, the one who lives in Ohio."

"Well," she said, "I wish you the best of luck on that score."

I stood on the porch for a moment after the door closed behind me. Nothing about the interview had turned out the way I'd expected. Instead of despising Roger Adams, I now found myself feeling sorry for him. As for Shelley Hollander Loveday Adams? She had coveted another woman's husband, and now that she had him, she seemed to be getting just what she deserved. As they say, sometimes karma is a bitch.

Chapter 19

It's about damned time," Twink muttered impatiently as I clambered into the Travelall beside her. "Did you happen to use the facilities while you were in there?"

"No, I didn't," I told her.

"Well, I need to pee like crazy," she said, "and we're not going anywhere else until I have a pit stop, understood?"

"Yes, ma'am," I told her, but the truth was, now that she mentioned it, I needed a pit stop, too.

Twink drove straight to a McDonald's, where we both used the facilities without buying anything. I felt guilty about that, but after the superior burgers we'd had at Zig's Place earlier, neither of us was the least bit hungry. Not only that, whatever McDonald's had on offer would have been a real letdown in comparison.

There had been a line for the ladies' restroom, so I beat Twink back to the Travelall.

"Where to now?" she asked when she finally showed up.

After my conversation with Shelley Adams, the ground had shifted, and so had my game plan. Roger Adams as he was now wouldn't have the mental or physical capacity to pull off a homicide, but twelve years ago he probably would have. Regardless of whether he was ever charged or convicted, I wanted the matter settled in my own mind once and for all, for myself as well as for Jared and Danitza.

In my experience a man's wife may *think* she knows everything there is to know about her husband, but I've learned over time that if the guy in question happens to have a secretary, she's likely to know infinitely more. To that end, speaking to Roger Adams's former secretary now moved to the top of my list.

"Next up will be a visit with someone named Helen Sinclair," I told Twink before reading off the address Todd had sent me.

"Who's she?" Twink asked.

"Roger Adams's longtime secretary."

"Wait, Roger Adams? Isn't he some kind of big-deal criminal defense attorney around here?" The way Twink asked the question implied she already knew the answer.

"Used to be," I said. "He's retired now."

"Is that the old guy who came to the door in his jammies?"

Since not much seemed to get past Twinkle Winkleman, there was no point in denying the obvious. "Yes, he was," I admitted.

"Didn't look like he was in very good shape."

"He's not," I said.

We headed back into town. "You're not going to call in advance and let Helen Sinclair know we're on our way to see her?" Twink wanted to know.

"In my line of work," I replied, "it's usually best to show up unannounced."

Twink thought about that for a moment before adding, "By the way, I booked a room for you at the Driftwood Inn. I already had your credit-card number, so I used my name and your card to make the reservation. That way they'll give you my professional discount."

"Thanks," I said. "I meant to do that, but I hadn't gotten around to it. But my room? What about yours?"

"Things aren't what they used to be," Twink replied. "Now all their rooms are nonsmoking. I'll be staying over with a friend. We both smoke, and it saves your having to fork over money for a second room."

"Thanks," I said. "Appreciate it."

And I did. After all, it was already verging on midafternoon. With that weird sort of pinkish dusk coloring the sky, staying overnight made sense. By my count we had at least three more interviews to do. The prospect of driving back to Anchorage in the dark of night with huge critters meandering across the highway wasn't all that appealing.

Helen Sinclair's place turned out to be a permanently installed mobile home on a street called Fairwood Drive. A white picket fence surrounded the place, but only the top six inches of each pointed post was visible above the accumulated snow. Twink parked on the street out front and once again settled into the driver's seat with her paperback while I bailed out, opened the gate, and made my way up the cleared walk.

Three wooden steps led up to a sturdy covered porch, where a pair of Adirondack chairs sat just to the right of the front door. Unlikely as it might seem right now, it was evident that during less frosty parts of the year the porch functioned as an outdoor seating area. The bell was a hand-operated ringer attached to the door itself. When I pulled the lever back and forth, the halfhearted jangle it produced didn't sound at all promising, but seconds later I heard approaching foot-steps.

The door was opened by a cherubic-looking little old lady with a ready smile and a halo of curly white hair. Appropriately dressed for the holiday season, she wore a bright red outfit trimmed with white fur. Somewhere in the background, I caught the aroma of freshly baked cookies.

"Mrs. Santa Claus, I presume?" I asked.

"That's me," she answered with a smile before glancing at her watch. "My granddaughter runs a day care," she explained. "My cookies and I are due to make an appearance there in about an hour's time, just before the kids go home. May I help you?"

I extracted a business card from my pocket and handed it over. "My name is J. P. Beaumont," I told her. "I'm from Seattle, and I'm here investigating the 2006 disappearance of Danitza Adams's then-boyfriend, Christopher Danielson. May I come in? This shouldn't take more than a few minutes."

"Of course," she said, "but as I said, we can't be long. I'll need to leave soon."

Over the course of my career, I've encountered some pretty dilapidated mobile homes, many of them so dere-lict as to be barely habitable. That was not the case here. Helen Sinclair's home was tastefully decorated and neat as a pin, without a hint of dust anywhere in sight. Todd's information on Helen had included the notation that she was a widow. Prominently displayed on the wall over the couch was a framed wedding picture. From the clothing and hairdos, I estimated that the wedding must have occurred sometime in the fifties. The sweetly smiling young bride barely came to the groom's shoulders, and she couldn't have been a day over eighteen.

"You and your husband?" I asked.

Helen nodded. "Michael and I were married forty-six years before he passed. He was a firefighter here in town. He was already in ill health and had been forced to retire when 9/11 happened. I think having to sit here day after day and watch those smoldering buildings on TV really got to him. I believe his not being able to do a single thing to help broke his heart. He passed away in his sleep in February of 2002."

As I took a seat on the sofa, I did some quick math in my head and arrived at the conclusion that this sprightly Mrs. Santa Claus, who had to be somewhere in her early eighties, appeared to be far more healthy and vital than her former boss, the much younger Roger Adams.

"So what would you like to know about Chris Danielson?" she asked, settling into a worn recliner. "I knew of him, of course, but I never met the boy in person."

Those were almost the same words Shelley Adams had used.

"But you did know Danitza?" I asked.

"And still do," she replied. "I met Nitz almost as soon as she was born, while she and her mother were still in the hospital."

"You've known the family that long?"

Helen nodded. "I went to work for Roger Adams when he was still single, fresh out of law school, and just opening his practice. I actually attended his and Eileen's wedding. As for Danitza, I couldn't have loved that girl more if she'd been my own grandchild."

"So when the whole estrangement thing happened between Nitz and her parents, that must have bothered you."

"It bothered me, all right," Helen agreed. "I was really disappointed that Roger and Eileen treated Nitz as an outcast. She's certainly not the only young woman in Homer to become pregnant out of wedlock. I thought Roger and Eileen should have done what the rest of us do under those circumstances, namely take their medicine and make the best of it, but they didn't. As a friend of the family who also happened to be an employee, I had to keep those opinions to myself."

"From what I've been able to learn, Roger was infuriated by Nitz's pregnancy, and I have reason to believe

that Roger might have been behind Chris's disappearance."

"I don't doubt that a bit," Helen agreed. "I believe
Roger handed Chris a fistful of cash and suggested he
go elsewhere."

"You don't think Roger might have done something
more permanent?" I asked.

"As in kill him?" Helen asked. "Is that what you
mean?"

I nodded.

"Absolutely not," Helen declared. "Roger Adams
may be an exceptionally stubborn and unforgiving
man, but there's not a murderous bone in his body.
Roger has defended a killer or two over the years, but
he could never be one."

"So a bribe yes, but murder no?" I asked.

"That's how I see it," Helen said. "And you can't
really blame him. As far as husband and father material, Chris wasn't a very likely prospect, and I'm sure
Roger did what he felt was necessary in hopes of keeping his child from making what he regarded as a stupid,
life-changing mistake."

"You don't fault Roger for that?"

"For shutting Nitz out his life?" Helen asked. "I
certainly blame him for that, but when it comes to his
having sent Chris packing, I don't begrudge him that

at all. Under similar circumstances, had I been in a position to pay the piper, I might have done the same thing."

"Let's talk about Danitza for a moment," I said, changing the subject. "I understand you went to see her not long ago."

"I did," Helen said with a nod. "I felt as though she needed to be aware of what's going on with her father."

"What *is* going on with him?" I asked.

"The man is seriously ill," Helen answered. "I wanted to give Nitz a chance to make peace with him before it's too late, not for his sake but for hers. If she doesn't at least try to put things right between them, I'm afraid she'll live to regret it."

The Roger Adams I had observed earlier in the day was in no condition to have a meaningful discussion with anyone, much less his estranged daughter. In fact, if Nitz showed up on his doorstep, I doubted he'd recognize her.

"It was the best I could do," Helen continued. "I probably shouldn't have meddled, but as I said earlier, I've known Roger since he was a very young man. In many ways I've been closer to him than to my own son."

"You worked for him the whole time?"

Helen nodded. "I could have retired years ago, but

I really enjoyed my job. I liked being part of something that felt important, and going to work each day made better sense to me than just sitting around here at home here waiting for the Grim Reaper to come calling. When Roger took on a new partner, Thomas Haley, several years ago, nothing much changed for me because I still reported primarily to Roger, but last summer when Roger decided to let Tom buy him out of the practice, I didn't care to take on a new boss at that time in my life. That's when I finally decided to retire."

"Roger is what, in his fifties?" I asked. "Isn't that a little early to retire?"

"The law firm has never been Roger's only source of income. Over the years, between him and his father, the family amassed an extensive collection of real-estate holdings—both residential and commercial—all over Alaska. Rental income from those surpassed his law-firm earnings years ago, but he kept on working for the same reason I did—because he loved it."

"So why quit?"

"I think he was already dealing with health issues of some kind—digestive problems and some personality issues, too. He just wasn't himself. I suggested he go see Doc Moody, the guy who used to be Roger's personal physician, to be checked out, but of course Shelley wouldn't hear of it."

"Why not?" I asked.

"Because Shelley Hollander Loveday is a Christian Scientist. She doesn't believe in medical doctors, and she doesn't think anyone else should either."

The way Helen spit out her response was notable on three counts. For one, the venom in her voice was surprisingly apparent. For another, despite the fact that Roger and Shelley had been married for almost a decade, Helen still referred to Shelley by her previous married name. For a third, I remembered clearly that Shelley had used the word "doctors" in describing her husband's early-onset dementia diagnosis.

"I take it you don't like Shelley very much," I observed.

"You think?" Helen responded. "I don't trust her any further than I could throw her, and I believe Roger was beginning to come to that same conclusion."

"How so?"

"I think he suspected she might be seeing someone on the side. That wouldn't surprise me in the least. Once a cheater, always a cheater."

"I take it you knew that Roger and Shelley were involved prior to his first wife's passing?"

"Well aware," Helen replied with a shake of her head. "Who do you think answered his phone calls and paid his bills? At least I used to," she added.

"Once I retired, I don't know who took over the bill-paying function, probably Shelley herself."

It was gratifying to realize that I had been right. In this case Roger's secretary seemed to know far more about his business than Shelley suspected.

"You said Roger might have had an inkling Shelley was cheating. Did he mention that to you straight out?"

"He didn't, but I was able to put two and two together and figure it out."

"Which two and two?" I asked.

"Roger had me set up an appointment with Jim Brixton, his life-insurance guy. I didn't think that much about it at the time, but while I was filing the paperwork, I noticed it was a change of beneficiary. When I saw that Roger had cut Shelley out of it completely in favor of Danitza, that certainly caught my attention. It made me wonder if maybe he was considering filing for a divorce—I wondered but didn't ask. In any case, he never got around to it."

"What would have happened if he had?" I asked.

"Shelley would have been up a creek. There's a prenup, you see. When she and Roger married, they both had money. Jack Loveday had just died. Since she had cleaned up financially and was known to be a bit of a spendthrift, he thought keeping their assets separate was a good idea."

"Is that prenup still in existence?"

"As far as I know."

"Where is it?"

"In a file in the office, right along with his will."

"Did he change his will when he changed the life-insurance beneficiary?"

"Not so far as I know."

"And that leaves everything to Shelley?"

Helen nodded.

So maybe Roger had started to feel guilty about cutting Danitza out of his life, and changing the beneficiary on the life insurance had been his way of making amends in lieu of facing his daughter.

"So what kept him from apologizing?" I asked. "Pride?"

Helen nodded. "Exactly," she said.

"Back to the prenup. Was that his idea or Shelley's?" I asked.

"His, I'm sure," Helen answered.

"Why? Because he was afraid from the beginning that the marriage would fall apart eventually?"

"Believe me, Roger has handled more than one contentious divorce in his time," Helen replied.

"Wait," I objected. "I thought he was a criminal attorney."

"In a town like this," Helen answered, "you have to be a jack-of-all-trades."

No doubt that was true. Roger had probably dealt with plenty of ugly divorces, but there was something else here as well. Past history is not an automatic predictor of future behavior, but in the case of cheating spouses, straying isn't usually a one-time-only thing. Since Shelley had cheated on Jack Loveday with Roger, what were the chances she'd cheat on him with someone else?

When I saw Shelley and her husband earlier, I'd wondered what a relatively young, good-looking, and vibrant woman was doing with a frail husk of an old man, but the existence of that prenup went a long way to explain why she would stick around. If she divorced him, she'd be out of luck. If she stuck it out with Roger till he died, she'd make out like a bandit, despite not receiving the life-insurance payout.

I brought Helen's and my conversation back to that very topic.

"What's the face amount on that life-insurance policy?" I asked.

"Five hundred thousand dollars."

Receiving that kind of unanticipated death benefit would make a huge difference in Danitza Miller's bottom line and life. I wondered how much of a dent it would put in what Shelley was expecting to receive.

"Do you think Shelley is aware of the change in beneficiary?"

"I doubt it. *I* certainly didn't tell her, and I shouldn't be telling you either. The only reason I am is I believe there's something seriously wrong here—that things with Roger aren't what they should be. When I went to see Danitza, I was planning on telling her about the insurance issue, just to get her to go see her dad to check on him, but at the last minute I decided against it. I would have been bribing her to come visit her father in almost the same way Roger bribed Chris Danielson in order to get him to leave town. For Nitz's sake, I wanted her to come see her father for the right reasons rather than the wrong ones."

"Earlier you mentioned that you thought there might be something ailing Roger," I said. "Would you mind being more specific about that?"

Helen sighed. "By the middle of last summer, I noticed he was often out of sorts and just not himself. I told you earlier that he'd been having digestive issues, and those didn't seem to let up, but the night he came to my retirement party, he acted like he'd tied one on before he and Shelley ever arrived. He started telling off-color jokes and making inappropriate remarks. I'd never seen him act like that before, and I was relieved when Shelley finally hustled him out of the room and took him home. I didn't want him to embarrass himself any more than he already had."

"That was the end of September. Have you seen him since?"

Helen shook her head. "I haven't seen him or spoken to him in months, but not for lack of trying. Whenever I've tried calling, Shelley is the one who answers the phone, or she answers the door when I show up in person. There's always some reason he can't talk on the phone or come to the door—either he's sleeping or he's not feeling well. It's like she's running interference to keep me from seeing him. I'm pretty sure she answers his e-mails and texts, too."

"If he has early-onset dementia of some kind, maybe he's deteriorated to the point where he can't answer for himself," I suggested.

"That's what I'm worried about, too," Helen agreed, "and that's exactly why I think Nitz needs to come see him now—while she still can and while he still knows who she is. I figure if Nitz were the one to show up instead of me, Shelley would pretty much have to let her inside."

"What about Roger's other friends and acquaintances?" I asked. "Have any of them seen him in the flesh recently?"

"Not so far as I know," she said.

"And when you saw him that last time at the party, how much would you say he weighed?"

Helen frowned. "That was one of the reasons I suggested that he go see a doctor. Long before the party, I noticed he was losing weight, and as far as I know, he wasn't dieting."

"So how much?"

"Two-ten, maybe," Helen answered with a frown, "but that's probably ten or fifteen pounds less than he's weighed most of his adult life. He was always concerned about the way he dressed. I noticed that his suits were getting baggy, but he didn't seem to care."

The Roger I'd seen earlier in the day, the guy in that pair of oversize pajamas, couldn't have weighed in at one-seventy soaking wet. If he'd dropped forty pounds between the end of September and now, that meant he'd undergone a precipitous weight loss. It could be the result of radical dieting or indicative of some underlying health issue, but now I was wondering if it might be due to something else entirely. With that prenup in effect, maybe the easiest way for Shelley to lay hands on her husband's money would be for him to cork off. What if she was actually starving him to death?

"How exactly did Jack Loveday die?" I asked.

"He was in a plane crash," Helen answered. "EMTs rescued him and airlifted him to a hospital in Anchorage, where they amputated both legs below the knee. He committed suicide a few weeks after they released him from rehab."

"Who took care of him once he was released?" I asked.

"Shelley was there, of course, but I believe a visiting nurse came by every day to help out," Helen answered.

"A visiting nurse, as in a regular RN?"

Helen nodded.

"So Jack didn't share his wife's Christian Science beliefs?"

"Evidently not."

Suddenly I found myself wanting to know a whole lot more about Jack Loveday's death.

"Was Shelley Jack Loveday's only heir?" I asked.

Helen shrugged. "As far as I know," she said. "He and his first wife, Lois, never had any kids."

At that point Helen glanced at her watch and rose to her feet. "You're going to have to excuse me now," she said hurriedly. "If I don't leave right this instant, Mrs. Santa Claus will be missing in action."

Given everything she'd just told me, I wanted to ask

a whole slew of additional questions, but those would have to wait.

"By all means don't let those kids down," I told her, "and don't worry about me. I can show myself out."

I stood on the porch for a moment, pondering what I'd just learned. If divorcing Roger was a nonstarter and if hanging around long enough for him to die was the only way for Shelley to make good on the years she'd invested in the man, I had the disturbing feeling that the poor guy was in the care and keeping of someone who might not have his best interests at heart. That left me with only one question: What, if anything, was I going to do about it?

Chapter 20

I paused on Helen's front porch and punched Todd's number into my phone. He answered, but only briefly. "I'm on another call," he said. "Hang on. I'll get right back to you."

I was prepared to stand there and wait for Todd to come back on the line, but at that point the Travelall's horn blared and Twink waved for me to get moving.

"What's the rush?" I asked once I was in the car.

"I ran out of smokes," she explained. "I thought for sure that I had another pack stowed in my purse, but I didn't, and if I don't get some soon, I'll explode."

Still holding the silent phone to my ear, I told her, "By all means let's go get some."

The Travelall had just started moving when Todd came back on the line. "What's up?"

There I was stuck between a rock and a hard place. Either I could tell Todd what I needed with Twink listening in on every word or I'd have to wait until she went inside somewhere to buy her smokes. *What the hell,* I told myself, and opted for the former.

"I'd like whatever you can find on two people—Shelley Hollander Loveday Adams and her deceased first husband, Jack Loveday. I also need to know if Christopher Danielson was ever issued a U.S. passport."

"And you need this information immediately if not sooner, right?" an exasperated Todd wanted to know.

"Absolutely."

Twink stopped at the first convenience store we saw. While she went inside, I scrolled through Todd's e-mails, looking for the three remaining unaffiliated boys—the ones who still lived in Homer. The first of those was a guy named Alex Walker, who according to Todd's notes was married, had three kids, and managed the local Firestone franchise.

When Twink returned with a cigarette already clenched between her lips, I told her that's where we were going.

"Do you think the manager will be there on Saturday afternoon?" Twink wanted to know.

We drove straight to Firestone. Surprisingly, Alex

Walker *was* at work. When I introduced myself, the man was pleasant enough, but it turned out he remembered nothing about Chris Danielson.

"We might've had a class or two together," Alex said, "but nothing stands out. From what I remember, he was kind of a loner. He lived with his grandparents for some reason and didn't have many friends. Why are you asking about him?"

"He went missing a dozen years ago, and nobody seemed to notice."

"I guess I heard about that at the time, but that's pretty much all," he said. "Wish I could help."

In the course of the next two hours, Twink and I tracked down the other two Homer guys—Ron Wolf and Phil Bonham. Like Alex, they, too, had vague recollections of Chris, but neither had had any close connections with our missing person. Phil's place was a long way out in the boonies. As we headed back into town, Twink asked, "Where to now?"

"Back to the barn, I guess," I told her, "although I'm not all that sure where the barn is."

"I believe that Chad, my brother, knows Shelley Loveday," Twink said, apropos of nothing a mile or so later.

Obviously she'd been listening in on my conversation with Todd. Even so, I was flabbergasted. By now

I was beginning to think that the state of Alaska was very much like an oversize version of the small town where, as the old joke used to say, even if you dial a wrong number, you end up chatting anyway.

"Really?" I asked.

"At one time everyone in Alaska knew of Shelley Hollander even if they didn't know her in person," Twink said. "She was a looker, all right. Shortly after she got her pilot's license and went to work for Jack Loveday, she entered the Miss Alaska beauty pageant and walked away the winner. Everybody was so surprised that a bush pilot could end up being Miss Alaska. I thought that was a crock. As far as I'm concerned, women can do any damned thing they want."

Twink paused as if giving me a chance to respond to that. When I wisely declined to take the bait, she continued.

"Anyway, Jack was a big gun in the bush-pilot world, and once Shelley got her claws into him, she didn't let go. He ended up divorcing his first wife and marrying Shelley. She probably thought she'd made herself a pretty good deal, except for one thing. In airplane circles everyone knew that Jack Loveday made money, all right, but they also knew he was so tight his farts squeaked. According to Chad, when it came to spending money, he kept Shelley on a very tight leash."

"Wait," I said. "I heard he gifted her with a Piper for a wedding present."

Twink laughed. "Jack wanted that Piper for himself. He only *said* he bought it for her. Anyway, Jack ended up biting it big time. He was doing a volunteer Flight for Life trip and carrying blood products from Homer to Fairbanks when his plane crashed. He was trapped inside and terribly injured but still managed to radio for help. Rescuers found him in time and airlifted him to the trauma center at Anchorage General, but he ended up losing both legs. From what I understand, he committed suicide a short time after he was released from the hospital."

That was the same trauma center where Danitza worked now, but this would have happened long before she completed her nurses' training.

"So your brother knew Jack. Is that how he met Shelley?"

"As I said earlier, Chad's in the airplane-resale business. After Jack's death Shelley decided to unload his inventory of aircraft. That's when she came to Chad looking for help."

"When did all this happen?" I asked.

In the illumination of a passing streetlight, I saw Twink shrug. "Beats me," she said, "maybe ten years or so ago, but the whole thing turned out to be a good deal for Chad. Shelley was worried that people would try to take advantage of her, and she was happy to pay Chad a commission on each of the sales. By the time everything was signed, sealed, and delivered, he was sitting in tall cotton."

Moments later we pulled up at the front entrance of the Driftwood Inn and parked on the street. It was a humble clapboard-covered place, a long way from the far more upscale Hotel Captain Cook. Since Twink wasn't staying there, I opened the back passenger door and retrieved my luggage.

"Breakfasts here are usually pretty good—at least they used to be," Twink told me. "Once you know what the schedule is for tomorrow, give me a call."

Walking into the lobby was like walking into my grandparents' long-ago living room in the north end of Seattle. It was filled with homey upholstered furniture. There was a cupboard crowded with all sorts of teas. In front of the tea display was a buffet with an electric kettle on it as well as an assortment of cups. A hand-lettered sign invited guest to help themselves. The varnished front desk was straight out of the fifties, with the clerk standing behind a window like an old-fashioned bank teller.

When I got upstairs, my "view" room, like the lobby, was homey and comfortable if not particularly posh, and in the dark of night the view part of the description was entirely meaningless. I showered off that day's layer of secondhand smoke, donned the terry-cloth robe I found hanging in the closet, and settled in to give Mel a call.

"I was beginning to think you'd forgotten all about us," she said.

"I've been busy," I said. "What have you been doing?"

"Sarah and I just came in from playing fetch out in the snow. At first she was very reluctant, but I finally managed to convince her that walking in snow won't kill her. Right now, though, she's completely tuckered out and snoozing in front of the fireplace. What have you been up to?"

For the next twenty minutes or so, I recounted my day's worth of work.

"What are you going to do about all this?" Mel asked when I finished.

"Beats me. I've been asking myself the same question."

"If you think Roger is in imminent danger, you could always call in a welfare check."

"I could, I suppose, but I don't have any real reason to do so. Other than looking like he hasn't had a decent meal in years, there's no reason to think he's in immediate jeopardy. Incapacitated? Yes. Should he be under a doctor's care? Absolutely. And if he's in danger of wandering outside on his own, barefoot in the snow, then the use of restraints of some kind is probably justifiable. But still, something's out of whack in that household, and I can't quite put my finger on what it is."

"JDLR," Mel said.

I chuckled at that little bit of law-enforcement lingo. "Yes, I agreed. It just doesn't look right."

"If Shelley was able to manage carrying on an extramarital affair for years without her husband's ever figuring it out," Mel surmised, "she's most likely one pretty cagey operator. If Homer PD sent out some newbie patrol officer to do a welfare check on Roger, she'd be able to pull the wool over the cop's eyes without having to think twice about it. In which case you'd be the one with egg on your face."

"That's my assessment, too."

"What about Danitza?" Mel asked. "Have you called to let her know what's going on?"

"Not so far."

"Maybe you should. She's an RN, right?"

"Correct."

"Just by seeing Roger in person, she might be able assess what's going on with him from a medical standpoint. And as his daughter she might be able to override Shelley's veto of medical intervention. Besides . . ."

Mel's voice faded away for a moment.

"Besides what?" I asked.

"The sudden weight loss you described sounds similar to what happened to my dad. According to his wife, he'd been trying to shed pounds unsuccessfully for years, so initially he was really happy about losing weight. By the time he went to see a doctor who finally figured out what was really happening, he was already in acute kidney failure. By then it was too late for him and for me, too. I've always regretted that I didn't try to patch things up with him while I still could."

Since this was Mel speaking, I knew I was hearing the voice of bitter experience.

"You're probably right about my bringing Danitza into the picture," I agreed. "Once I can give her a final answer about whatever happened to Chris, I'll let her know about what's going on with her father."

The sound of an arriving text pinged on my phone, and the notification in the corner said it was from Todd.

"Hold on a sec," I told Mel. "Todd just sent me a text." When the text was open, I read his short message aloud. "'No U.S. passports ever issued under the name Christopher Anthony Danielson.'"

Once I finished reading it aloud, Mel and I remained silent for a moment while we both considered the message's implications.

"So even with that ten-thousand-dollar bribe in his pocket, you don't believe Chris ever made it out of the state alive," Mel concluded finally.

"Correct, " I agreed, "which makes it all the more likely that the skeletal remains in Harriet Raines's lab are his and nobody else's."

"Have you heard anything from Gretchen at the crime lab about Jared's DNA profile?"

"Not so far, and I don't really expect to," I replied. "After all the uproar over the lab's mishandling of evidence in the Mateo Vega case, I'm sure she's going a hundred percent by the book—crossing all the t's and dotting all the i's. Once Gretchen has the profile in hand, it'll go straight to Professor Raines, but Harriet strikes me as a straight shooter. As soon as she has the information, she'll forward it to the Alaska State Troopers, but I'm betting she'll let me know, too."

"Still," Mel said, "the instant the remains come back to Chris, you'll be booted off the case. What'll you do then?"

"Come home," I said. "Alaska's a beautiful place, if you like snow, but I wouldn't want to live here, at least not in the winter."

"That makes two of us," Mel said with a laugh, "so what are you and Twink doing for dinner?"

"I'm on my own."

"How come?"

"She's not staying here. The rooms are all nonsmoking. There's a breakfast room here at the hotel, but no real restaurant. The girl at the desk said there's a steak house across the street. I'll probably grab a bite there before I hit the hay."

We talked for a while after that, exchanging meaningless pleasantries the way married people do. It wasn't so much about what was being said as it was that we were chatting. The truth is, I've become something of a homebody of late, and I would much rather have been home in Bellingham and in front of the fireplace with Mel and Sarah that cold winter's night instead of hanging out on my own at the Driftwood Inn in Homer, Alaska.

When the phone call ended, I turned on the TV set briefly, but there wasn't anything scheduled that I found remotely interesting. By then it was almost eight. Those Ziggy Specials were now a long way in the rearview mirror. I got dressed, bundled up, and made my way across the street to AJ's OldTown Steakhouse & Tavern. If you're looking for white linen tablecloths and crystal glassware, AJ's isn't the place for you, but it worked for me. I ordered a ginger ale, a house salad, and a small plate of what the menu referred to as "drunken clams drowning in a white wine, garlic, butter sauce." As long as the clams were the ones swilling down the white wine and I wasn't, we were good to go.

I was done with dinner and considering my dessert options when my phone rang.

"Hey, Todd," I said. "How's it going?"

"I've been working the Shelley Loveday Adams problem, and I just hit on something interesting."

Todd sounded excited enough that it piqued my curiosity. "What?" I asked.

"On April seventh, 2006, Shelley Loveday was involved in a minor traffic incident in Las Vegas, Nevada. There was evidently a big pileup on the Strip. The accident probably wasn't her fault, but she rear-ended somebody and came away with a DUI conviction. It was a first offense. She probably could have taken a safe-driving course and had the citation removed from her record. Instead she let it ride, and that's why I was able to find it."

"The timing's pretty interesting," I said. "That's only a week or so after Chris disappeared."

"Exactly," Todd agreed. "So I checked with the major hotels in Vegas. Turns out Shelley Loveday was staying in a suite at Caesars Palace, the kind of accommodations casinos usually reserve for and routinely comp to their high rollers."

Suddenly I was making the same connection that Todd had. Shelley had told me straight out that Roger had paid Chris off in order to encourage him to disappear. She'd also mentioned that the payment would have been made from the "just in case" funds that Roger stowed in the safe at home. But what if Roger hadn't made the payment in person? What if he'd used a courier to make the payoff and had delegated his mistress to deliver the goods?

After all, what about that unidentified woman Bill Farmdale had told me about, the one claiming car trouble who'd shown up at the back door of Zig's Place the night Chris disappeared? What if Roger had dispatched his mistress to deliver the payoff money to Chris but she'd pulled a fast one? What if while Chris was working on her car, she'd attacked him from behind? With him on the ground and her standing over him, she would have been at the proper angle to deliver that fatal blow, the results of which were still visible in Harriet Raines's patched-together skull. As for Chris? In that position he would have been totally oblivious to the danger and completely unable to defend himself.

And just like that, with that one blow, Shelley Loveday would have accomplished two very different things.

Roger Adams had wanted Chris Danielson gone, and killing him handled that thorny issue once and for all. As a very important side benefit, however, Shelley now found herself in the possession of a sum of cold, hard cash to spend on whatever she wanted, including an expensive junket to Vegas.

According to Twink, as long as Shelley had been married to Jack Loveday, the guy had kept her on a very short leash as far as spending was concerned. Would someone like that hand over money for his wife to squander on a weekend of gambling in Vegas? Not on a bet, I told myself. I suspected that Jack Loveday had known nothing at all about that weekend junket, and there was a good chance Roger Adams, Shelley's longtime lover, hadn't heard a word about it either.

Prior to that moment, I had considered Roger Adams, Danitza's aggrieved father, to be the only person of interest in the likely death of Chris Danielson. While I was still on the job, I would have regarded that kind of investigation with disdain, saying the detectives involved were suffering from tunnel vision. Hadn't I been doing the same thing?

Most homicides revolve around one of three things—drugs, sex, or money. Here was number three staring me straight in the face—money, ten thousand dollars' worth! Compared to that a father's simmering anger might have to take a backseat, because now I had two things I hadn't had before—motivation and an actual suspect.

I was still holding the phone with those ideas flashing through my mind when I heard Todd's impatient voice in the background. "Beau, are you still there?"

"Sorry, yes, I'm here. Great work, Todd," I told him. "Keep digging. I think you've just handed me the name of my possible killer."

"Shelley Loveday Adams?"

"Yes, indeed."

"Okay," Todd said. "I'm on it."

He hung up then. Instead of ordering dessert, I waved for the waitress to bring my check. After paying the bill, I headed back across the street to the Driftwood. There might have been snow on the ground. It could have been frigid weather, but I didn't notice and didn't care, because now I had a real sense of purpose.

I was on the job again, and the old killer-chasing bloodhound had just caught a scent.

Chapter 21

B ack in my room at the Driftwood Inn, I hied myself to the desk chair and began going through the documents Todd had sent me. I worked from the bottom up, starting with the ones sent earlier in the day and gradually arriving at the later ones, all the while searching for any telling details that might provide a smoking gun that would point suspicion at Shelley Adams.

In my years as a homicide investigator, I often went to a prosecutor with what I thought to be a solid case only to be told it wasn't enough—that I needed more in order to prove the suspect guilty beyond a reasonable doubt. This time I was several rungs on the investigative ladder below that. All I had at the moment were suspicions—plenty of those—but nothing concrete and nothing solid enough to rise to the level of probable cause. This was a cold case for sure, one with no forensics or DNA or eyewitnesses. It would have to be solved the old-fashioned way, by tracking down friends and relations of both victim and suspect in order to establish exactly how the fatal encounter might have occurred.

A lot of crooks get caught because they're just plain stupid. Shelley was anything but that. Homer, Alaska, is definitely a small town. With the notable exception of Penny Olmstead's accidental sighting in Anchorage, Shelley and Roger Adams had managed to carry on an extramarital affair for years without anyone being the wiser. No, Shelley was smart, all right, and excellent at keeping secrets. Fortunately, I'm an expert at unearthing same.

There was no scene of the crime as such. Even had there been video surveillance cameras rolling nearby at the time when Chris went to help that supposedly stranded motorist, those tapes—that's what they generally were back then—would have long since been overwritten and disappeared. What I had to do was recreate the crime scene in my mind, and in the quiet of my room at the Driftwood Inn that's what I did.

I knew Chris had disappeared after his shift at Zig's

Place on March, 27, 2006—a Monday night. Consulting my notes, I verified that Bill Farmdale had said Chris had come back into the restaurant after taking out the trash. That's when he'd mentioned he was leaving early so he could help the lady in distress. Now that I was paying attention to Shelley Adams, I thought the wording was telling. Chris hadn't said a girl needed her tire changed. He had specifically used the term "lady." That implied that this was someone ten or more years older than Chris was and most likely someone he didn't know personally. If it had been a regular or occasional customer at the restaurant—someone Chris recognized—he would have identified her as such. No, the woman with the flat had been a stranger to Chris—someone he didn't know at all

Now I wanted to know more about Chris's final interaction with Bill, and the only way to verify that was to speak to the sole survivor of that verbal exchange. I picked up my phone, located Bill's phone number, and called him. Fortunately, it was Saturday and not all that late, so I doubted I was risking waking someone.

"Hey, Bill," I said when he answered. "It's J. P. Beaumont calling again. I hope I'm not disturbing you, but I need a little more information."

"Not at all," he said. "Happy to help."

"By the way, I had lunch at Zig's Place today—the

Ziggy Special. It was great. I also met your uncle. He seems like a hell of a nice guy."

"He is that," Bill agreed. "What do you need?"

"I believe you told me Chris came in toward the end of his shift to say he was leaving early."

"That's right."

"About what time was that?"

"Eight thirty or so. He was due to get off at nine."

"You said that he was taking the trash out when he was approached by a woman saying she had a flat tire."

"That's correct," Bill answered.

"Do you happen to remember how Chris was dressed at the time?"

"Dressed? He was wearing his uniform. That's one of the things about working at Zig's. Everybody wears uniforms. Uncle Sig says that's how you build an effective team, by having everybody dress the same way."

"But when Chris came back from taking out the trash, was he dressed for going outdoors?"

"Sure," Bill said easily. "I didn't see his uniform, but he was probably still wearing it. He also had on his jacket and a pair of boots. I remember there was snow in his hair and on his jacket. It snowed like crazy that night—ten inches at least—and it was windy, too," Bill added. "I ended up running off the road and landing in a snowdrift on my way home. Had to call a tow truck to pull me loose."

Danitza had been out walking that night, too. I could have asked her the same question, and she could have told me about the snow and wind, too, although for this phase of my investigation I needed to leave Danitza Miller in the dark.

But if it had snowed heavily that night, visibility from any motorists passing the scene most likely would have been limited. And if the car had been parked on the shoulder of the road, any crime-scene evidence to be found there would have vanished the moment the snowplows came by the next morning. Ditto for any remaining blood spatter. Later in the spring, when the piles of accumulated snow finally melted into the earth, the blood evidence would have disappeared into the ground along with it.

"Anything else?" Bill wanted to know.

"One other thing," I said. "How big was Chris back then?" The last time I'd seen Chris Danielson, he was a little kid.

"Taller than I was by at least three inches, maybe more," Bill said. "He was always teasing me and calling me Shorty."

"Do you remember how tall you were back then?"

"I was only five-eleven when we ordered our caps

and gowns for graduation. Everyone else claimed they were six feet, even guys who were shorter than me."

"And how was Chris built?" I asked.

"Tall but really skinny," Bill replied. "So I'd say he weighed about one-forty, give or take. Anything else?"

"That's all for the time being," I told him. "Thanks."

I ended the call and sat there thinking some more, trying to imagine how a smart killer might have come up with a plan to get away with murder. Wanting to lay hands on the money, Shelley would have thought all of this out in advance, and she would have been careful about the location. To avoid eyewitnesses, she would have chosen a place off the main drag, one that wasn't well traveled.

I tried to reconstruct the exact chronology of events. The scene would have to have been close enough to Zig's Place that Chris and his killer could walk to the stranded vehicle together. I had seen streetlights on most of the major thoroughfares in town, but off the beaten path I suspected they were few and far between. Once the two of them reached the woman's vehicle, Chris would have knelt beside it to examine the tire with his killer standing directly behind him. But if it was dark that night—really dark—wouldn't Chris have needed some kind of illumination to see what he was doing? And suddenly a picture of the scene formed in my brain. Chris was next to the vehicle on his knees As for the woman? She was standing slightly to one side with a flashlight in her hand—maybe one of those high-powered Maglites that cops carry on patrol, something powerful enough to provide plenty of illumination in the darkness but heavy enough to function as a weapon as well.

I took a breath. Yes, this was all conjecture on my part, but I had the sensation that I was finally getting somewhere. So what would have happened next? With Chris sprawled on the edge of the road, either dead or unconscious, Shelley would have needed to move him away from the scene in a hell of a hurry.

I thought about the bathrobe-clad woman I'd encountered earlier at the house on Diamond Ridge Road. She had been five-eight, about the same height as Twinkle Winkleman. Unlike Twink, however, Shelley Adams was not particularly muscular and probably weighed somewhere around a hundred thirty-five. From Bill Farmdale's description, it was safe to assume Chris had been six-two and weighed in at somewhere around a hundred forty pounds. The math didn't add up, if you will. There was no way someone like Shelley alone would be strong enough to lift something that weighed more than she did. Was it possible she'd had an accomplice? After a moment's thought, I dismissed that idea. If she had done this in order to lay hands on that ten grand, she wouldn't have wanted to share her spoils with a partner in crime.

Once more I closed my eyes and envisioned my mental crime scene, again with the snow falling all around and with Chris lying dead or dying on the side of the road. Desperate to get him out of sight, his killer would need to move him. The problem is, human bodies— especially newly dead human bodies—aren't easy to maneuver. For one thing they're ungainly. Before rigor sets in, arms and legs tend to flop around in an unpredictable fashion. It's hard to get a firm grip. Not only that, if there's blood involved, they can be slick and slip out of your grasp.

The killer's best bet for getting away would have been to load the victim into a vehicle, but what kind? It was snowing that night. An all-wheel-drive sedan of some kind? Nope. Lifting the victim up and over the lip of the trunk opening would have been difficult, and dragging him into the backseat would have left behind a bloody mess. What about an SUV? With adrenaline coursing through her body, someone Shelley's size might have been able to climb in and drag him into the luggage compartment, especially if she'd been able to lift him partway up onto something else—a toolbox maybe—so she didn't have to pull him the whole way from the ground to the SUV all at once.

I made a note to see if we could find out what kinds of vehicles Shelley and Jack Loveday had owned back in 2006.

Now what? I asked myself. *Where does our killer go once she departs the scene of the crime?*

Leaving the body in the back of the SUV would be too risky. What if someone looked in through the windows and saw it? It made sense that she'd want to ditch the corpse at the earliest opportunity. I opened my iPad and Googled the distance from Homer to Eklutna Lake, where I discovered that the estimated driving time was four hours and forty minutes, about the same amount of time it would take to drive between Anchorage and Homer. But it would doubtless take much longer on a night with ten inches of new-fallen snow on the ground. It didn't seem likely that she would have embarked on that kind of perilous journey alone in the middle of a stormy night alone and with a dead body rolling around in the back of her vehicle.

If Shelley had spent an hour or so wrestling with a bloody body, she certainly wasn't afraid of getting her hands dirty—and her clothing, too. She would have been a blood-soaked mess. It made sense that she'd have driven home, but if the tire was really flat, how was that possible? So maybe Shelley had come prepared for just such a contingency. If she was an airplane pilot, she'd have some mechanical ability. Maybe she'd let the air out of the tire herself and then brought along a cigarette-lighter-powered compressor to refill it. I was pretty sure Twink had just such a device among the equipment stowed in the Travelall's rooftop luggage rack. Once Shelley reinflated the tire, she most likely drove home, parked her vehicle in her garage out of sight of prying eyes, and cleaned herself up. That way she could ditch her filthy clothing and wait for better weather in which to dispose of the body.

Had Jack Loveday been at home to greet Shelley late that night when she showed up after murdering Chris? I doubted it, and with him dead there was no way to ask. Since no alarm had been sounded in the wake of Chris's sudden disappearance, his killer was gifted with the luxury of time. Shelley would have been able to get rid of the body and Chris's personal effects at her leisure, eventually abandoning the corpse in the middle of nowhere for the bears to find. She'd also had ample opportunity to clean up the vehicle she'd used to first entrap Chris and later to transport his body.

At this point, a dozen years down the road, Shelley was resting on her laurels, convinced that she'd committed the perfect murder. Unfortunately for her, there was a fly in her ointment—yours truly.

If Shelley Hollander Loveday Adams had murdered Sue Danielson's son, I was determined that she pay for it—come hell or high water.

Chapter 22

I spent the next hour or so going through the material Todd had sent along during the course of the day. While looking into Roger Adams's life and times, Todd had researched details about his second marriage, to Shelley Hollander Loveday, which had occurred in July of 2009, a bare two months after the death of Roger's first wife in May of that same year.

The dossier included details concerning the death of Jack Loveday, starting with the crash of his aircraft in early November of 2008 and his subsequent suicide in February of 2009. With my new focus on the possibility that Shelley might be a cold-blooded killer, that seemed like two too many deaths in her proximity in far too short a time for them to be dismissed as mere coincidence, so I studied with avid interest the details Todd had provided.

After the plane crash that resulted in the loss of both his legs, Jack Loveday had been hospitalized for three weeks before being transferred to a rehab facility in Anchorage for an additional three weeks. Following his release from there, he'd been sent home to Homer to for his stumps to heal completely so he could be fitted with his prosthetics. A fitting appointment for those had been scheduled two months down the road, but Jack died before that day arrived.

On February 15 his wife claimed she had awakened in the morning and found him unresponsive in the master bedroom of the home they shared. She had immediately called 911, but arriving EMTs had been unable to revive him. Initially the medical examiner had listed Jack's cause of death as undetermined. Six weeks later, after the toxicology results came in, the cause had been amended to suicide by means of an overdose of sleeping aids and painkillers combined with alcohol.

I sat back and thought about all that. Shelley had been home with her husband at the time he died, which meant she was most likely the last person to have seen Jack Loveday alive. She was the one who called 911 to report the incident. She was also the spouse. Twink had already told me that Shelley had benefited from her husband's death by selling off his collection of aircraft. Taking all those things together, she should have been a person of interest in his death from the get-go, and I was sure she must have been questioned then. I wanted more than anything to have access to what had been said in those initial interviews—the ones that had been conducted immediately after Jack's death.

There was no way anyone in Homer was going to grant that kind of official access to a private detective visiting from out of town, especially one who was there presumably investigating another matter entirely. But if not official access, what about unofficial?

I scrolled back through my messages and found the one from Hank Frazier that had given me the name and contact information for Lieutenant Marvin Price, Homer's senior detective of investigations. A glance at my watch said it was ten o'clock. This was Saturday night. If you happen to be in law enforcement, that's generally the busiest night of the week. Hank had provided two numbers—a cell phone and a direct number at work. After a few moment of consideration, I dialed the second one.

"Lieutenant Price here," a voice answered.

I had already decided that if I was going to ask for Lieutenant Price's help, I was going to have to be straight with him, cop to cop with no pulled punches.

"My name's J. P. Beaumont," I told him. "If you're working a case, I don't want to interrupt, but—"

"No case," he said, "just sitting here shuffling paperwork. What's up?"

"I used to be a homicide cop for Seattle PD," I explained. "After I left there, I worked for the attorney general's Special Homicide Investigation Team. Now I'm a private investigator, and I'm here in town looking into the disappearance of a kid named Chris Danielson, who never came home from working an evening shift at Zig's Place in March of 2006. Hank Frazier is a friend of mine. He's the one who gave me your contact information."

"Hank's a good friend of mine," Price told me. "I was relatively new on the job and still working patrol back in 2006. I don't remember a case like that, but I can put you in touch with the missing-persons guy from back then—"

I cut him off in midsentence and did some strategic name-dropping. "You've never heard of Chris Danielson's case because he was never officially reported missing, but does the name Harriet Raines mean anything to you?"

"Harry?" he asked with an amused chuckle. "Of course I know her. Everybody in law enforcement knows Harry Raines. Why?"

"Because I believe that Chris's disappearance can now be classified as a homicide, and so does Professor

Raines. She's in possession of unidentified human remains that were found in a black-bear den near Eklutna Lake in the spring of 2008. We're in the process of comparing a DNA profile obtained from Chris's older brother, Jared. We expect to have a DNA confirmation within the next day or so."

Over the phone I heard a squawk of some kind. I imagined it was the sound of Lieutenant Marvin Price sitting up straighter in whatever decrepit chair was behind his desk. And that actually made me smile, because that's what real homicide cops do when they get word of a case—they come to attention.

"You say that Chris Danielson disappeared in 2006?"

"Yes, Monday, March twenty-seventh, to be exact."

"You're working the case on whose behalf—the brother's?" Price asked.

"Initially that was true, but now there's another person involved—make that two people. A young woman named Danitza Adams Miller and her son, Christopher, have been added to the list. At the time Chris went missing, Danitza and he were boyfriend and girlfriend. On the day Chris disappeared, Danitza's parents had just learned that their sixteen-year-old daughter was pregnant."

"Wait, did you say Danitza Adams? Any relation to Roger Adams?"

"Danitza is Roger and Eileen Adams's only child."

There was a momentary pause. "If you've been investigating a missing-persons case that you now believe to be a homicide, have you identified any persons of interest?"

It was time for me to either put up or shut up.

"Actually, I have," I told him. "I have reason to believe that someone named Shelley Loveday might have been involved. She's currently Mrs. Roger Adams the second, but at the time Chris disappeared, and even though Shelley was married to someone else at the time, she and Mr. Adams were involved in a long-standing affair."

There was another pause on the line. I wondered if I had lost him. "Where are you right now?" he asked a moment later. "Didn't you say you were here in town?"

"I am," I told him. "I'm at the Driftwood Inn."

"Don't go anywhere," he said. "I'll be there in ten minutes."

And he was, too. In the meantime I hustled down to the desk and collected a few more Keurig pods along with some extra containers of whatever passes for hotel-room cream and sugar. Price's reaction over the phone told me that whatever discussion we were about to have probably shouldn't be conducted in public. That meant a table in AJ's or one down in the cozy lobby at the Driftwood were both out of the question.

While I was down in the lobby, I told the desk clerk that I was expecting a visitor, and he sent Lieutenant Price straight up to my room. When I opened the door, the guy I found in the hallway was an all-too-familiar figure—a homicide cop through and through who definitely looked the part, rumpled cheap suit and all. Most likely in his mid-forties, Marvin Price was about my height and a bit on the lean side. He was handsome enough, with dark wavy hair going gray around the temples.

"Mr. Beaumont?" he asked, extending his hand.

"Call me Beau, please," I told him. "What about you?"

"Marve works, but most people call me Marvin."

With introductions out of the way, I ushered him into the room. As I did so, I noted the lingering faded groove on the ring finger of his left hand indicating that a long-worn wedding ring was now MIA. That told me Marvin Price used to be married but wasn't anymore. No wonder he was hanging around his office late on a Saturday night. Back in those days, I would have been hanging out in a bar.

"Have a seat," I told him. Fortunately, my view room at the Driftwood came with a small pullout sofa and a reasonably comfortable chair. "Coffee?" I asked.

"Yes."

"Straight or decaf?"

"I don't do decaf."

"Neither do I. Cream and sugar?"

"Black, please."

"My kind of guy," I told him. We both laughed, at that, and I set about getting the Keurig to do its stuff.

"I gave Hank a call on my way over," Marvin said. "He says that you may be a PI now, but that back in the day you were the real deal."

I didn't take offense. From where Marvin stood, I must have looked as old as Methuselah.

"I like to think I still am the real deal," I replied, "but as Joe Kenda says, 'Homicide is a young man's game.' That doesn't mean, however, that I don't like keeping my hand in on occasion. When I took this case, I had no idea it would lead me to a possible homicide."

"Or two," he added quietly.

The word "two" certainly grabbed my interest. "I could tell by your reaction to the name of Shelley Loveday Adams that it rang a bell with you," I suggested.

He nodded. "You can say that again, because I'm pretty sure that woman had something to do with her husband's death. Unfortunately, as far as I can tell, she's going to get away with it."

Obviously, Hank Frazier really had put in a good word for me. Marvin's coffee finished brewing. I handed him his cup and started mine.

"So tell me about that Jack Loveday case," I urged. "Was it yours to begin with?"

Marvin shook his head. "At the time I was still working patrol, and Barry Caldwell was in charge of investigations. When I moved up from patrol to investigations in 2011, he was still there, and he was still pissed about the case. As far as he was concerned, the Loveday case was a screwup from day one."

"I knew that Shelley's first husband was dead," I ventured, "but everyone I've spoken to so far seems to be under the impression that he committed suicide."

"Yes," Price told me, "that's the official story, but in my opinion it ain't necessarily so."

"Care to tell me about it?"

Marvin stared into his coffee cup for a moment before he answered. "If I tell you this, I'm talking out of school," he said finally, "and there are any number of people in town—powerful people at that—who aren't at all interested in having that story rehashed."

"Like Roger Adams, for instance?" I asked.

Marvin favored me with a wry grin. "Precisely like Roger Adams," he said.

"So tell me about it," I said.

"First off," Marvin said, "you need to know I'm not exactly unbiased here."

"You've got a dog in this fight?"

"I do," he admitted. "My dad's best friend growing up was a guy named Larry Earling, whose sister, Lois, happened to be Jack Loveday's first wife. Dad was invited to their wedding. He and Jack hit it off, and they became good friends as well. Makes sense, of course. They were birds of a feather—both bush pilots and both hard drinkers who loved their tequila. They drank it the old-fashioned way—straight with a dab of salt and a section of lime. My dad sobered up before he died. Obviously, Jack never did."

The subject of drinking too much was familiar territory for me, although José Cuervo was never a friend of mine. I always favored a cheap Canadian blend called MacNaughton's. As for drinking buddies? Those kinds of friendships generally come to an abrupt end when one or the other of the drinking pals either sobers up or croaks.

"You said obviously Jack never quit," I observed. "How come 'obviously'?"

"Hold on," Marvin said. "I'm getting ahead of myself. In the old days, my folks and Lois and Jack all palled around together—playing cards, fishing, camping, that sort of thing. Once Shelley came into the picture and got her claws into Jack, my dad and he called it quits as far as friendship went.

"As soon as Jack and Lois divorced, he married Shelley. That was ten years or so before his crippling plane crash, which occurred in November of 2008. In January of 2009, he was released from rehab and sent home to continue his recovery. Due to mobility issues, he needed a hospital bed, which was installed in the master bedroom while Shelley slept in a guest bedroom down the hall.

"On the morning of February fifteenth, she went into his room, purportedly to help him out of bed and into his wheelchair. That's when she found him unresponsive. She dialed 911. When EMTs arrived, they were unable to revive him. Jack was declared dead at the scene, and that's when Lieutenant Caldwell entered the picture. Inside the bedroom he noticed an empty tequila bottle tipped over on the bedside table along with two separate pill containers lying empty on the bedding. Barry Caldwell, like my dad, wasn't a big fan of Shelley's either. Before leaving the scene, he declared the cause of death as undetermined and ordered the body shipped off to the medical examiner's office in Anchorage so an autopsy could be performed. Then he brought Shelley in for questioning."

"What were the pill bottles for?" I asked.

"Oxy and Ambien," Marvin answered. "Jack had prescriptions for both of them."

"Wait a minute," I commented. "I doubt either of those should be taken with a chaser of tequila."

"That's what Lieutenant Caldwell thought, too. According to his visiting nurse, once Jack was out of bed, he could get around all right in his wheelchair. So Caldwell asked Shelley about the tequila bottle. Where had that come from? She allowed as how, after having a Valentine's dinner together, Jack had asked her to bring the tequila to the master bedroom so they could share a nightcap."

"Sounds very romantic," I said.

"Right," Marvin muttered. It was one of those sarcastic "Rights" that doesn't mean right at all.

"In the interview Shelley claimed that even though Jack was on those prescribed meds, he continued to have difficulties with ongoing pain and falling asleep. She said that was why whenever he asked for tequila, she brought it to him—that it helped him sleep."

"I'll just bet it did," I said, "but the whole bottle?"

"That's what Barry thought," Marvin said.

"Were there fingerprints?"

"Yes, Shelley's prints were on both the booze bottle and each pill bottle, but those were easily explained because she was the one who usually dished out his meds. And in all cases, his fingerprints overlaid hers. His were the only prints on the shot glass."

"If there was a visiting nurse," I said, "why wasn't she administering the meds?"

"Have you ever dealt with a visiting nurse?" Marvin asked.

I shook my head. "Not really," I said. "Why?"

"When my father came down with cancer, he ended up dying at home after being bedridden for the better part of a year. Visiting nurses came by on a regular basis, all right, but as far as I could tell, they did very little nursing. They mostly came by to check the house's inventory of pills to make sure no one was saving them up in case my father wanted to use a handful of them as an early ticket out.

"Lieutenant Caldwell theorized that since Jack wasn't getting the kind of relief he needed from the pills, maybe Shelley wasn't dispensing his meds properly."

"You mean like maybe she was hoarding up enough pills to be able to get the job done?"

"Something like that," Marvin replied.

"Was there a note?"

"No note."

"So why would Jack take his own life?"

"Shelley claimed he was terribly depressed. She maintained that he was devastated by the loss of his legs because it meant he would never fly again. Lieutenant Caldwell was working the case and trying to prove that wasn't true—that Jack really did have something to live for. Barry said he'd heard from an airplane mechanic over in Anchorage who maintained that with the right prosthetics there was no reason Jack couldn't fly again."

Wait. This was sounding vaguely familiar. An airplane mechanic in Anchorage who knew Jack and Shelley Loveday? "Not Chad Winkleman!" I exclaimed.

Marvin Price looked at me in utter amazement. "How the hell did you know that?" he demanded.

"Never mind," I said. "It doesn't matter. Just tell me what happened."

"The initial autopsy results came in as undetermined, too, but once the toxicology report arrived, the medical examiner in Anchorage ruled the manner of death to be suicide and the cause of death to be an overdose, due in part to mixing alcohol with the prescribed medications."

"And that was the end of Lieutenant Caldwell's case?"

"You've got that right. Barry argued until he was blue in the face. Shelley was Jack's only heir, and she came into a bundle of money as a result of his death, which gave her motive aplenty. In addition, Lieutenant Caldwell believed that since Shelley had provided the liquor, even if she wasn't guilty of murder, at the very least she was guilty of involuntary manslaughter. The brass basically said that believing that and proving it were two different things."

"So Caldwell never got to first base?"

"Correct," Marvin said. "Especially with the M.E.'s eventual determination that Jack's death was a suicide. Next thing you know, Shelley's very good friend, Eileen Adams, dies in the hospital while undergoing treatment for cancer, and—"

"And two months later Eileen Adams's widower and Jack Loveday's widow just happen to tie the knot, which sounds a little too convenient to me."

"Me, too," Marvin agreed glumly.

"What about Eileen's death?" I asked. "Anything dodgy about that?"

"Could be, but who knows?" Marvin responded. "Eileen Adams was in a medical facility and under a doctor's care at the time she died. Her passing was reported as an expected medical death, so no autopsy was required."

"You're thinking that could have been murder, too," I asked.

Marvin nodded. "I think it's possible."

"In that case," I said, "our main worry now is making sure Roger Adams doesn't wind up being victim number four."

Marvin looked startled. "Wait a minute. You think he might be in danger, too?"

"I do."

"So tell me," Marvin said.

"I will," I said, "but before I do, I think we'd both better have a refill. I've got a feeling this is going to be a very long night."

Chapter 23

And I wasn't wrong about that. Marvin and I talked steadily until the wee hours of the morning, with neither of us paying the slightest attention to the passage of time. When homicide cops are working a case, the idea of punching a clock disappears. As we spoke, I was amused to notice that I was consulting notes and e-mails from Todd to provide names and dates. Meanwhile Marvin was using a ballpoint pen and a tiny spiral notebook to jot down his own items of interest.

The irony wasn't lost on me. Here I was, the old guy who'd had to be dragged kicking and screaming into the computer world, relying on high-tech devices to jog my memory while my much younger compatriot was old-school all the way. Marvin Price had made a great first impression, but his using that notebook caused me to like him even more.

I started at square one and told him everything from the beginning, starting with Sue Danielson's death and explaining how her older son, Jared, had charged me with looking into the disappearance of his younger brother. Then I recounted every detail of what my investigation had unearthed so far. In the process I made note of a couple of additional people who should probably be interviewed now that Shelley Loveday Adams had become the center of not only my investigation but of Marvin Price's, too.

Among those individuals was one Betsy Norman, Shelley's good friend who'd been responsible for notifying Penny Olmstead of her sister's passing. It occurred to me that I should also get in touch with Roger Adams's life-insurance guy. In the process of doing that change of beneficiary, it was possible that Roger might have mentioned something about what was going on in his personal life at the time. As far as I know, life-insurance salesmen don't qualify for protection due to client privilege. The third person on my list was Twink's brother, Chad, who was familiar with both Shelley and Jack Loveday. If his changed physical situation hadn't left him permanently grounded, then the whole motivation for Jack's suicide suddenly evaporated.

Marvin took a lot of interest in the description of my visit to the Adamses' home earlier that day, or the previous day, depending on what time of the morning it was by then.

"You think Roger is being confined against his will?" Marvin asked.

"I can't say that for sure," I admitted, "but something doesn't seem right. Listen to this. I recorded while I was at their place. I had noticed bruising on Roger's wrists, and I was worried that things weren't right, and I wanted to have documentation to back me up in case I called for a welfare check."

With that I pulled out my phone, located the recording, and played it back. "You hear that?" I said when the recording ended. "She says that doctors diagnosed Roger as having early-onset dementia, but according to Helen Sinclair, Roger's longtime secretary, both Roger and Shelley are now practicing Christian Scientists."

"So she's lying about the doctor part," Marvin mused. "I wonder what else she's lying about? And about that wellness check. Do you think one is in order?"

I thought about that for a moment before answering. "From what I could tell, Roger isn't in any immediate danger, although my having shown up asking questions earlier might have put him in a more precarious situation than he was in before."

"What do you mean by precarious?"

"Helen Sinclair also told me that when Roger and Shelley married, she signed a prenuptial agreement."

"So divorce would be out as far as she's concerned," Marvin surmised, "but she'll come into a bundle when he dies, the same way she did with Jack Loveday."

"Not as much as she thinks," I said. "According to Helen, Roger did a change of beneficiary on his life-insurance policy last summer, something Shelley may or may not be aware of. There's a chance he might also have rewritten his will. That means the only way for her to make out financially is for Roger to die. She did so when Jack Loveday died, and she may be expecting the same kind of windfall when Roger kicks off, but as for the wellness check? I think it's safe to say that Shelley Adams is a very capable liar. If some young patrol officer showed up to do a wellness check, she'd have him eating out of her hand and believing up was down in two shakes of a lamb's tail."

"What about notifying Roger's daughter about what's going on?" Marvin asked.

"I was holding off on that, waiting for the DNA results on Jared to turn up. If the Eklutna homicide victim turns out to be Chris Danielson, I intend to give her a full report. At that point it won't matter, because AST will be on the case and I'll be out of it.

By then any number of people will be parked at the Adams house asking all kinds of difficult questions. When Danitza turns up, she'll be one of many."

"About that DNA profile," Marvin said. "Do you think Harry Raines could have it in hand as early as Monday?"

"Most likely," I replied. "I have a lot of faith in the lab tech who's handling it at the Washington State Patrol Crime Lab."

"Well, then," Marvin concluded, "if you and I are going to solve this thing before the AST comes around sticking their noses in my business, we'd better get busy, because we only have tomorrow . . ." He paused long enough to glance at his wrist. "Make that today, to get her done."

I could write a book about law-enforcement turf wars, the kind of interjurisdictional wrangling that occurs when local cop shops and outside agencies are forced to work together. The local guys tend to regard the outsiders as unwelcome intruders, while the outsiders more often than not consider themselves as experts sent down from above to school local yokels in the finer points of how to get their jobs done. The only thing those warring factions share in common is an utter contempt for private investigators. In other words, in this situation—with two competing agencies and a private eye involved—the working dynamic for me was going to be crap.

"You've got that right," I agreed, "Sunday's it. That's all we've got. By Monday it'll turn into a free-for-all."

At that point in the discussion, I did a recap of my mental reconstruction of Chris Danielson's murder, and Marvin listened to every word with rapt attention.

"Your suppositions on how it all went down make sense," he agreed once I'd finished. "If the homicide occurred on a spur-of-the-moment basis and within walking distance of Zig's Place, the perpetrator would have needed to remove the victim from the crime scene in a hurry. You and I both know that head wounds bleed like crazy. By the time the victim's body was wrestled into a waiting vehicle, it would have been a bloody mess, as would the killer."

"Right," I assented.

"On the assumption that Shelley Adams is our doer, I'll check with the department of licensing to see if I can find out what vehicles were registered to Jack and Shelley Loveday back then. With enough bleach and elbow grease, you can scrub away blood evidence until it's invisible to the naked eye, but a spray with luminol can make it pop even years after the fact. On the off chance that the vehicle in question is still in existence . . ."

We both knew that when it came to expecting the vehicle to still be around this long after the fact, the words "off chance" counted as a gross understatement.

Marvin let the rest of his sentence go unfinished while he jotted a reminder into his notebook, but I knew he was right as far as the luminol was concerned. I once witnessed a case where it lit up like crazy at a crime scene that was more than a decade old. And although Marvin's strategy of attempting to track down the Lovedays' former vehicles was a good one, to my way of thinking it didn't go far enough.

"You should probably do the same for any vehicles registered to Roger and Eileen Adams at the time as well," I suggested. "If Roger dispatched Shelley to deliver the payoff money, he might have let her use one of his vehicles rather than her own."

"Good point," Marvin agreed.

Our discussion ended just after 2:00 A.M. Once Marvin was gone, I was utterly fagged. I stripped off my clothes and flopped into bed. The caffeine we'd swilled down had absolutely zero effect. I was asleep before my head hit the pillow. The next thing I knew, it was 7:00 A.M., and the phone on the bedside table was ringing off the hook. I was hoping for an early-morning wake-up call from Mel. Unfortunately, the landline phone in my room didn't come equipped with caller ID.

"So what's the deal?" Twink demanded irritably once I picked up the receiver. "Am I hauling your ass back to Anchorage today or not?"

I started to say, "Well, good morning to you, too," but thought better of it. Twink already sounded pissed, and that kind of response would have lit her up even more.

"A few other things have come up," I answered once I got my head in the game. "There are some additional people I need to interview." *Including your brother.* That's what I thought without saying it aloud. "If you need to get back home, I can probably rent a car here and get myself back to Anchorage once I finish up."

"Like hell you will," Twink snarled. "You're more trouble than you're worth, and so far our relationship has lasted longer than one of my marriages, but I said I'd get you back and forth, and I will."

I thought maybe she was kidding about the marriage bit but didn't dare ask.

"Just checked my friend's fridge," Twink continued. "Believe me, the cupboard is bare, so you're taking me to breakfast at Zig's Place. I'll be at the hotel to pick you up in ten minutes flat. Got it?"

"Yes, ma'am," I said. "Ten it is."

Thirty minutes later Twink and I were both ensconced in a booth at Zig's Place. On Sunday mornings in Homer, it was clearly the go-to destination.

The restaurant was jammed with customers, and uniformed staff members were working their butts off.

We both had coffee. Twink ordered the Sunday special—ham and eggs with hash browns and a short stack of buttermilk pancakes on the side. I settled for bacon, eggs, and toast—hold the hash browns. Twink devoured her food with a level of enthusiasm that reminded me of the "starving children in China" line my mother always used when she was trying to guilt me into cleaning my plate. As I watched Twink polish hers off, I suspected that if she hadn't been a chain smoker, she would have been a very large woman, which, pound for pound, would have made her that much scarier than she already was.

"So who's on the agenda for today?" she asked, mopping up the last of a puddle of maple syrup with a final forkful of pancake.

While we'd been waiting for our food, I had sent an SOS to Todd asking for address information for Betsy Norman, Shelley's high-school cheerleading pal, and for Jim Brixton, Roger's life-insurance guy. I had both of those at the ready, but now that I had Twink properly fed, I figured it was safe to ask a potentially explosive question.

"I'd like to speak to your brother," I said.

Twink spat a mouthful of coffee back into her cup. "You want to talk to Chad? How come?"

"I need to know if he can shed any light on Jack Loveday's suicide."

"I thought you were looking for a missing kid," Twink said. "What the hell does Jack Loveday's suicide have to do with anything?"

"That's not something I can go into right now," I told her, "but trust me, they might be related."

Twink glowered at me. "It's winter. I checked and found out that Chad's in Palm Springs right now, but what makes you think I'll just haul off and give you his number?"

"I could probably get it eventually from another source, but getting it from you would be faster and simpler all around."

"I'm going outside for a smoke," she said.

I decided to stay right where I was and waved to our waitress that I was ready for a coffee refill. Eventually Twink returned, still scowling. She sat down across from me and crossed both arms over her chest.

"Well?" I asked. "Did you come to any conclusions?"

"I'll give you Chad's number on one condition."

"What's that?"

"That I get to listen in when you call him."

I should have expected that, and it certainly wasn't an optimal arrangement, but it was probably the best deal I was going to get. Marvin Price and I had determined that today was it as far as having the investigation to ourselves, and wasting valuable resources tracking down a telephone number wasn't an effective use of our valuable and limited time.

"Done," I said.

Twink reached for her phone. "Not here," I said, motioning for our server to bring the check. "We'll call from the car."

"Good idea," she said. "It's Sunday. If Chad was out drinking last night, he's probably still asleep, and he won't be happy to be dragged out of bed."

Once in the Travelall, rather than reaching for the ignition, Twink punched the lighter instead. Then, with a lit cigarette held between her fingers, she tapped a button on her phone.

"Wait," I objected. "Are you calling him from your phone?"

Twink nodded.

"I thought you said you'd give me his number."

"You want him to answer or not?" At that point she put the phone on speaker, and I heard a muffled hello.

"Top of the morning to you, bro," Twink said cheerfully. "Sorry to wake you, but I've got someone here who needs to talk to you. His name's Beaumont, and he's a private investigator from Seattle. He wants to talk to you about Jack Loveday's suicide."

With that dubious introduction, she handed the phone over to me, instantly putting me in the hot seat.

"I don't like talking to private eyes," Chad said. "So thanks but no thanks."

"I'm working with Lieutenant Marvin Price," I said quickly. "He's a homicide detective for Homer PD. We're looking into the possibility that Jack Loveday didn't commit suicide."

Chad's change in attitude was like flipping a light switch. "Hot damn!" he exclaimed. "Why didn't you say so? I thought that case was closed for good and there was no way they were going to reopen it. What happened?"

"Some new evidence might have surfaced," I answered, still trying to be cagey, gathering information without giving too much away.

"What do you need?"

"My understanding is that during the initial investigation you told Lieutenant Caldwell that you didn't believe Jack's death was a suicide. How come?"

"Shelley had given them some sob story about his being depressed about not being able to fly again, and that's bullshit."

Chad Winkleman, like his sister, didn't believe in mincing his words.

"Why's that?"

"Who says amputees can't fly planes?" Chad returned. "Shelley had filled his head with all kinds of crap about never being able to fly again. With the sorts of prosthetics they make these days, amputees can do damned near anything they want, including running in marathons, and that's exactly what I told him, but I don't doubt the man was depressed. If I'da been stuck with a bitch like Shelley, I'd be depressed, too. I think he was finally seeing the writing on the wall, that she had only married him for his money. He was fixing to do something about that when he crashed the plane."

"You know this how?"

"He told me."

"When?"

"A couple of weeks before the crash," Chad replied. "It felt like great news. to me, I'll tell you—like he was finally catching on to what she was really like. Next thing I knew, he was in the hospital with both legs hacked off below the knee. I was over in town on business one day and went to see him in the hospital in Anchorage. Shelley was there, acting like she was Jack's self-appointed guardian angel. It made me want to puke."

"Was there ever any indication that someone might have tampered with his aircraft?"

"None," Chad answered. "The Air Transportation Safety guys ruled it an accident, a combination of bad weather and pilot error."

"Was anyone else privy to that conversation between you and Jack where he told you his marriage was going south?"

"Nope," Chad answered, "it was just the two of us. He had some upcoming maintenance work he wanted done, and he'd stopped by my office to talk about that. Before it was over, he ended up crying in his beer about what was going on at home."

"Beer?" I asked.

"Not beer," Chad admitted. "Jack was always partial to tequila, and so am I."

Evidently tequila is something of a big deal in Homer.

"My understanding is that at some point after the crash he asked you to do some modifications to one of his planes."

"I told him that was so much balderdash—that with the right prosthetics he'd be able to fly just fine, but there were a few adjustments that would have made it easier for him to get in and out."

"When did he ask you about that?"

"Not sure," Chad said. "We talked about that on the phone. I'm pretty sure he was out of the hospital by then. Maybe he was home, maybe he was still in rehab. I can't say. But like I told the cops back then, a guy who's asking you to fix his aircraft isn't someone who's ready to do himself in because he can't fly anymore. Unfortunately, once the M.E. in Anchorage determined Jack's death as a suicide, that was the end of it. Next thing I knew, Shelley was on my doorstep asking for help unloading his planes."

"What did you do?"

"What do you think?" he asked. "Jack was a friend of mine. Shelley might have been a ring-tailed bitch, but she was off the hook as far as law enforcement was concerned, and money's money. I made whatever repairs were needed the planes and then sold 'em. Truth be told, I mighta charged a higher commission than I should have. Does my conscience bother me about that? Not one damned bit!"

"You sold them all?" I asked.

"All but one," he replied. "She held back the newest Piper to keep for her own use."

"Just to confirm, no matter what the M.E. says, you don't believe that Jack Loveday committed suicide."

"Absolutely not! Jack was a serious drinker. He wasn't someone to sit around sipping fancy cocktails. I think she laced his tequila with a dose of whatever, and he drank it down without even tasting it. Hell of a way to treat your valentine."

I couldn't have agreed more.

"Do you need anything else?" he asked.

"Not at this time."

Chad took a breath. "So how'd you meet up with my sister?"

"Just lucky," I said. "I needed a driver, and she happened to be available."

"She's a good driver," he allowed, "as long as you don't mind breathing all that cigarette smoke. Why don't you put her back on?"

I was tempted to tell him, *You can say that again about the cigarette smoke,* but I knew better. I kept my mouth glued shut and handed the phone over to Twink.

Chapter 24

Breakfast had taken longer than expected, and by the time Twink and I left Zig's Place, it was verging on nine. Naturally Todd had provided addresses for that day's worth of interviewees. While Twink navigated us to Betsy Norman's place on Bonanza Avenue, I decided to give Mel a call.

As soon as I heard her groggy hello, I knew I had awakened her out of a sound sleep. "What time is it?" she mumbled.

"Nine here," I told her, "so ten there. I didn't mean to wake you."

"I just crawled into bed an hour ago," she said. "I got a call out to a DV hostage situation around midnight. It didn't end well."

I heard the sorrow in her voice. Mel's the chief of

police in a small city. When something goes wrong, she's there on the scene, working with her people and usually handling the media.

"How bad?" I asked.

"The wife bled out from stab wounds while we were negotiating with the asshole husband. He shot himself in the head as the Emergency Response Team was making entry. My guys found a four-month-old baby unharmed in a back bedroom. She's an orphan now, currently in foster care."

The heartbreak in Mel's voice made my own heart ache as well, and the accompanying pang of guilt took my breath away. I should have been in Bellingham with her, backing her up, instead of off up here in Alaska on what suddenly seemed like a pointless wild-goose chase.

"I'm so sorry," I managed. "I'll hang up and let you go back to sleep."

"No," she said. "I needed to hear your voice. As for Sarah? I took her along on the call and left her in the car because I had no way of knowing when I'd get home. Once we got here, I let her out, but when I went to bed, she climbed up here right beside me. She must have known how upset I was. She helped me fall asleep."

"Damn dog!" I muttered. "I'm away from home for just three nights, she's already taken over my side of the bed."

Mel laughed aloud at that, and the sound was music to my ears. Right then a tiny bit of laughter was what we both needed.

"As long as I'm awake now, what are you up to today?" she asked.

At that moment we were motoring down Bonanza Avenue, and Twink's Travelall was pulling over in front of a small frame house set far back from the street. "I'm doing a few more interviews in Homer," I told her. "We're just now coming up on one of the residences. You go back to sleep. Call me when you're up and about."

"Will do," she said.

I ended the call. "Something wrong with your wife?" Twink wanted to know.

"She had a rough night," I answered. "She's the police chief in Bellingham. There was a domestic case. Two people died on her watch last night, and a baby girl has been left an orphan."

"Sorry," Twink said. From the tone of her voice, I knew she meant it.

I bailed out of the car and made my way up a long shoveled walk to the house. I rang the doorbell twice before I finally heard footfalls inside. The door was opened by a red-haired, freckle-faced kid who appeared to be about fifteen. He was dressed in the bottom half of a pair of pajamas and looked as though he'd just crawled out of bed.

"Yeah?" he asked. "What do you want?"

"I'm looking for Betsy Norman."

"That's my mom. She's not here. She's at work."

"I need to speak to her. Could you tell me where she is?"

"Who are you?" he asked. "Are you a friend of hers?"

"My name's J. P. Beaumont. I'm a private investigator from Seattle," I told him. "Who are you?"

"Noah."

"It's not a big deal, Noah," I assured him. "I just need to ask her a few questions."

"Is she in some kind of trouble?"

"No, I want to speak to her about one of her patients from years ago."

Noah looked relieved. "You could call her, I guess," he said. "Do you have her number?"

I did, but I decided to let him help. "Not on me," I said.

He gave me the number, and I keyed it into my phone.

"But she's really not in any trouble?"

"None at all, Noah. Thanks for your help."

I dialed the number on my way back to the car. The

call went to voice mail. "This is Betsy Norman. I'm either on the phone or doing patient rounds. Leave your name and number. I'll get back to you."

I left my name and number. "Where to next?" Twink asked.

I gave her Jim Brixton's address on East Danview Avenue. For the first time ever, Twink was stumped and had to dial up Siri on her iPhone to get directions. We didn't talk much as we drove from the first house to the second. I was still preoccupied with what was going on with Mel.

We pulled up in front of the Brixton residence just as a late-model Lexus entered the driveway and parked in the attached garage. A man, a woman, and three kids exited the vehicle. They were all dressed up as though they'd just come from church—Mass, most likely. The woman and the kids went on into the house. As I exited the Travelall, the man came walking up to me with a puzzled expression on his face.

"May I help you?" he asked.

"I'm looking for Jim Brixton," I said.

"That would be me. Who are you?"

"My name's J. P. Beaumont," I explained. "I'm a private investigator from Seattle. I'd like to ask you a question about one of your clients."

"Which client?"

"Roger Adams."

"Do you have any ID?"

I presented my ID wallet and passed along a business card as well.

"Has something happened to Roger?" he asked, handing the wallet back to me. "Is he all right?"

"As far as I know," I answered. "At least at the moment."

Brixton frowned. "Then why . . . ?"

I cut him off in midsentence. "I'm doing some work for Roger's daughter, Danitza. I understand you did a change of beneficiary on a life-insurance policy for Mr. Adams last summer and that Nitz is now the owner and beneficiary of a half-million-dollar policy on her father's life."

"That's correct," Brixton said, "but if you already know that . . ."

"Mr. Adams and his daughter have been estranged for a number of years. Would you be able to tell me what triggered this action on his part, this sudden change of heart?"

"Mr. Beaumont, my dealings with my clients are confidential, and—"

I ignored his objection. "Before you made the

change," I asked, "was Mr. Adams's current wife, Shelley, the previous beneficiary?"

Brixton gave me an exasperated sigh. "Yes, she was," he replied resignedly.

"Do you know if she's aware that she's no longer listed as the beneficiary on that policy?"

"I have no idea what Roger might or might not have shared with her, and I don't understand—"

"When you came to his office to do the paperwork, did he mention if he and Shelley were having any kind of marital difficulties?"

"This is outrageous," Brixton objected. "I really can't answer these kinds of questions. As I said, dealings between my clients and me are private transactions."

The fact that he was trying to avoid answering my questions provided more information than might have come from straight answers. I was reasonably sure that Shelley Loveday Adams was up to her old tricks by cheating on this husband the same way she had cheated on her previous one, and Roger was finally beginning to catch on.

"When did you execute that change order?" I asked.

Brixton frowned. "Back in June, I believe. I'd have to check my calendar in order to give you an exact date, but I don't understand. . . ."

I had a feeling Jim Brixton knew way more than he was saying. I needed to get him to spit it out today, because once the Alaska State Troopers rode into town, I'd be kicked to the curb, right along with Lieutenant Marvin Price. With that thought in mind, I decided to go for broke.

"Are you aware that Shelley Adams was married before?" I asked.

"Yes," Brixton answered. "I forget his name, but I believe the man was a bush pilot."

"His name was Loveday," I supplied. "Jack Loveday."

"That's right. I remember now. He committed suicide."

"He *might* have committed suicide," I corrected. "Lieutenant Marvin Price is considering reopening that case as a possible homicide, and Shelley Loveday Adams is the primary person of interest."

Dropping Marvin's name was the right thing to do. Brixton seemed taken aback. "I hadn't heard a word about any of that," he said.

"That's because it just happened, and here's my concern. I went to see Roger Adams yesterday. It struck me that he's in very ill health at the moment. If his primary caregiver thinks she's looking at a half-million-dollar insurance payday when Roger kicks off . . ."

"Roger thought Shelley was having an affair," Brixton blurted out. "That's what he told me. He said he'd checked her phone and her computer and hadn't found anything, but he said she was spending a lot of time going back and forth to Anchorage, and he was pretty sure she was seeing someone."

"No idea who?"

"If he knew, he didn't say, but do you think Roger is in danger?" Brixton asked.

"He may be," I said, "and that's why I'm working with Lieutenant Price on this. We both consider it a matter of some urgency. With that in mind, is there anything more you'd like to add?"

Brixton grew hesitant again. "The change of beneficiary was just the first step. He told me that he intended to write her out of his will as well. If he did that, Shelley would lose all the way around, and in that case what would be her motive?"

Good question, I thought. "We're looking into it," I said.

"Do you think I should stop by and see him?"

"No," I said. "For now let sleeping dogs lie. If Shelley is up to something, I don't want to raise her suspicions any more than they already are."

"But if she means to do him harm . . ."

"Believe me, Mr. Brixton, Lieutenant Price and I

are doing everything in our power to prevent that from happening. Just hold tight, but thank you for your help. What you've told me has been very informative."

With that I gave him a half-baked salute and headed for the Travelall. Jim Brixton might have answered most of my questions, but I didn't want to be trapped into answering any of his.

Chapter 25

As I fastened my seat belt, I was dreading Twink's next question about where we were going because I had no idea. Fortunately, a phone call saved me.

"Mr. Beaumont?" a woman's voice asked.

"Yes."

"This is Betsy Norman. You asked me to call?"

"Yes."

"What's this about?"

"I'm doing some work for Danitza Adams Miller," I told her. Had Betsy been able to see my face, she might have seen that as a big fat lie, but over the phone I figured I could get away with it.

"Her aunt, Penny Olmstead, mentioned you're good friends with Nitz's stepmother," I continued. "I wondered if I could visit with you about that for a few minutes."

"*Were* good friends," Betsy corrected, "not so much anymore." I found that to be an interesting tidbit as Betsy continued. "These days Danitza and her father aren't exactly on the best of terms either, you know."

"I'm aware of that," I said. "I believe Penny is hoping we might be able to find a way to resolve that situation."

That was the honest truth. Penny really did want to end Nitz's long estrangement from Roger Adams.

Betsy sighed into her phone. "I don't know how I can help on that score, but it can't hurt to talk. Does it have to be today?"

"Yes," I replied. "I'm on a deadline, and I really need to get this sorted."

"I have about half an hour between now and my next appointment," she conceded. "I suppose I could meet you for coffee. Do you know where the McDonald's is on Old Glenn Highway?"

I personally had no idea, but I was pretty sure Twink would be able to find it.

"I'm on the way," I said.

"How will I know you?"

"Just look for a bright yellow vintage Travelall," I told her. "I'll be the guy climbing out of that."

We arrived minutes later. Entering the restaurant, I saw a woman waving in my direction from the far side of the room. I nodded at her, but I stopped off at the counter long enough to pick up my own cup of coffee. I had swilled enough coffee at Zig's Place that I really didn't need any more caffeine right then, but I wanted this conversation to seem more like a casual visit than an interrogation, and a steaming paper cup of coffee functioned as a suitable prop.

When I got to Betsy's table, I put my cup down and then presented her with both a look at my ID and a business card before taking the opposite seat. I noticed that Betsy Norman, Penny Olmstead, and Shelley Adams were all of an age, but it occurred to me that of the three Shelley was the only one whose good looks were being helped along by professional augmentation.

"It says here you're from Seattle," Betsy said, frowning at my card.

That's another prop, by the way. Mel and I still have the condo in Seattle, and from a business standpoint using Seattle as a base of operations has more cachet to it than Bellingham. Also, people know where it is.

"What's this all about?" she added.

"I was friends with Danitza's son's father," I replied.

"Back before Chris disappeared into the woodwork, you mean?" she asked.

"Yes," I said. "That was an unfortunate situation all the way around."

Betsy nodded in agreement.

"So I'm working on behalf of Danitza and her son. She's considering attempting to reconcile with her father, and I'm trying to smooth the way."

"That would be wonderful," Betsy said. "The rift with her daughter broke Eileen's heart, but Roger was absolutely adamant about it, and Eileen went with the flow."

"I understand that growing up you were friends with both Eileen Phillips and Shelley Hollander?" I asked.

Betsy nodded. "Shelley and I go way back," she said. "I knew who Eileen was, of course, because I was also friends with her younger sister, Penny, but I didn't really get acquainted with her until I met her as a patient when she started showing up at the hospital for chemo. She was such a fighter as far as the cancer was concerned, and it surprised me that she didn't go to war with her husband about burying the hatchet with their daughter. I sure as hell would have."

"You knew Roger had forbidden Danitza to visit her mother in the hospital?"

Betsy nodded. "Yes, everyone at the hospital was aware of that, and we all went along with it. Roger was in the state legislature at the time. He was a big deal statewide, not just here in Homer, and what he said went. Had Danitza tried to visit, she wouldn't have been allowed to enter her mother's room."

"But Shelley was."

"Of course she was," Betsy said. "She and her husband and Roger and Eileen had all been great friends—up until Jack died. After he was gone, Shelley was lost. I think being there for Eileen and Roger was one way she helped herself deal with losing Jack. She was a constant visitor in Eileen's room, especially when the legislature was in session and Roger was off in Juneau. During that last round of chemo, when Eileen was so sick, Shelley was at the hospital every single day. Eileen considered her a godsend, and so did I."

"Were you surprised that Roger and Shelley married so soon after Eileen died?" I asked.

Betsy shook her head. "Not really," she answered. "Widows and widowers who come from happy marriages tend to remarry sooner than those whose marital lives were troubled. Besides, the two of them had a lot in common—not only that long history of the four of them being friends together but also having lived through the devastating loss of a beloved spouse."

Betsy's response made me think that even now she still had no inkling that her good friend Shelley and Roger Adams had been involved in an affair long before either one of their spouses was out of the picture.

"So as far as you knew, Jack and Shelley had a solid marriage?"

Betsy gave a small shrug. "For the most part," she said finally. "Jack was a little rough around the edges, and there was a big age difference. He was a homebody, and she was more of a good-time girl. He kept her reined in."

"Socially or financially?" I asked.

"Both," she said. "Jack had a reputation for being something of a tightwad."

"Are you and Shelley still good friends?" I asked.

"Not as close as we used to be," Betsy admitted.

"What happened?"

"Nothing really," she said. "Once she married Roger, she started moving in a different social circle, and we drifted apart. I still see her around town occasionally, but we're not that close. In fact, the last time I saw her, sometime last fall, she mentioned Roger was having health issues."

"Did she give any specifics?" I asked.

Betsy frowned. "I believe she said something about Alzheimer's, although Roger's pretty young to be dealing with that."

The word "Alzheimer's" grabbed my attention. Shelley had told me Roger was suffering from some form of dementia. My understanding is that those two ailments are two distinctly different propositions.

"Naturally I didn't ask for any more details."

"Why not?"

"Religion," Betsy replied. "That was a big part of why Shelley and I fell out. I'm a nurse—an RN. Sometime after Eileen died, Shelley and Roger walked away from regular medicine and turned to Christian Science instead. I took it personally. People are free to believe whatever they believe, and I should probably have just let it go. But what's this all about, Mr. Beaumont? I'd hate to think Shelley is in some kind of trouble."

The Christian Science lie again, with slightly different twist—Alzheimer's instead of dementia—but I didn't want to alarm Betsy for fear she might warn her former good friend that I was going around asking questions.

"Not at all," I fibbed. "I was just wondering if you thought Shelley would have any problem if Danitza showed back up in her father's life."

Betsy shook her head. "I can't imagine why she would." At that point she paused long enough to check her watch. "Oops," she said, "I have to go. I'm due at my next patient's home in ten minutes."

"Home?" I inquired. "I was under the impression that you worked at a hospice."

"I do hospice care," she corrected, "but I do it in my patients' homes. We don't have a brick-and-mortar hospice facility here in Homer." She stood up and gathered her purse. "I hope this was a help."

"It certainly was," I told her. "Thank you."

Once she was gone, I noticed that while I'd been talking to Betsy, Twink had entered the restaurant. I walked over and sat down at her table.

"Do any good?" she asked.

"Not really," I said. The truth is, I was discouraged. Neither interview had been particularly fruitful, and I felt as though I was just spinning my wheels. And the fact that I was functioning on less than five hours of sleep didn't help.

"Look," I said. "How about if you take me back to the hotel and then give yourself some time off and maybe hang out with your friend. If I need you later today, I'll call. Tonight I'll treat you to dinner at AJ's."

"Sounds good to me," Twink said. "After all, Sunday is supposed to be a day of rest. As for dinner? I'm ready. I finished up the rest of the leftovers from Simon & Seafort's yesterday."

We saddled up and headed back to the Driftwood.

Twink seemed to be in a somewhat cheery mood, so I decided to take a risk. "Mind if I ask you something?"

"What's that?"

"I'm curious. You told me earlier that our relationship had lasted longer than one of your marriages. Is that true or were you just pulling my leg?"

"God's truth," Twink replied. "The day after the wedding, I found out the son of a bitch was still married. I messed him up pretty good before I was done with him. Not enough to put him in the hospital, but close enough to make me feel better. After that, I had to hire a lawyer and go to court to get it annulled. Took me six months. Talk about insult to injury."

"I'll bet he never tried a stunt like that again."

"You'd better believe it," she declared. "He most certainly did not!"

Chapter 26

Back at the hotel, I slipped off my jacket and boots and lay down on the bed to rest both my eyes and my feet. It turns out I'm not accustomed to wearing boots, and I had a suspicion that once I got home to Bellingham, the ones I'd bought in Anchorage would disappear into the far corner of my walk-in closet, never to surface again. By the way, that's one formula for maintaining marital harmony—separate bathrooms and separate walk-in closets.

I wanted to text Mel and see how she was doing, but I also didn't want to disturb her if she was still asleep. I had just closed my eyes and was about to doze off when my phone rang. The caller turned out to be Marvin Price.

"Hey, Beau," he said. "We may be in luck."

I couldn't help but notice the excitement in his voice. "How's that?" I asked.

"I just got off the phone with a guy named Nate Bucknell."

"Who's he?"

"The guy who bought a Subaru Forester from Shelley Adams in 2010."

"He still has it?" I asked.

"Yup, he sure does. I ran the VIN numbers of all vehicles registered to either the Lovedays or the Adamses back in '06, and this is the only one of those still in existence. So maybe that commercial is actually true—the one that says most of the Subarus manufactured in the last ten years are still on the road."

It was actually twelve years now, but why quibble?

"According to Mr. Bucknell, Shelley said that she and Jack Loveday bought the Subaru new in 2005, and she was still driving it when she and Roger Adams married. At that point, between driving the older Subaru or one of her new husband's Range Rovers, it wasn't a contest. She wanted to unload it and gave Nate a good price even though the vehicle had fairly low mileage at the time. By the way, it's not much higher now. Ever since Nate bought it, the vehicle has spent most of the time sitting in a friend's garage here in Homer, hooked up to a trickle charger."

"Why buy a car if you're not going to drive it?" I asked.

"Mr. Bucknell lives part-time in Palm Desert and part-time in a place called Halibut Cove. It's about five miles from here, across Kachemak Bay. People who live there mostly get around either by boat or in ATVs. Bucknell's place there is right on the water, and he goes back and forth from here in his own boat. Nate pulls up to Red Bolger's dock here in Homer, ties up his boat, then off he goes on his own set of wheels."

"So what now?" I asked.

"I told Nate that the car had surfaced as possibly being connected to a homicide investigation, and I asked him if he'd mind if we took a look at it."

"And?"

"He said sure, no problem. He said something else that I found interesting. He wanted to know if this had anything to do with Jack's death. 'I always thought that bitch of a wife of his had something to do with it.' Quote, unquote."

I was excited now, too. "If we can look at the vehicle, how soon?"

"Not immediately," Marvin replied. "Nate tried calling Red. Unfortunately, he's off ice-fishing this weekend and isn't due back until sometime this afternoon. Nate gave Red my number and asked that he give me a call once he gets home. As soon as Red calls me, I'll call you."

"Good enough," I said, "but you and I both know odds are that all this will come to nothing."

"Maybe so," Marvin agreed, "but what else have we got? Not a damned thing. What you said this morning about our suspect's being able to load a dead body into the back of an SUV rather than into the trunk of a sedan makes all kinds of sense, and that Subaru is definitely an SUV. I'll give you a call once I hear from him."

"Sounds good," I said. "I'll be here."

I put down the phone and had no more than closed my eyes when it rang again. This time it was Todd. "I just sent you a whole wad of stuff," he said. "I think you're going to want to take a look at it."

"What kind of stuff?"

"My public-records search has turned up a whole batch of real-estate transactions," he said. "It appears that Roger Adams has been unloading numerous properties over the course of the last few months, starting in November—fifteen so far. "

I thought about the dazed and confused pajama-clad guy I'd seen the day before. The Roger Adams standing in the doorway had been in no condition to conduct business transactions of any kind.

"Fifteen?" I repeated. "What is it a fire sale."

"Seems like," Todd replied. "Three of those sales closed in just the last week, and I checked the comps. All three of them sold at well under market value. Even so, taken together those proceeds alone still add up to a cool million five."

"Under market value?" I asked. "That sounds like a red flag."

"I agree," Todd replied, "but here's the really cool part. Would you like to know how the closing documents were signed?"

"Tell me."

"By Shelley Loveday Adams, acting with Roger's power of attorney!"

I was beyond stunned. "Good work, Todd," I said. "I'll get right on these."

Clambering out of bed, I made straight for my iPad. It was almost out of juice, so I had to sit at the desk to keep it on the charger. During that morning's interviews, I'd kept both my phone and iPad on silent, so I hadn't heard the arriving pings of Todd's barrage of e-mails.

I started with the ones labeled "Real Estate Transactions." When you're reading through page after page of legalese, it doesn't take much for your eyes to blur over and your mind to go numb. In each instance the closing had been finalized by an employee at the same office of Alaskan Title in Anchorage. The sales agreements had all been signed by Shelley, and a copy of the notarized power-of-attorney document accompanied each bill of sale, verifying her ability to sign in Roger's stead.

Prior to this I had never seen a power-of-attorney form before. It appeared to be a readily available template that had to be filled out, signed, witnessed, and notarized. The notary turned out to be someone named Tracy Hamilton, whose place of employment was listed as an Anchorage branch of the First Alaska National Bank. The names of the two people who had signed the form as witnesses weren't familiar to me, but I suspected they were most likely some of Tracy's fellow bank employees who'd been drafted to guarantee the authenticity of the signatures on the documents. I was about to move on when I noticed the date on the document in my hand—November 6, 2018. That made my weary eyes pop wide open.

November 6? That was only a little over a month ago. The last time Helen Sinclair saw Roger Adams in the flesh had been at the end of September. If he'd become ill at some point after that, his decline had to have been incredibly rapid. When I saw him yesterday, Roger had appeared to be at death's door. So how had he been a little over a month ago? What had been his physical condition then? Would he have been well enough at that point to travel back and forth between Homer and Anchorage and to show up in person at a bank branch? And why go that far? I wondered. If someone living in Homer needed a notary public, wouldn't they go looking for one that was less than a four-hour drive away?

I made a note of Tracy Hamilton's name and the bank-branch location on my Reminders app so I'd be able to call her first thing on Monday morning to ask about all this. Then I returned to analyzing the sales agreements. They were full of the usual gobbledygook, boilerplate legalese that in my opinion is usually designed to cover the behinds of the real-estate agents involved rather than to offer any genuine protection for either buyer or seller. It wasn't until the very last page of the first one that I hit the bombshell—and that came in the final section, the one outlining the disbursal of funds.

Proceeds of all three sales were to be wired to a numbered joint account belonging to Roger D. Adams and Shelley Lorraine Adams. So far so good, but the kicker came in the address details. It turns out that the joint account was held in trust by the First Commercial Bank of Sri Lanka, with headquarters in Colombo!

Sri Lanka? I'd heard the name, of course, but I had to check on my iPad to come up with the country's exact location on the planet—just north of a group of islands called the Maldives where the Arabian Sea and the Indian Ocean meet up. Once I knew that much, it didn't take long to sort out that in terms of offshore banking, institutions located in the Maldives are considered to be among the top ten of preferred options for one simple reason: Funds deposited there are well out of reach of scrutiny and oversight from the IRS!

Bingo. Who do you suppose had opened that account? Todd had yet to provide an answer to that question, but I for one was reasonably sure that Roger Adams himself had absolutely no idea that his name was attached to a numbered account in the wilds of Sri Lanka. And right now I was willing to bet good money that he hadn't been physically present at that notary's office in Anchorage either.

And suddenly I had a clearer view of what Shelley's game plan was. She didn't need Roger dead. She was keeping him alive and under wraps while she systematically liquidated his assets and looted his estate. Once the funds landed in Sri Lanka, she'd be able to transfer them to an account listed in her name only. Ultimately, when Roger died, it wouldn't matter in the least if he'd rewritten his will, because what had once been a multimillion-dollar estate would have been drained dry.

So Shelley Loveday Adams wasn't just a suspected serial killer, she was most likely also engaged in wire fraud. As long as there were some properties still in Roger's name, the man probably wasn't in immediate danger, but I wanted that woman brought to justice before she had a chance to grab all his money and run. Suddenly waiting around until Monday to speak to the notary from the bank branch in Anchorage was no longer acceptable. I needed her number, and I needed it now!

Law-enforcement agencies have access to databases that aren't available to the public. There's better than a fifty-fifty chance that Todd Hatcher shouldn't be able to utilize some of the ones he uses on a regular basis. But this time things were different. If in the near future someone from the FBI came around asking how it was that I happened to know so much about Shelley Adams's clandestine dealings, I needed to be able to show them that I had connected all those dots in an aboveboard fashion.

With that in mind, I picked up the phone and dialed Anchorage detective Hank Frazier's cell.

"Hey, Beau," he said. "What's up? Did you ever cross paths with Marvin Price?"

"I sure did," I told him. "He's been a huge help. We have a lead on a vehicle that might have been involved in my missing-persons disappearance. We're hoping that we may still be able to obtain forensic evidence from that."

"Good to hear," Hank said, "though from your tone of voice, I expect there's a but coming."

"You've got me there," I said. "I do have a but, and it's a big one. I still need your help."

"What kind?"

"There's a good chance my person of interest in the original case is now involved in some fraudulent real-estate transactions that will deplete her ailing husband's estate and leave him virtually penniless while she's living it up on proceeds transferred to offshore accounts."

"You think she's getting ready to make a run for it?" Hank wanted to know.

"I certainly do."

"What do you need?"

"The real-estate transactions are being made in the husband's name using what I believe to be a fraudulently obtained power of attorney. I need to speak to the notary public who witnessed the signatures on that POA."

"Someone here in Anchorage?"

"Yes," I said. "All I have is a name—Tracy Hamilton. She evidently works at a branch of First Alaska National Bank, the one on West Tudor."

"Probably the midtown branch, then," Hank concluded. "Give me a few minutes. I'll see what I can do."

Only ten minutes elapsed between the end of that first conversation and the time he called me back. Even so, it seemed like forever.

"Here's Tracy's home number," Hank announced. I fed it into my phone as he reeled it off. "If she asks how you got her number, feel free to tell her it came from me. One of my newbie detectives, Darrell Russell, has worked security in that branch for years."

"Thanks, Hank," I told him. "Appreciate it."

The moment our call ended, I dialed the number Hank had given me. I was relieved when a woman answered almost immediately. "Hello?"

"Is this Tracy Hamilton?"

"Yes, but who's this?"

"My name's J. P. Beaumont. I'm a private investigator from Seattle—"

"How did you get this number?"

"From a guy named Darrell Russell," I said. "I believe he's done security work for your bank branch."

"What's all this about?" Tracy wanted to know. Her tone was almost as icy as the panorama currently visible outside the picture windows of my "view" room.

"I'm working on behalf of a young woman named Danitza Adams Miller," I said. That was fudging things, but so be it. "I understand that earlier this fall—back in November—you notarized a power-of-attorney document for her father, Roger Adams from here in Homer. I believe he and his wife, Shelley, came into your bank branch to sign the document."

At worst I expected Tracy to hang up on me. At the very least, I thought she'd tell me to get lost. Instead she surprised me.

"Oh, my goodness," she said, "I remember them well. How is he? The poor man looked so ill at the time I saw them that I doubted he was long for this world."

"Roger's hanging in there," I said. "What can you tell me about that visit?"

"I remember they didn't have an appointment. They dropped by after visiting Mr. Adams's physician's office. I felt incredibly sorry for them both. Clearly Roger had just been given some kind of devastating diagnosis, and arranging for that power of attorney and having it in place was first on their list of getting things in order."

"You're certain they said they were coming from his doctor's office?"

"Absolutely. They mentioned the office complex, and it happens to be the same one where my doctor is located."

"Had you ever seen either one of them before?"

"No, but they have accounts with our branch in Homer, and that qualifies them as customers at every branch."

"In order to notarize their document, you had to verify that they were who they said they were, right?"

"Of course."

"How did you do that?" I asked.

"I'm pretty sure they both presented me with driver's licenses at the time. That's all that's required—some form of government-issued photo ID."

"Do you keep a copy of those?"

"Of course," she said. "I have it in my file. Why do you ask? Where is this going?"

It was time for me to drop the bomb. "I believe the man who came to your bank that day claiming to be Roger Adams was an impostor. I also believe that Shelley Adams is using that fraudulently obtained power of attorney to divest the real Mr. Adams of literally millions of dollars' worth of real estate."

The phone went silent for a moment.

"No!" Tracy said finally. "That can't be true."

"I'm afraid it is. I believe the fake ID for him they presented to you might well have been a professionally created one that looked legitimate enough to fool even a pro."

"If that's the case, it's dreadful," Tracy said, sounding shaken, "and I'm partially responsible."

I did my best to reassure her. "As I said, I'm working on Danitza's behalf and trying to keep her stepmother from robbing her father blind. It's not exactly elder abuse, because Roger Adams isn't that old, but I do believe that Shelley Adams is taking advantage of her husband's somewhat limited mental capabilities. I'm not a law-enforcement officer, but if what I suspect is true, I'll be turning my findings over to Anchorage PD at the earliest possible moment. Since it appears from the closing documents that offshore banks are involved, I suspect the FBI will be brought in as well."

"But do you have any proof?" Tracy asked.

"I don't," I admitted, "not in my possession at this time, but if you still have copies of that phony ID, I'm pretty sure you do. Hold on a minute. I'll text you a photo of Roger Adams taken from his law firm's Web site. Take a look and let me know if the Roger Adams pictured there is the same man who came to your office."

In the mountain of received messages from Todd Hatcher, it took a few seconds for me to locate the correct one. Once I found it, I copied it and pressed send. Moments later I heard the sound of an arriving text on Tracy's end of the line.

Tracy's response was instantaneous and pure gold. "Oh, my God!" she exclaimed. "That's not him at all! What should I do now, call the cops?"

"Where do you keep your notary files?"

"In a desk drawer at work. Why?"

"Can you get into your bank branch today?"

"Of course," she replied. "I'm the manager."

"If you could text me copies of Roger Adams's supposed driver's license, that would give me a better idea of who Shelley's co-conspirator might be. Once I know that, I'll have an idea of where to take this next."

"But what about contacting law enforcement?" she said. "Shouldn't that be done first?"

"I'm working with a Homer PD detective named Marvin Price. As soon as I have the information from you, I'll pass it along to him. Or, if you like, I can give you his information and you can forward what you have directly to him."

There was another moment of silence on the phone before Tracy Hamilton made up her mind. "It'll take me about forty-five minutes to get to the office, copy the photos, and send them to you. Will that be all right?"

Her offer was way more than all right, but I was afraid that a display of too much enthusiasm on my part would spook her.

"That would be incredibly helpful, Ms. Hamilton," I told her. "And I appreciate your help more than I can say."

Fifty-five minutes later a text announcement pinged my phone. I was still opening the text when the phone rang.

"Is it him?" Tracy asked.

In order to see the photo more clearly, I needed to enlarge it, so I opened the text again on my iPad. As soon as I did, I recognized the face, because I had seen the guy in the photo only the day before—the husband of Shelley Adams's cousin. She had referred to the guy as Dunk when she told me he did odd jobs for her, like keeping the wood boxes full and the vehicles running. From the photo I knew at once that his other task assignment was helping to cheat Roger Adams out of his hard-earned assets.

"No," I said after a moment. "This guy is most definitely not the real Roger Adams."

"Do you know who it is?"

"I've seen him, but don't really know him," I answered. "His first name is Duncan. I don't have a last name."

"So what should I do?" Tracy asked desperately. "Who should I call?"

"Please don't do anything or call anyone right now,"

I begged. "It's going to take law enforcement time to pull all these threads together and build a case. Based on the closing documents I've seen on Shelley's real-estate dealings, these people have more than enough cash on hand to flee the country. If they have any inkling that someone is onto them, I'm afraid they'll take off."

"I don't want them to get away with this," Tracy said, "so I should just keep quiet?"

"For the time being," I told her. "As soon as Lieutenant Price gives me the go-ahead, I'll be in touch. At that point you'll have my wholehearted permission to tell anyone you like. In fact, you can sing it to the high heavens as far as I'm concerned."

"All right," she agreed. "I'll wait to hear from you."

Chapter 27

There comes a time in every case when I realize I've finally made a breakthrough, and that phone call with Tracy Hamilton was it. Suddenly I knew exactly how Eliza Doolittle felt when she finally said that "rain in Spain" line correctly. That's when Professor Higgins jubilantly announces, "By George, she's got it!" Because right that minute, I knew we did.

Maybe what Marvin Price and I had didn't add up to enough on Shelley Adams to for sure link her to the disappearance and/or death of Christopher Danielson—or to the supposed suicide of her first husband either—but we had enough to put her away for a long time on fraud charges, and that was good enough for me.

But now if this was about to turn into a court case, I had to have all my ducks in a row. I went back through Todd's e-mails and scrubbed away anything that hadn't come from regular, open-to-the-public sources. I copied everything else into e-mails addressed to Marvin Price, which I stored in my waiting-to-be-sent file. I wanted to be able to talk about what was coming and let him know some of Todd Hatcher's background before I actually sent him the info.

About that time Mel called. She had just woken up, but she sounded weary beyond words—the kind of tired that comes from an overdose of despair rather than hard work. "How are you?" I asked.

"I've been better," she said.

My heart ached for her. I wanted to be there with her and tell her that it would be all right, even though it wasn't right and never would be, not with an orphaned four-month-old baby involved.

"Care to talk about it?" I asked.

Mel took a deep breath. "A shots-fired call came in about midnight from an apartment complex near campus."

Bellingham, Washington, is a college town and home to Western Washington University.

Mel continued. "Since Christmas break started

Friday afternoon, responding officers initially hoped it was just some of the kids left in town over the holidays letting off steam. Unfortunately, that wasn't the case. When my officers approached the apartment, the guy said he'd already shot his wife and would kill anyone who tried to enter."

"Doesn't sound like he was looking for a happy ending," I put in.

Mel didn't say anything aloud, but I guessed she was nodding in agreement.

"The watch commander called me as soon as he summoned the Emergency Response Team. By the time I got to the scene, officers had cleared the neighboring apartments. They had managed to establish communication with the guy, and our hostage negotiator was already talking to him. In the beginning Dave Willis, my negotiator, knew that the female victim was still alive because he could hear her moaning and pleading for help in the background. Dave could also hear a baby crying.

"Eventually the sounds from the wife gave out. She'd been shot three times and bled out on the living-room floor. At that point the strategy was to keep the shooter talking until he finally fell asleep. Unfortunately, he was high on something, and sleeping wasn't part of the program. Finally, this morning, just after five, the baby started crying again. When the shooter threatened to shut her up for good, that's when ERT made entry. Thank God the shooter turned the weapon on himself. He was pronounced dead at the scene."

That's the hard thing about being a cop—you can never unsee or unhear what you've seen and heard, and you can never unfeel what you've felt.

"Any idea what the shooter was high on?"

"Won't know for sure until the tox screen comes back, but he had a little bit of everything in that apartment—meth, ecstasy, crack, you name it."

"So he was both a dealer and a user?"

"Right," Mel muttered. "Selling drugs is a great way to support a growing family."

"What's going to happen to the baby?" I asked.

I heard the slight catch in Mel's throat before she answered. "Her name is Cara. Child Protective Services took her into foster care from the scene early this morning. That's where she is now—with a foster family, but her maternal grandparents are flying in from Hawaii late this afternoon. They're set to arrive at SeaTac around five. I've dispatched officers to meet them at the airport and bring them to Bellingham. I'll have some time with them privately once they're here. My understanding is they're willing to take custody of the baby, but that will all have to be sorted out with

CPS. In the meantime I just got out of the shower. I have a press conference coming up in about an hour. That's the only reason I crawled out of bed."

"What about the shooter's parents?" I asked. "Have they been notified?"

"They're both professors at the university. Unfortunately, they were at the scene this morning when it all went down."

In a university town, with professors and students involved, this would be a public-relations nightmare for Mel's department. I didn't envy her presence at the up-coming high-profile press conference or her having to deal with either set of grief-stricken parents. Even now I was working a case that had originated from eerily similar circumstances. Just as it hadn't been a walk in the park for me, this one wouldn't be for her either. But I also knew that Mel would be up to the task. By the time she faced the cameras and microphones, I expected she'd be wearing her dress uniform and appear to be in total control of her emotions. I wasn't too sure about her ability to maintain emotional control when it came to dealing with the two sets of parents.

"Let me know how it goes."

"I will," she said. "I just needed to hear your voice."

"Are you taking Sarah with you?" I asked.

"Nope," she said. "Much as I'd like to, I'm afraid

she's on her own this evening. With snow still on the ground, she may choose not to use the doggy door, but I'll deal with that when it happens."

We hung up then, and for a long time afterward I sat there as a slew of my own nightmare scenarios replayed themselves in my memory. In the old days, those were the kinds of traumatic events that would send me seeking solace in a bottle of booze. Even revisiting them secondhand, the temptation was still there. Fortunately for me, there wasn't an honor bar in my "view room," so I went looking for relief by brewing another cup of coffee.

There was nothing I wanted more right then than to be at home with Mel so I could hold her and comfort her in this time of need. But that wasn't an option. I was just swilling down the last of my coffee and wondering about starting another cup when the room's landline phone rang on my bedside table.

"Mr. Beaumont?" the caller said when I answered. "This is Michael from down at the desk. Your guest is here."

Marvin Price had arrived in the nick of time.

Chapter 28

When I entered the lobby, Marvin stood staring out the window, lost in thought. I tapped him on the shoulder to let him know I was there, and he started as though he'd been miles away.

"What's up?" I asked.

He shook his head. "Looking for ghosts, I guess," he said.

"How so?"

He glanced around the lobby. "The last time I was here was for my honeymoon," he explained. "Lisa and I were both eighteen, and she was three months pregnant. We got married by a judge with only our two sets of parents as witnesses. We were young and broke, and the best we could do for a honeymoon was to spend our wedding night here. Not surprisingly, the marriage didn't last. Lisa divorced me and moved to Seattle when my son was six."

Lars Jenssen, my stepgrandfather, emigrated from Norway when he was in his early twenties. When Jeremy, my son-in-law, first met Lars, he did his best to get to know the old guy. At one point I happened to enter the family room in time to overhear a conversation between the two of them.

"What did you do in the old country?" Jeremy had asked, making a stab at engaging Lars in conversation.

"In the summer we fuck and fish," was the curt reply.

For a moment Jeremy had been too stunned at hearing those completely unexpected words that he couldn't say a thing. "So what did you do in the winter?" he asked finally.

"Too cold to fish," Lars answered.

That was good old plainspoken Lars in a nutshell, and boy, do I miss him, but the look of shocked dismay on Jeremy's face at the time is something I'll never forget. Now, based on what I knew about Danitza Adams and Christopher Danielson's history and about Marvin Price's own shotgun wedding, it occurred to me that teenagers in Homer were still in much the same fix as those kids in Norway, with the emphasis most definitely on something other than fishing.

"Where's your son now?" I asked.

"He's a pilot in the air force, stationed at Nellis Air Force Base near Las Vegas. He doesn't speak to me—hasn't for years. He maintains everything that happened between Lisa and me is all my fault and considers me to be the devil incarnate."

When it comes to dealing with estranged offspring, I have more than a little experience. "Give him time," I said. "Maybe he'll come around. My kids all did eventually."

"Really?" Marvin asked hopefully.

"Really," I said. "Now, where are we going?"

"Just up the road apiece," Marvin said. "Red Bolger's place is right on the water."

Marvin's work car, an Interceptor, was parked outside. It was a big step up from Twink's Travelall. Along the way I told him about my conversation with Tracy Hamilton. It was good news, but not enough to pull Marvin out of his dark mood.

When we parked in the driveway at a house on a bluff overlooking the bay, I followed him around to the back of his vehicle and watched while he mixed up a concoction of Blue Star and water, which he poured into a spray bottle. According to experienced forensics folks, Blue Star does a better job of illuminating older bloodstains. With the bottle prepared and in hand, he passed me a flashlight-shaped instrument that I knew to be a Bluemaxx alternate light source that makes luminesced bloodstains visible. He also passed me a small video camera. Laden with the tools of the trade, we approached Red Bolger's front door, where he stood waiting.

In my experience guys who bear the nickname handle of "Red" usually start out in life with red hair. That might have been true in this case, too, but at this point in life Red Bolger was completely bald.

"Hey, Red," Marvin said. "Good to see you."

"Same to you, Marve," Red said. "Who's this?" He nodded in my direction.

I kept forgetting this was a small town.

"He's my associate, J. P. Beaumont."

"He a cop, too?" Red wanted to know.

"I'm a private investigator from Seattle," I told him. Since both my hands were full, I couldn't very well offer a handshake.

"Well, come on through," Red said. "What kind of crime do you think Nate's car might be mixed up in—a homicide?"

The question was addressed to Marvin, and I left him to answer it.

"Yup," he said. "An unsolved case from 2006."

"When Nate called, he told me Shelley Hollander might be mixed up in something. No surprise there.

I thought that gal was trouble from the time Jack first hooked up with her," Red said. "She's always been a looker, all right, but if some female looks too good to be true, she probably is."

The tangle of personal connections in town made me grateful I'd spent my entire career working in a large metropolitan area rather than in this kind of a fish-bowl, where literally everybody knew everyone else. And I was also struck by the fact that so many people still referred to Shelley by her maiden name as opposed to either of her married ones.

Red led us through the cluttered, dingy house—a living room, dining room, and kitchen—that hadn't seen a woman's touch in many a year. I didn't know if Red was divorced, widowed, or even a lifelong bachelor. No doubt Marvin could have told me, but it wasn't any of my business. As soon as Red stepped into the garage, the door opener's automatic lighting system came on, revealing two parked cars—a ten-year-old white Jeep Cherokee and an even older Subaru Forester. The ve-hicle was covered with a thick layer of dust with a hint of red paint visible beneath that.

"The key's under the floor mat," Red said. "Do you want me to disconnect it from the charger?"

"No need," Marvin said. "We won't have to start it."

"All right," he said, "but be prepared. After it's been

locked up for a while, the smell of bleach will knock your socks off."

Marvin and I both stopped short, but he was the one who spoke first. "Bleach?" he asked.

Red nodded. "Shelley told Nate that a friend of hers borrowed the car to go fishing and ended up spilling a bucket of fish bait in the luggage compartment. He tried to clean it up, but the smell of dead fish is tough as hell to get rid of."

So's blood, I thought.

I was afraid Red was going to hang around and dog our heels the whole time, but instead he turned and went back inside. Marvin handed me a small video camera. "You ever used one of these?"

"Once or twice," I said.

"You're on camera duty, then," he told me. "We need to start by time-dating this. Go ahead and start filming."

I would have preferred using the video option on my phone, but that's just me. Rules are rules. It took some fumbling around before I managed to get the damned camera up and running. Finally Marvin was able to begin the narration. "The time is four fifteen P.M., Sunday, December sixteenth, 2018. The location is 4041 Ocean Drive Loop, Homer, Alaska. Present is Lieutenant Marvin Price of the Homer PD investigations unit.

With me is a private investigator named J. P. Beaumont of Seattle, Washington. We're about to make entry into a vehicle belonging to Nathaniel Bucknell housed in a garage at the residence of Grover Bolger in Homer, Alaska. Both men have given their verbal consent for us to search this vehicle on suspicion that it might have been involved in a possible homicide."

Marvin paused for a moment and then nodded in my direction. "Okay," he added. "Here goes."

Saying that, he walked over to where the garage door's electrical cord was connected to an outlet. The moment he pulled the plug, we were plunged into total darkness. Marvin managed to stumble his way back to the rear of the Subaru, where he located the latch and punched the button.

Alternate light-source implements need total darkness in order to function. Had the vehicle's interior lights come on, we would have been screwed, but thankfully, due either to age or some missing connection, they didn't. By the time the tailgate swung open, my eyes had adjusted enough that I could just make out a dim image of Marvin's hand holding the spray bottle as it suddenly appeared in the camera's viewfinder.

At that point I was holding my breath, and Marvin probably was holding his, too. It felt a little bit like standing on a bouncing diving board for the first time and knowing you're about to plunge into the deep end. The moment Marvin hit the spray button, the carpet on the interior of that old Subaru lit up like a damned Christmas tree, and it sure as hell wasn't caused by fish blood!

"Holy crap!" I exclaimed aloud without meaning to. "She really did do it!"

In that instant I knew it, and Marvin knew it, but nobody else did, and it would take a whole lot more evidence to prove the case beyond a reasonable doubt.

Marvin immediately stopped spraying. If these bloodstains belonged to Chris Danielson, they were more than twelve years old, and we didn't want to do anything that would degrade them further in case there was a chance that a DNA profile could still be obtained from the sample.

"Due to the visible presence of a substantial amount of blood," Marvin continued for the benefit of the recording, "this vehicle will immediately be towed to the Homer PD impound lot for further processing. Video filming is ceasing at four twenty P.M."

I turned off the camera, Marvin plugged the garage door's electrical cord back into the wall outlet, and then he and I exchanged high fives. Harriet Raines had given me the gift of a weekend to conclude my own investigation. With Marvin Price's help, I'd done just that, but he and I both knew that we were a long way from being able to say case closed.

Not surprisingly, in the immediate aftermath I was shuttled off to the sidelines while Marvin summoned additional officers and proceeded to cross the necessary t's and dot the i's, a process I knew would most likely keep him occupied for the next several hours. After he'd called for a tow truck, Marvin's next order of business was a call to Nate Bucknell in Palm Desert. I could tell from Marvin's side of the conversation that Nate was dismayed to learn that in his absence his vehicle had just been declared a crime scene and was about to be impounded.

"I'm sorry," Marvin told him. "This is now an active homicide investigation, and I'm unable to give you any additional information at this time."

Meanwhile Red Bolger's neighbors were beginning to gather outside the house, gawking and wondering what was the cause of the sudden police presence milling about in this otherwise quiet section of Ocean Drive.

At five fifteen I was still stomping around in the snow and trying to keep warm when my phone rang.

"Where are you?" Twink demanded. "I'm here for our date, remember? I tried calling the hotel, but you're not in your room."

"I'm at a crime scene," I told her. "Where are you?"

"At AJ's," she replied, "where do you think? I called to see if you'd made a reservation, which of course you hadn't. By the time I called, the choices weren't great—either five thirty or eight thirty. I chose the former. Does this mean you're standing me up?"

"Not exactly, but the guy who gave me a ride here is a bit preoccupied at the moment. I don't know when I'll be able to get there."

"I have no intention of missing a good dinner because you can't hitch a ride, so how about if I come fetch you?"

"Sounds good," I said, giving her the address. "See you when you get here."

Chapter 29

Once we arrived, it seemed to me that for a Sunday night AJ's was surprisingly busy. I was grateful for the din of conversation around us, because as Twinkle Winkleman chowed down on my nickel, she was also full of questions.

"So what was going on back there on Ocean Drive?" she asked. "That guy's garage didn't look like any crime scene I've ever seen—no blood, no guts, no bullet holes. Is this somehow connected to your missing person?"

Fortunately, the bloodstains had been totally out of sight by the time Twink arrived, but at this point in our somewhat odd partnership, I decided to come clean and fill her in on the rest of the details about the murder of Chris Danielson and our belief that the Subaru in the garage on Ocean Drive had been used to transport his body.

"I'm guessing you used luminol to locate the blood-stains," she observed.

"Close," I told her. "Blue Star. It works better on older stains, and these are more than a dozen years old."

"Are arrests imminent?"

"Unfortunately, no. We've got a long way to go between here and there."

I hadn't told her everything, but it was enough to turn off the question spigot and get her to pay attention to her surf and turf—a rib-eye steak topped with king crab—rather than continue putting me through an interrogation meat grinder. Dinner was over, the server had cleared our plates, and Twink was studying the dessert options when my phone rang.

I had added Danitza Miller's name to my contacts list, so I knew who was calling before I even answered.

"What's up, Nitz?" I asked.

"It's Jimmy," she said breathlessly. "He ran away, and I don't know what to do."

"Slow down, slow down," I advised. "Tell me what's going on."

"Someone at the hospital was out sick today, so I worked an extra shift. When I came home, Jimmy wasn't there."

"How do you know he ran away?"

"He left a note. It said he's on his way to Homer."

"Homer," I echoed. "Why is he coming here?"

"To meet his grandfather," Danitza managed through a half sob. "Whenever he asked me about my parents, I always told him they were both dead, but he must have been eavesdropping the other night when you were here. That's how he learned my father's still alive."

"What exactly did the note say?"

"'How come you lied to me? Now that I know I have a grandfather, I'm going to go meet him.'"

My heart sank. "You mean he's headed for your father's house?"

"Evidently."

"Where are you?" I asked.

"Where do you think? I'm on my way to Homer, and I'm coming as fast as I can. I only just now thought to call you, but I'm still at least forty-five minutes out."

The last thing I wanted to happen was for Christopher James Danielson to show up at his grandfather's house, which was now or soon would be the epicenter of a homicide investigation. There was still a good chance that Roger Adams had been involved in Chris's homicide, although I was beginning to doubt that. On the other hand, I was convinced Shelley Adams was involved in that plot all the way up to her pretty little neck.

"Can you track Jimmy's phone?" I asked. "It might be possible for us to intercept him before he gets to the house. Does he even know where your father lives?"

"He left the phone on his bed along with the note," Nitz said. "But I checked the search history on his desktop. The last thing that came up was my father's address on Diamond Ridge Road."

"Okay," I told her. "I'll see what I can do to find him. In the meantime stay in touch. If you hear from him, call me right away."

"I will."

When the call ended, Twink was in the process of ordering the sticky pudding, that night's specialty dessert. "She'll take that to go," I told our server. "And we need the bill right away."

As we waited for the bill and dessert to arrive, I considered calling Marvin Price to alert him to the situation, but since he was probably still fully occupied with his newly confirmed but very old murder, I decided against it. He was a homicide cop, after all, not a juvenile-detention officer. When I came back to the present, Twink was sitting across the table, giving me the stink-eye.

"I've never liked to eat and run," she said. "What's up?"

"We need to go back to Diamond Ridge Road," I answered. "ASAP."

"Oh, we'll go there, all right," she said, "but not until you tell me what's really going on."

And just like that, Twinkle Winkleman had me over a barrel. "Okay," I conceded. "I'll tell you on the way."

I paid the bill, Twink collected her carry-out sticky bread pudding, and we made for the Travelall. Suddenly the abbreviated overview of the situation I'd given her earlier was no longer adequate. It was close to ten miles from the restaurant to the Adamses' place. Along the way I filled her in on much of the family's troubled history and on how an unsuspecting twelve-year-old hoping to meet his grandfather for the first time ever was about to blunder into the middle of a murder inquiry.

"You really think Shelley Hollander killed the boy's father?" Twink asked.

"In March of 2006 when Chris Danielson disappeared, the vehicle in that garage on Ocean View Drive—the one filled with human bloodstains—was registered to Shelley and Jack Loveday."

"My, oh, my," Twink muttered after a moment's thought. "So much for being a former Miss Alaska!"

When we arrived at the house, there were plenty of lights on, so I knew that someone was home. Twink stopped the Travelall, and I piled out. When I rang the doorbell, no one answered. I gave it thirty seconds or so, then hit the button again—this time really leaning on it. Eventually I heard footsteps inside. After that the porch light came on, the dead bolt clicked, and the door swung open. Standing before me was a fully dressed and very pissed-off Shelley Adams. Wearing a high-necked sweater, a pantsuit, and a pair of fashionable boots, she appeared to be dressed more for a night on the town rather than a long evening at home keeping watch over an ailing husband.

"You again!" she growled when she saw me. Tone of voice is everything, and hers indicated that she had zero intention of inviting me inside. "What are you doing here?"

"I need to speak to Roger."

"He's asleep," she said.

At six forty-five in the evening? I wondered. *Asleep or handcuffed to his bed?*

"Then wake him up," I told her. "I need to talk to him about his grandson."

"Roger doesn't have a grandson," Shelley said.

"Roger may not like the idea, but it turns out he does have a grandson," I asserted. "He's Danitza's twelve year-old-son. His name is Jimmy, and he ran away from home earlier today, supposedly to come here and meet his mother's father for the first time ever."

"Well, he's not here," Shelley declared, making as if to slam the door in my face. "We haven't seen him. Now, leave."

I had no intention of leaving. Liars lie, and I figured if Shelley Loveday Adams's lips were moving, that was the case now.

At that point Shelley did actually try to slam the door in my face. I had worked my way through college doing door-to-door sales for Fuller Brush. I may be among the last of that dying breed, but I still have the moves. Before she could close it all the way, I had the toe of my boot between it and the jamb. Once the door bounced back open, I brushed past Shelley and entered the house.

"Jimmy!" I called out. "Jimmy, are you here?"

"You can't come inside like this," Shelley hissed at me. "Get out or I'll call the cops."

"Maybe you should," I said. "When they show up, I'll let them know that they should probably do a welfare check on your husband. Several people have mentioned that you might be holding him here against his will."

Shelley's face contorted in fury. "I said get out."

"I'll go when I'm good and ready," I told her. "Jimmy!" I called again. "Are you here?"

Again there was no answer, making me hope that

Twink and I had made it to the house before the boy had.

"Shut the hell up or you'll wake him," Shelley snarled, and she wasn't talking about waking Jimmy. She was talking about Roger, and that's when I noticed the collection of luggage parked on the far side of the entryway. Shelley was dressed to go somewhere, all right, because she *was* going somewhere.

"Taking a trip?" I asked.

"None of your business," she snapped.

"Maybe I'm making it my business."

"If you really want to know, I'm going to Anchorage for a couple of days. Nadine and Dunk will be staying here to look after Roger."

"Going there to sell off a few more of his properties?" I asked innocently.

Of course, I shouldn't have goaded her. It's like one of those fight scenes on TV where one guy has the drop on another. Then the second guy says, "Go ahead and shoot me," and is surprised as all heck when that's what happens and he gets shot. But now that I was fairly sure Jimmy Danielson wasn't inside the residence, I was willing to take that risk. For one thing, I doubted she was armed. Shelley's tight-fitting clothing was designed for maximum effect in showing off her considerable assets, leaving little to the imagination and no room at all for a concealed weapon. Besides, maybe I could provoke her into saying or doing something stupid, because angry people tend to do stupid things.

Shelley was staring at me in absolute fury when the ping of an arriving text came in on my phone. Feigning indifference, I pulled the device out of my pocket and checked the screen. The text was from Twink:

Got your missing kid in the car. He's eating my dessert. Come when ready.

Bless Twink's heart! I barely managed to avoid heaving a sigh of relief. With Jimmy clearly out of danger, I decided to take another swipe at Shelley.

"Since Jimmy isn't here," I said, pocketing the phone, "just so you know, a lot of Roger's friends are beginning to ask questions about what's going on with him."

Shelley tried to keep her face expressionless, but it didn't quite work. Having dropped what I regarded as an appropriate exit line, I turned on my heel and beat it out the still-open door behind me. As the heavy oaken door slammed shut, I couldn't help but smile.

She'd heard me, all right. Shelley Hollander Loveday Adams was on notice now, because she'd heard me loud and clear.

Chapter 30

I was concerned about what I would find once I got to the Travelall. Would Jimmy be upset because he was being held captive by a strange woman? Would I find a kid who thought he was being kidnapped by people he didn't know? What I found instead was a calm middle-schooler sitting in the rear passenger seat, happily chowing down on Twink's generous serving of AJ's sticky pudding.

"I told him he couldn't go inside because his grandfather's ill," Twink explained. "He said he was hungry, so I gave him my dessert. Where to?" she added.

I thought about Shelley's luggage sitting packed and ready to go. Obviously she was headed out of town, and I wondered if my parting remarks might have accelerated her departure. If so, I wanted to have some idea where she was headed.

"Shelley may be leaving soon," I said to Twink. "Pull off the road somewhere out of sight but close enough for us to still be able to see the driveway. If she leaves the house, I want to know which direction she's going."

Then I turned around and studied our passenger. "Hello, Jimmy," I said. "Your mom's really worried about you."

"I don't care. If I'm not supposed to lie, she shouldn't either," he replied. "But she did. When we did an ancestry thing in social studies, we were supposed to write an essay about our grandparents. I don't know any of my grandparents. Mom said her mother died of cancer and that all my other grandparents died on accident, but it's not true. Why did she lie?"

It occurred to me that Nitz wasn't the only one who'd maintained that falsehood as the truth. So had Jimmy's beloved Aunt Penny and Uncle Wally. As for people dying "on accident"?

I had to grit my teeth at his use of that term. I suppose "on accident" has something to do with confusing "by accident" with the phrase "on purpose." My grandkids say that, too, and it drives me nuts. Maybe I'm turning into a grammar cop in my old age. In this case I let Jimmy's phraseology, go but I did take issue with his facts.

"Your dad's father, Richard, shot your grandmother, Sue, to death and then turned the weapon on himself. For the record, Sue Danielson was my partner at Seattle PD and one of the bravest women I've ever known. And it turns out you're wrong about having no grandparents, and not just Roger Adams. One of the reasons I came to Alaska this week is a woman named Annie Hinkle, your great-grandmother on your mother's side. She's still alive and living in Ohio. She has no idea you exist any more than you knew she did, but I'm sure she'd be thrilled beyond words to meet you. The same goes for your dad's brother, your Uncle Jared."

"I have an uncle?" Jimmy asked hopefully. "For real?"

"For real," I assured him. "But if your mother never told you any of this, how did you hear about what happened to your dad's parents?"

"How do you think?" Jimmy replied. "After you were there the other night and I heard you and Mom talking, I went online and looked stuff up."

"Including your grandfather's street address here on Diamond Ridge Road?"

Jimmy nodded. "I'm not stupid, you know."

The idea that this twelve-year-old kid could locate

information on the Internet that would elude far too many well-seasoned adults was downright alarming. In the meantime Twink had moved the Travelall from the Adamses' driveway to another one two doors up, where she pulled in, switched off the engine, and doused the lights.

"Is he really sick?" Jimmy asked as he used a plastic spoon to scrape the last morsels of sticky pudding out of the bowl and into his mouth. "My grandfather, I mean."

"Yes, he's really ill."

"Is he going to die before I get to meet him?"

"I don't know about that," I said, "but I do know this. You need to call your mom."

With that I turned on my phone and passed it to Jimmy.

"Do I have to?"

"Yes, you have to."

"She's going to be mad at me."

"I don't blame her a bit."

Jimmy was in the process of dialing when I heard Twink say under her breath, "We've got movement."

I looked out the driver's window in time to see a light-colored SUV, a rapidly moving Range Rover, go speeding past.

"She isn't headed for Anchorage," Twink muttered.

"Seward Highway is in the other direction. Do you want me to follow her?"

"Please," I said, "but not too close. I don't want her to spot us."

"I'm not stupid, you know," Twink said, mimicking Jimmy perfectly. Then she put the Travelall in gear and off we went.

I could hear Jimmy in the backseat tearfully pleading his case. "But I didn't hitchhike," he was saying. "Ty's older brother gave me a ride. I had him drop me off downtown, and I walked the rest of the way. I didn't want him to know exactly where I was going, but it took longer than I thought. That's why I just now got here."

There was more than a little irony in that. Years earlier Jimmy's mother had caught a ride to take her from Homer to Anchorage without her parents' knowledge or consent. Now Jimmy had done the same thing in reverse. It wasn't exactly karma, but it came close.

There was a long silence on Jimmy's end of the line while his mother gave him an earful, so I turned my attention to Twink. "Any idea where she's going?"

"If she's leaving town, probably the airport," was the reply.

"Are there commercial flights in and out of Homer?" I asked.

"Limited," Twink answered, "and not at this time of night."

"So why . . . ?"

And that's when I remembered something Chad Winkleman had said—he'd sold off all of Jack Loveday's aircraft—all but one. Shelley had been a bush pilot once, too, and she'd held back one of the planes for her own use. By morning she'd be on her way out of Anchorage, probably flying with a fake ID and headed somewhere far out of reach of U.S. extradition proceedings—a place where she'd be able to cash in on Roger's stolen monies at her leisure.

"The airport," I said. "Is that where Jack Loveday's flight school was located?"

"You've got that right," Twink replied. "And unless I miss my guess, she has that Piper of hers all gassed up and waiting."

If Shelley was on her way to the airport, so were Twink and I, but we couldn't very well go racing after a fleeing felon with a twelve-year-old innocent bystander doing a ride-along.

"Is the Driftwood on the way to the airport?"

"It could be."

I gave the problem some thought. If Shelley was planning on hiding out somewhere in the interior of Alaska, a BOLO would eventually turn up her vehicle.

But I know enough about airport issues to understand that even when using private aircraft, getting into and out of airports takes time. It seemed to me that pausing our tail long enough to unload Jimmy was worth the risk of possibly losing sight of our target.

I swung around and held out my hand. "Give me the phone," I said.

"But I'm not done—" Jimmy began.

"Give me the damn phone," I repeated, "but don't hang up. I need to talk to your mom."

After a moment's hesitation, Jimmy complied.

"Nitz," I said. "How close are you?"

"Probably fifteen minutes out. Why?"

"Do you know where the Driftwood Inn is?"

"Yes, of course."

"That's where I'm staying. My driver and I have an errand to run, and we need to drop Jimmy off. We'll let him out there and have him wait for you in the lobby."

"Wouldn't it be simpler if I just went to my dad's place to begin with?" Nitz asked. "I need to have it out with him sooner or later, and I could just as well get it over with."

"Trust me on this," I said. "Going to your father's place right now is not a good idea. We'll drop Jimmy at the hotel lobby and ask the desk clerk to keep an eye on him until you get there."

"But I'm so mad at him—" she began.

"Don't be," I advised. "I think he's a pretty squared-away kid, and you haven't been straight with him. If I'd just learned that the people I love had been lying to me my whole life, I think I'd be pissed off, too. So why don't you start by telling him the whole story?"

"All of it?"

"All of it," I said. "After all, it's his life, too."

Chapter 31

By the time the call with Nitz ended, I realized Twink was talking on her phone. "That's right, Fred," she was saying. "We'll pull up at the door and drop him off. His mom's on his way."

"Who's Fred?" I asked.

"The nighttime desk clerk," Twink answered. "Who do you think? He'll give the kid some hot chocolate and have him wait in the lobby.

With my phone still in hand, I tried dialing Marvin. The call went to voice mail just as we pulled up to the Driftwood Inn. Fred was standing outside waiting to take charge of Jimmy the moment he stepped out of the Travelall. Clearly Twink's boots-on-the-ground knowledge had saved the day.

"How far to the airport?" I asked as we peeled away from the hotel.

"Fifteen to twenty," Twink replied.

"Make that fifteen," I told her. "I'm going to try Lieutenant Price again. We need reinforcements."

I dialed his cell phone and was frustrated when once again my call went straight to voice mail. "It's Beau," I told him. "Call me. It's urgent."

Of course I knew what he was up against at that point. Once a homicide cop has been handed a case, that instantly becomes his whole priority. Everything else fades to insignificance. Nothing else matters. The problem was, I didn't like being on the wrong side of that otherwise completely understandable barrier.

"Do you think Shelley's armed?" Twink asked.

"She wasn't when I saw her at the house, but she might be now."

"What about you?"

"Twice over," I replied, meaning of course weapon and backup weapon. I didn't need to ask whether Twink was carrying. She'd already told me about the rifle under her seat and the Colt .45 in her glovebox.

"What I'm really missing right about now is a Kevlar vest," I added.

"Let's hope it doesn't come to that," she said. "Do you think Price will be able to arrest her?"

"I don't know about an arrest," I admitted. "Everything we have on Chris Danielson's possible homicide is circumstantial. There might be enough there to take her in for questioning. Right now the best we can hope for is wire fraud. We have actual evidence on that. With any luck that will be enough for them to issue an arrest warrant."

The phone rang just then with Marvin Price's name in the caller ID window. "Great minds," he said. "You were going to be my next call. For a change the AST is riding to the rescue instead of giving me grief. Harry Raines contacted Captain Blake Fordham earlier this afternoon and told him that the DNA profile from Jared Danielson has confirmed that the human remains previously known as Geoffrey 4/25/2008 have now been identified as belonging to Christopher Anthony Danielson."

I allowed myself a sigh of relief. Chris was dead, but at least he was found.

"Harry suggested that a good starting point would be to contact you or Homer PD," Marvin continued. "Between calling in Homer PD or a visiting private eye . . ."

"Never mind," I said impatiently. "I know the drill, get to the point."

"Once I told Fordham what we had, particularly the

blood evidence in the back of the Subaru, he was willing to go for a homicide arrest warrant. He's faxing it over, and I'm waiting to have it in hand before I head out to take Shelley Adams into custody."

"Sounds good," I said, "but you'd better get a move on. I have it on good authority that Shelley Adams is on her way out of Dodge. She's headed for the airport."

"Here in Homer?"

"Yes," I answered. "Her Piper's tied down there, and she's probably planning to fly herself out. We're en route there now."

"Who's we?" Marvin asked.

"My driver and I. Her name's Winkleman."

"Not Twink?" Marvin replied. "Really? Tell her I said hello. She gave me a lift from Anchorage to Homer once. I was bringing an escaped convict back to Alaska from Arkansas. When the plane finally landed, the only driver in Anchorage willing to go the distance from there to Homer was Twinkle Winkleman."

Clearly my traveling companion was every bit as much of an Alaskan legend as the late Jack Loveday had been. Marvin remembered Twink, and she probably remembered him, too.

"Marvin Price says hello," I told her, putting the phone on speaker.

"Right back at him," came the reply.

"So where are you?"

"About three miles out," Twink said, answering for both of us.

"And you're sure she's there?"

"Reasonably sure," I said. "Not one hundred percent, because we don't have eyes on her vehicle."

"One hundred percent or no, I'll dispatch units as soon as I'm off the phone here, and once I have the warrant in hand, I'll be on my way there, too."

The gods had been smiling on me when I lucked into Marvin Price. There are plenty of good guys in law enforcement, but there are also plenty of jerks. Lieutenant Price was definitely one in a million. For that matter, so was Harriet Raines.

Because Twink was who she was, when it came time to turn off the imaginatively named FAA Road, she bypassed the exit to the terminal and headed straight for the civil-aviation end of the airport where the fixed base operator handled fuel and flight issues.

"The FBO will be straight ahead," Twink informed me, gesturing. "The flight school is on the right. If she's got a plane based here, my guess is that's where it will be, near the hangar that Jack used for the flight school.

I've traveled aboard private aircraft enough that I know what it takes to navigate airport entry rules. In a post-9/11 world, security at airports, even small ones, is paramount. Everybody knows about security in airport terminals, but the same holds true in the world of civil aviation. Vehicles don't enter or exit airport properties without the drivers being properly identified, and all entrances and exits are controlled by locked and remotely operated electronic gates, usually installed in sturdy chain-link fences.

Twink was pulling up right outside the entrance to the FBO. "Just drop me here," I told her. "With any luck she's still inside handling paperwork."

I hit the ground running before the wheels came to a full stop. It was nighttime, and the building's doors were locked. I had to wait seemingly forever to be buzzed in.

"May I help you, sir?" the clerk behind the counter asked.

"I'm looking for Shelley Adams," I said, glancing around an otherwise empty room. The woman Shelley was nowhere in sight. Neither was her luggage.

"Ms. Adams came through here a few minutes ago," the clerk informed me. "She borrowed one of our luggage carts. She's probably on the taxiway by now."

"I need to catch her," I said. I started for the exit that led out to the landing strips. I hit the door full force, but it refused open, and I bounced off it like a Ping-Pong ball.

"Sir," the clerk said, sounding alarmed. "Please step

away from the door. You're not allowed out there without showing government-issued ID."

The fact that a cold-blooded killer was about to fly off into the wild blue yonder was of no concern to her. The clerk's job was to enforce the FAA's rules, and she was going to do so no matter what.

Shaking with frustration, I dug my wallet out of my pocket and extracted my driver's license. I stood there shifting impatiently from foot to foot while the clerk took her sweet time examining my license. Then she pulled out a form. "And what is the purpose of your visit?" she asked.

"I already told you," I barked "I need to speak to Shelley Adams!"

"Good luck with that." Her reply was accompanied by a syrupy smile as she handed back the license. "I think you've already missed her, but when you're ready to leave, you'll need to check in with me again."

"Right," I muttered.

As I stuffed the license back into my wallet, I couldn't help thinking about the car-rental agent in that old Steve Martin movie *Planes, Trains and Automobiles.* I could cheerfully have pulled a Twink and decked the woman on the spot. Instead I made for the door. Once again I had to wait for her to take her sweet time in pressing the button.

When the door opened, I dashed out into the night. The part of the airport where I was standing was reasonably well lit and mostly silent. But then, standing at attention and listening with all my might, I heard the distinct *put-put* of the engine on a light aircraft of some kind. Seconds later a set of landing lights appeared, as the plane in question rounded a hangar and taxied forward—toward me yes, but also toward the open runway.

I knew it had to be Shelley's Piper. Who else would be out here flying on a cold winter's night? I needed to stop her. I had to stop her, but how? And then, as if taking a page out of an action movie featuring some aging superhero, I set off at a dead run.

The Piper was moving straight ahead while I was approaching it at an angle. Weirdly enough, as I raced along, I remembered the sole remaining takeaway from my high-school geometry class: The hypotenuse is the longest side of a triangle, and that's what I was on—the hypotenuse. I was on foot and limping along to the best of my limited ability on that while Shelley was taxiing along on the straightaway. There was no chance on God's green earth I was going to catch her.

And that's when a pair of full-beam headlights lit up the tarmac in front of me. Off to the side, I heard the sound of a revving automobile engine, but I didn't dare look in that direction. Grateful for the additional illumination, I kept on running, but only for a step or two before a resounding crash split the night. At that point I had no choice but to stop and look.

I turned to my right just in time to see the Travelall come barreling through the locked security gate, with the snowplow throwing broken pieces of metal into the air as if they were nothing sturdier than a handful of Tinker Toys. I had no doubt that the ground around the ruined gate was now littered with the crumpled remains of signs bearing the messages EXIT ONLY and DO NOT ENTER. None of those had fazed Twinkle Winkleman. They hadn't even slowed her down.

Too stunned to move, I was still standing there thunderstruck when the speeding Travelall squealed to a stop beside me. Twink gestured wildly in my direction, and I got the message. Wrenching open the passenger door, I scrambled up and into the vehicle. I was barely inside when Twink jammed the gas pedal to the floor, pinning me against the seat back and slamming the still-open car door shut beside me. By the time I took another breath, we were hurtling toward the moving Piper.

Gasping for air, I panted, "What are you going to do?"

"Hide and watch," she told me, "but hang on to this."

With only one hand guiding the speeding Travelall, she dragged the 357 Magnum out from under her seat and handed it over. "You do know how to use one of these, don't you?" she asked.

"Yes, but—" I began.

"Well enough to shoot out one of her tires?" Twink demanded.

It had been a long time since I'd visited a shooting range with my Glock, to say nothing of doing so with a rifle. "Maybe," I allowed dubiously through gritted teeth.

"I'll try to pull up alongside her so you can get off a shot," she told me. "You'd best roll down that window." I was in the process of doing so when Twink groaned, "Crap. Not these guys!"

Instead of looking at the moving Piper, she was now staring into the rearview mirror. I turned and glanced over my shoulder. Behind us two maintenance men, both dressed in signature orange jumpsuits, were pounding after us, waving wildly at the Travelall, and, as it turned out, yelling, too. Through my now-open window, I could hear them frantically ordering us to stop, but we didn't. Twink, with her jaw set, jammed the Travelall's gas pedal to the floor, and off we went. We were blasting along now, but we were still traveling on that damned hypotenuse, and the Piper was headed in a straight beeline for the runway. We were never going to be able to come up alongside the aircraft in a position that would give me a clear shot at the tires. That wasn't going to happen.

Then, without a word of warning, Twink jerked the steering wheel hard to the left. I hadn't had time to fasten my seat belt when I'd jumped into the vehicle. Now the abrupt change in direction pitched me forward almost face-first into the windshield. By the time I got my new bearings, I saw that Shelley was still traveling on her straight line, but now so were we. After speeding across an expanse of ice-dotted tarmac, Twink jerked the wheel sharply to the right and then brought the Travelall to an abrupt halt at the edge of the runway directly in front of the Piper's nose.

We stopped, the Piper stopped, and there we sat, head to head, for a long tense moment. Our vehicle's glowing headlights gave us a clear view of Shelley Adams's anger-distorted face staring at us from behind the aircraft's windshield. I leaned out my window, took aim with the rifle. I fired off a single shot without coming anywhere close to the rubber on that critical front tire.

"Can't you do any better than that?" Twink demanded.

Just then the maintenance men caught up to us and

started pounding on the Travelall's side panels and windows. Shelley must have expected the orange men to carry the day. At that point she put the Piper in gear and nosed to the right as if preparing to go around us.

The problem is, neither Shelley nor the maintenance men were blessed with a full understanding of exactly who Twinkle Winkleman was. As the plane moved, so did the Travelall. By the time Shelley maneuvered the Piper around so it was once again facing the runway, we were right there, too, directly in front of the idling aircraft and blocking its path.

Years ago I had the opportunity to watch some sheep-dog trials at an outdoor event in Coeur d'Alene, Idaho, and that's exactly how Twink behaved that night, like one of those cagey sheepdogs. The trials were held in an open field, with those low-to-the-ground, black-and-white border collies darting this way and that, instantly cutting off any straying sheep and forcing them back to where they belonged. Each of Shelley's attempts to go around us was easily countered by Twink because, as it turns out, on the ground automobiles are far more maneuverable than aircraft.

I finally leaned out my open window again and yelled at the nearest orange man, "That woman's a sus-pected killer!" I shouted, pointing in Shelley's direction. "Cops are en route, but if we don't stop her now, she's going to get away."

Fortunately, the man got the message. "Okay," he called back. "Hold up a minute."

The Piper and the Travelall were once again stalled in a face-to-face standoff. Just then the two maintenance men charged past us. When they did, I noticed that each of them was carrying what I recognized to be a pair of aircraft chocks. It took them bare seconds to shove the chocks in place, leaving the Piper immobilized. As a chorus of sirens blared in the background, I knew right then that Shelley Loveday Adams was toast. Within a matter of minutes and after all these years, Christopher Danielson's murderer would finally be in police custody.

At that moment I was tempted to lean over and give Twinkle Winkleman a kiss out of sheer gratitude. It's probably a good thing I didn't. She was so wound up on adrenaline right then that if she'd punched me in the chops, she would have knocked me out cold.

Chapter 32

Once the squad cars arrived, I walked over to the plane while Twink remained with the Travelall. As the scene bustled with sworn officers, I was once again relegated to fifth-wheel status, just as I had been earlier in the day at Red Bolger's garage. That was only to be expected. I watched from the sidelines as Marvin Price led a handcuffed and obviously furious Shelley Adams out of the Piper, placed her in the back of his waiting Interceptor, and closed the car door behind her. Only then, for the first time since his arrival, did Marvin acknowledge my presence. He came over to where I was standing with his hand outstretched and a triumphant grin on his face.

"We got her, Beau," he said as we shook.

"Was she armed?" I asked.

"No, unless you consider the plane to be a deadly weapon."

With the ghosts of 9/11 still in our heads, we both knew that using an aircraft to murder innocent people was an all-too-real possibility.

"At least not this time," I replied.

"But without you and Ms. Winkleman here, there's a good chance Shelley would have gotten away clean. Where is Twink, by the way?"

"Over there," I said, nodding toward the Travelall. "The airport authorities are giving her hell big time about crashing through the gate."

"I'll leave Shelley to cool her heels for a while," Marvin said. "Let's go see if we can bail Twink out of hot water with the feds. They tend to take a very dim view of people busting their way onto airfields."

When we fought our way through the crowd of people encircling the Travelall, I spotted a truculent Twink, arms folded stubbornly across her chest, standing guard next to her beloved vehicle's left front fender, which had suffered some damage during its close encounter with the security gate. I surmised that the raised blade of the snowplow had tossed some of the flying debris in that direction. Knowing Twink, I wouldn't have been the least bit surprised to find she had a spare fender lashed to the Travelall's roof along with the rest of her vast collection of spare parts.

As we arrived on the scene, Twink was being berated by a towering, finger-pointing black man who turned out to be the airport manager—a guy by the name of Conrad Jones. Homer being Homer, Marvin and Conrad were on a first-name basis.

"Hey, Connie," Marvin said, edging his way between them. "Don't be giving her so much grief. Responding units were on their way, but if Ms. Winkleman here hadn't acted in a timely fashion, our homicide suspect would have made good on her getaway."

Mr. Jones was not mollified. "That damned snowplow not only wrecked my gate, it yanked two of the posts completely out of the ground, and it's going to cost a good five thousand bucks to fix it."

"And you know that because," Marvin observed, "unless I'm sadly mistaken, a city-operated snowplow took out that very same gate sometime last year. I understand that you'll have to deal with all kinds of paperwork. I'm sorry about that, but for right now how about if I have my guys help your guys set up a temporary barrier? Then we'll need to haul that Piper out of the weather into an empty hangar so it can be impounded and processed for evidence."

"What about her?" Conrad wanted to know, sending a glower in Twink's direction.

"Believe me," Marvin assured him, "I'll have all her information available should it be needed."

"Okay," Conrad grumbled, "but she hasn't heard the last of this."

As the airport manager and Marvin walked away to deal with the barrier issue, my cell phone rang in my pocket. A glance at caller ID told me Nitz was on the phone.

"Danitza?" I asked.

"No, it's me, Mr. Beaumont—Jimmy," was the reply. "Mom's busy with the EMTs right now. She asked me to call you."

"The EMTs!" I yelped in alarm. "What's happened? Did your mom have an accident on her way to the hotel?"

"No," Jimmy answered, "she's fine. We're at her dad's place. The EMTs are working on him right now. When we got here and found him, he was un . . . un. . . ."

"Unresponsive?" I supplied.

I had been too preoccupied with everything else to call for a welfare check on Roger Adams, but clearly someone else had done so.

"Yes, that's what he said," a shaken Jimmy agreed,

"unresponsive. As soon as we got inside the house and found him like that, Mom called 911. They'll probably take him to the hospital. She wanted you to know what's going on."

I felt a sudden surge of anger. Shelley Adams had struck again—or at least she had tried to—on her way out of town.

"Okay," I said, "I'll come to the house as soon as I can, but there's a bit of a hang-up on this end. If you wind up heading for the hospital before we arrive, call back and let me know."

"Okay," Jimmy murmured. "Will do." He terminated the call.

The crowd around the Travelall had melted away along with Marvin Price and Conrad Jones, leaving just Twink and me. She was bent over, examining the damaged fender. She was also smoking a cigarette. What a surprise!

"Is it drivable?" I asked.

"It will be," she said determinedly, "as soon as I hammer out the fender so it isn't catching on the tire. Why, are you in some kind of hurry?"

I allowed as how I was. I told her about Jimmy's call and said that I needed to get back to Diamond Ridge Road in one hell of a hurry. "I could probably ask one of Marvin's patrol officers to give me a lift."

"Hold your horses," Twink growled at me. "Just give me a minute. I'll have Maude here back in shape in no time."

Marvin must have managed to work some kind of magic. By all rights the Travelall should have been impounded.

Twink had come to AJ's wearing what passed as dress-up attire for her—a plaid western shirt, jeans, and a pair of cowboy boots. Within moments she had donned the gray coveralls she retrieved from the backseat and had ditched the cowboy boots for what I assumed to be a second pair of insulated work boots—probably stored in one of the boxes in the rooftop luggage rack

After wrestling her toolbox down to the ground, she opened the lid and extracted both a metal rod and a wooden mallet. She took those with her as she scrambled under the vehicle's front end. For the next minute or two, a series of thumps—wood on metal—filled the air before Twink emerged once more.

"All good," she announced before returning the rod and mallet to the toolbox and the toolbox to its designated place on the roof. "Now, do you want me to drive you like this or ditch the coveralls?"

It was dark, and as much of a hurry as I was in, she could have driven me stark naked for all I cared. "You're fine," I told her.

Thanks to the snowplow's having done the heavy lifting, the trusty engine was damage-free, and it roared to life as soon as Twink turned the key in the ignition. When she put the vehicle in gear and we began to move, the ride was smooth as silk, with zero thumping or bumping. Obviously Twink's two-minute hammer-and-tongs repair job had filled the bill.

"So what's the deal?" she asked after we cleared the wrecked gate and were speeding along.

"Jimmy called from Roger's house," I told her. "He and his mom went there and found Roger unresponsive."

"So are we going to the house or to the hospital?" she asked. "The hospital's a lot closer."

I called Nitz's number, and Jimmy answered.

"Hullo."

"It's Mr. Beaumont," I said. "Where are you?"

"We just now got to the ER," he said. "Mom went inside with the EMTs. She said I have to wait in the lobby."

"We're on our way, Jimmy," I said. "Stay put."

I ended the call. "The hospital," I told Twink.

"Figured as much," she replied. "We'll be there in less than five."

Which meant I had less than five minutes to prepare whatever I was going to say to a twelve-year-old kid who'd spent his whole life being lied to by all the people he loved—by his mother, his Aunt Penny, and his Uncle Wally. Everything real he'd been able to learn about his background was information Jimmy had gleaned on his own from the Internet.

Twink dumped me out at the entrance to the ER. "Call when you're ready to go," she said. "I'll be in the visitors' parking area out front."

After exiting the car, I stood for a moment gathering myself before approaching the door and recalling those unyielding words—the truth, the whole truth, and nothing but the truth, so help me God. On the other hand, how much truth could a twelve-year-old take? Struggling to find middle ground between the two, I squared my shoulders to walk into the hospital and face down Sue Danielson's grandson.

Chapter 33

When I entered the hospital lobby, there were three groups of concerned family members huddled around the room worrying about their own ailing or injured. Jimmy Danielson sat in desolate isolation in the far corner, staring down at his feet. He didn't glance up when the entryway doors slid open behind me.

"How's it going?" I asked as I approached.

He looked up at me briefly, shook his head, and then dropped his gaze.

I sat down beside him. "Have you heard anything?"

Jimmy shook his head again and said nothing. So far this was turning out to be a very one-sided conversation.

"Did they say anything about his condition?"

"They're pumping his stomach. Will that work?"

"Let's hope," I said, "but it's hard to tell. It's probably a good thing you and your mom went to the house when you did instead of waiting for us to get back to the hotel. By then it might have been too late."

"Did they catch her?" Jimmy asked. "His wife, I mean?"

I wasn't sure how much Jimmy had overheard as Twink drove us to the Driftwood Inn, but obviously he'd been paying attention.

"Yes," I answered. "She's been taken into custody."

"Good," he said. Then, after a pause, he added, "Mom's father was handcuffed to the bed when we found him. Mom said his wife was trying to kill him."

I nodded. "I believe your mother is right. That's exactly what Shelley Adams intended."

At that point Jimmy seemed to be talked out. In the moments of silence that followed, I thought about the house on Diamond Ridge Road. It had looked more like a log-walled fortress than a house. I remembered the heavy oaken door, to say nothing of the dead bolt.

"Was the door locked?" I asked.

He nodded.

"How'd you get inside?" I asked.

"Through the window in what used to be my mom's bedroom," Jimmy answered. "There's a big tree next to the house. We climbed that, and then she used a tool from the car—a putty knife—to jimmy the window. When she said that, I thought she was making fun of me."

"No," I told him. "That's what it's called—jimmying. It's when you get into a locked house through a window by messing with the lock rather than breaking the glass."

"Anyway, that's how we got in. Mom climbed in first, and then she helped me. She said that's how she used to sneak in and out of the house when she was a girl."

"Have you ever snuck in and out of a house like that?" I asked.

In reply Jimmy ducked his head and shrugged his shoulders. In other words, asked and answered.

"If that's how you and your mother got in, how about the EMTs? Was she able to find the dead-bolt key?"

Jimmy shook his head. "Mom remembered the door code on the garage because it was her mom's birthday. We were able to let the medics into the garage, but they had to break down the kitchen door to get into the house."

The old code was probably Roger's doing. Had Shelley known about that, she would have changed it.

Jimmy paused for a moment before continuing. "Anyway," he said, "we found Mom's father in one of the bedrooms. He was asleep with one arm handcuffed to the frame of the bed. Mom tried to wake him up but couldn't. She tried to call 911 from the bedside table, but the phone didn't work. It had been unplugged. We had to plug it back in."

That made sense. Even if Roger Adams had tried to call for help, he wouldn't have been able to.

The boy shivered, and not from the cold either. "Why would anyone do that, Mr. Beaumont?" he asked.

Because they're evil, I thought. "Greed," I answered aloud. "We've uncovered evidence that Shelley Adams has been using fake IDs to sell off your grandfather's properties without his knowledge or consent."

"She's been stealing from him, too?"

I nodded.

"Will she go to prison?"

"Ultimately that decision will be up to a judge and jury, but when she goes on trial, it won't be just for what she did or tried to do to Roger Adams."

That was the moment when I came to the fork in the road, when I could have wigged out on doing the hard part and left the remainder of the telling to Jimmy's mother. Instead I forged on.

"There's a whole lot more to the Shelley Adams story," I said.

"Like what?"

"Like your father," I answered.

"What do you mean?"

"You know that your parents were very young when they fell in love."

Jimmy nodded. "She told me her parents didn't approve of him—like they thought he was some kind of juvenile delinquent."

"And they were worried about her having a baby when she was still little more than a child herself."

"Me?" he asked.

"You," I agreed. "But your mother wanted to keep you. That's why she ran away and went to live in Anchorage with Aunt Penny and Uncle Wally."

"But what happened to my father?" Jimmy insisted. "Mom said he just left, went home to Ohio, and never came back."

I was relieved to hear that at least the boy knew that much—the broad outline of the story if not all the gory details. In reality it was as much as anyone in official-dom had known until today, until the moment Gretchen Walther had forwarded Jared Danielson's DNA profile to Harriet Raines. Now it was time to do Chris's next-of-kin notification. I'd never done one of those with a twelve-year-old survivor, but I had traveled too far down this path to back off now. Jimmy Danielson was

Christopher Danielson's son—and he had a right to be told.

"Your father never made it to Ohio," I said quietly.

Jimmy gave me a wide-eyed, disbelieving look. "He didn't?"

Obviously that was the story Jimmy had always been told. No doubt he'd believed it, most likely because the person who'd told him that tale had believed it, too.

I took a deep breath before continuing. "We now believe that on or about the twenty-seventh of March, 2006, Christopher Danielson was murdered, most likely by Shelley Adams."

Jimmy seemed taken aback. "You mean the same woman who just tried to murder my grandfather?"

I nodded.

"But why?"

"She wasn't your grandfather's wife back then, but the two of them were very close," I answered. "My understanding is that your grandfather's plan was to pay Chris a sum of money in order to get him to go away and leave your mother alone."

"Like a bribe you mean?"

"Exactly," I agreed, "and Shelley was the one who was supposed to deliver the money. Instead we believe she murdered Chris and kept the money for herself."

"How did he die?"

"Of blunt-force trauma," I answered. "Do you know what that means?"

Jimmy nodded. "I've seen it on TV. It means someone bashed him over the head, but where's he been all this time? And why didn't we know about it?"

"Your father's skeletal remains were located in a bear den near Eklutna Lake two years after he disappeared, but they remained unidentified until today, when DNA from those remains were matched to Chris's brother, your Uncle Jared."

I watched Jimmy's face as his eyes flooded with tears. "So my father's really dead, then? He's never coming back?"

"Not ever. I'm sorry."

Jimmy, sobbing brokenly, leaned over and rested his head on my shoulder. "Mom always hoped he'd come back someday," the boy managed through his tears. "I did, too."

Jimmy had at least had that myth to cling to—that someday his father would return. Now he no longer had even that.

As one fatherless child to another, I knew exactly how he felt.

Chapter 34

There's a reason hospital lobbies and waiting rooms are stocked with unending supplies of tissues. When Jimmy finally started to settle down, I passed him a handful of those. He wiped his face and blew his nose.

"Do you know what happened to my dad?" Jimmy asked at last.

I sighed. He was just a kid, but still he wanted to know the whole story.

"Your father was working in a restaurant at the time, something called Zig's Place. It's still in business here in Homer. That evening when he was about to get off work, a woman asked him to come help her change a tire."

"Was it Shelley?" he asked.

I nodded. "That's what we believe."

"Did anyone else see her besides him?"

"No, but when he left the restaurant a few minutes later, that's the last time he was seen alive."

"How come you finally figured it out today?"

"We had to connect a bunch of dots," I answered. "That's what homicide detectives do—assemble all the pieces of the puzzle and then put them together. When your uncle first consulted me about your dad, we had no idea he was dead. First I contacted the authorities here in Alaska and discovered that a set of unidentified human remains, the remains of someone who'd died of homicidal violence, had been found near Eklutna Lake in 2008. That's when I asked your Uncle Jared to provide a DNA sample. Next we had to assemble a timeline for when your father disappeared. That's when I learned about the unidentified lady who asked him for help changing a tire. In the process we learned about the sum of money—ten thousand dollars—Roger Adams was prepared to pay Chris to leave town."

Jimmy was clearly impressed. "Ten thousand dollars?" he asked. "That's a lot of money. Is my grandfather rich?"

"Maybe, maybe not," I replied. "At that point I really thought that if your father was deceased, Roger Adams had something to do with it. But then we found out about the money. At the time Shelley was living with her previous husband, Jack Loveday, in what she regarded as straitened circumstances."

"What does that s-word mean?"

"Straitened? It means that she didn't have much spending money. But then, a couple of weeks later in early April, just days after your father disappeared, she took a very expensive weekend trip to Vegas."

"On the money she was supposed to give my dad?"

"I believe so."

"If she'd given the money to him like she was supposed to, do you think my father really would have left?"

I didn't have to give my reply to that even a moment of consideration. "No," I answered at once. "I think he really cared about your mom, and he cared about you, too. Money or not, I don't believe that Christopher Danielson would have left town and not taken both of you with him."

"But if you know now that Shelley did it, how did you figure it out?"

"I've been working with a police detective here in Homer, a guy named Lieutenant Marvin Price. When we heard about the woman asking for help with that supposedly flat tire, we realized that whatever occurred must have happened somewhere near the restaurant. If he was murdered here in town, that meant his killer would have needed to move the body fast, before any witnesses spotted it. By then we had Shelley in our sights. Lieutenant Price ran a check on all vehicles belonging to Jack and Shelley Loveday in 2006. This afternoon we used luminol to examine one of those vehicles."

"Luminol," Jimmy repeated. "Isn't that the stuff that lights up when it touches blood?"

I suppose Jimmy had seen instances of that on TV as well.

"It is," I said, "and that's what we found in that old Subaru of hers—bloodstains."

Way too much, I thought. *More than someone could lose and still survive.* The amount of blood we'd seen in the luggage compartment indicated to me that Chris had most likely still been alive at the time he was loaded into the vehicle. That wasn't an ugly detail I needed to share with either the boy or his mother.

After that, Jimmy fell silent for a very long time. Finally he gave a heartfelt sigh. "If you think Shelley did it, will you be able to prove it?"

"I don't know," I said. "It's primarily a circumstantial case. That means a case without a lot of physical evidence, but I'm hoping we'll be able to convince a judge and jury that she's the culprit."

"Good," Jimmy pronounced. "She deserves to go to prison for that, but what about my mom? Have you told her about any of this—her or my Uncle Jared?"

"Not yet," I said. "I should have, but I've been a little busy."

"When you tell my uncle, do you think he'll come here—to Alaska, I mean?"

"I wouldn't be surprised," I said, "especially if I called him and told him you asked for him to come."

"Would I be able to meet him?"

"I can't imagine that you wouldn't," I replied. "He only recently found out that you exist."

At that moment Nitz entered the lobby. When she saw me, she smiled gratefully. "Thank you for being here with him," she said.

"How's Roger?" I asked.

She shook her head. "It was a near thing. He's on a ventilator in the ICU. We'll have to wait and see."

I could tell from the concerned expression on her face that the professional nurse in Danitza Miller had some-how replaced the aggrieved daughter. Roger Adams was no longer her estranged father. He was her patient, and Nitz was going to fight for him tooth and nail.

At that point, however, she focused on the face of her son. "You look like you've been crying, Jimmy. Are you all right?"

The boy shook his head as his tears returned. "I'm not all right," he blurted, racing into his mother's arms and holding her tight. "Mr. Beaumont just told me about my dad. He says my father is dead. He thinks that woman named Shelley murdered him!"

A bewildered, slack-jawed Nitz gazed wonderingly at her son and then stared openly at me. "Is that true?" she whispered. "Chris is really gone?"

It wasn't at all the way next-of-kin notifications are supposed to go, but the deed was done.

"I'm afraid so," I murmured. "So sorry for your loss."

The next thing I knew, all three of us were standing there in the ER lobby, holding each other in a group embrace, crying like babies. It was the right thing to do. Chris Danielson had been dead for twelve long years. It was high time someone grieved for him properly.

We were still in that huddle when someone tapped me on the shoulder. I loosened my grip on Nitz and Jimmy and turned to find Twinkle Winkleman, still in her grimy coveralls, standing there peering up at me.

"Sorry to interrupt," she said.

"It's okay," I muttered, brushing away my own tears. "What's up?"

"I just had a call from the FBI office in Anchorage. The resident agent in charge is requesting that I turn up there tomorrow morning to discuss my security breach at the Homer Municipal Airport. I'd like to drive there tonight rather than in the morning. It'll still be dark, but there'll be less traffic now than on a Monday morning."

It occurred to me, as someone from Seattle, that what Twink regarded as traffic was far different from my version.

"I'm sorry I got you into so much hot water," I apologized.

"You?" she said. "I didn't see your hands on the steering wheel when I crashed through that gate. In fact, you weren't even in the vehicle. That's all on me, and I'm prepared to suffer the consequences. If some candy-ass agent tries to give me too much trouble, I'll tell him to put it where the sun don't shine."

"Or her," I suggested. "I believe you're the one who told me women can do anything they want."

Twink actually grinned at me then. "Roger that," she said. "But here's the deal. I'm still on your payroll. Do you want me to drive you back to the hotel before I head out, or should I leave you here?"

"You go on back to Anchorage," I told her. "Someone here will give me a lift to the hotel, and one way or another I'll make it back to Anchorage, too."

"Okay, then," Twink replied. "I still have your credit card on file. Is it okay if I charge it?"

"Charge away," I said, "but only after you're safely home in Anchorage."

"Will do." Twink held out her hand. "Driving you around has been interesting," she added as we shook. "More fun than I've had in a long time." Halfway to the door, she paused and turned back. "There's a Hertz outlet back at the airport, but you should probably have someone else take you there." With that she was gone.

"That was Twink?" Nitz asked as the sliding glass doors closed behind her. "Shouldn't I go thank her for rescuing Jimmy?"

"No need," I said. "I'm pretty sure she enjoyed every minute of it."

"But what's this about an airport security breach?"

"It's a long story, and one of the things I need to talk to you about, but probably not here," I said, glancing around the lobby, where at that very moment everyone in the room seemed to be watching all of us with undisguised interest.

"I just came out to get Jimmy," Nitz said. "There's a separate ICU waiting room. It'll probably be a bit more private there."

"Good," I said. "Privacy is exactly what's needed."

Chapter 35

The ICU waiting room was smaller than the ER lobby, and because there were no sliding glass doors leading to the outside, it was warmer, too. After his long day, Jimmy was done for. When Nitz disappeared into one of the patient rooms, Jimmy curled up on a love seat. Using his arms for a pillow, he was soon fast asleep.

I took advantage of those few moments of privacy to call Mel. "Are you home?" I asked.

"Just kicked off my shoes, lit the fire, and poured myself a glass of wine," she answered. "The snow is finally starting to melt around here, and you'll be happy to know Sarah was a good girl and let herself out through the doggy door as needed."

I decided to accept that as positive news and not ask if Mel had checked for deposits on the front porch. If they were there, they'd still be waiting for me when I got home.

"How was it?" Asking that unnecessary question was a lot like asking someone who's just lost a spouse, *How're you doing?* I already knew it had been bad. I just didn't know how bad.

"Heartbreaking," Mel said, and I heard the depth of weariness in her voice. "I spent the day with two separate but equally devastated families. Paul's parents knew their son was troubled but had no idea about his drug use. They believed Amy was the best thing that ever happened to him and that she and baby Cara were the answer to their prayers. Amy was an only child. Her parents are beyond devastated, but they're determined to take the baby back home to Hawaii. They may be in for a fight on that score. I'm not sure if taking the child out of state will fly with either Child Protective Services or with the shooter's parents."

"Wait," I said, suddenly irate. "You mean CPS would rather keep the baby in foster care than send her home with her grandparents?"

"Come on," Mel said. "You and I both know that bureaucracies aren't smart on that score."

She was right about that, because we had seen it

firsthand. Alan Dale, my granddaughter Athena's other grandfather, had battled for months before being granted permission to take the child back home to Texas.

"I hope they have a good lawyer."

Mel actually laughed. "Believe me, they do," she said. "I already gave them some suggestions about that. But the good news for me is that an autopsy has confirmed that the shooter took his own life, so at least I don't have the added complication of an officer-involved shooting. What's happening on your end, and where are you?"

"In the waiting room for the ICU at the hospital in Homer." After that I gave her a brief overview of everything that had happened, and I'd gotten as far as Shelley Adams's being taken into custody at the airport when Nitz emerged from her father's room.

"Sorry, Mel," I said. "I have to go. I'll talk to you again in the morning."

Nitz glanced at her sleeping son then went back to the nurses' station and returned with a blanket. After covering Jimmy, she came over to the chair next to me and sank into it.

"How's your dad?" I asked.

She bit her lip and shook her head. "He's nothing but skin and bones," Nitz murmured. "It looks like Shelley's been starving him to death."

"That's how it looked to me, too," I agreed.

The word "alleged" was notably missing from the conversation. In my mind Shelley had already been tried and convicted.

"When Helen Sinclair tried to warn me that something was wrong," Nitz continued, "I should have listened, but I didn't. I was still harboring a grudge, and now . . ." The remainder of that sentence went unfinished.

I started to tell her she shouldn't blame herself, but knowing she would anyway, I didn't waste my breath.

"Do the doctors have any idea about what she used?"

"They're analyzing his stomach contents and checking his blood work, too. My best guess would be that she gave him an overdose of something, we're not sure what, although how she could lay hands on illegal drugs, I don't know."

All she'd have to do is place a call to her friendly neighborhood drug dealer, I thought. *The same guy who works as her supposed handyman.*

"At least he's off the ventilator," Nitz continued. "And I can't thank you enough. If you and that Twink woman hadn't gone to the house looking for Jimmy, my father would be dead by now and maybe Jimmy would be, too. I don't even want to think about what might have happened if you hadn't been there."

I had to agree. We'd all been lucky on that score.

"So tell me about Chris," she said. "How did you find out he was dead, and who killed him?"

That was a very long story, and as I launched off into telling it, I realized that the next person I'd need to call was Father Jared Danielson. When I finished relating all of it, Nitz was aghast.

"So you don't think my father had anything to do with killing Chris?" she asked.

I shook my head. "I doubt it," I said. "I think that was all on Shelley. Your father thought the best way to get rid of Chris was to buy him off with ten thousand bucks. I suspect there might have been something going on at the house that night that caused him to delegate Shelley to deliver the money. Right then, though, she was strapped for funds. She saw all that money and couldn't bear to simply let it pass through her hands."

Boom! Just like that, as the word came out of my mind, I made a critical connection between what had happened at the airport and what must have occurred on that cold March night in 2006. Shelley Loveday hadn't driven home with Chris's body in the back of her Subaru—not at all. Instead she'd driven him to the airport! I had no idea how she'd managed to transfer the body from the Subaru into the plane, but that had to be how she'd transported it from Homer to Eklutna

Lake—by plane. Once the body had been loaded onto the aircraft, there would have been no reason for her to fly him out of town that snowy night. She would have waited for better weather. Then, at a more convenient time, she could have dropped the body off at or near where it had been found, landing on and taking off from the lake's iced-over surface.

"If Shelley killed Chris," Nitz was saying, "what about her husband? Was he in on it, too? Aunt Penny told me Jack Loveday committed suicide."

It took a moment for me to change gears. "I doubt that Jack had any idea about what was going on. As for his committing suicide? That's the general consensus, and it's what the M.E. put on his death certificate, but several of the people I've spoken to over the past few days think that's so much bunk, and I tend to agree with them.

"At the time of Jack's death, he was at home recuperating from having his legs amputated after a plane crash, with Shelley supposedly looking after him, but I'm wondering about that. What if she was looking after him the same way she's been looking after your father? The M.E.'s conclusion about Jack's death was that he committed suicide by mixing too much alcohol with his prescribed meds. I've been told that his drink of choice was always tequila—as in straight shots of tequila. After tonight it's not out of the question to think she might have added some of some extra meds to his usual evening nightcap, and he would have gulped them down without even tasting them."

Nitz fell silent for a moment before concluding, "She really is evil, isn't she?"

"Most definitely," I agreed.

"Will she be convicted?"

"In connection with Jack's death? Probably not, but with Chris's you'd better believe Lieutenant Marvin Price of the Homer Police Department is doing everything in his power to make that happen. And speaking of Marvin, I should probably call him and see if he'll give me a lift back to the hotel. It's a little farther than I care to walk."

"After all you've done for us today, I'll be glad to take you," she said.

"What about Jimmy?"

"I'll have to wake him."

"Are you planning on spending the night here?"

Nitz nodded. "There's a foldout visitor's chair in my dad's room."

"Why don't you leave Jimmy with me, then?" I asked. "I have it on good authority that there's a pullout sofa in my room at the Driftwood Inn. That's bound to be more comfortable than sleeping on a love seat in a hospital waiting room. He can stay with me and sleep in a real bed. And I'll be sure to feed him breakfast before I bring him back to you tomorrow morning."

"You're sure you don't mind?"

"Not at all," I told her. "As far as I'm concerned, nothing's too good for Sue Danielson's grandson."

I don't think Jimmy was even aware of being walked out of the hospital and loaded into his mother's SUV. On the way to the hotel, with Jimmy sacked out in the backseat, Nitz asked a difficult question.

"What about a funeral?" she asked.

"It can't happen until Professor Raines releases the remains," I answered.

"What should I do about that? I mean, I'm not really his next of kin."

"I think I should put you and Chris's brother Jared in touch so you can work it out," I said. "Why don't I give him your number so the two of you can discuss it?"

"Okay," she said. A moment later she added, "Should I see him?"

"See Jared?" I asked.

"No, Chris. Should I ask to see his body?"

When I had told the story, I'd stuck to the words "human remains" for a reason. I imagined that she envisioned a human skeleton neatly laid out in an understandable fashion. I'm sure Nitz had no idea that all that existed of the first love of her life was a glued-together partial skull. I wanted to shout to the heavens, *For God's sake no, don't do that!* In this case I went for understated elegance.

"I would strongly advise against it," I said. "You're better off remembering Chris as he was rather than the way he is now."

"All right," she said.

I hoped she meant it rather than simply saying the words she knew would shut me up.

"And about that funeral," I added. "Once you and Jared decide on a mortuary, put me in touch with them. I'll be happy to handle the funeral expenses."

Nitz thought about that for a moment. "You really liked his mother, didn't you?"

"I did more than just like her," I said. "Sue was my partner. When you're a cop, that's a sacred bond. She saved my life more than once, and I'll always regret not saving hers."

"I don't believe that what happened to Chris's mother was any of your fault."

That was easy enough for Nitz to say, but it wasn't something that was easy for me to believe. I had many years' worth of bad dreams and sleepless nights to prove it wasn't true.

Chapter 36

When Nitz dropped Jimmy and me off at the hotel, I stopped by the desk to talk to Fred about the car-rental situation before going up to the room. I believe I've mentioned before that Homer is a small town. As it happened, the Driftwood's night clerk was good friends with the guy who ran the Hertz operation at the airport. They were able to work out an arrangement to have a vehicle dropped off at the hotel overnight.

Once in the room, I pulled out the sofa bed, while Jimmy went to the bathroom to undress. I didn't blame him for not wanting to shed his clothing in front of me. Fortunately Nitz had had the foresight to bring along a backpack with some of his clothing in it. Once dressed in pj's, Jimmy fell into bed and was out like a light.

Obviously his day of being a runaway had been a tough one for him.

Next up I called Marvin Price's number. I expected he'd be wide awake, and he was.

"Any news about Roger?" he asked at once.

I passed along everything Nitz had told me.

"Anything else?" he wondered.

"As a matter of fact there is," I said. "I had a brainstorm tonight. What if Shelley didn't drive Chris's body to Eklutna Lake?" I asked. "What if she used her plane? Maybe someone should check that for blood evidence, too."

"Lordy, Lordy!" Marvin breathed. "Why the hell didn't I think of that? Thanks, Beau. I'll get someone right on it!"

By the time that call ended, it was almost eleven in Homer—an hour later in Seattle. I knew I needed to talk to Jared, but calling someone who was a guest in a monastery at midnight didn't seem like a good idea. Besides, Chris had been dead for a dozen years. Jared could wait a few more hours to hear the bad news. As a consequence I followed Jimmy's example and went to bed.

By six the next morning and with Jimmy still sawing logs, I was awake and fully dressed. I left a note for

Jimmy and then went down to the lobby to dial Jared Danielson's cell phone.

"Is it Chris?" he asked as soon as he answered.

"Yes," I answered. "I'm so sorry."

I heard Jared sigh. It was the news he'd been both expecting and dreading. "I'll call Gram and let her know," he said. "It'll break her heart, of course. Do you have any idea who's responsible?"

Actually, I did have some idea, and over the next many minutes I told him everything I knew. As a homicide cop, I'd always been unable to share much if any information on the progress of a case with grieving relatives in order to maintain the integrity of the investigation. As a private investigator, I was under no such obligation, so I told Jared what I knew with a clear conscience. Besides, at that point in the investigation I was as much in the dark about what was really going on with Lieutenant Marvin Price and the AST as anyone else.

There was silence once I finally finished. I guess I shouldn't have been surprised when the recently ordained priest finally responded by quoting a Bible verse.

"'For the love of money is the root of all evil: which while some coveted after, they have erred from the faith, and pierced themselves through with many sorrows.' First Timothy, chapter six, verse ten. If Shelley Adams is sitting in jail right now and looking at prison time, it sounds as though she's certainly pierced herself with sorrows."

"Amen to that," I told him.

"What happens now?"

"I don't know exactly," I replied. "With the remains identified and the autopsy already conducted, there shouldn't be much delay in releasing the body. You should probably be in touch with Professor Raines about that. I'll text you her contact information." I found her information in my contacts and sent it along.

"What should I do about a funeral?" he wanted to know. "What about that?"

"I'm of the opinion you should discuss that with Danitza Miller, your nephew's mother. Legally, you're Chris's next of kin, but she and Jimmy certainly have a vested interest in what follows. I'm texting you their contact information as well. I told Nitz, and I'm telling you, that I'll take care of any and all funeral expenses—"

"Wait," Jared objected, "you can't do that."

"I can and I will," I told him, "but there's one

stipulation. You can choose cremation or burial, that's up to you. If you pick the latter, however, I want you to order a full-size casket with no viewing."

"Because Danitza and Jimmy don't know how little is left of the body?"

"Exactly."

"So what should I do today?" Jared persisted. "Should I get on a plane and come to Alaska or what?"

"By all means," I told him. "I know for a fact that Jimmy is eager to meet you, and you'll need to speak with the official homicide investigators as well. And since you're probably not too flush for cash at the moment, you can plan on billing me for the airfare. As far as I'm concerned, your coming here is all a part of wrapping up my investigation."

"Thank you. So I fly into Anchorage?" Jared asked.

"I know Nitz's address information gives an Anchorage address, but right now and for probably the next several days she'll be spending most of her time here in Homer."

"How far is that from Anchorage?"

"A long way," I said. "Look, once you have your flight arrangements, let me know your ETA. I'll have someone meet you at the airport and bring you here, and I'll book a room for you at the same hotel where I'm staying."

It made me smile to think that Twinkle Winkleman wasn't quite done with me yet.

"All right," Jared said. "I'll be in touch as soon as I call Grandma and get my flight details sorted."

"Good enough."

About that time the elevator door opened and Jimmy Danielson wandered into the lobby. His hair was still tousled from sleeping. He paused for a moment, looking anxiously around the lobby. When he spotted me, his face brightened and he hurried over.

"Was that my mom on the phone?" he asked.

"No," I said, "it was your Uncle Jared. He's checking to see how soon he can catch a flight from Seattle to Anchorage."

"He's coming here, really?"

"Really."

Twink had told me that the Driftwood had a breakfast room, and somewhere it smelled as though someone was making waffles. Jimmy must have caught the same scent.

"Can we have breakfast?" he asked. "I'm starving."

I was sure he was. It had been a very long time since he'd downed Twink's sticky pudding and whatever goodies he'd been able to extract from the hotel's vending machines.

But suddenly I had another idea—a very bright idea.

"Yes, we can have breakfast," I told him, "but not here. I know just the spot. It's called Zig's Place."

"Really? Isn't that where my dad was working?"

Clearly he'd been paying attention to everything I'd said. "Yes, it is," I told him. "It's also where he and your mom met."

"Really?"

Jimmy's food-starved brain seemed to be stuck on "really."

"Yes, really," I repeated. "So let's get our coats and head out."

A few minutes later, when we walked outside to my latest version of the Ford Exploder, even I could tell that it was noticeably warmer. Snow was starting to melt and drip off eaves. Not long after that, we were seated in a booth at Zig's Place. When the waitress came to take our order, I asked if Mr. Norquist was working that day.

"He's in the back," she told us.

"Would you tell him that Chris Danielson's son, Christopher James, is here and would very much like to meet him?"

"Will do," she said. "Now, what can I get you?"

Jimmy ordered everything but the kitchen sink—OJ, ham, eggs, and hash browns with a pecan waffle on the side. I ordered bacon and eggs.

"I can't believe my father actually worked here," Jimmy commented once the waitress left. He looked around the room in wonder, as if taking in every detail.

"You know that framed pencil drawing of your mother?"

"The one that says 'Would you like to hang out sometime'?" His mouth screwed up when he repeated the words, as though it was weird to have to consider his parents in those kinds of terms—as though the idea that they might have been young and in love once was somehow beyond the pale.

I nodded and held up my place mat. "This is what it was drawn on," I told him, "a place mat from Zig's Place. Do you draw?"

"A little," Jimmy admitted with a self-conscious shrug, "but I'm not very good at it."

"Your father was terrific when it comes to drawing. You'll need to ask your Uncle Jared to show you the portrait your father did of your grandmother."

"Your partner you mean," Jimmy asked quietly.

He had me there. Jimmy's Internet search about the clash between Sue and Rich Danielson was still bearing fruit.

"Yes," I agreed with a lump in my throat, "she was definitely my partner."

Just then a gigantic human shadow fell over our

table. Jimmy and I both looked up to see the looming figure of Siegfried Norquist standing there. When I noticed he was cradling something in the crook of his arm, I knew exactly what it was.

"You must be Chris Danielson's son," he said, beaming down at Jimmy, holding out his massive hand. "I'm so glad to meet you. You look just like your father."

"Is it true that he worked here?" Jimmy asked.

Ziggy smiled. "It certainly is. Your father was a fine young man—upstanding and dependable, and talented, too. Here's something he drew for me."

With a flick of his hand, Ziggy turned the framed pencil portrait so Jimmy could see it.

"Who's that?" the boy asked.

"My wife," Ziggy explained, "my late wife. Her name was Sonja. She managed the restaurant at the same time your dad worked here. One night when we weren't very busy, he sketched this. He tossed it in the trash, but one of the waitresses spotted it and gave it to me. Sonja died two years ago, and I keep this in the kitchen with me. I was so sorry when he disappeared."

"He's dead now, too," Jimmy said quietly. "Someone found his body a long time ago, but they've only just now identified it."

Marvin Price and the AST might not have made any

official announcements about Chris Danielson's homicide up to that point, but the story was out in public now, and I didn't care. After all, this was Jimmy's family and his story to tell.

The welcoming smile vanished from Ziggy's face. "I'm so sorry to hear that, so very sorry. Is there anything I can do?"

Jimmy shook his head. "I don't think so," he said.

Our waitress showed up just then, carrying our order. Ziggy stepped aside and watched as she delivered the plates of food to our table. The last thing she put down was our ticket.

"There's one thing I can do," Ziggy said, grabbing the tab and stuffing it into the pocket of his pants. "Breakfast is on me."

I have to say, cold winter weather or not, the little burg of Homer, Alaska, was starting to grow on me. Or as Jimmy Danielson would say, *Really starting to grow on me.*

Chapter 37

With Christopher James Danielson finally stuffed to the gills, we left the restaurant and drove to the hospital. When we arrived, we found an Alaska State Trooper vehicle as well as one from Homer PD parked end to end in the tow-away zone outside the front entrance. Inside, the woman at the reception desk informed us that Mr. Adams had been moved from ICU to a regular room. When we started in that direction she called after us, "Wait, children under sixteen aren't allowed."

With cop cars parked right outside the front door, I figured I was golden. "Jimmy here is a witness, and the detectives need to speak to him."

"Okay, fine," she relented. "Go ahead."

In the hallway outside an open door, I spotted Nitz engaged in a low-voiced huddle with two individuals, one of whom was Marvin Price. The one I didn't recognize was a woman wearing a pantsuit and a pair of boots that were more of a fashion statement than they were weather-related. Nitz broke away from her companions as soon as she saw us and hurried over to gather her son in her arms.

"Jimmy," was all she said as she held the boy tight. Nitz looked weary beyond words but far better than I would have expected after an all-night vigil.

"How are things?" I asked.

"He's sleeping right now," she answered. "The doctors have upgraded his condition to fair."

"So he's going to make it?"

She nodded, then added, "But there may be some residual long-term damage."

I was puzzling over that when Marvin approached. He, too, looked as though he'd pulled an all-nighter but with far more visible ill effects than Nitz displayed. He clearly hadn't gone home to change. By contrast the woman accompanying him—perfectly made up and with every hair in place—looked fresh as a daisy.

"Glad to see you," Marvin said. "You were scheduled to be our next stop. Allow me to introduce Detective Sergeant Genevieve Madison of the AST. And this is J. P. Beaumont from Seattle, the private investigator who brought this matter to our attention."

Detective Madison offered me a firm handshake with a grip that wasn't quite as forceful as Twink's but close.

"Glad to meet you," she said, with a welcoming smile. "Call me Jenny."

"And I'm Beau," I told her. "So what's going on?"

"We were just discussing Mr. Adams's latest lab results with Ms. Miller here," Marvin explained. "It appears that Shelley has been controlling her husband for some time by administering low doses of both scopolamine and LSD."

Those initials took me back several decades. I knew people who tripped out on LSD in the sixties and never returned to any semblance of reality. No wonder Roger's doctors feared there was a possibility of long-term residual consequences.

"But here's the good news," Jenny Madison offered. "We ran the photocopies in Tracy Hamilton's notary file through our facial-rec program and hit pay dirt. The guy posing as Roger Adams for the power-of-attorney application turns out to be Duncan Langdon."

I nodded. "I met him," I said. "He's married to Shelley's cousin Nadine and goes by the name of Dunk.

According to Shelley they did odd jobs around the house."

"Boyfriend and girlfriend rather than husband and wife," Jenny supplied. "Oddly enough, they were booked on an early-morning Alaska Airlines flight out of Anchorage headed for Seattle with a final destination of Cancún. They spent the night inside the terminal. We had a team of officers intercept them before they were able to board."

"Cancún," Marvin added. "It's the same place Shelley was going. I'm sure they were expecting their big payday. Turns out Dunk Langdon is, as we say, 'someone known to law enforcement.' He's Homer's resident drug dealer—mostly a small-time operator who deals in more exotic things than, say, your basic methamphetamines."

"Like LSD and scopolamine, you mean?" I asked.

"Exactly," Marvin replied, "to say nothing of fentanyl. So we put both Nadine and Dunk in separate interview rooms and, after a certain amount of persuading, offered them the same deal. Surprise, surprise, they both took it."

"What deal?" I asked.

"The two of them agreed to plead guilty to low-level drug-possession charges in exchange for testifying against Shelley Adams on charges of both attempted murder and elder abuse with regard to Roger Adams. We have no idea what the feds plan to do on the wire-fraud and money-laundering charges, because Dunk was obviously involved in those as well. They're examining all the closing statements on those fraudulent real-estate transactions and trying to retrieve those off-shore funds so they can be returned to Mr. Adams's custody or, if necessary, into the custody of whoever is put in charge of handling his affairs. But I suspect that the feds will also offer Langdon a similar deal on those. Shelley's clearly the major doer here, and she's the one whose feet we all want to hold to the fire."

Having the feds along with the state authorities working hand in glove with the local cops? In my book that was virtually unheard of.

"What about Chris's case?" I asked.

"It may be circumstantial, but the blood evidence we found in Shelley's vehicle and in the plane is pretty powerful."

"The plane?" I asked. "There *was* blood evidence in the plane?"

"Yes, there certainly was," Marvin answered. "Not as much as in the Forester, but enough. Not only that, our CSI also discovered traces of blood on the business end of a Maglite found on board the aircraft. We've already sent the dimensions of that to Professor Raines so it can be checked against the damage to Chris's skull. If that matches up, it'll be more than circumstantial. It'll give us actual physical evidence. Not only that, our prosecutor is weighing in. Even though Chris's murder and Roger's attempted homicide are two separate incidents, he's hoping they can be tried together. The defense will object, of course, but Shelley's willingness to commit one murder speaks to her willingness to do two."

"What about Jack Loveday?" I asked.

Marvin shook his head. "Unfortunately, without additional evidence that one's still off the table." He checked his watch. "Right this minute Jenny and I need to be on our way. We have an upcoming joint press conference, and the two of us are expected to be front and center."

I understood that a press conference would open a whole new can of worms for both Nitz and Jimmy. Suddenly they would be thrust into the limelight and targeted by all kinds of unwelcome public attention—attention they'd never expected nor wanted. Still, if that was the cost of finally solving Chris's homicide, it seemed like a small price to pay.

"Wait," I said as the two detectives started to walk away. "What about Twink's nine A.M. appointment with the FBI?"

Marvin paused long enough to look back at me. "Not to worry," he replied with a grin. "That's been handled."

Just then a cell phone began chirping. At first I thought it was one of theirs, but Nitz was the one who turned away to answer.

"Hello," she said, sounding a bit uncertain. Then, a moment later, she added, "Oh, hello, Jared. I'm so glad to hear from you. Not under these circumstances of course, but yes. . . ." There was another pause, a longer one. "This afternoon at three? That's wonderful news. Jimmy and I would love to meet you, but we're not actually in Anchorage at the moment. . . . Yes, we're still in Homer and will probably be here until at least tomorrow and maybe the next day as well."

She and Jared were still talking as I keyed in Twink's number. "You again?" she asked with typical brusqueness as she answered the phone.

"Yes, me again," I replied. "Are you booked for later on this afternoon?"

"Are you kidding? After the last couple of days, I figured I deserved a day off. What have you got in mind?"

"Chris Danielson's brother, Jared, is coming in on a flight from Seattle that's due to land in Anchorage at three. Could you meet him at baggage claim?"

"What's the flight number?"

"I don't know. I can get it—"

"Never mind," Twink barked. "I'll figure it out. Where do you want me to take him?"

"Bring him here to Homer."

"To the Driftwood?"

"Yes, please."

"Still on your charge card?"

"Yes, ma'am."

"All right," she allowed. "I guess I'll keep on giving you the multi-day discount, but only on one condition."

"What's that?"

"Dinner at AJ's," she answered, "and this time I plan to stay long enough to eat my own damned sticky pudding."

Chapter 38

That night, after once again feeding a kid who was evidently a bottomless pit where food was concerned, I was waiting with Jimmy in the lobby at the Driftwood Inn for Twink and the Travelall to deliver Father Jared Danielson door-to-door, airport to hotel. Nitz was still at the hospital. Fortunately for me, she'd brought Jimmy's phone and charger along with his clothes on her panicked trip to Homer, and he was happily sprawled in a nearby chair, playing video games to his heart's content.

As we sat there together in what now felt like companionable silence, I couldn't help but think about how private investigators are portrayed on TV. Boob-tube PI dramas are always filled to the brim with fistfights, gunfights loaded with automatic firearms, and scene after scene of macho mayhem. It's usually one death-defying act of derring-do after another. In all those scenes of never-ending drama, there are hardly ever any moments for quiet introspection.

A lot of what both cops and PIs do is boring—following one strand of inquiry or another just to see where it leads. When one thread dead-ends, you find another one to follow. Eventually those paths lead you from threads to dots and then from one small dot to another until you finally arrive at important ones. In this case those threads had involved paper chases rather than car chases—examining real-estate transactions and vehicle registrations until the puzzle pieces had finally come together in three separate homicides—two possibly provable and one not.

In addition, being a PI means showing up fully prepared to do whatever is necessary, which in this case meant looking after a middle-schooler who, without my being there, would have been either left to his own devices or stuck enduring two long nights in hospital waiting rooms.

The television and movie crime dramas seldom include stellar moments like the one I'd witnessed earlier in the evening when Danitza Adams Miller finally introduced her twelve-year-old son to his grandfather for the very first time. When Roger held out a frail, bony hand, Jimmy gave it a gentle shake. "I'm happy to meet you, sir," the boy had said gravely. That one took my breath away.

As for Roger? At times he seemed somewhat more lucid than he'd been when I first met him on Saturday, but when an orderly appeared a few minutes later and deposited a food tray on his table, Roger had looked under the service plate's cover and then dropped it as though it were hot to the touch.

"What's wrong?" Nitz asked.

"I can't eat that," Roger objected, pointing at the food.

"Why not?"

"Because Shelley will be mad at me."

"Why?"

"It's my ulcer," he said. "She says regular food makes me sick. That's why she gives me that chocolate-flavored stuff to drink. Have them bring me some of that."

Obviously there was still some confusion in Roger's mind about what was really going on, but what he'd just said answered one lingering question. No wonder Roger Adams resembled a starving prisoner straight out of a Nazi concentration camp. He actually *was* starving and for months had existed on a liquid-only diet.

"It's all right, Daddy," Nitz assured him. "The hospital doesn't have any of that chocolate stuff, and Shelley's not here. Go ahead and try the food. You might like it, and if Shelley turns up, we won't tell her about it, will we, Jimmy?"

"No," a wide-eyed Jimmy agreed. "We won't tell, cross our hearts."

I couldn't help but notice Nitz's casual use of the word "Daddy." In the previous hours, something important had occurred and the long estrangement between father and daughter had unobtrusively come to an end.

Moments later Roger was digging into his plateful of food. It was hospital fare—probably incredibly bland and mostly tasteless as well, but he downed it with obvious gusto. He was clearly disappointed when Nitz declared he'd eaten as much as he should and removed his plate with some food still on it.

"It's all right," she assured him. "If this doesn't upset your stomach and you're hungry again a little later, I'll bring you something else."

Shortly after that, Jimmy and I left the hospital. With the convenience of AJ's just across the street from the hotel, I offered to take him there for dinner, but there was only one place in Homer where Jimmy Danielson cared to dine—back to Zig's Place, so that's where we went.

Just after nine the Driftwood's glass doors slid open. Father Jared Danielson entered the lobby, followed by Twink carrying an armload of luggage. She went straight to the check-in desk while Jared headed for us.

"Is that him?" Jimmy whispered.

I nodded.

With that, Jimmy pocketed his phone, shot out of his chair, and went to greet the new arrival.

"Are you my uncle?" he asked.

Jared looked down at the boy and smiled. "If your name happens to be Christopher James Danielson, I certainly am," he said, extending his hand.

"I'm glad to meet you, sir," Jimmy said as they shook.

"You're welcome to call me Uncle Jared. What should I call you?"

"Jimmy."

"Okay," Jared said. "Jimmy it is."

Believe me, I had another huge lump in my throat during that brief encounter,

A few minutes later, I left Jared and Jimmy to get acquainted and hurried across the street to AJ's, where Twink had arrived just in time to place her order before the kitchen shut down. I stopped at the hostess stand and made arrangements to cover Twink's tab, sticky pudding and all. Then I wandered over to her table.

"Hey, Trouble," she greeted me. "What are you doing here?"

"I came to pay my bill."

"Sorry," she said. "I don't have my credit-card gizmo on me."

"No problem," I told her. Slipping into the booth across from her, I pulled out a business card and scribbled a series of numbers on it. Then I passed the card to her. "When you do charge the account, that's the amount you should use."

Twink looked at the number, and her eyes bulged. "That's way more than you owe!"

"And you did work that was above and beyond just being my driver."

"But—"

"No buts, Twink. Having you and Maude at my disposal made all the difference. If nothing else, use the extra moolah to take that ding out of the fender and give the old girl a new paint job."

"Thanks," Twink said at last, pocketing the card. "Maybe I will."

"And if you speak to that brother of yours, you might suggest that he get in touch with Lieutenant Price here at Homer PD. I'm not sure it'll do any good, but someone needs to let investigators know that Jack Loveday wouldn't have committed suicide just because the doctors whacked off his legs."

"I'll do that, too," she said.

Rising to my feet, I held out my hand, and she gripped it with knuckle-grinding force. "This is it, then?" she asked.

"I'm afraid so."

"Too bad." She grinned. "Doing business with you has been more fun than a barrel of monkeys."

Chapter 39

O n Monday of that week, Twink headed back to Anchorage while Father Jared and Nitz sat down and sorted out Chris's final arrangements. He had supposedly been on his way home to Ohio when he'd disappeared a dozen years earlier. Now he was finally making that trip. In death his body would be returned to his mother's hometown of Monroe, Ohio, where his funeral would be held, and he would be laid to rest next to his mother in the Hinkle family plot. The timing on all that was up in the air, but Nitz had agreed to go there for the funeral, which hopefully would give Jimmy a chance to finally meet his great-grandmother, Annie Hinkle.

A local mortuary had been brought into the picture to make arrangements for transporting the casket once Professor Raines released Chris's remains. In the meantime the mortuary would host a small memorial service on Friday afternoon, with Father Jared officiating. I placed a discreet call to the owner and made it clear that I would be handling all charges related to Chris's final expenses.

The service was being hastily organized, but it was no problem getting out the word. Chris Danielson's long-ago murder was now headline news all over Alaska, and I was sure his memorial in Homer would be well attended. Siegfried Norquist had come forward and offered to close Zig's Place to the public for the afternoon in order to host a post-service reception at no cost to the family.

I wasn't planning on hanging around long enough to attend. I'd done as much as I could for Sue Danielson's family. Now I needed to pay attention to my own. Mel was still hurting, and I wanted to be home with her where I belonged.

On Tuesday morning Shelley Loveday Adams, a former Miss Alaska who had once won the Miss America swimsuit competition, showed up at her arraignment in Homer wearing an orange jumpsuit and handcuffs, after a short stay in the Kenai Correctional Center. She was escorted into the courtroom by uniformed members of the AST.

What happened next was incredibly gratifying. Shelley ended up pleading not guilty to one charge of murder in the first degree in the death of Chris Danielson and one charge of attempted murder and another of elder abuse against Roger Adams. She also pled not guilty to fifteen counts each of fraud and theft based on her shoddy real-estate dealings. Despite her not-guilty pleas, the prosecutors thought they had a good case. Their request to try both cases together was granted. Not only that, claiming Shelley was a flight risk, they also asked for and were granted no bail, meaning Shelley would remain in custody while awaiting trial. All I can say to that is bravo!

Roger was still in recovery mode—physically at least. Mentally he was still lost in the woods, and his confusion persisted. Despite being told that Shelley was in jail, he kept asking for her and wondering why she didn't come to the hospital to see him. I suspected the poor man would be living with a certain amount of mental impairment for the remainder of his life. Fortunately for him he now had Nitz to watch over him.

Speaking of Nitz, while trying to get a handle on Roger's financial situation she'd gone through the desk in his home office, where she discovered a hidden compartment containing a handwritten revised, signed, and properly witnessed will. It was dated the same day as the change of beneficiary on his life-insurance policy. It specified that any properties not held in common with Shelley were to go directly to Danitza. Shelley must have somehow gotten wind of that arrangement and launched her scheme to liquidate as much of Roger's solely owned real estate as possible. Fortunately, there was still a good deal of it that she hadn't managed to unload.

On Tuesday night Jared, Danitza, Jimmy, and I had a farewell dinner together at Zig's Place. The evening special was beef Stroganoff. The food was delicious, and the company was even better. On Wednesday morning, as I packed to leave town, I was tempted to abandon the boots in my room at the Driftwood Inn, but in the end I wore those home and packed the shoes I'd brought with me.

After that I drove from Homer to the airport in Anchorage, where I dropped off my rental, cleared security, and arrived at my gate in plenty of time. My flight left at eleven thirty. I had booked a first-class ticket, meaning I qualified for lunch, but as soon as that was over, I wrapped myself in a blanket and went nighty-night. I'd been in Alaska for a solid week, from Wednesday to Wednesday, but it felt like forever. Although I could give myself credit for a job well done, I knew that the case had taken a lot out of me. I was tired. I wanted my wife, my dog, and my very own bed, but most of all I wanted to be rid of those damned boots.

As we neared SeaTac and broke through the low-hanging cloud cover, it was raining like crazy—no surprise there—but I was relieved to see that the Pineapple Express churning in off the Pacific had done its work, as there was no snow on the ground. Sure there was visible snow in the Olympics and the Cascades, but not in the lowlands. It would be months yet before what Harriet Raines called the "big breakup" happened in Alaska. In western Washington it looked as though it was well under way in mid-December.

Once on I-5 headed north and expecting Mel to be at work, I punched her office number into my phone. The call went straight to voice mail. "I'm currently out of the office," Mel's cheerful recorded voice told me. "If this is an emergency, please hang up and dial 911. Otherwise leave your number and a message. I'll get back to you as soon as I can." Obviously she hadn't forwarded calls to her cell as she usually does, which meant she probably wasn't answering that either.

I admit to being a little annoyed. I hadn't called earlier because I hadn't wanted to interrupt her at work. A lot of good that did me. I made the rest of the drive in silence, without even bothering to turn on the radio. By the time I opened the garage door, I was a long way down the road to being Mr. Grumbly Bear.

But then a miracle happened. Mel's Interceptor was already parked in her spot. She hadn't answered the phone in her office because she was already home! When I pushed open the door, two things happened, one after the other. First my nostrils were assailed by the peppery aromas of fresh Thai takeout. At Mel's and my house, that qualifies as home cooking.

For a brief moment after that, I caught a glimpse of Mel standing at the far end of the entry hallway. An instant later my view of her was completely obliterated when a mass of galloping gray fur launched itself in my direction. As Sarah's wet nose touched mine, her front paws landed square on my shoulders and almost knocked me over.

Coming from the garage, I had planned to announce my arrival with that old Desi Arnaz line, "Honey, I'm home." Thanks to Sarah I never had a chance. Mel and I were both laughing too hard.

Once the doggy greeting subsided, I dropped my luggage and gathered Mel into my arms. "How are you doing?" I asked.

"Better," she said, "but I gave myself an excused absence from the planning meeting I was supposed to attend tonight. I figured we both needed some time to debrief."

"You're right about that," I said.

And that's exactly what we did. We had a quiet dinner, then we talked, and then we went to bed. I can tell you for sure it was wonderful to be home.

Chapter 40

It seemed like only a matter of minutes from the time I got home until it was Christmas Day, and we had a blast. Contrast is everything, but the brightness of the holiday compared with the darkness of what had happened in Alaska made everything seem extraordinarily special. Kelly and Jeremy weren't there, of course, because that year they were spending the holidays with his folks. But even with the Ashland, Oregon, contingent of the family missing, we all had a glorious time.

First thing in the morning, we used modern technology and FaceTimed while Athena, grandchild number four, opened her gifts in the presence of her other grandfather, Alan Dale, in Jasper, Texas. Next up we watched grandkids numbers one and two, Kayla and Kyle, open their gifts under Jeremy's folks' Christ-

Please use code in blue box on left when ordering.
Prices in this insert in effect until 3/31/22

Woman Within®
a FULL**BEAUTY** brand™
500 S. MESA HILLS DRIVE, EL PASO, TX 79912

womanwithin.com **or**
1-800-248-2000

622-220190

Save $20^ when you open & use a Woman Within card today!
Being a Cardholder has its benefits!
- Earn rewards every time you shop*
- No annual fee**
- Special birthday surprise***

Not a Cardholder yet? Apply today! Call **1-800-253-4195** visit www.womanwithin.com/apply

Please use code in blue box when ordering. Prices in this insert in effect until 3/31/22

FREE SHIPPING!
WITH PURCHASE FROM THIS INSERT USE CODE **WWCP3SHIP** See details below.

totes.

TOTES®
3-SEASON
JACKET

TRY US
WAS $~~54.99~~
NOW ONLY
$**34**⁹⁹

Storm Blue

Merlot   Plum

erglade   Black

TOTES® 3-SEASON JACKET.
20-19351-622
Water-resistant and lightweight. Fleece lined. Full-zip front. Zip-off hood with adjustable pulls. 31" length. Elastic cuffs. Woven poly. **Sizes M-5X**
~~54.99~~ 34.99

WATER-RESISTANT OUTER SHELL

FLEECE LINED ZIP-OFF HOOD WITH ADJUSTABLE PULLS

COZY FLEECE LINING

44

Account Number 00888226060
Invoice # 8739645   Invoice Date February 21, 2022

1   L7 E-Z open   #SO 16445 7062

Location	Description	Selection	Price
	Nothing to Lose (Large Pr	14265583	$23.99

Subtotal	$	23.99
Shipping/Processing	$	0.99
Tax	$	1.50
Previous Balance	$	180.42
TOTAL DUE		**$206.90**

USPS TRACKING # eVS

9241 9901 7237 3887 3964 59

BZNBQLM
0008 7396 4500 5807
ROSEMARY HOLMES
31 NORTHCOURT LN
LEVITTOWN PA 19054-3310

14265583 Nothing to Lose (Large Print)

YRK

PRSRT BPM
U.S POSTAGE PAID
OSM
E-VS

02

CHANGE
SERVICE REQUESTED

YP	51
BP	

iild number three, Jon
grand personally in at-
as Scotty and Cherisse
eir baby after his two
herisse's dad, Pierre—I
nas Pierre would des-
nd of name-challenge
I'm eternally grateful

d already prepared
d before serving) was
, which it turned out
ton State. Scotty and
neal, and so was the
y adult but only re-
ni, who also happens
n Athena is in Texas
State is a long story
so in attendance was

it Naomi's existence,
to learn that he had
ut. I was a little ner-
because our family
ie longest period of
Naomi had spent in the same room. I need

not have worried. The meal was perfect, and everyone got along. And when it came time to unwrap gifts, everyone loved the presents I'd obtained during my pre-Christmas shopping spree in Anchorage.

Naturally some of the conversation swirled around Christopher Danielson's homicide, which had also surfaced in Seattle's news media. I would have preferred it if Scotty and Naomi had peppered Jared with fewer questions about his younger brother, but Jared seemed totally at ease in answering them. Long before we knew for sure that the human remains found at Eklutna Lake belonged to Chris, Jared had resigned himself to the idea that his brother was probably deceased. He had less need to grieve now because he'd done that years earlier. Even so, grieving is never completely over.

By five o'clock in the afternoon, the guests had gone home, the table was cleared, the leftovers put away, and both dishwashers were loaded and running. In the living room, Scotty had cleared the floor and furnishings of every smidgeon of torn wrapping paper and ribbon by stuffing it all into an enormous plastic trash bag. Sarah, worn out by so much hubbub, was snoozing in front of the fireplace while Mel and I—she with a glass of wine and me with a cup of coffee— enjoyed each other's presence in the enveloping silence.

Without presents stacked under and around it, the Christmas tree looked a bit sad. That's when I noticed that a single gift still lingered there, hidden almost out of sight.

"Oops," I said, getting up to retrieve it. "Someone forgot something."

"Nobody forgot it," Mel said as I returned with the box in hand.

"I don't know who it's for," I said. "There's no tag on it."

"It's yours," Mel said. "It's a surprise. I put it under the tree while you were loading the dishwashers."

"How come?" I said. "Why wasn't I allowed to open it when everybody was here?"

"Orders from headquarters," Mel said mysteriously, "but you're welcome to open it now."

So I did. Mel had obviously wrapped it. The paper was the same pattern we'd used on several other packages. With the holiday wrapping removed, I was left holding a small rectangular box. It was about the size and shape that an expensive ladies' necklace might come in, but this was plain unadorned cardboard with no identifying markings of any kind.

I shook it. There was no rattle, but I could hear a sort of soft shuffling sound coming from inside.

"Do you know what it is?" I asked.

Mel nodded. "But I'm not going to tell. Go on. Finish opening it."

So I did. Inside was a soft leather pouch, colorfully beaded on one side. With it was a small envelope. In the envelope I found a piece of notepaper with Harriet Raines's name embossed across the top. On it was written the following note:

Dear Beau,

Thank you for your efforts in successfully identifying Geoffrey 4/25/2008 and returning him to his family.

Yesterday I visited with a medicine man and told him about your situation with the other medicine man's curse. He gave me this pouch and told me that the pouch and the items inside it should help with your nightmare. You don't need to open the pouch. Just sleep with it under your pillow.

> *Yours respectfully,*
> *Harry Raines*

Dismayed, I looked at Mel. "Harriet Raines sent this to you?"

Mel nodded. "She mailed it to me at the office. She asked that it be given to you in private, and it was."

I handed Mel the note, and she read it. "You must have told her about your recurring nightmare."

"I didn't intend to," I said self-consciously. "I told her about Sue Danielson and the medicine man's curse, but I don't remember mentioning the dream."

But I did remember what Hank Frazier had told me—that Harriet Raines was one of those people who seemed to see all and know all.

"Still, the idea of sleeping with this bag of whatever under my pillow seems a little much."

I stuck to my guns, and hours later when Mel and I went to bed, the leather pouch still sat on the coffee table in the living room exactly where I'd left it. But sometime overnight, when Sarah cold-nosed me on the elbow saying she needed to go out, I walked her to the door. (The dog has yet to have a complete understanding of the magic of doggy doors. She much prefers having a doorman.)

It was a clear night with an almost-full moon overhead. When I came back through the living room, a tiny splash of moonlight illuminated the glass-topped coffee table—the table holding the beaded leather pouch.

"Okay, okay, Harriet," I muttered to myself. "I guess I've got nothing to lose."

Reluctantly, I grabbed up the pouch, carried it into the bedroom, and stuffed it under my pillow, grateful that Mel was sawing logs and wasn't awake to see my capitulation.

Not long after I fell asleep, the dream came again—the same awful dream that has haunted me for years, and it started the exact same old way. I drive up to Sue Danielson's lighted residence and switch off the engine of my vehicle. Holding my breath, I step up onto Sue's front porch and discover that the door isn't locked. I turn the knob and push the door open to reveal a scene awash in blood.

Sue—shot, bleeding, and dying—sits propped against the far wall as Richie Danielson, her ex, disappears from view down a short hallway. I hand her my backup weapon and then pause for an indecisive moment, torn between trying to help Sue and going after Richie. I have yet to move one way or the other when a gunshot rings out as Richie takes his own life, and then I turn back to Sue and race in her direction. Usually at that point my firearm slips from her lifeless fingers because she's already gone.

But this time something is different. When I reach her and kneel beside her, Sue is gravely wounded and dying yes, but she's still breathing—not only breathing but smiling up at me.

"You've got this, Beau," she whispers. "You've got this."

Those were her last words. I awakened out of the dream with my face wet with tears, but with sudden a sense of calm and with the certain knowledge that Sue was right. I hadn't been able to save her life or her son's, but I had returned her long-lost Christopher to his family, and that was what she'd really needed.

For the first time ever, the dream didn't send me sweaty, sleepless, and shaken to spend the remainder of the night pacing the living-room floor. Instead I rolled over onto my side, threw one arm over Mel's soft shoulder, and fell right back to sleep.

It turns out Harriet Raines was right, and so was her medicine man—that beaded leather pouch worked like a charm.

About the Author

J. A. JANCE is the *New York Times* bestselling author of more than sixty books. Born in South Dakota and raised in Bisbee, Arizona, she lives in the Seattle area with her husband and their two long-haired dachshunds, Mary and Jojo.

HARPER
LARGE PRINT

We hope you enjoyed reading
our new, comfortable print size and found it
an experience you would like to repeat.

Well – you're in luck!

Harper Large Print offers the finest in
fiction and nonfiction books in this same larger
print size and paperback format. Light and easy to read,
Harper Large Print paperbacks are for the book lovers
who want to see what they are reading without strain.

For a full listing of titles and
new releases to come, please visit our website:
www.hc.com

HARPER LARGE PRINT

SEEING IS BELIEVING!